hidden

hidden

TOMAS MOURNIAN

KENSINGTON BOOKS
www.kensingtonbooks.com

KENSINGTON BOOKS are published by

Kensington Publishing Corp.
119 West 40th Street
New York, NY 10018

All Kensington titles, imprints, and distributed lines are available at special quantity discounts for bulk purchases for sales promotion, premiums, fund-raising, educational, or institutional use.

Special book excerpts or customized printings can also be created to fit specific needs. For details, write or phone the office of the Kensington Special Sales Manager: Kensington Publishing Corp., 119 West 40th Street, New York, NY 10018. Attn. Special Sales Department. Phone: 1-800-221-2647.

Kensington and the K logo Reg. U.S. Pat. & TM Off.

ISBN-13: 978-0-7582-5131-2
ISBN-10: 0-7582-5131-9

First Kensington Trade Paperback Printing: February 2011
10 9 8 7 6 5 4 3 2 1

Printed in the United States of America

To Hugo

ACKNOWLEDGMENTS

Timing being everything, I'm most grateful to John Scognamiglio's generous gift of time to find the hidden truth of *hidden*. Mitchell Waters, my most excellent consigliere, makes me laugh as he walks me through my paces. And Rachel Cohn, to whom I'll be forever grateful for giving me a voice.

It took a village to write *hidden,* and mine was far-flung: Daniel Lee, Stacey Szewczyk and Alan F. and Eder Azael all read—and reread—the manuscript and gave insightful comments. Kristine Mills-Noble designed a cover that is nothing less than a gift. Amy Maffei's copy edit was both precise and mindful of my intention. And Craig Bentley: Everyone should be so lucky to have a publicist who sounds like a movie star.

Friends and fellow earth signs Jose Jimenez, Andrew Harburn and Lou Hunter listened to me all the way through.

Patricke said "Ahmed" at precisely the right moment, and Orlando gave me J.D.'s glance. Likewise, the City of Angels has blessed me over the years with the guidance of Marilyn R. Atlas and Kylie Mackenzie and John Turck, Eileen Rapke, and Joao Neto. Also, Kathryn Galan, Octavio Marin and Alfredo de Villa, and Chris Soth, Linda Palmer and Darren Stein. San Francisco sent good juju, too, sustaining me with signals and crucial information from Shannon Minter, Regina Marler and DeeDee Shideler.

For showing me the value of fighting the good fight, I'm indebted to editors Colleen Curtis, Kevin Koffler, Tim Redmond,

Gabriel Roth and Bruce B. Brugmann, and Gia Lauren Gittleson, Bob Roe, Michael Caruso, Barbara Walters, and Glenda Bailey.

Special thanks to Greg Beal, Joan Wai, Shawn Guthrie and Catherine Irwin.

Fellow yogis who reminded me to breathe: Abbe Britton, Noah Maze, Ross Rayburn, Jeff Fisher, Sita White and Durgidas.

Those three great spirits who reached out and refused to let me slip, there they were: George Michael, Nancy Jo Sales, and Siri Sat Nam.

The Corporation of Yaddo.

And, finally, in memory of Lance.

RUN

Chapter 1

I am high.

"I—"

My voice catches. I cannot string together a whole sentence. My eyes open. I've been deposited in the back of my parents' black Mercedes. I look at the dashboard clock. Where did the last forty-five minutes go?

Beyond the windshield, gates swing open. The car rolls forward. I turn: I want a parting shot. Through the back window, I see twenty-foot walls lined with electrified barbed wire.

The Mercedes picks up speed. Desert surrounds us. No wonder Serenity Ridge was built in the Nevada outback. Even if a kid manages to escape, there's no way you can survive the run.

"I need to use the restroom."

My parents stick with their preferred mode of communication: the nonresponse. I won't know if it's a "yes" or a "no" for several minutes. Did I already say, I am high? Medicated, mobilized, and tranquilized?

This morning, when the nurse slid the needle into my ass, I thought about Raoul. I met Raoul in fourth grade. Raoul loved waving Magic Markers under his nose, acting stupid and saying, "Chil', this'll make ya high." The drugs jumped into my bloodstream, and all I could think was, "Chil', this'll make ya the Reluctant Junkie." And then I passed out.

Now, I'd say, "I feel like shit" but the drugs make me so woozy, I don't know *what* I feel. But that's what they want: separate me from my feelings so that I don't "act out" or run. Fortunately, they have yet to figure out that feelings are different than ideas. Being stripped of my feelings is a good thing. Because now I can focus on Idea Numero Uno: *ESCAPE.*

You'd probably be similarly obsessed, too, if you'd been in my place. For eleven months, twelve days, four hours, two minutes and twenty-one seconds, I've been locked up in Serenity Ridge, an RTC (short for residential treatment facility, a.k.a. pay-as-you-go-prisons-for-queer-teens.) In my head, I hear, *"Baby, you're on the brink."*

Brink? More like, *abyss.* And I'm not sixteen, I'm *fifteen* (going on sixteen). Minor detail. I wasn't cured of my "crime" (see above, "gay teens"). Coz I resisted. I lived in fantasy. I knew what was beyond Serenity Ridge's walls and barbed wire: Swimming pools! Laughter! Music! Beach balls! Fun! Nekkidness! Tan golden skin! (Or, Boys! Boys! Boys!)

"Ahmed?"

Haifa's eyes meet mine in the rearview mirror. Haifa is Stepmother Number Four. Or, five. I've lost count. See, Moustapha, my father, believes in marriage, harem-style. IDK. I can't place Haifa's face because she's the *new* Haifa? Or, because she's had a radical nip / tuck? During my time in the queer penitentiary, this Stepmother has either acquired a new face or *is* a new Stepmother. Haifa Whoever twists her face into an expression that's a cross between a grimace and a smile. Looks like? Aging supermodel with bad face-lift.

"Um, yes?" I press my index fingernail to thumb and remind myself to: Pause. Think before I speak. Sound / act obedient. And bright. And alert. Even if I am loaded on downers and the car feels more like a coffin than a luxury four-door sedan. And I really, really want to scream. . . .

I feel a second set of eyes. Hidden behind mirrored, aviator-shaped shades, those eyes scan me for signs of "trouble." Am I talking Green Beret? Special Forces Military Paratrooper? Or,

Saddam Hussein's ghost? No, just Dad, or Moustapha. Today, he wears one of his tacky Village People (the gay cop) getups.

Moustapha waits for me to throw up my arms and drop my wrists, a Middle-Eastern Marilyn Monroe. In fact, he'd *love* nothing more than for me to spontaneously queen out with a shrill "*Girrrlllll!!!*" He'd pull a hard U and drive back. Moustapha would have no problem leaving me at S.R. to rot on the forever and forgotten treatment plan.

He hates me. He really hates what I am. Or, what he *thinks* I am: a wannabe cocksucker and buttfucker. What Moustapha really hates about me is that I remind him of my mother. (Or, "that bitch.") The bitch who decided she had enough, stood up and left his hairy ass. Her "See ya!" still drives him crazy. And he doesn't know, but I plan to leave, too. Leave as in, Escape. You know. "Junkie whore," he said. "Just like your mother."

Moustapha believes his silence convicts me—for sins I have yet to commit (buttfucking, cocksucking, etc.). In Moustapha's world, gay ("queer" in my world) equals sex. He could never understand how it's possible I've had sex but am also a (emotional) virgin. By Moustapha's dated definition—circa 1998?—gay is nuthin' but a messed-up 'mo.

"Did you *enjoy* Serenity Ridge?" Haifa asks. Amazing, she thinks I just got back from a trip to . . . Hawaii! Her question reminds me: I can't feel the beige leather seat (but I *can* hear). Convenient. Allah forgot to turn off the audio.

"Yes, I did. *Very* much." I've mastered the Good Boy tone: flat, humble and certain. Now, if only I could get the straight dude part of my act down, everything would be fabulous. "Thank you for sending me there."

My stepmother nods, "pleased." I study her hair. It's rock hard. A helmet. I can't figure out the look. Accidental motorcycle mama? Or, escapee from the *Planet of the Apes?* Then, I see the netting, and realize, that's not Haifa's hair but a wig! Thank G-D, no homosexuals were involved in her 'do. I blame Moustapha. I bet he told her that a bad wig counts as a head scarf. That reasoning fits with *The Phantom of the Opera* soundtrack. This being the couple who tell everyone they're "strict, *observant* Muslims"—and so fake I want to barf.

Hating them changes nothing. I shift my thoughts to the car's alloy wheels. Beneath us, those wheels speed over asphalt—miles and miles of black . . . tar. I pray the road liquifies under the brutal late August heat.

Flash! Black letters on a yellow face. The sign reads: LAS VEGAS, 30 MILES.

Two days ago, in the cafeteria during breakfast, Eric leaned toward me and whispered, "There's a store a couple miles after the sign that says, 'Thirty miles to Vegas.' " I'd said, "Uh-huh," and promptly forgot. Everyone said Eric was crazy. But damn if crazy Eric wasn't spot-on *correct*.

"Uhhh!" My body shivers. The sign signals escape (mine) is mere minutes away. Boy Scout, be prepared. Problem is, I got kicked out of Cub Scouts for trying to kiss a boy, Timmy. Also: I can barely keep my eyes open.

"*Wake up!*" A girlie-boy voice. Oh, fucking hell. I'm hearing voices. Figure, it would belong to Lance. "*Wake up, darling! Rise and shine!*"

I want to shout, "Lance, would you shut the fuck up!" But I don't. Talking out loud to my (invisible) roommate from Serenity Ridge would be the perfect excuse ("He's crrrraaaaaazzzzzz yyyyyy") for my parents to turn around, drive me back to Serenity Ridge and drop me off.

All I need to do is keep my eyes open, my mouth shut and—What!?! I muffle my shriek. Where my male Mata Hari eyes should be (in the rearview mirror), there's two squinty blue eyes. Blink: Corn-colored eyelashes come down like a pair of giant, frilly fans. Lance.

I must be *really* loaded. Because I know he's not here in this luxury car slash coffin. Lance, he of the square-jawed, blond flat top, football player body of death and . . . lisp! I met Lance the day I "officially" checked into Hotel d'Serenity Ridge. Looking at him, I'd expected a deep-voiced dude. Then he opened his mouth and a purse fell out. Looked like: Thug. Sounded like: Bitch.

"*Wake up,*" Lance trills. Bitch is per-*sist*-ent. For the next twenty-nine miles, Lance's voice keeps me awake, repeating the horror story. What Happened. To him, to me, to all of us: "*You couldn't hide. . . .*"

I look away from the rearview mirror. No good: Lance's face is there, in the window's tinted glass. I surrender, listening to our story unspool like a book on tape, " '*Cause even if you didn't get a boner when they were showing you the pornos . . .*"

The Mercedes lurches, rolls onto a large, dirt lot and parks between two semis. "Miller Time!" promises the side of the semi with its bright, painted letters. Beer is *not* what the doctor ordered. I need something to wake me up. Ritalin. Or, speed. Surely, there must be a meth lab tucked away somewhere in one of those desert trailers.

I look back, blinded by the windshield field, bright and migrainey. What am I doing here? Can I really escape? My confidence dips. Lance's voice pipes up, "*. . . this little thing tracked your pulse, telling them when you got excited.*"

I reach for the door handle. Locked. In the rearview mirror, my father's eyes drill into me. This pit stop is a test. See Ahmed Run. Knock Ahmed Down. Watch Ahmed Crawl. If only Moustapha knew how much energy it takes just for Ahmed to grab the handle. The lock clicks. The handle moves. The door swings open.

My right leg steps out. Somehow, the rest of my body follows. I stand, suspended in hot air, dusty from the semis' tires churn. My legs buckle and my lungs seize up. Cold to hot. My body's shocked by the abrupt change in temperature.

Sorry, Lance, but I can't follow through on my half-assed plan. I'm too weak. Or, I might have caught a cable movie disease. You know, when the adult playing the child actor starts aging prematurely and dies in the quick ninety minutes that passes in-between commercials?

"*And then they'd shock you.*" Lance's lisp makes me remember: the dark room. The wires that creep up and reach between my legs, electric tentacles.

I reach, grip the door, then the roof. I hold up my body. I feel like an old man. I can't do this.

"*It felt like when you drag your feet over carpet.*"

Oh, yeah. Now I remember. The electric shocks. To my dick and balls. The pain. Every time I looked at the pictures on the wall.

I can't go back. No *fucking* way am I going back.

White dust cakes my lips, tongue and mouth. Fuck it, I breathe deep *because I can.*

Suddenly, I really am outside, alone, almost free.

Soon, I'll be able to walk anywhere, speak with anyone, live.

Chapter 2

Moustapha's hand tightens on my tiny left bicep. He "guides" me across the parking lot, grip crushing both my arm and self-confidence.

"Moustapha!" Haifa shouts. "Wait! I need something."

She's stepped out of the car. I can't believe my luck: Inside a store, Haifa always demands an escort. She won't go anywhere alone.

Glad as I am, I can't help but think, My *real* mother wouldn't pull this crap. Even though she left when I was like, *two,* I know her. Know what she's like. For one, I inherited her common sense.

This is how my stepmother shops: She drags my father into the liquor section and leaves me to wander the aisles. Moustapha acts tough, but he cannot resist the gravitational pull of my stepmother's planet-sized demands.

Our family's shopping habits haven't changed in eleven months. At some point, I will be left alone. And left alone to wander the aisles means *Escape.* My heart rate speeds up. I cannot, for the life of me, control my pulse.

"*My dick started bleeding and they blamed me, called me 'uncooperative,'*" Lance says, reminding me what happened the last time my heart sped up: It triggered a virtual fireworks display of electric shocks.

"Make it quick!" Moustapha barks. He's a die-hard fan of the bark-shout. I guess he thinks I'm not just gay but deaf, too. Add that to my case of premature, movie-of-the-week aging disease and I have so many health problems that it'll be a miracle if I can make it inside the bathroom. He gives me a shove. I mouth a silent, "Thank you." *Really.* I am that exhausted, grateful for every extra bit of help.

The bathroom's a cubicle-sized room. One toilet with matching sink. It stinks of shit, piss and vomit. Footsteps. Moustapha's behind me. Is he here to change my diaper? Or, help me unzip?

I don't dare raise my head or look him in the eye. Still, I manage to survey the layout. The window over the urinal is propped open. Fresh air squeezes through the crack. The second it hits the bathroom's warm, disgusting soup, it collapses.

I suck at math. Today, however, panic turns me into a human calculator. I'm able to instantly calculate the distance from floor to window. Too far. I nix that escape route.

I push, opening the stall door. No hand'kins. Fuck! I'd planned to splash my face with cold water and wash off the sleep. I am not *about* to touch the faucet knob. The round push button's smeared with bacteria, trillions of invisible germs. I look for a stack of cheap doily napkin wipes (you always need a handful 'cause the first five dissolve). I don't mean to, but I look in the toilet.

Soggy turds float in the yellow-brown water. They're pressed up against one another like dead coy fish. My stomach revolts. I taste bile, the pre-vomit stuff that dances in your throat *right* before you barf. Which only guarantees that you *will*, in fact, barf. If only I'd known today I'd be so barf obsessed, I would have stolen a barf bag from the seat pocket on my flight back from Honolulu. Oh, silly me.

I turn to leave. Moustapha stands outside the stall. Oops. The stall door slams into his Santa Claus–sized paunch: While I was away and Haifa (or, her twin) got to work transforming her face into an Arabian Wonder Woman, Captain Cuckoo's been pigging out on Ding Dongs and Ho Hos. Suddenly, I understand why he's agreed to stop. Junk food raid.

"Sorry." My apology's drowned by the outside roar of several semi engines. Moustapha's eyes are invisible behind the sunglasses' mirrored panes. I'm face-to-face with Darth Vader.

"Done?"

The Force of Darkness does a double take. He sees the shit-filled toilet bowl. Oh joy! Darth puts out an arm and blocks my body.

"Flush it," he commands. "Or didn't they teach you that?"

"But—"

He spins me around, and shoves me back, into the stall. I hold down the flusher. It's stuck. The toilet gurgles, churning, tossing up shit chunks and dirty water.

"See?" I step aside. "It won't flush."

Darth's thick lips press together, his Bert unibrow knitting. This is his "serious" look. The "don't give me any lip" expression.

"I think it's broken." I instantly regret voicing my opinion. Ever since Haifa opened my journal and read the scrawled words, "I might be queer," Moustapha's lived for confrontations that pit his anger (righteousness and hypocrisy) against my budding sexual identity.

"We're not leaving till—"

"Ahmed?! Moustapha?!"

Haifa possesses the instincts of a homing pigeon. I wonder if she knows that my father hires hookers. *That* I wish I'd written down in my journal: the afternoon I walked into his office and found him face fucking a tranny.

I bet that incident crosses Moustapha's mind, too. He grabs my head, shoves me down and holds my face near the cloudy brown water. My stomach tightens, forcing up breakfast and tranquilizers. I taste the stew just before it hits the cloudy water. The shit soup splatters, up and onto my face.

My eyes are tightly shut. Still, I feel hot tears burn my cheeks. I just lost hope that my father might ever look at me as anything other than an animal. I remind myself I'm lucky to be alive and, literally, eating shit. We've all heard stories about Arab parents who think nothing of killing their queer kid.

My head jerks up. Blind, I cannot see him. But I hear his low, nasty laugh.

"Feel better?"

Arms out, I step forward and touch . . . nothing. He's gone.

I stagger to the sink and throw water on my face.

"Is he all right?" Haifa's voice drifts into the bathroom through the open window. I'm surprised by the concerned tone of her voice. Then again, she's so good at faking everything else, even her concern's probably a put-on.

"He claims he's sick. Hurry up!"

"One—" I stop short, cut my impatient tone. Readjust, Ahmed, use the Good Boy tone (flat, humble, certain). "Please, could you give me one minute?"

"We'll meet you in the store!" My stepmother's voice is crisp and round, Broadway style, Janice Dickinson on mood elevators.

I step out the bathroom. The water ran out every two seconds and I only had ten. So I'm not sure if I cleaned off the shit slime. Again, my will to run slips. Doubt rushes in—nature abhors a vacuum—and I know, I can't follow through.

"*But after a while,*" Lance says. "*They didn't know how to make the bleeding stop.*"

I walk toward the Shop 'N Go. Flies swarm my face. They're drawn to my skin. It must be glazed with shit slime. Although I'm anxious to flee the flies, I slow my pace and look, taking notes. Rows of semis form long alleyways. Each one is a potential escape route. I could run right now, but I'd risk getting lost. I might turn the wrong way.

I shoo away a cluster of flies. My hand touches my left jaw, grazing my throbbing tooth. Again, I reconsider my half-assed escape plan. If I stay with my parents I will get my tooth fixed. Relief from the constant, throbbing pain. That, or I'll overdose on Haifa's sleeping pills.

Nearby, I hear a chorus of gunning engines, race cars anxious to blast the starting gate. I'm starting to feel like I stepped into a video game.

I feel someone staring at me. I glance to my left. Two girls, tough looking and sexy, stride between the trucks. They work a look that screams, "Dyke!" I know this because I've never seen a straight girl who dresses like supermodel truck driver—I am a secret fashionista.

In every way, they're extreme. The blond isn't just blond, she's PLATINUM blond. White hair bristles her head like ice picks. Backlit, the brunette's shoulder-length mane looks a devilish blue in the sun. They both wear tight, faded jeans, frayed bottoms licking the top of steel toed, black motorcycle boots. The white tank tops plastered to their taut torsos barely contain their breasts. The material is so sheer I see matching sets of four, quarter-sized areolas.

Barbed wire and flame tattoos circle their biceps, and their wrists are bound with three-inch-thick leather bands. Evenly matched in height and stride, one looks like an angel, the other a demon, both spit from chariots and sent from heaven and hell to meet—who, *me?*—in this dusty parking lot.

"Hurry up!" Moustapha stands between the Shop 'N Go's stuttering automatic doors.

I resume walking, toward the store and away from the dykey supermodels. I sneak a peek. They're looking at *me*. They smile, *Sly*. I imagine that's their signal, my invitation to run and join them. I'd leave with them, for sure, but I don't know how to signal them back. Except . . . left hand behind my back, I twiddle my fingers. Lame, it prolly makes me look like a dork. But I gotta do something, let them know, "Yeah! I'll go! Wait for me, um, somewhere nearby!"

I pick up my pace. The plastic bracelet slams my ankle bone. If I manage to escape, I need to figure out how to quickly remove the tracking device.

I enter the store. My orange kicks skid on the waxed white floor. The electric doors close, and the silent *Whoosh!* seals off the hot outside air. The store's a giant fridge.

I stop. Overload. Rows of vivid red soda cans, dazzling orange lotto tickets and potato chip bags puffed up with salt and cancer.

The tranks make me stare—a lot. Plus, I've been off consumer culture for a year and that's a whole other detox. Hello, Ahmed, and welcome back to the house of addiction!

Next to the register, there's a cornucopia of jazzy-colored lighters, cigarettes, gum, mints, fudge and Slim Jims. Next to *that,* a magazine rack stocked with more temptation. Pornos, fashion and celeb porn.

A large TV hangs from the ceiling. On-screen, a singer writhes around on a soapy car. She wears a tiny loin cloth, and her long, blond wig is glued to her plastic tits.

Oh, *now* I get it. My people aren't offended by American infidels so much as their bottomless appetite for junk and skanks who crave dick. (Or, me.)

"Ahmed, what do you want?" Haifa asks.

"The hot boy in aisle ten." I could say it, but I don't. Haifa doesn't care what I want—only that I say I want something. Anything. Exercise my native-born right to consume. The family that shops together numbs out together. Sugar comas. Alcohol poisoning.

I walk the aisles, looking at the boys (all blond and perfect; a Mormon boy convention?) who wander amidst shelves crowded with stuff. Bright orange Sno-Cones? I've been gone so long from the world, I didn't know Halloween's in two months.

Near the end of aisle one, thick rubber slats divide the store. Midshelf, next to my left hand, a notebook. Blue. College ruled, 150 sheets, three subjects. 9 ½ x 6 inches. It fits perfectly under my shirt.

The rubber parts. A girl steps out. She reeks of cheap perfume and cigarettes. Her long hair brushes my arm. Past her, I see the back. The room's crowded with boxes—a lifetime supply of corn nuts, Slim Jims and boxed Kool-Aid. Bright light—white, of course—pours through the exit, makes my eye snap. If I can master my pounding heart ("Dude! Get a grip!"), my escape plan (RUN >>>> FAST) might work.

I case the store. My eye strips the junk. Now I just see the basics. People, layout, exits.

Up where the wall meets the ceiling, there are bugs. Well, not bugs, but bug eyes. Round, mirrored insect eyes hiding cameras. Reflected in one, I see my parents. They huddle in the liquor section, heads pressed close together, comparing vodkas. For such observant Muslims, they're singularly obsessed with grain content.

I step to the glass beverage door, hand out, like I'm going to open it. But instead of reaching for the handle, I part the rubber curtains. I slip out of the light, into the dim storage room.

"Ahmed?" Haifa's voice pierces the dark. "Ahmed!" (Like I said, instincts of a homing pigeon.) I run. Already, her voice chases me. "Ahmed!!!"

I trip on empty boxes, slide, trip. My knee slams a metal prong. Fuck!

My eyes aren't adjusting to the dark. Blind, I trip through this painful obstacle course. Too fast, too slow? I don't know, I've lost track of my body. I am all forward movement. Terror is my fuel, smell is my guide. I follow the scent of cigarette smoke and cheap perfume. That girl with the long hair was outside, smoking on her break.

Arms out, my palms touch flimsy aluminum. The doors swing open. I stumble out, into light and heat.

I look over the loading dock. It's a five foot drop to the ground. *I cannot do this.* I'm terrified of heights. I look around, where are the steps?

"*AAAAHHHHMMMMEEEEEDDDDDD!*"

Oh, Haifa. Give it up. Allah, kindly tap her shoulder and let her know, "Ahmed's left the building."

I close my eyes and jump. My body lands, flat and heavy, on the hard dirt. I don't even stand. I scramble, run for the semi alley, low to the ground. I have no idea where I'm going. I'm lost in the engines' roar and air thick with exhaust.

Out of nowhere, a hand grabs my shirt and lifts me up. The claw-hook-hand holds me over the dirt. I land on a passenger's seat, face-to-face with an enormous man. Or woman. Her / his gender is an elevator that's stuck in-between two floors. There's a beard but it looks glued on. Well, Halloween *is* soon. Stomach fat spills over the steering wheel. S / he smiles, a wolfish grin that glints gold and nicotine stains. The meat hook / hand reaches up and jerks a cord.

HONK! HONK! HONK!

The truck lurches and rolls forward. Large Marge reaches around the seat and opens a small, second door.

"Git," s / he orders, picking me up again by my neck and tossing me out as quickly as s / he took me in. "Run straight that'er're way. Three trucks, thar's ya ride, waitin' fer yew."

I leap out the back door, run that'er're way, the length of three semis, and turn right.

My ride: a cherry red convertible. Xena and her warrior gal pal, the supermodel dyke duo, sit in the muscle car's front seat. The motor's running. They wave me over.

I jump in the backseat and pull the door shut. The car peels out. My body slams against the hot, black leather.

The world becomes a blur of alloy wheels and metal.

I feel like James Bond's bitch.

Chapter 3

The brunette—the one who looks like Xena's twin—turns and reaches over the seat. She holds out wire clippers.

"What the fuck?!" Xena ignores me, lifts the bottom of my jeans and clicks the clippers. Snip, the white plastic ankle bracelet drops. She tosses it out the car. I love the dykes, they're so fucking can-do.

"Here." She dumps clothes on my lap. We're still in a James Bond movie. The car's moving at the speed of sound or near to it.

"Whoa!!!" Xena screams. "Sandy, grrrrl, you gon' win the derby!" Pirates, the women thrust bare arms up, into the air. Sun gleams on their tan skin and black, barbed wire tattoos.

I look back. My parents, those two clueless fucks, stand on the Shop 'N Go's loading dock. Moustapha's mouth is pulled down into his "I'm pissed off" face. Beside him, Haifa's slipped into her helpless act. I can practically hear her whine, "Honey, *what* should we *do?*" as she reaches into her clutch for the cellie. I bet she's got Serenity Ridge on speed dial and has already plotted her refund request: "He's still gay! He escaped!"

I turn back and face the front. I can't be bothered.

Sandy drives so fast the car sucks wind, and hot air thrashes my face. I claw, desperate to peel off the stiff blue denim jeans and shapeless, polyester shirt. I want nothing more than to shed these lame-ass Mormon boy clothes.

My spontaneous nudist behavior shocks me. My whole life I've been shy about undressing in front of strangers. But now I can't wait to take off my clothes. I want nothing more than to feel the hot wind lick my body. A pukey lime green, my olive skin's starved for sun. In seconds, I'm nearly naked and *really* confused. For the second time in as many minutes, I lose track of the moment.

Meaning, I don't know where I am. I don't know who I am. I know I'm "free" . . . and still high, on hospital drugs. Or, I'm losing my mind. I go with it.

"Here," the brunette says. I get a better look at her face. She's gorgeous. A cross between Salma Hayek and Penélope Cruz. *Ola, chica, donde Latina?* She holds out an Evian. I take it and tilt the bottle, guzzling la agua.

"Hey, pilgrim!" Sandy shouts. "Take a fucking look! America!"

Our eyes meet in the rearview mirror. I know her. She's the crazy white girl who grew up in a trailer park with an alcoholic father who molested her while Mom waitressed in a casino.

"See, they'll *never* get'cha!" Sandy yells.

I know what *that* means. Sandy won't be satisfied until she's certain that *I* see what *she* sees. Dutiful, I turn and look back. Five semis split off into opposite directions, creating an enormous dust ball. *Whoosh!* The opening sequence of James Bond #39, "Dust Ball."

"See, we tricked 'em! Hi, I'm Elena!"

Up front, the girls chatter, laughing. Sandy cranks the music. The speaker blares, bad rock (screechy guitar solos). Heat waves glimmer on the road and empty desert. The speedometer's eighty-five M.P.H. Every mile the car travels puts more distance between me and my parents. And, I know my parents. They won't stop until I turn eighteen. Or catch me. Or I'm dead.

I should be grateful I've been rescued by these female pirates but . . . where the fuck am I going?

The leather seat sticks to my naked back and hamstrings. I close my eyes and spread my arms. I savor the feeling of hot air mixed with the thrill of escape. Silent D.J., I work the reluctant junkie feeling into the mix. Delicious. I feel like I'm in a mobile spa.

Blink: The back of my eyelids go white and take me back to the private screening room. On it, a sea of men in butt-hugger swimsuits. I was twelve when I started riding my bike to the park. I rode around the fruit loop and stared at men sunbathing on the grass slope. They all wore tiny bits of stretchy fabric that were designed to show off their muscular bodies and big dicks.

In my mind's eye, beneath its bright, midafternoon sun, the men's bodies glisten, their tan skin slick with oil. I set myself down in the middle of them. I'm no longer a skinny kid wearing saggy granny briefs but a hot, young muscle boy surrounded by tons of studly admirers.

"Doll!" Elena's voice breaks the bikini brief spell. "Ya betta get dressed, *now.*"

I open my eyes and reach for the light brown chinos. I slide my orange kicks through the legs and hike them up over my slim hips. The pants are ten sizes too large. I need a belt.

"Here." Elena holds out a heavy leather belt with a brass buckle. On it, the cowboy rides a broncing stallion. "That was my bro's, Luis's, so you better take good care of it."

Our hands touch. Something besides the belt passes between us. Her sad, beautiful eyes say everything. She doesn't need to explain Luis is the reason she's helping me.

"I don't wanna be gettin' this back from *you.*" Her stern voice trails off. The hard prison matron shell cracks. Tears well up and threaten to spill out her almond-shaped eyes.

I look away, embarrassed. I can't bear to look at her face. It's an open wound. I mumble, "Sure," turn my body away from the front seat and thread the belt through the back loops.

Elena takes my chin and gently tilts it up with her elegant fingers. Tiny golden sunsets and palm trees are painted on the nails. She looks me in the eye. "You better."

The engine growls, a deep, steady hum. The speedometer inches toward a hundred M.P.H. The ladies grasp my need to travel, fast.

"Here." Sandy holds out a trucker's cap. "Put this on."

The wind shatters Sandy's stiff hair, churning the blond ice picks into a white froth. In the rearview mirror, my brown eyes meet hers. They're emerald green, mischievous as a cat's. "You can tip me later," she says, arching her back, pushing out her boobs and licking her lips.

OMG! I've been rescued by lesbian strippers!

Elena leans over and takes Sandy's face between two deadly claws. She pulls the other girl's glossy, pink lips toward her dark red ones. *Finally,* the lezzie moment. The women kiss, passionately and without shame. Fortunately, the road *is* straight so we don't get into an accident. They part. Elena turns to me. "See, you could have that, too. But with a guy, if that's what you want." Oh, you think?

She reaches back, yanks the trucker cap down and hides my face. Now that I'm fully dressed, I'm ready for my racial profiling. People constantly mistake me for Mexican. These loose, baggy clothes make me look like a wannabe cholo. I feel . . . how *does* E'sai feel? He doesn't know. His feelings are loose change that drop out dime-sized pocket holes.

"After we let you out on the street," Elena says, "go down the side of the house, jump the back fence and *run—*"

"*Book,*" Sandy adds. Her voice—sharp, momentarily sane—makes me look up into her nutty emerald eyes. "You listening?"

Like most crazy people, Sandy's keenly aware of other people's behavior, especially the attention they are or aren't paying her.

"Yes, of course, I'm listening. Go down the side of the house, jump the back fence—"

"Right, and after you jump the fence—this is *real* important—it's a hundred seventy steps to the top. Got that? You just go, *up.* Climb. There're steps carved in the hill. All you gotta do is focus on counting. One to one hundred seventy. Don't look back, don't think, jus' keep movin'—forward. *If* ya get caught, it'll be 'cause ya stopped. I'll be straight with you. The guy who owns Serenity Ridge, his house is near the one with the side path. Takes you right to the top. And I got the feelin' you know *exactly* what I'm talkin' 'bout, right?"

"Yeah, for sure."

"Right. But then when you go down the hill, slow down, 'cause it'll be dark and you're not gonna be able to see your way so good."

Elena reaches back. She holds out a wallet. "In there, that's your fake ID." I take the leather square and slide it in my back pocket.

"Hurry up, baby, we're almost there."

I've listened to Sandy so closely I missed seeing how the landscape mutated: from desert to suburb.

The car slows, veers to the right and exits the freeway.

We drive down an off-ramp.

Redwhiteblue lights flash.

A cop.

My heart seizes.

The car slows, pauses at a stop sign.

I knew it. I'm gonna get caught.

Chapter 4

1 776 Liberation Drive.
I stand on the sidewalk outside a tacky tract house. The red muscle car drives down the street, turns and vanishes. Maybe they're following the cop car that pulled up and sped by the Mustang.

Gold light casts shadows on perfectly manicured lawns and leafy trees. The sun's on the verge of setting. I glance at the enormous, fiery orb, turn and run up the driveway. There, just like Sandy said, is a path that runs parallel along the side of the house. My spirits lift.

I run, crouched down, close to the ground. The pebbled path crunches underfoot. Halfway to the gate, I see a rectangle of light on the wood fence. I stop at eye level with the picture window's bottom ledge.

I look through the window and see a dining room. A family of four (mother, father, one boy, one girl) sit, about to eat dinner. White napkins lie on their perfect laps of creased slacks and ironed dresses. Heads down, hands clasped, they pray. I do a double take: I *know* the father! Edward Parker Jones. He runs Serenity Ridge! WTF! Sandy said "near," not "living in."

I stare at these All-American Robots and remember my own. At Ahmed's house, dinnertime wasn't scheduled for eating but for fighting. Someone was always getting mad, shoving back his chair, boycotting dinner or sulking in his room. We were ideal candidates for the most disastrous reality TV show, ever!

Prayer over, the family drops their hands and reaches for the food. The boy reminds me of me when I was eight, shy with hair parted on the side. He feels my gaze and looks up. I stick out my tongue and pull my cheeks apart. He sees me and points. His sister—also blond, hair pulled into two, doll-like ponytails—follows her brother's tiny finger to the window. She sees me—Arab, probably a *terrorist*—and screams.

I run to the gate and lift the metal latch. It swings open. I run across the lawn and around a kidney-shaped pool. I'm tempted to jump into the blue-green water, toss the rainbow-colored beach balls and hump the giant, inflated walrus. Then, I see a hill over the fence. I am one hundred seventy something steps away from freedom.

I know I shouldn't look back, but I do. On the back patio, three vicious Dobermans strain at their leashes, long snouts snapping. They make no sound except for an awful hacking sound. Their voice boxes have been cut out.

I know how they feel. They did that to us at the hospital—removed our voices. I often wondered where they stored those voices. In a room? Or, did they flush them down the toilet, all our cries swirling through the sewers, and out to the ocean?

The sliding glass door opens. Mr. Jones steps out. I feel his eyes on my back. He's on the phone. His calm voice floats across the pool. "He's in the backyard." He doesn't chase me. Mr. Jones always preached solution. His solution to this situation is to reach down and unhook the Dobermans' collars.

The dogs sprint—toward me. I'm inches from the fence. Arms up, hands open, I leap. Splinters dig into my hands, but—being numbed by drugs—I feel nothing.

Behind me, the dogs' nails click on pavement. They leap, their sharp fangs nipping at my butt. They fall away and land on their raised ridged backs, pockets hung out their foaming mouths.

Crazy amounts of adrenaline pump through my body. I haul myself up, plant my left foot on top of the fence and hoist my body over.

The dogs recover and leap. Their heads butt, skulls cracking. I feel sharp teeth slice the fabric, digging into my calf, hamstring and ankle. I yank, and pull my leg out their mouths. It feels like razors are dragged over my skin.

The dogs have tasted blood and want more. Sure enough, they go mad sketchy crazy and bounce back up. Aloft, the dogs are Olympic pole vaulters jumping high as the ledge. But their snouts miss my legs and hit the orange sneakers, nudging me up and over the fence.

I drop, land on the hard desert floor and sprint across the sandy stretch between fence and hill. Warm wetness drips off my right leg. Blood. Fuck it. I'm pure, forward movement. Unlike the store, I can see where I'm going. Great. More heights. Nausea. I run.

The ground is lined with rows of cacti and dozens of other nasty, snapping, Dobermanish plants. A snake springs up, jaws open, fangs dripping venom, tongue flickering. But I'm too damn quick and escape. Adrenaline propels me, human rocket fuel. I'm stopwatch ready and reckon I'll reach the hill in under a minute.

I climb.

Step up, one.

Step up, two.

Step up, three.

Four, five, six, seven, eight.

The faster I count, the higher I climb.

I slip. I stop. Look back. DON'T. It's *so* far down! One misstep and I could fall. Who would be there to care? Catch me? Edward Parker Jones? No, no one. Forget it. I focus on what I *can* deal with. Like the fact that the hill's covered with sandy pebbles that roll underfoot like marbles. I put out my hands and steady myself. Up, up, up. I lean forward, body close to the ground.

Close up, this hill is more of a mountain. It's also a lot steeper than it looked from the house. Scaling the incline, I feel like a monkey on a vine, a Curious George of the Suburban Jungle. Halfway to the top, a wave of weariness washes over me. Behind me, the light fades, casting a golden hue on the brown hill. I want to look back. Don't look back! I feel my energy fade with the sun as it slips under the horizon. I want to stop, rest.

"I remember when they brought in a doctor, a real one, to look at me. He said, 'I've never seen damage like this.' " I want to put up my hands, cover my ears and block out Lance's voice. But he won't be quiet, and if I did, I'd lose my balance. *"The best that he could do was cover the head of the penis with a Vaseline-soaked gauze."* I shout, "Leave me alone!" But Lance continues, *"He said, 'Loss of sensation was not uncommon and often permanent.' "* I hear his words and my weariness evaporates. The exhaustion drops off my head and my legs obey and I scramble up the hill just as the light on my back peaks, fades and vanishes.

I am near the top.

Then.

Gunshots.

Chapter 5

*B*ang! Bang! Bang!
Bullets kick up the dirt. It's night. He can't see me. I escape into the dark. For once, youth is on my side.

"One hundred sixty-eight, one hundred sixty-nine and ..." No air, no breath, I drag oxygen into my burning lungs. At the top, I exhale, *"One. Hundred. Seventy!"*

I'm on the other side of the hill. Safe. But at the same time, not. Eleven months ago, I learned safety comes and goes. Safety is temporary. I must be vigilant.

Hands to knees, my mouth hangs open. I suck up air—giant gulps—my abs contracting without expanding, lungs and throat burning.

I look back. My eyesight's blurry, but I can see Mr. Jones well enough to know that he holds a gun. Behind him, in front of the house, there are flashing lights.

Blueredwhite redbluewhitered.

There's a clusterfuck of cop cars on the street.

Another memory. Eleven months ago, the cops smashed my bedroom door, pulled me off my bed and out into the hallway. They slapped handcuffs on my wrists and dragged me down the steps to a silver sedan.

I turn away from the memory. Spent, I hobble down the hill.

This side of the mountain is dark. The steps down are un-even, tricky. I remember Sandy's advice to go slow. I navigate them with help from the city's blinking, neon light. I don't know why, but going down the hill becomes easier than going up. Maybe coz you're going down?

Each step brings me closer to the Vegas strip. Where, I won-der, who or what awaits.

Chapter 6

I am hungry. Starving, really. My stomach was about to go cannibal. Turn and devour itself.

I shove the rolled-up tortillas into my dry mouth. The soft, warm bread wet with butter and stuffed with rice and beans. Mexican food's never tasted so good. I choke. I forget—burrito numero cuatro in as many minutes. One of the men holds out a water bottle. I take it and suck, hard, till the plastic crinkles. Fluid floods my throat and pushes the food down, into my bloated stomach. I burp. My tummy's ready to explode. I don't care.

The men tug at my clothes. "Jouvencito, cambiate la ropa!" Yeah, I comprende. (I took three years junior high school Spanish.) I ignore them. They tell me I need to change. My clothes, my identity, my everything. I'm sick of people telling me what to do. Another one holds out clothes, stacked and folded. They smell clean.

I take the clothes and strip. Back in the desert, I ditched my modesty. Or, maybe my modesty went even earlier than that, in Serenity Ridge. Then, it was different: My modesty was *taken* from me. I reset the button, back in the desert. I *chose* to surrender my modesty. I feel a little flicker and my power come back. Yeah, I *chose*.

I switch trucker hat for safari hat. Blood runs down my leg.

The skin's covered with red dots, crescent shaped, the dog's teeth marks. I rip off a piece of fabric and wrap it around the flesh wound.

New outfit, new person? Not really. These clothes couldn't be any more obvious. Even I know that. The jacket might as well have stenciled RUNAWAY TEEN on the back.

"Eh! Vamos!"

The truck slows, the men part the cloth curtains. Below, I see blurred asphalt. Empowered by my paramilitary G.I. Joe getup, I jump, land on a sidewalk and survey the landscape.

Vegas. The old, bad part.

I turn. I want to say, Thank you, but the truck's already gone, merging into traffic. Hand to temple, I salute, *Ciao, Che!*

Inside the bus station, there aren't any showgirls handing out twofer fliers. I do notice two roaming Rent-A-Cops. Officer Dick and his partner, Head. My heart leaps. DickHead strolls through the lobby. It's a cross between a city dump, a mental hospital and casino (Totos Los Desperados). Filthy, the floor and wood benches are crowded with bums. Dressed in rags with smudged faces, they all look the same. Anemic light comes from the blinking-bleeping slot machines.

"San Francisco," the PA announces. "Boarding, Gate Two."

Time is short. If I'm not at Gate Two, and on that bus, then I will be caught. If I'm caught, I will be sent back to Serenity Ridge. And if I go back there, mostly likely I will die.

I join the line to the ticket window. I look up at the enormous clock looming over the main entrance. The second hand travels over the white face and black Roman numerals. The hand consumes one minute in one second.

Sweat runs down my neck. Sick or hot? The tourniquet brushes my pant leg. I glance down. Blood's soaked through the fabric. The stain makes me look like I peed my pants. Yeah, if my dick hung down to my knees.

My heart, already beating at a quick rat-a-tat-tat rate, speeds up. The Rent-A-Cops walk toward the line. Interesting: Death wears ugly, brown polyester uniforms.

"Next!" I step to the narrow metal counter. A prissy clerk sits behind the thick plate glass partition. Name tag. Randy. Randy gives me a look that's a cross between recognition ("Girlllllll!") and hate (jealous that I get to walk around in public wearing this butch getup). Randy wears a gold wedding band.

"Destination?"

"First," I want to ask, "does your wife know you're gay?"

"San Francisco."

Randy is Mormon, has eight kids, and wants to come with.

"Round trip or one way?"

"One way."

"ID." His voice is flat, inhuman. I look close: robot? Or, Tom Cruise?

I reach into my back pocket. Empty. The wallet's gone! Panic in the disco. It's in the pants I left in the truck.

"I—I—I'm sorry. I can't find it."

"Can't sell you no ticket without ID."

"I have money. Cash. See—"

"Don't matter." Randy purses his lips. He loves this. Finding a reason to say no. "Step to the side. Next?"

"But—" I check the other pocket. There. The wallet.

"There a problem?" The Rent-A-Cops loom, human bookends or gladiators with prefrontal lobotomies.

Much as I hate these two minimum-wage morons, I know they can stop me—from buying the ticket. And I need that ticket to get on the bus. And I *must* get on that bus. Because I cannot stop moving. Because if I stop for even one second, I will die. Forward momentum being everything right now.

I ignore Officer Dick and Head. The LAPD drop-outs won't take the hint. They don't move. Death is a stubborn SOB.

I focus, remove the wallet, open it and slide out the (fake) ID. I drop the plastic rectangle on the metal tray. My hands shake: Parkinson's or paranoia, I need to get a grip.

Randy takes the ID without looking at it, fingers flying over a keyboard like a concert pianist's.

"How are you paying for this, sir?"

Sir? And I thought I was cast to play "boy" for the next fifteen years.

"Oh—"

Out the corner of my eye, Rent-A-Cops move, hands on holsters. Death is armed and moves in sync. Death is careful, watching my every move.

I kneel, lift the camouflage pants and unzip the kicks' velcro side pouch. Birthday money. It arrived that day, right before I was "sent away."

I found the plain white envelope, no return address, stuck between catalogues. The crisp bill was stuck inside. She knew; somehow my mother *knew*: Her son would need that money. Coz someday, he would need to escape, run for his life. Same as her. Daddy Saddam has that effect on people.

I slip out the hundred. Deliberate, I place the bill on the tray. Green against silver. There. Now, please hand over my ticket.

Right now, I *really* feel Death's stare-glare. But Officer Dick-Head's so dumb I can hear its thought: "Runaway." Rent-A-Cop Number Two leans down. His mastodon-sized head nudges my chest like a pushy Labrador.

"Lemme see that."

Not a question ("May I see that?"), but a demand.

Focus.

Randy ignores the request. Still, I know I'm three seconds from being caught. In Serenity Ridge, I guarded that money with my life. I never took off my kicks. One kid tried to steal them. I kicked him in the groin and crushed his left testicle. That landed me in solitary for three weeks. I wonder how long this little trip will net: life?

"My mother gave me that hundred for my birthday!" I want to shout. "Really, I'm not a prostitute!" But the Rent-A-Cops haven't asked me any questions. I keep my mouth shut. People only know what you tell them.

Randy pushes ticket, change and fake ID onto the metal tray. "Ticket's nonrefundable. The bus is boarding at Gate Two."

I count the change. I fumble putting it back. The laminate falls out, tumbles to the floor. Before I can, the Rent-A-Cop picks it up and examines the picture. My stomach drops.

"Excuse me," I say. "That's mine."

"What's yours," he says, suggesting nothing belongs to me.

"That picture. It's my mom. It's the only one I have."

I look to the crowd for support.

"Sure." He drops it, grinding it under his boot. He moves his shoe. I kneel, pick it up.

"Attention all officers in the Fremont vicinity," the walkie-talkie on the Fake Cop's hip squawks. "Armed robbery, repeat, armed robbery in progress at—"

"We'll be seeing you," Rent-A-Cop says, Officer DickHead's voice in stereo. They turn and march off. From the back, Death's fat ass looks like a pair of overweight marching band majorettes.

Under the baggy clothes, my body is out-of-the-shower wet. I run toward Gate Two. The bus doors pull shut. The engine revvs.

"Hey!" I pound on the door. The giant metal creature lurches, moves back. It's going to leave without me.

"HEY!" I pound harder, running backward with the bus. "LET ME IN!"

Abruptly, the bus stops—not because of me, I realize, but because the driver needs to make a two-point turn and pull onto the road.

"LET ME IN!" I shout, pounding hard, one last time.

The door wheezes and . . . opens.

"Go on, get in," the driver says, impatient behind his silver aviator glasses. Like I was lingering or taking my time. I grab the handicap bar and pull myself up, into the stairwell. Behind me, the door shuts and seals out the hot air.

I head to the back. I sit and look back, out the rear window. The red brake light licks the black asphalt. The bus rolls into the desert, moving away from Las Vegas, an empty giant slot machine made of bright, blinking lights.

Head. Rest. Eyes. Shut.

My vision goes white, blank as a movie screen, same as when the red curtains pull back and the theater dims. An image flickers on the white screen and—

The movie starts.

The boy drives a cherry red Karmann Ghia. Sunlight explodes on his hair. He's smiling, singing.

I look in the rearview mirror. A woman sits in the car's tiny backseat. Wind ruffles the scarf tied around her head. She wears glamorous sunglasses, bright red lipstick and a low-cut white dress with a red cherry print.

"Mom?"

She smiles but says nothing. She doesn't need to: I know she's over my shoulder, *there,* a guardian angel, Djinn, or protective pagan faerie.

My eyes tear up.

"I miss—"

"Shhh," she whispers, and drapes sleep over my eyes.

Then, just as quickly as it appears, the image vanishes and the white screen goes black.

Three angels hover over the highway. They guard the bus. The bread box shape rolls down the two lane blacktop. They watch the gray beast lumber toward the morning sun, bright orange over the desert landscape.

My head slumps against the greasy window.

Sleep, death, bliss.

Chapter 7

"**S**AN FRANCISCO, LAST STOP, SAN FRANCISCO!"
"*You!*" A hand grabs my shoulder, shakes me. My ass squirts—*poop*. Yup. Baby Boy shit his pants. Bound to happen. Now it has. I held it in for as long as—"Get up! You gotta get off."

"Mom?" I rub my eyes and look up. No, not Mom, the bus driver. Not even—he's the *maintenance* guy. His name tag. Earl. I push myself, roll off the seat. I'm so not ready to wake up. I'm so tired I could sleep for another hundred years, but Earl's not leaving my seat until I vacate it.

I step off the bus. The door slams. Some welcome. Isn't this city famous for its hospitality? And sourdough bread? My stomach's knotted with hunger. Where's my loaf? While I'm at it: Where's the Golden Gate Bridge? The "fabulous" Victorian architecture? And the streets filled with queer people? Just guessing but Gay Pride's been rescheduled.

Thus far, San Francisco is fog (gray), pigeons (gray) and concrete (gray and covered with white pigeon shit). The only people I've seen are a crazy woman pushing a stroller with a dog and dozens of office drones who wear dark blue business suits and carry briefcases.

Two cops slowly cruise by on bicycles. They wear shorts. I'm distracted by their muscular legs. Their walkie-talkies squawk.

Starfleet's Calling. "All points bulletin! Be on the lookout for an Arab boy who answers to Ahmed! He's escaped from Serenity Ridge! He also answers to Ben!"

The cops roll forward. Even if I'm hearing voices and imagined the Ahmed APB, I know they'll snatch me if they see me. Intuition. I. Gots. To. Go. I step around a corner, vanish into the shadows and escape my paranoia. I look for a pay phone. But that just leads me back into the dirty bus station. It's the same setup as Vegas minus the slot machines. Same trash, same bums sleeping on the same benches. "Hell," I'll testify (Hallelujah! Praise Jesus! Or whoever you're into, just get me out of here), "is The Bus Station."

There. Pay phone. My grubby hand digs into my grubby pocket and fishes for the scrap of paper. I hold it up. I read the telephone number and scrawled instructions. "Hi, my name is Ben." Any chance I'll have to permanently escape Serenity Ridge rests in these seven digits—and my new, generic American identity. I chant my name: Ben. BenBenBen. A Ben in the Road.

I lift the receiver, drop two quarters and *carefully* (quarters being hard to come by right now) punch in the number. Rings one, two, three—"Click, the Page Net account you're trying to reach is out of service. Message four four—"

I replace the phone and slump back against the casket-shaped booth. I'm fucked and so tired, I'm ready to give up and call my father. His number's the only one I know by heart. Even if I knew it, my real mother's number would be unlisted. Stuart? He's the one who got me into this mess. Think. Who to call. I pick up the phone and dial 4-1-1. "Directory assistance, city and listing please."

"Oh, um . . ." I blank. Why am I calling? I stand there, hold the phone and breath. Very stalkerish.

"Hello? Hello?"

I imagine the operator asks, Is this an emergency? I want her to ask because I want to tell someone, even a stranger, "In fact it is an emergency. I escaped from Serenity Ridge, a Nevada Residential Treatment Facility where I've been locked up and subjected to treatments meant to turn me from gay to straight."

"Page Net," I remember. "San Francisco."

"Please hold for—" The operator cuts herself off. Left, a flash of blue. Cops! I drop the phone. CALM. DOWN. Not a cop. Businessman carrying a briefcase and dressed in a dark blue suit (another uniform). I'm surrounded by clones. 4-1-1. Redial.

"Page Net, howmayIhelpyou?" I read the number. "How may I help you, Ms. Smith?"

"I have a question about my bill. I wanted to double-check the home phone number with the one you had on file?" I hear my upturned voice and wince. I sound like a girl. I'm worried I sound like I believe my own question.

"One moment, plea—" The operator's voice is gone; another automated voice comes on and recites the number. I drop my last coins in the slot, dial and listen. Ring one, two, three . . . ten. I'm about to hang up / give up. *Click.* The line picks up.

"Hi, I'm—"

Bleep! A machine. Silence. Maybe someone's listening. Maybe there is a place. Maybe it's safe. Maybe—

"Hi, this is, uh . . . me. Ben. I'm at the bus station. Downtown? Someone gave me your number—well, your other number—but it was out of order. Anyway, I'm gonna wait here. Um, well, I guess I'll hide in the men's room. Last stall. On the right. I'll stay there till you show up. I'm wearing orange kicks and a safari hat."

I stretch out my message. I hope, if I keep talking, someone will hear me and pick up.

Beep!

The machine cuts me off. I hang up.

Chapter 8

L eft, a big man steps around a corner and walks toward me. His look shouts, "Bounty Hunter." I look around. There's nowhere to go. I am trapped. I step back, duck into the men's room, run to the last stall. I could be on a spaceship: It's one of those industrial bathrooms. The reflective silver surfaces are scratched. I close the door, careful not to make a sound. Then, I wait, and stare at my schizo-scratch'up'd reflection.

Rubber sneaks skid-screech on the floor. I look through the crack in the door: a boy. He looks around the bathroom. Too late, he realizes, "I'm trapped." I see it on his face: There's nowhere to hide. Dead. End. We hold our breath. A second set of footsteps breaks the quiet. *Click-click-click.* Official sounding. Dress shoes. Or, Shirley Temple.

I peek through a crack. A man, his back is turned away from me, grabs the boy and holds a knife to his neck.

"I want my money's worth." He pushes the boy against the sink and yanks down his jeans. The bunched-up denim pools at his ankles. He tries to move, but the thick fabric stops him.

The man squeezes the boy's neck. The trench coat cloaks their bodies. I know what's happening coz I see the boy's face in the broken mirror. His eyes are shut, his mouth screwed up with pain.

"Ah!" The man's head drops back, his body shudders. The

boy's hand grips the sink. The man steps back and zips up. The boy drops to the floor. Blood and shit dribble out of his butt.

The man ignores the boy and reaches for soap and water. Calm, he washes his hands. The boy looks up. Our eyes meet. He puts up his arm.

"Help—" the boy rasps, a strangled cry for help. His arm drops, dead next his limp, lifeless body.

The man turns, away from the sink, to the stall. I can't see his face, just his eyes. Blank, they're android blue and tell me he feels . . . nothing. For the boy, for what he just did.

"Ah!" I cry. I can't help it. It's just a peep, but the sound gets the man's attention. He grabs the knife and steps toward the stalls.

My heart beats so loud, I'm sure he can hear it. There's nowhere for me to hide.

Click. Click. Click.

He walks down the line, tapping the knife on each stall door.

Click. Click. Click.

He walks the line, opening each door.

I squat on the seat. His shadow moves along the floor. He stops, one stall from mine.

Creak . . .

The door swings open, its shadow moving over the floor. This is way worse than any movie. I can't pick up the remote and press Pause. Real life, I need to act.

Click. Click. Click.

The man's heels tap dance on the floor. My stall's last in the line. He knows. I know that he knows. And he knows that I know. Both of us know. Someone saw and now they're hidden in the last stall.

Click—

The door handle turns. Slow. Time. To. Die.

No.

Last second, I dip and slip under to the next stall, moving back as he steps forward—

Click—

The knife taps, metal-on-metal door.

Tap—

I slip under the partition. The safari hat's knocked off—

Creak—

The door opens. I don't know what's worse. Capture, rape or death—or the knowledge right before one or all happens. I'm starting to believe death *is* my destiny. Another runaway, found on a bus station in a pool of blood.

He raises the knife, ready to kill, and I know he will if he sees the hat. Act, Ahmed, you have one chance. Live or die, you choose—

I reach, grab it—

And the door slams, *WHOMP!* Heels *click-click-click,* he barges into the empty stall. The shadow turns and turns and turns, an animal furious about losing its prey. Or, a ballerina, spinning along in a jewelry box, crazed by the music.

Ballerina or predator, IDK because I'm gone.

And this time, I don't need anyone to tell me.

I don't look back.

Chapter 9

I know I can't ask for help. I just follow a cute guy to an escalator. It stretches so far down I can't see where it ends. Down, the bottom, a train pulls into the station. Orange and white doors slide open. Black letters spell out CASTRO. Castro's Ground Zero for The Gays. For safety (or, something like it) the Castro's my Number One destination. I hope.

I step inside. The doors slide shut. My eyes meet blue robot eyes.

The train pulls away. I *know* him. I've seen those blue eyes. But where? I want to take another look. Maybe he wasn't bathroom stall man. It's official, I'm losing my mind.

"Civic Station! *Ciiiivick* Station! Next stop! Civic Station."

I jump off. I figure, I'm safer above ground than trapped underground. The escalator's slow. I hurry, up-up-up, pushing past more men in dark blue suits.

" 'Scuse me, 'scuse me."

At street level, I see a sign: YOUTH DROP-IN SHELTER. Yeah! Safety! Salvation! Forget the Castro, I don't need you. I cross the street without looking. I enter. I *belong* here. If anyone's a Drop-In Youth who needs shelter, I am.

The receptionist is a black girl with cornrows. She sits at the front desk, regal as a queen on her throne. She doesn't look up from the computer screen. Scrabble.

"How may I help you?" she says, the voice of an off-duty gospel singer. I guess it's not totally obvious who I *am*: a runaway teen ISO shelter. She's confused me with the cable guy? I bite my lip. I'm outside, on the street. I need to get back there, behind the Plexiglas and locked door.

"Oh, um, I'm here about shelter?"

She looks me over, like I'm some reality TV reject, calculating statement with the obvious fact of my youth. The phone rings. She answers it and smiles. I can tell, she'll forget about me.

I make my helpless face. It's not tough to pull off. I *am* helpless.

I try not to, then I do: look over my shoulder. Is he outside? The stalker-rapist? Easy, he could reach inside, grab my arm, snatch—

BZZZZZZZZZZZZ!

The door clicks. I step inside. It's official: Ahmed's off the street.

"Wait there." She gestures over her shoulder, at a bench. I stumble forward. My legs give out. I collapse on the wood slats. I lean back. I close my eyes.

"You'll need to wait there for an intake counselor. It might be a while."

I nod, Okay. I don't care how long it takes. So long as bulletproof glass separates me from the street. Here, I can see anyone who walks through the door. Like, for example—oh, shit!—Mr. Blue Eyes. His mouth moves, voice muffled. Underwater.

"No, sir, I will *not* let you in, I do not *care* who—"

I open my eyes and shit my pants for the second time. Mr. Blue Eyes looks at me. Miss Gospel Singer's big head blocks his face. I see those blue-blue eyes. Ice cubes. They bore into me. I drop my head, chin to chest, but he's seen my face, taken his picture. His eyes move down, to his left. Mine follow. There, hidden from her sight line, he pushes back his trench coat and strokes the knife handle.

I pass out.

Chapter 10

I wake. I've been moved to an office. A white lady with fake dreadlocks sits behind a messy desk. Before she opens her mouth, she bugs me. Reword. She bugs the *shit* out of me. I know her type. Even so, I give her a Once-Ovah (my version of racial profiling). Tragically, Ms. Irritata thinks just because she invested in dreads and shapeless hemp "fashion," she's doing "good work."

Reality? She'd look so much better with a blond bob and dark blue suit. She could work in a bank. Ms. Irritata's a classic, fat-ass example of white-people's-crimes-against-humanity, the most serious count against her being Really *Bad* Fashion (not to be confused with "bad ass"). Call me classist, racist, ageist—maybe even a little bit antifeminist—but that's what I see.

Rat-a-ta-tat. She types (loudly) on a laptop. She's probably chews her food loud, too. And farts in public, clueless to the sound because she wears a *Walkman* and listens to Sade 24 / 7. Three strikes. Silent, I sentence her to twenty years. I glance at the screen. My life hangs in the balance and she's . . . searching for *apartments?!?*

"Uh—"

"I'll be with you . . ." Her bored-but-brisk tone's meant to make me—oh, hi? Runaway teen? In shelter?—feel like I am the one bothering her. Done, she looks up. "How may I help you?"

"That man, he—I—" I don't know how to tell her. I'm not even sure I saw what I saw. Clearly, I'm supposed to tell her what happened, why I'm here and what I want.

"*Two* minutes," she says, impatient as a waitress at lunch hour. Then what? I wonder. You need to take the eggs off the stove? Run a mini-mile marathon? Her left eyebrow cocks, Mr. Spock style. "Your pimp said—"

"Pimp?" I am confused. The left eyebrow drops and she cocks the right. If she takes requests, I want to see her do it real fast. Work it, Ms. Irritata, work your fancy eyebrow dance! "He? Who?"

I stop. Fuck her, there's no way I can explain *everything* in two minutes. Besides, where would I start: Haifa's Hasidim helmet hair? The supermodel dykes? Bloodthirsty dobermans? Gunshots? Illegal immigrants? Downtown Vegas, rent-a-cops and slot machines? Or—oh, yeah!—Mr. Blue Eyes. Deadly, you've heard about him? He carries a knife, and rapes and kills boys in the men's room.

"Can I stay here?"

"I can't help you if you won't tell me what happened." She narrows her beady banker eyes. *Now* I get it. I'd better barf up some trauma *now* or get the fuck out. She expects me to wrap my story with a little bow and hand it over. Here, for you, Ms. Irritata, for your collection. Merry Christmas! But I don't celebrate Christmas, Jesus is the same as Buddha, and the twelve disciples were all drunks.

I do, however, remember the telephone number. I tap the digits in my palm, silently repeating the sequence. To her, I prolly look like a crazy kid who thinks he's the male Helen Keller. I don't care what she thinks about me: I know what I think about her, starting with the upper lip: "Lady, hasn't anybody ever told you that you should get your mustache waxed?"

"Listen, um—" Busted! She doesn't know my name. She has so many *other* items on her mind. Dry cleaning. Organic groceries. What's on cable TV tonight. Where's the vibrator (to go with the cheesy lesbian porn). Clearly, I am the least of her worries. "What's your name again?"

The safe sex poster hangs crooked on the wall, directly over Ms. Irritata's dreads. I noticed they're flecked with lint. Cool! I choose the smiling boy on the left.

"Edward," I say. We're friends. Why stand on ceremony? I ask, "Can I stay here?"

"Edward, *by law,* after seventy-two hours, we are required *by law* to notify your parents."

The hair prickles on my neck. She should *know* this stuff. She should be *prepared* for kids like me. Be ready to *roll out the red carpet.* Know there are those of us who *don't* want their parents notified for—a lifetime would not be long enough—of their whereabouts.

"Unless you disclose your circumstances, we can't help you." She smiles. Or, grimaces. I can't read the face. She has gas?

"Oh." We? Really. *We.* I give her my spaced-out / those crazy kids smile. Truth, I'm not willing to disclose anything, circumstances or circumcision, to this self-coronated queen. Her principality being The White People's Wannabe Banjo Republic of Hemp and Linty Press-On Dreads.

"You can tell me what happened," she says.

Yeah, I think, holding my spacey smile. I've heard that before. "Trust me. It's okay. Tell me your secret. I won't tell. I *promise.*" I shake my head. "Go fuck yourself, Rasta poseur."

"Take these." She plants her hands on the desk, gives it a hard shove and rolls her chair back. She reaches into the desk and removes a stack of rectangle-shaped packets. She places them down on the desk. Her gesture's care reminds me of a flight attendant's long fingers closing an overhead luggage compartment. I hear a voice. Dude! Rouse thyself! Ye not on thy ladies plane!

I look at her. Her mouth moves. For a moment, I think— She's talking?—but all I hear is a *wah-wah-wah.* A *Charlie Brown Christmas* special teacher voice. I tune in and hear, "*Wah-wah-wah* you can get food with these vouchers, but honestly, Jeremy, I think your best bet's calling your parents. Go home. The streets aren't for you."

Done, she sits back. That's her pitch: Go home. The streets

aren't for you. Who, I want to ask, are the streets for? I love that she called me "Jeremy." Was he the kid in the bus station? The one who got murdered? Did she suggest he go home, too? I look at her. *All* attitude. Yeah, I have it in me: I can be a shady biatch. I feel like I should tell her that this *job* isn't "for her." She sucks. There hasn't been one "sweetheart" or "honey" in all of her canned "advice." Which sounds like something you'd hear on a community access show. When this little interview's over, I plan to fill out the comment card with a simple "YOU SUCK."

I look at the vouchers. She looks at me. I'm supposed to answer. *Now*.

"Can I make a phone call?"

"Local?"

No, I want to say, you stupid fuck, I'm calling Saudi Arabia to order a prop plane jihad on this lame-ass shelter.

I nod. She gestures at the phone but doesn't move from her seat. I tilt my head down, and look up. Not to be confused with my helpless look, this is my shy face.

"I kinda need to be alone, so could you . . ."

I glance at the door.

She must be desperate to leave and pick up her organic dry cleaning, because she stands and leaves, no questions asked.

I pick up the phone and dial. Listen. One ring.

" 'lo?"

"Hi," I say. I try to sound as normal (relaxed, not desperate or panicked) and gay (done) as possible while asking for help from a stranger. "I'm, uh—" What's my fake name again? "Ben! I called before. Left a message. But I had to leave the bus station."

"Where are you?"

I search for something that will tell me where I am. There. Blue letters stamped on white pen.

"Larkin Shelter."

"Tell them you need to use the restroom. There's a set of stairs at the end of the hall. On the third floor, there's a women's room. Hide in the last stall. Don't move."

"But, should—"

The line goes dead, the door opens and Ms. Headda Dreadful steps into the room.

"Are we good?"

"Can I use the bathroom?"

"Down the hall and to the right."

Chapter 11

I reach into my pants and pull out the blue notebook I "borrowed" from the Shop 'N Go. Plus, the pen I stole from the social worker's desk. Go ahead. Say it. Natural Born Klepto.

I plant my kicks on the toilet seat, open the notebook and prepare to write. Sitting this way is awkward. I close the notebook and sit, ass flat on the seat. This is G-R-O-S-S since there's no t.p. or any of those wispy coverlet things. I force myself to ignore the fact there's nothing between me and billions of E. coli. I open the notebook and lay it flat on my knees. White paper with light blue lines. It's been almost a whole year since I could write what I want to in a notebook. Pen to paper.

i

The gesture fills me with dread. At any moment, cops or bounty hunters might break down the door, take the notebook and use what I wrote inside as evidence.

FUCKING HELL!!!!!!!!!

I'm mad. I want to throw the notebook against the stall. Hard. Kill it. I worry this is how Mr. Blue Eyes got his start. Calm down. This notebook's cousin is the whole reason I was

locked up and tortured in Serenity Ridge. Fool, I *trusted* my
thoughts to the notebook when I wrote

i might be queer

Not

i am queer

Just

i MIGHT be queer

One. Two. Three. Four words. "Evidence." Of what, I never
got an answer, but my stepmother, father and a whole bunch of
adults were convinced those words meant everything. The
worse part, I was *so* careful. Porn and gay chat rooms? Before I
logged off, I'd erase the browser history and clear the cache.
Every time. And I didn't do anything ridiculously stupid like
create a blog (The Secret Diary of All-American Gay Arabian
Teen). I left no clues. I got caught only because I wrote with pen
on paper. Dummy. Moustapha and Haifa were so obsessed with
my computer, I never dreamed they'd even think to open a notebook. Diaries and journals being just so last (20th) century.
Cool and kinda retro! I assumed they thought, no one as smart
as our son would be dumb enough to write down his thoughts.
Deep breath.

four FUCKING words

There. My hand feels looser now. I could never have written
those words in the hospital. I could never have spoken those
words. Deceitful notebook. I could rip this one to shreds and
flush it, but I don't because then I'd really be alone. I'll vomit my
thoughts and *use* this dumb-ass notebook—*then* I'll flush it.
Attn. notebook: You're safe. But when I'm done with you,
you're D-E-A-D. Dumb-Ass Word Turd, I'll LMAO and flush—

forget it
i have to forget the hospital for right now because i
do not know—the silver door. i can see me. well, not
really me. more, a dark shape in the surface. the blot
is more like a ghost. i am the ghost looking at its
reflection. startled to see how he looks. real but not.

I reread the words. They make perfect sense.

i feel—

The pen stops. Feelings? Mine are global and quickly expanding. Chaos, soon to equal those of creation. Deep breath.
My alma mater, Serenity Ridge, *remember*. There, feelings were
like yesterday's trash, a chore. Your job was to stuff them in a
plastic bag, tie the top and take them out to the curb. Problem
was, the psychic trash collector never showed. Budget cuts.

I can't write about my feelings, because there's *one* feeling
that makes sense. At Serenity Ridge, I was "taught." Who am I
kidding? I wasn't taught; I was brainwashed. For months, someone told me what to feel. But here, alone in the women's room,
with a kazillion chaotic feelings (and germs), the real problem is
feeling what *I* feel. Or . . . Everything. For a moment, I consider
hopping off the seat, diving into the toilet and flushing myself.

Get A Grip
what do you feel?

IDK. IDK. IDK. I. Don't. Know. Answer Fail. I'm the one
asking the question.

FEAR. i am afraid. what will happen to me?
this is so damn scary. i am hungry. "wait."
but for who? "someone"

Now I remember why I chose to use journals in the first
place. Class assignment, one. But more, I needed to tell *me*. My

Story. I was both audience and actor. If I could make sense of my life, then . . . If I could—can—tell myself a story, I could—will—survive.

BE GONE FEAR
LOVE AND HAPPINESS

> i will write about serenity ridge. but I will write
> about middle school. i remember, I walked down the
> hallway. there were so many people. a blur. faces. all
> i had to do was get through the day and i would be
> okay. i am fourteen. i am in ninth grade at _____

I pause. Write.

i might be queer

Tap tap, knock knock. Oh, shit! I've been found! "Hey, you in there?" A girl's voice. "Ben?" Ben? Who's Ben? Oh, yeah. Takes me a second, then I remember.

I. Am. Ben. Ben is me. The new me. The Ben Me. The Ben-E-me of Ahmed. Parry, thrust, Ben stands over Ahmed. Triumph! Long live Ben! Etc. I lift my shirt and slide the notebook underneath.

"Yeah? Who's that?"

"C'mon, move it," she says, "open up. We don't have much time."

I lift the latch and open the door. Short and fat, Miss "C'mon Move It" wears Chunky, Nerd Girl glasses and rumpled clothes. She smiles. "Ben?"

"Ah—" I catch myself, reminding myself to say my new name. "*Yes.* I am Ben." I sound so FOB (fresh off the boat) but then, I guess I am. Except in my case, it's fresh off the bus.

"Hi, I'm Marci."

She turns and I follow her out the exit, down another hallway and into a stairwell.

WAH! WAH! WAH!

An alarm goes off. Except, I know it's not a fire but me they're looking for. I am the emergency. I was so close. I want to go back, have a moment with john. I really needed a private moment, to take a dump.

"*C'mon*," she says, calm, like she rescues runaways on a daily basis. Like a movie, everything shifts to—

Slo-mo—

Death—

He's farther back, as I—

Pull out in front. I might just win this race. We scramble down three flights, our footsteps echoing in the empty well. On the ground floor, we burst out the building, onto an alleyway. A blue beater van is parked by the curb.

We climb inside; the van drives away. Past the patrol car that pulls up and the cops who jump out, guns drawn. You'd think it was a bank robbery. I can't figure out what was stolen.

Except, maybe—

Me?

Chapter 12

The VW beater van pulls up to a curb. The engine sputters, dies. We're in a forest. Or, a park. Overhead, the street lamp's dim light filters through a canopy of leaves. I sit in the backseat, next to Marci. The boy driver sits up front. He ignores me.

There's something fishy about this setup. Panic! Adrenaline surge. Get out! Before I become a sex slave. Marci runs a brothel stocked with runaway teenage queer boys. We're locked inside and forced to service men. Yes, I need to jump out and—

"Did anyone see you?"

Sure, I almost say, lots of people *saw* me. A knife-wielding serial killer, for instance.

"No."

"How'd you get my number?"

"Serenity Ridge." I hand over the wrinkled paper. "A boy gave it to me the night before I left. He told me, 'Call this.' "

She examines the paper under the dim light. Everybody's paranoid. Full moon? I never thought *she* might be nervous about meeting *me*. I could be a baby-faced cop posing as a runaway queer teen who's been sent to *bust* the teen boi brothel. She holds up a lighter, flame to paper and drops it out the window.

"That's out of service. How'd you find me?"

"I called the phone company, cross-checked the correct name and address against the bill and—"

A car drives toward us. Lights strobe across our startled faces. A warning? A trap? Marci grabs my head and pulls me down to the floor. We don't move.

"We're good," the boy says.

My face is close to Marci's. She exhales. Pizza breath.

We sit up. I glimpse the boy's face in the side mirror. He's really cute.

"We need your statement," Marci says, facing forward. "It will be transcribed and sent to an attorney via certified mail."

"Why?"

"Why?" she says. She sounds surprised I (dare) question her.

"I don't want a record of my dirty deeds."

"It's so, in case we—you—need to go to court."

"Or, what, coz you really don't believe me?"

"No." The Cute Driver Boy speaks. His deep voice doesn't match his baby face. "Kids change their story. Maybe they tried to kill themselves. Or, they ran away from home. Or, *whatever.*"

On *whatever,* his dark eyes meet mine in the rearview mirror. I thought all I had to do was run away from Serenity Ridge, get myself to San Francisco and the van people would take care of the rest. I want to request, "Some disinterest, please. Some of Ms. Wanna-be Rasta's don't-bug-me-I'm-looking-for-a-new-apartment attitude."

Marci holds up a tiny tape recorder. The red light's on. Cue tape, people, we're live in five, four, three, two, one—Ahmed / Ben's life story. Problem is, I need a nap.

Luckily, I wrote down what happened in the notebook. That's it. I'll *read* my story. I reach under my shirt. An alarmed look crosses Marci's face. She *definitely* thinks I'm undercover— the cop who hides his handcuffs under a tee shirt. She sees the blue notebook and exhales a big gust of Domino's. Extra large relief, hold the anchovies.

"Can I read what I wrote?"

"Sure."

"It's kind of dark." I open the notebook. Light. Driver Boy

holds a flashlight overhead. The pages are covered with scrawl. Doesn't matter, my handwriting or somebody else's, I can barely keep my eyes open. I stare at the page and try to focus. On the words. But I can't. My eyes can't—

"What!" My body jerks. "Epileptic. I caught it in the hospital."

"No," she says. "You dozed off. You were about to read?"

"My story?" Again, I wonder, which one? Supermodel dykes? Large Marge? Downtown Vegas? Blue-Eyed Bathroom Rapist?

"Why'd they put you in Serenity Ridge?"

Oh, that's easy.

"I wrote, 'I might be queer,' for a class assignment."

Marci nods. I can't see her face now. She sits with her back turned, away from the window.

"And how'd they find that out?"

"My stepmother read it." If this is how the interview goes, we'll be done in five minutes. "And she *really* overreacted."

"Right. What happened to you in Serenity Ridge?"

"They gave me a shot. Thorazine or something." I yawn. "I w-w-ant to—"

"Coffee." She holds out a styrofoam cup. "It'll help you stay awake. We can't take you back with us unless we know your story."

I tilt the cup and taste cold, bitter coffee. Neat. Caffeinated cough syrup. Marci's thought of everything. How to keep me up, how to suck out my story. I look at the blank page, where the words—my words—should be. If I'd had more time in the bathroom to write, I would have the luxury of reading it aloud.

I do the next best thing: close my eyes, open my mouth, and let the words tumble out. Out my weary head, down my dry throat and through my heavy, heavy lips.

Chapter 13

"Mrs. McIngle walked through English class, dropping those blue test notebooks on our desks. 'These are your new journals. What you write is between *you, your notebook* and *me*. If you don't want me to read something, staple the pages.'

"The class groaned. Not me. I was excited. I had a *lot* to say and no one to say it to. 'Perfect,' I thought. 'I can write anything in there and . . . they'll never know. Because the parental unit's obsessed with my *computer*. They'll never look in a notebook. Everyone 'knows' the Internet is the 'danger' spot.' Online porn, woo-hoo! Hah. Not for me. I was careful. I always emptied the cache and cleared the history.

"I left class and walked to my locker. I opened it. A dildo fell out. People laughed in the background. Stuff like dildos, all that crap, started in fifth grade. I looked at the dildo. I nudged it with my big toe. It was shaped like a sausage and rolled away.

"Next. The walk of shame. My face felt hot. I knew it was red. 'Later, haters,' I said. I wrote off the dildo. It meant nothing except . . . it was a worse-than-usual 'one of those days.'

"School was a daily dose: same sex harassment run riot. Same as yesterday, same as the day before, same as tomorrow, school sucked. I knew this, so I never fantasized it would ever get *better*. I just never thought it would get *worse,* but it did when people got older. Dildos, Brie-filled condoms—"

"Brie?"

"It melts and looks—kinda smells like, too—sperm. Stuff like this happened—"

"You never complained?"

"To who? A counselor? Sure, I tried. Once. He rolled his eyes and told me to go back to class. What happened was, during the day, my body was there but my head was elsewhere.

"So I get to the end of the hall. I'm thinking. Why a dildo? Why today? Then I think—no, I *know*—'Oh, it's my outfit!' I wore a pink polo shirt with turned-up collar and snug, stove-pipe jeans. The kicks didn't fool anyone. Basketball players—*they* could wear pink. Their pants could hang half off their asses. Not me. I was The Fag. Least, that's what people said. Others were The Slut. Or, The Gigolo. The Methhead, The Pot-head, The Loser, The Dropout, The Brain. I'd cornered the market on The Gay.

"I'd worked it out. Maybe that's why it didn't bug me so much. Kids want to look different for adults but the *same* with each other. You want to fit in there but stand out here. I was the frommage who stood alone."

"You mean," she interrupts, "you had *no* friends? No one? What about the gay–straight club?"

"Right, there was a gay–straight club. But the only people who went were future fag hags and computer geeks padding their activities for college apps. I wouldn't be caught dead there."

"There weren't any other gay kids?" Marci asks.

I'm starting to wonder how many gay teenagers she's met. Have I not spelled out the State of the Teenage Gay?

"There was another one—a gay—and people just 'knew' about him, same as me. We stayed away from one another. I always thought, maybe he's jealous. I got all the attention. Dildos, condoms—oh, and one day, shit smeared on my locker. The janitor pointed out the alfalfa sprouts in the feces. Maybe it was coz I dressed the part. If I was gonna be The Fag, I'd own it. Fuck 'em, y'know?"

"People said stuff?" Marci says. Is she deaf?

"Uh, yeah."

"A lot? Or, just sometimes."

"*All* the time."

"How'd they know?"

I give her my "You've got to be kidding" look.

"I don't know. People, they just *knew*. And I knew they *knew* coz when they called me 'faggot' everyday, they weren't kidding."

"Yeah, but how'd they know? Did you . . ."

"Did I what? Open my mouth? Yeah, and when I did, people knew. Most of the time I was quiet. You know how people are. Like on cop shows. The special light they shine on murder scenes."

"Yeah." She nods. "It lets them see blood."

"Right." I gesture. There I go, "talking" with my hands. I'd point out, another giveaway, but decide to skip it. "With the special light and glasses. These days, all the kids have that special light and glasses. They can just *tell*. Fag. It started and I didn't know what it meant. I was like, 'Fag? What's that?' It's, it's—"

Her face remains blank. I'm frustrated.

"You've never heard this? How kids label you? Like that movie, *The Breakfast Club*. Except, now it's the nerd, the joke, the sosh, the freak and the . . . *fag*."

Her silence asks, How *did* they know? I realize, she wants me to repeat it. Say it twice. Prove I'm not lying.

"Okay, gay people, it's not like they're all secret. They're everywhere. On TV. I guess, I filled the slot. Yeah. I was the school's designated faggot."

"After the dildo . . ."

"The dildo. Yeah, so it fell out, I ran from the hallway to my bike. I jumped on it and left. Cranked my music, hit the road and rode to this cafe. In the gay neighborhood. Gayborhood. Hah. That's a stretch. One block and half a street corner.

"The cafe was empty. I sat down at the end of the bar and coached myself. 'Don't let them see what you're feeling. *Ever.*' Told myself, I'm developing inner strength. I imagined high school was my baby mama moment. If I could get through—"

"What?" she asks.

"*High school.* Anyway, I looked up and right. At the old cigarette machine. A naked lady was painted on the side. She was something, too. Wore a see-through nightie. *Pink.* You couldn't miss the pink. She winked, and held a pinkie finger to her bow-tie-shaped mouth. Naughty. She dared me. 'Write it.' What did I have to lose except . . . everything? I remembered the blue notebook. I pulled it out my backpack and wrote, 'I might be queer.'

"She dared you?"

"Yeah, I knew, I *knew*—the way you know—when I wrote those words, I was daring my parents. Which is kinda why, I think, I wrote them down. I knew there'd be hell to pay if they read those words. I wanted to get caught *and* I wanted to tell them."

"They were really that ignorant?" says Little Miss Contrarian. Or, the Straight Devil's Advocate. "I'm sure they watch TV. On TV, practically the *whole* world's gay."

"Plus, gay porn," I joke. "Gay porn drove my father crazy. Gay people are fine so long as they're not your son. And you don't know what they do. Gay porn made it way worse. It was always popping up on his computer. All that gay, what do you call it? Visibility? It's great. But if you're a teenager, the TV and Internet can't save you from your parents if they're homophobic. You know, most people are. It's a straight world. I didn't have anyone watching my back. And I knew all *that* because I *knew* my U.S. history."

"Wait." Marci touches my arm. I flinch. It's gonna take a while to get used to her touching me. "What does U.S. history have to do with you coming out?"

"Us—kids—anyone under eighteen? Basically, we have the rights of slaves. As in, no rights. Parents can do whatever they want with us. You parents' rights rule."

"Dependency relationships," she says. "Go on."

I don't know dependency relationships from Depend diapers, but I continue, "I felt this urge—to leave. I waved good-bye to Miss Pinkie. I stood up, walked to the cash register, pulled out my wallet and . . . oh, wow! The guy at the cash register was *so* cute. How'd I miss him? His name tag read 'Stuart.' Stuart smiled—at me! And he got even cuter!

"I handed him the money but I couldn't look him in the eye. He held out my change. I took it and turned to leave. 'Hey there,' he said. 'Wait up a sec.' I felt it! The beat that my heart skipped. Stuart said, 'I see you in here all the time and . . .' He flashed me this friendly-flirty smile. I was sure he was about to ask me to be his boyfriend. I would have said, 'Sure,' because I never say 'yes,' only, 'sure.' I said, 'What are you smiling at?' He looked at me and said, 'Are you queer?'

"I was so embarrassed. I didn't know what to say. People didn't *ask*. Ever since fifth grade . . ." My voice trails off. I'm getting tired of proving I'm not pink enemy number one.

"Fifth grade," Marci says. "What was so special about that?"

"The *first* day of fifth grade, I dressed up. I looked *so smart*. Madras shorts, button-up Oxford cloth dress shirt. It was like everyone's head turned, took one look. 'Ah, *no*. He didn't.' My fashion tipped them off. I landed splat on the Fag Fashion No Fly List. I was naive. I didn't know. I'd never get off. Coz Fashion = Fag. Social Fail. My bad. I could have faked it."

"How so?"

"If I just didn't open my mouth, for one. Tip off number one. I mean, *look* at me: I had facial hair . . . at eleven! I could have worked it. Hidden myself under another look: Natural Born Terrorist. Maybe, it was more simple. If I'd just worn . . . less pink. After a while, I just said, 'Fuck it.' I wasn't about to walk around looking . . . *drab*. Wearing gray. Or, beige. That's how I ended up leaving school, in that cafe, writing in the blue notebook. Looking back? I should have surrendered. Just worn the straight dude's headscarf, the baseball cap."

I shut my mouth. I'm done. I don't ever want to think about

being called a fag. Or, the color pink. I close my eyes. The fashion flashback's destroyed me. My nap's short. Her finger jabs my shoulder.

"What'd you say?" Marci asks. "To Stuart?"

"I thought he was some emo guy who worked in a coffee shop. He knew nothing about me. I paid cash so—"

Thump! Something hits the van. I jump. Like I've been shocked. My left eye twitches. The muscle starts pulling, crazily yanking under the skin. The fast tug-tug-tug prolly makes me look like I'm squinting *really* fast. My body knows. I'm gonna get caught and returned to Serenity Ridge. I reach over her and try to get out. "Move! Let me out!" Marci turns her body. She's not in my way. I feel trapped but . . . I'm not. I can leave.

"Pine cone. Then what?"

"Oh." I look down at my journal for words that (still) aren't there. I close my eyes. Remember. Where I left off. The German headrest is soft as a rock. Deep breath. In my mind's eye, I step back, into the cafe, back to that moment.

Chapter 14

"I didn't think. I said, 'Yeah.' Right away, I wanted to bolt. Leave my change. But I didn't. I stayed. Stuart was too damn *cute*. Funny thing was, *nothing* happened. He didn't laugh. Nothing. Then he goes, 'I get off at five. You want to go for a walk?' I wait, we rode our bikes to the park and walked across this bridge. I remember we stood in the middle of it. I looked down at rush hour traffic. The lights glittered like a moving Christmas tree. The sunset was *so* romantic. I waited for him to lean over and kiss me.

"He didn't. I couldn't figure out why he was so timid. I gave him a hint it was okay to make a move. I told him, 'I want to have sex *so bad*—' He grabbed my arm and said, 'Don't ever just have sex. Make love.' I didn't know what he was talking about. I just wanted him to kiss me. I had a boner. I leaned against the bridge and tried to hide it.

"He reached over and messed up my hair. I got the message. 'THIS IS NOT A DATE.' He was treating me like his younger gay brother. We weren't in hook-up territory. Maybe he liked blonds? He didn't seem like the child molester type—even though I *was* fourteen, I wasn't a little kid, but some people might say I was. He goes, 'I know this group. You can meet other queer kids.' I said, 'I'm not a kid.' He laughed. 'Until you turn thirty, people think you're a kid.' I guess I had a lot to learn. I thought the age of consent was eighteen. 'Are you interested?'

" 'Why,' I asked, 'would I want some group when I can chat with people online?' He said, 'But have you ever actually *met* those people? Face-to-face? Gone on a date?' I admitted, no, I hadn't. I told him, 'I'll go to one of your meetings.' I wasn't sure when, but I would. He said, 'Whenever you want.'

"That kinda confused me. I always had it in my head—I guess from what my parents told me—or, looking at gay Web sites, gay people were always trying to, like, get you to join them. Or, hit it, you know, get with them. They were only ten percent of the population. They needed to recruit people and build the numbers. I thought about it. One night, a week later, I went to that group and when I got home, I—"

"Wait," says Marci.

Wait, I wonder, for what? Another pine cone?

Chapter 15

She flips the tape. The red Record light pops back on. I feel like I'm testifying in court. But I'm not proving my innocence so much as my existence. "Continue." The way she talks makes me feel like I'm on TV. Or, on trial.

"I crawled through my bedroom window. Who knew. My parents were waitin' in the hallway. My father knocked on the door. 'We need to talk.' The moment I heard his voice, I froze. Their bedtime was between seven and eight p.m. So I knew something was wrong. I stood next to the door. I heard this big *OOMPHHH!* This sound. I jumped. My stepmother yelled, '*OPEN THIS FUCKING DOOR RIGHT NOW!*' She kept screaming, the same thing, over and over. 'Open the door right now!' I don't know what purpose that'd serve. Except to give them the opportunity to kill me. Douse me in gasoline, toss a match and light me on fire. I'd heard about other Arab parents doing that to their kids. I think, my real mom's white. I'm only half towel head. Can I choose what part they burn?

"Finally she stopped. I could still hear them. Standing there, on the other side. I guess my stepmother was out of breath. Or, they needed to go pray. Maybe they could convince Allah to throw a lightning bolt and strike me down. I felt sad. All we were separated by was a door. Thin plywood. Close yet far apart. I couldn't face them. And I felt sadder by the second.

"My father spoke. 'Are you there?' I didn't answer. Was I 'there'? I felt less 'there' by the second. I was melting on the spot. Somehow, I'd become the Wicked Witch and their words were water.

" 'Come out,' he said. 'We *know*.' I wondered if he felt like he had to say this. Or, did someone coach him? In case, I hadn't figured it out on my own, were they there to tell me? Either way, I suspected my parents didn't think I was all that bright.

"His, 'We know,' set off my stepmother. The words were a cattle prod. '*OPEN THE DOOR!*' she screamed, pounding on the door. She was possessed. 'Help,' I think, 'somebody please call an exorcist.' Sharing her knowledge of 'family values'—the gay hating ones—StepMonster ran through the dictionary. She spewed every nasty, angry, bad word for faggot. F, F & F.

"She switched gears. I guess she'd been saving up. She started asking me questions. 'Where were you tonight?' I told her, 'Work.' She said, 'You left early.' How could she know this? 'I did?' 'Yes,' she said, certain, the way you choose a diamond or pick your mugger out of a lineup. 'We *called*. Last night and the night before. Where were you tonight?'

"I couldn't answer her questions. Not truthfully. I couldn't. So I ended up feeling like a liar. That was my first mistake: thinking *they* were telling the truth. I thought, I don't have a choice. I wanted to tell the truth. I knew if I did, StepMonster's head would explode. Messy. I said, 'Can we talk about this tomorrow morning?' My question set off another round of verbal gunfire. 'You've been lying to us!' I leaned against the door. Right then, I knew, I knew . . ."

I look away and out the window. I remember the moment, the exact second. I was back, in my bedroom. Then, I stood outside the house: I saw us. Me, my father, StepMonster. Some light goes out. Ahmed dies.

"Knew what?" Marci prompts.

"Everything," I say. I hear my voice. I sound empty. Hollow as I feel. Or, dead, same as what I saw. "I knew it was over. I had done something horrible. In their eyes, unforgivable.

"It was one thing to *be* gay, entirely another to *admit* being gay. Couldn't take it back. Any of it. When I wrote those words, I thought I'd voiced my desires. I hadn't counted on a giant—gay—gap would open up between us. We were survivors. Natural disaster. The fault line in our family was always there. I just refused to see it. Now, the Earthquake. My words—*I* caused it. They were swept away. I'd done it. All on my own. Four words. Made myself an orphan."

Marci touches my arm. Again, I flinch. I'm not scared. More surprised. I forget someone's there, listening.

"When what was over?"

I look away. How can I explain these facts to this American girl? Who will never understand? Actually, I know nothing about her, but I'm certain of one fact. How I was raised, in my culture, there was—is—*no* possibility of my being gay. TV shows can't protect me, celebrities can't protect me—this girl *definitely* can't protect me. Safety was adulthood and, even then, only in a fake marriage.

Writing those words proved . . . nothing. Except, I was—am—a fool. I'd gambled and lost. My entire family. I'd never fit. Maybe I *was* insane. In my heart, believing if I wrote those words, I cast a spell. A dare but also a hope—a wish—I could change them. I think, everything changed, American Girl, because I wasn't just an outsider, I was an outsider among outsiders. Alone.

I look at her. Arabs are direct. Even if I'm only half. They cannot rob my directness. I will explain. I'll use force. The truth.

"Our relationship, my childhood. There was me before. And there was me after. It was like we'd all been in a car accident. Afterward, my family walked one way and I walked the other."

I stop. This is hard. Harder than I'd imagined. This part—the part where I *tell* the truth—is not writing or thinking the truth. Speaking the truth about my family hurts. Is painful. The truth that my family *hates* me. Even after Serenity Ridge, after everything they've done to prove their hatred, some tiny part of *me* won't or refuses to believe. I struggle to find the words she can hear.

"I-I mean, today, you'd think parents . . . they'd just be cool about it. Glad, even. Coz, figure one in ten. A gay kid's like winning the lotto. You've won someone rare and special. Yeah!!! You'd think they'd celebrate. We won! But that's not how they saw it. They read those words, looked at me and saw their worse nightmare come true."

I look at Marci. Or, I should say, in Marci's direction. Right now, I couldn't look anyone in the eye. Even a sympathetic eye. My mouth wobbles, my face quivers. Tears. I hope I've said enough. I can't go on. I can't see her face. Even so. I can tell. We're not going anywhere. Not until I finish this.

"That night, I couldn't sleep. I knew, if I did, I might not wake up."

"What do you mean, 'Not wake up'?"

"Die. Might not wake up because I'd be dead."

"Killed?"

"Yes."

Chapter 16

"The next morning, I found a stack of presents at the bottom of my bed. I forgot it was my birthday. Fourteen! Two years and I could drive. I picked up the first present I saw and unwrapped it. Orange tennies from my grandmother. I put them on, left my room and walked into the house. It was empty. In the vestibule—"

"That church thing?" she asks.

I'm surprised she didn't ask, "That mosque thing?" I bite my tongue, don't say, "I didn't grow up in the projects."

"Um, no. It's a hallway thing. To the front door. The mail slot opened. I picked up the envelopes. I never looked at the mail. But for some reason, that day I did. I saw . . . my name? Yes. The envelope was nothing special. Plain, white, business sized. I turned it over: no return address. I went to my bedroom. I needed to open it before the StepMonster walked in and found me.

"I shut the door. Ripped it. There was a hundred dollar bill folded up inside a piece of blank stationery. The top was embossed with dark blue letters—M.G.—outlined in gold. M? Mary's my birth mother's name."

"She sent it."

"Yes," I say. "She must have known. Been counting the days. Known I'd need money. She was right, coz—"

"Was there anything else?"

I shake my head, No. I leave out the picture paper-clipped to the bill. Maybe I'm worried she'll tell me to hand over the snapshot. I could see her taking it and burning it.

I continue, "I touched the bill and thought, 'I should run away.' But as much as I was afraid of living there, I had school. I went outside. My bike was trashed. The wheels were removed. My father had done it. They must have suspected I'd try to escape. Maybe they felt it. How I was free. Because, after exposing my secret? What else could they do? Fine, I thought, I'll climb on my bike, ride away and never look back. I'll disappear into the land of missing children.

"I remembered another bike. An old one without gears. I lifted the garage door. It was shoved in between my father's lathe and band saw. The garage smelled of wood shavings. As I backed the bike out, I remembered how we spent every Saturday morning together last year. He was into woodworking. We made toy planes and cars. I was still a little boy. Everything was simple and he loved me and I loved him. That, actually . . ."

I look away. Wobbly faced. I'm about to cry. I don't wanna cry. That moment, of all the horrible moments—the ones before and after—was the worst. If not the worst, in the top ten. A You're-Not-Going-Back moment. I take a breath, continue.

"I rolled the garage door. It was half closed when . . . I saw yellow. The color was another painful reminded. The yellow something I saw was our tandem bike. *Our* bike. Father and son.

"I stood there, peering into the dark garage, and remembered last summer. Midnight. He woke me. 'Ahmed! Get up! We're leaving.'

"I took my time. I thought we were moving—again. We moved a lot. I was too tired to ask, 'What's the rush? Why are we moving in the middle of the night?' I dressed and met him outside. I felt drunk. Or, how I imagined being drunk. Groggy, I guess. I've never been drunk. When I saw him standing next to the two seater, I thought I was dreaming. He looked so . . .

proud. He had this smile on his face. I thought, finally, he's lost his mind. Totally.

" 'Ahmed, get on!' he shouted. We climbed on the bike and rode off, into the warm summer air. He was a bad father. His temper was horrible, he couldn't keep a wife or a job to save his life. But he knew something about surprise, adventure, the 'You're-*NOT*-going-to-believe-this!'

"We rode to a new freeway. There were other people. In secret, this group rode down these white, virgin concrete lanes. It was incredible. Here we were, riding *bikes* on a freeway at three a.m. Maybe that's why some part of me thought . . . my father, he'll accept me? I thought our dreamy, midnight bike ride was a signal. His way of saying, 'You and I, Ahmed, we are different.'

"I slammed the garage door down. On love, that night or anything good. My legs were heavy. My insides sagged. It took me forever to get to school. Riding, I realized I'd been safe so long as I stayed inside a black outline. The picture of me. My father had drawn it. The minute I'd stepped outside, I'd betrayed him. After that, I was, homo-cidal. I—"

"You mean," Marci interrupts, "*suicidal?*"

"No, *homo*-cidal. Drama! I was more into the idea of death. Doing it, not so much. In English class, we were reading *The Bell Jar.* And I listened to *The Virgin Suicides* all the time. It's a good soundtrack for—"

"When was this?" She jumps on the pop cultural references. Insight! She's an amateur psychologist. Whatever.

"A few weeks later," I say. "Two? I'd lost count. I'd stopped sleeping. I was wired. I was afraid something would happen if—"

"Happen? Like what?"

"Um, die."

"From natural causes or—"

"Coz they poured gasoline on me and tossed a burning match."

Behind the coke-bottle glasses, her eyes get "Oh, Wow" wide.

"You thought your family would burn you alive?"

"Yes." This girl has no idea what they'd do—for much less.

Or, what I'm really running from. "I avoided my parents in the house. I knew they wished I was gone. That I *would* run away. I felt shame. I knew. They didn't need to tell me. In their world, I'd done the worst possible thing. To them. To their *idea* of me. By writing those words—"

"You said you knew," Marci says.

"Yeah, I knew, I was the one who was responsible. I destroyed our family. Worse, I'd done it on purpose. My stepmother was nosey. I knew she'd find it. I could have asked her to read it. Or sat them down and told them. Same difference. But I like the drama: shock! discovery!

"One day I passed my stepmother in the dining room. She grabbed my arm and hissed, '*What a waste!*' With her, at least I knew her hate lived in her voice and face. My father? He wouldn't even look at me, much less speak to me."

"Be honest," Marci asks, "did you try to kill yourself?"

"I'd stand in the shower. Close my eyes and let the hot water pour down on my head. I'd pretend the water was blood. Or, tears. I'd crunch up my face. Fake cry. Really, I didn't feel anything. Just numb."

Those feelings come back. A wave. They wash over me. This time, I don't pretend. I'm not numb. I'm overwhelmed.

"What?" she says. Touches my arm. I'm getting tired of her talk show gesture. I know she means to comfort me. But I want to knock her hand. Slap her face. "Let's stop there."

"Okay."

I want to stop. Then again, maybe it will help—telling someone. My story. The big What Happened. Even though I know, after eleven months, talk therapy is total bullshit. I recall the words, "Transcribed and sent by certified mail to an attorney." This story is my evidence—testimony. Someday, it might come in handy.

"I might as well finish."

Chapter 17

"I woke up depressed. Couldn't get out of bed depressed. I tried. But I felt *heavy*. Like my body was filled with lead. I lay there and stared at the ceiling. It was white and I was black. Art class. The teacher showed up as a picture and said, 'Study in contrast.' Life, same thing. I heard someone pound on the door. *'Let us in! Let us in!'*

" 'Great,' I thought. 'My stepmother's going crazy. *Again.*' She had a nervous breakdown every other week. One time, I asked her, 'How many breakdowns do you have in you?' She hated me after that.

"Then, I heard something. This sound . . . the door? Wood . . . cracking? Yes, the door! It was splintering! Because an ax! Had split it in two! Two cops stood in the hallway. 'Are you—' "

"Not your real name," Marci cautions.

" 'Ben?' I didn't answer. I just stared at them. I guess that was all they needed. They stomped in. 'What'd I do?' I asked. I wasn't a criminal. Except, some part of me knew. I was. They lifted me up off the bed and handcuffed my wrists. I didn't resist, didn't try to get away. But I didn't help them. I played dead. I take that back. I didn't play. I *was* dead.

"They carried me out the house and down the front steps. The perfect neighbors stood on their perfect lawns and watched.

I should have been humiliated, but I wasn't. I didn't care. I knew it was the last time I'd see this place. I wasn't coming back. Ever.

"Even though I knew what was happening, I couldn't believe it. All *this*—the cops, the ax, the handcuffs—was because of *me*. Me. Three minutes ago, I lay on my bed and stared at the ceiling.

"The men led me to an unmarked sedan. Right then I realized, 'They're not cops. They can't do this. I'm being kidnapped.' Too late. One palmed my head like a basketball and shoved me into the backseat. They pulled a hoodie over my head. I was blind.

"My mind started going. I was Gitmo bound. They were moving me out of the country. Extra rendition. Water boarding. Torture. I started—I couldn't breathe. Panic—I had an attack. I screamed. I begged them, 'Please! Let me go! I'm dying!' I heard them laugh. Call me a liar. Finally, they pulled back the hoodie. They shoved a pill in my mouth; the car jerked and threw me back against the seat. The tires squealed. *Zoom!* We drove for a long time. I still couldn't see—they'd pulled the hoodie back down. Overnight, I turned into a gay terrorist.

"I couldn't hold it in anymore. I told them, 'Hey! I need to pee!' I felt the car pull over. The door opened. The hoodie came off. One man led me to a bathroom. Inside, he unlocked my wrists and closed the door.

"I couldn't believe my eyes. Behind the door, there was a pay phone! You'd think it would be easy—for me to save myself. But when I picked up the receiver, I shook so bad I could barely hold it. I was terrified I'd get caught. I was scared what they'd do to me. I forced myself to dial. I talked myself through it. 'At least *try* . . . if you don't save yourself, nobody will.'

"I called Stuart. I had memorized his work number. I couldn't believe it—he answered and accepted the charges. Amazing, he'd help, I was saved! 'Stuart, I've been kidnapped! Help me, can you—' He said, 'Your dad—'

"Right then, the man stepped into the bathroom and caught me. He dragged me back to the car. I wet myself. They laughed. 'Faggot's wet hisself.' I felt the air go out of me. Nobody needed to explain. *No one* could protect me. I was on my own. My family doesn't want me. Flip side was, I had nothing to lose. My parents abandoning me was bad enough. Them *knowing* these people would hurt me—some part of me, truly . . ."

My voice trails off. My thoughts continue: "I knew they chose to throw me away. Toss me out, like trash." But I don't say this aloud. I can't. Admit this horrible fact—not a guess, or a feeling but a *fact*—to a stranger.

For some reason, I reach up and touch my face. It's wet. Tears. I hate this. Feelings embarrass me. I want to keep them to myself. Private. I distrust my feelings. This time, they won't betray me. I'll *act*. Coz now I know better. Fact: I'm in another car, in the backseat. I am trapped. I reach—

Chapter 18

"Let me out! I gotta—"
She grabs my arm. Won't let me go. I fight. But not too hard. I start crying. I don't want them to see. I turn my head away. Toward the door. I know, if I really want, I can get out. Handle's right there. My body, I guess, I need to, I surrender, I let out—

"Uh! Uh! Uh!" I'm filled with shame. Since when did my feelings become a freak show? Me, naked. Oh, look at him! I know they're looking at me.

"Don't look at me!"

I cry. I want to stop. I can't. I hate them.

"I know what you're thinking. I'm not some—some pathetic little kid!"

I kick my feet. Hard. Slam! Against the backseat. Nobody stops me. I cry. I scream. I howl. The wind is louder. Forest, park, wherever we are. Nowhere. And I am alone—again—with my feelings.

I cry, curled up in a ball against the side. My balled fists pound the window. I cry until I can't cry. Until I'm out of tears. The way a storm gives way to drizzle and, finally, stops. I'm hella tired. The way I was before, in my bedroom, when I was so depressed I couldn't move. This feels different. Still dark. Clearer. Lighter.

Still, the van's silence makes me anxious. I glance down. The red light glows and the tape moves, unspooling, recording. I have more to say but no energy left to say it. I rub my temples.

"Are we done? Coz after that, I have a hard time, you know, remembering."

A lie. I remember everything after the gas station. But I don't owe her that story. Nobody gets that story. It's mine.

For the first time in the hour—or, three?—we've been together, Marci doesn't answer my question, ask one or touch my arm. The silence makes me uncomfortable. Pride's the other thing I'm keeping for myself. There are limits. In Serenity Ridge, they'd called me "manipulative." It's true. Right now, for example, I know what to say, but it's too humiliating to say aloud. My father marked me. A big, fat L—Loser—across my forehead.

"You really want to hear this? I still, I know it should be easy but . . . I can't believe. They did *this*. I'm having . . . after that, you know, a hard time, remembering."

"Can't think straight yet, huh?" She smiles.

I shrug, make a face: I don't get it. Of course, I do. I repeat myself, on purpose. She looks at me. I don't know if she believes me. I don't care.

"You can tell me the rest later." Finally—finally!—the tape recorder clicks. Off. Thank G-D, Allah, Praise Jesus Christ, Lord Shiva and Toys "R" Us. My story gets its well-earned rest. Hopefully, soon I will, too. The engine turns over and the van pulls away. I turn and look back. Same as Serenity Ridge, I want a parting shot. This time, of the interview spot.

The whole time, we were parked under a tree the size of a circus tent. Under a large, black pool. We were always perfectly hidden.

Chapter 19

I peer out the window, in search of San Fran-cis-co. The Gay Ground Zero. Queer Mecca. But instead of believers flocking to mosques and minarets, the streets should be filled with gays. It's a full moon. The streets are empty. The city's sexy, horny hotties must be sleeping. The passing landscape doesn't resemble a "City." All I see are houses with sloped front lawns and cars parked on severely angled driveways.

The van turns left, then right. The city jumps out. Now the streets look like the tourist brochure pictures. Smoke shops and windows with mannequins dressed in flashback fashion (flowing hippie chick dresses, '80s New Wave polyester), marijuana dispensaries and used record stores. Victorian architecture.

A group of straggly-looking college types drunkenly weaves down the street. They sing, *"Load up on guns and bring your friends."* Sure does, I think, "Smells Like Teen Spirit."

I glimpse a boy. About my age, he leans into a car window. My body shudders. I look away. I don't want to see him climb in. I'm forty-two dollars away from doing the same.

"What?" Marci asks.

"Nothing," I lie. Lying comes easy. Too easy. Get caught in a lie or don't. Lie, but only if you really need to (and remember the truth). I look back. The car's swallowed him up. The red taillights bob and blink, gone. Nothing? Why lie. I *know* what he's doing in the front seat. If I follow his example, then there's no point. I'm no better than Haifa's curse.

RULE #1: DO NOT SELL YOUR BODY. No matter what.

The van makes more turns, quick as on a TV cop show. Abrupt, the van stops in the middle of a street. Marci opens the van door. She jumps (and lands) with ease. She motions me out. Blind, I jump. I land. Hard. My fingers touch asphalt. The van door slides, slams shut and peels off.

I see: Semi trucks. Loading docks hung over barren side-walks. Metal curtains hide warehouse entrances. The street's closed up. Abandoned. Still, I feel eyes watching us from behind hundreds of warehouse windows.

Marci sets off. For a big girl, she sure walks fast. I run to catch up.

"What're you on? Thorazine?"

I shrug. I don't want to think about Serenity Ridge. I feel happy. I want to enjoy the night. I feel like I'm moving through taffy.

"The safe house where you're going to live," Marci says, "is a closed, long-term."

The stoplights blink, red, furious. We ignore their warning, cross the street.

"What's that mean?"

"Nobody leaves. You stay inside, twenty-four seven. You don't go near the windows, don't answer the phone, don't open the door."

A second intersection. There are so many bright, yellow lights, it could be day at Valencia and Sixteenth. The street's divided in two. On one side, hipsters. On the other, homeless people. That's America. I wonder, what side of the divide do I stand on? People sleep everywhere: on a brick, half-moon-shaped plaza, bus benches and cardboard boxes. Dealers slang weed, and panhandlers push shopping carts. Everyone looks *very* awake.

A giant man appears. His giraffe legs take four steps. He's next to us.

"Hey, baby." He smiles, gold capped teeth catching the blinking neon red light. Marci grabs my hand. "Wanna partay? Got chronic, PCP, rock, X, got G-H-B . . ." He rattles off a dozen more letters. I can't figure out if he's selling drugs or the alphabet.

Marci ignores Alphabet Man. Probably, I should, too, but I can't look away. I've never seen anyone like him. He looks like he escaped from that '80s movie, *Mad Max*. Great. My new reality. It's an apocalypse now, populated with crazy, hungry people. Who don't know they smell. Serenity Ridge was "hardcore" but nothing like this.

Alphabet Man moves toward us. Big, monsterish. White spit's caught between his teeth. He smiles, craaaazzzyyy. The spit pulls apart, taffy or spiderweb. Close up, his eyes catch light, two glittery marbles cock-eyed in opposite directions. His smile vanishes. His hand pushes back his jacket flap. His nails are eagle talons. His fingers wrap around a handle. He slides a knife out his waistband.

I freeze. Why run. We're gonna die anyway.

"Hey!" An Asian lady crosses the street. Alphabet Man sees her and steps back. Her enormous feet are shoved into stilt-sized high heels. Watermelon-sized boobs spill out a leopard print bikini top. She wears a silver thong. Her daddy longlegs eyelashes bat-ta-bat, flashing purple-gold lids. Asian Lady's blond wig and body jiggle, same as warm apricot Jell-O. "Motor! Where the fuck you been?!? You got my shit?"

Her question turns us into extras, background for an '80s video. Whatsit. She was a girl. And this girl was in . . . trouble? But her bad behavior (caught, cuffed, clink) was . . . a temporary thing. I saw the *Where Are They Now?* TV special in Serenity Ridge. Romeo Void. Asian Lady could be the singer's twin. Her sneer turned her eyes to slits; she sang, "She's got a face that shows what she knows."

Marci yanks my arm. We run, cross the street and vanish into the shadows.

I look back.

Alphabet Motor Man stands there, looking around, searching for us. But we're gone and the intersection's empty.

Chapter 20

L eaving the way we do teaches me how easy it is to disappear. Be quick. Have an escape route. Or, an alley. For instance, the one we're running down. We exit it, and run down another street, passing the SEXXXY LADY THEATER. It's slotted in-between an SRO and soup kitchen. The white marquee with capital orange letters promises ONE WEEK ONLY.

"In the safe house, you don't answer the door," Marci says between quick, short breaths. "You don't wear shoes."

"Why not?"

"People downstairs can hear you walking around. We keep the radio or TV on at all times so people don't hear you talking."

Forget talking. I'm exhausted. I can barely walk. We cover—five? ten?—more blocks.

"Here—"

I follow; we turn the corner. She stops outside a brick building: The Cretan. Cretan as in creepy. I'd guess it's been rundown since it was built . . . two centuries ago. Some places are like that. A bordello slash punk band hotel slash safe house for runaway gay teens.

"The apartment's not under my real name." She looks for her keys. "Same with the phone."

The front door faces Market Street, a four-lane boulevard.

It's empty except for a stream of cabs and the occasional street-car. They rumble by, empty and ghosty. I lean against the door-way, about to pass out. Marci opens the metal gate. Sleep calls my name. Reaches out for my body. I struggle to resist the promise of its sweet, dead embrace.

Marci steps through the open gate, grabs my arm and hustles me inside. We pass through a foyer, a second glass door draped with dirty lace curtains and into a lobby. The ceilings are vaulted, walls covered with billboard-sized mirrors.

I feel eyes on my back. I turn. See a face past the dirty lace curtain and metal grill.

My heart skips. It's the blue-eyed man from the bathroom!

Blink. He's gone.

I have a bad feeling. He'll be back.

Chapter 21

"C'mon!" Marci's halfway up the stairs. I struggle to make it up the first step.

"Are you, like, a triathlete?"

"Elevator broke."

We near the second floor. Voices. Marci grabs my arm and yanks me back, out of sight. Shadows move up the wall. The elevator groans. A door opens, slams, shuts. Another groan. Fades. A distant *Clunk!* She motions, move back. Feline, she tiptoes up the stairs, to the next floor. She looks both ways—at what, traffic?—then motions me.

"Hurry!"

I scramble up the stairs, reach the third floor and collapse on the carpet. Filthy, it's a thousand years old, beaten down by millions of shoes. Marci wheezes.

"Are you okay?"

"Yeah." She pants, tongue out against her lower lip like a dog. "I'm all right."

Happy to hear. Her, gasping for air, worries me: She stands one heart attack away between me and Serenity Ridge.

"Two of us run this safe house." Another wheeze. "If we catch you doing drugs, you'll be evicted—*no questions asked.*"

All these rules. Is the test multiple choice or T / F? Marci hangs on a square wood banister, exhausted by the climb or the effort it takes to explain everything. I get a better look: geek girl who wears big Velma glasses. She's so ordinary looking you'd never suspect she drives around San Francisco picking up queer kids who've escaped from gay-to-straight boot camps.

Marci pushes her body off the banister. We walk down the dark hallway, toward the EMERGENCY EXIT sign's green glow.

"You better!" Manic laughter, screechy voices.

"Is this place haunted?" Marci ignores my question and fumbles with the key, struggling to open the door. The voices become louder.

"Hey!"

I hide behind Marci's body. She could double as a chest of drawers. I keep my head down. I don't want them to see my face.

"Hey." She mumbles and looks down.

"What's up with the elevator?" A young guy's voice. His shadow's on the carpet. He walks toward us. I want to run. I peek around Marci. He's smiling. Cops, authorities, anyone who wants to lock you up—they always smile. Right before they reach out and grab you. We're about to get caught. I feel it. I *know,* this is it.

"Need help?" The male voice. I don't need to see him—I know, he's a bully. I've heard the tone before. " 'Cause I *can* help."

I cringe. He's drunk. Or, a thief. Another serial killer. At this moment, San Francisco doesn't seem psychedelic so much as plain Psycho. The voice is low, smooth.

Marci might be armed with street smarts but she's scared, too. I can tell. How? Coz I smell it. The scent peels off her pungent like my stepmother's perfume.

Click.

A gun. The safety. Cock. The shadow steps closer.

"Really. You need help."

"No."

HİDDEN

Chapter 22

Click.
The key turns, the door opens, we slip inside. My heart beats loud—so loud I know I'm doomed. The door clicks, dead bolts falling into place. I point down to the space between floor and door. Shadows.

"They're still there!" I whisper.

"Close." Marci exhales. Her body falls against the door. Our "friend" is outside: His shadow paces, pauses outside the door. He better not try to bust it down. Like I said, Marci could double as a chest of drawers.

"Fucking weirdo!" He hisses. The shadow leaves, voices fading. They're gone. She touches me. I flinch. My hand's a balled-up fist.

"Relax," she says. "You're safe."

Am I? I want to ask. Is anybody? Safe? I thought I was safe (enough) living with my father. Look at where that idea got me. Here. A runaway. Standing in the dark. Who knows where. I can't see at all. The only advantage is, nobody can see me, either.

The safe house is pitch black. But I sure as hell smell it. The safe house reeks of junior high hallways. Hormones, bad breath, and various body odors.

Marci takes my hand and leads me through the teenage mist.

"That's the bathroom," she whispers. "Someone sleeps in there. The closet: someone sleeps in there, too. This is the kitchen."

She drops my hand and steps away. My eyes adjust to the dimness. I stand in the middle of a large doorway. *Wop!* The sound of rubber unsticking. Marci peers into the fridge.

Something's stuck to the wall over the stove. A button? I look closer. The button crawls down, toward the stacked dishes. A roach, the gross kind.

I sit at the round table beside a window. I reach out, lift the curtain and peer out at other apartments. She knocks my hand away.

"What's there?"

"A courtyard."

"So who cares?"

"Someone might look out their window and see *you*."

Honey, I shrank the world. Mine's now itty-bitty size. I want to leave. I'd turn and leave if—if I knew where I'd go. Already, I feel trapped. The instant the front door shut, I became a different person.

The safe house scent isn't just grotty kids. It's . . . poverty? Yeah, the safe house smells poor. If I stay, the middle-class part of me—the boy who orders a five-dollar triple espresso percent, no foam latte—dies. Living here, I'll learn to count. Watch, look, jump. Fear.

I need sleep. Marci has other plans. She walks to the table. She holds a stack of Tupperware containers in her left arm and a tiny candle with her right hand. She practically skips. I'd guess, whatever comes next is a high point of her sad life.

"Make yourself comfortable." She places candle and containers on the black-and-white-striped tabletop. "Take off your shoes."

I slide off my kicks and cross my legs, yogi style. My eyes droop and I can barely keep my head up. Either she doesn't notice my exhaustion or she's really lonely. There were nurses at Serenity Ridge who'd trap you. They loved to order the boys around. They were hungry for male attention; a fourteen-year-old boy's would do. Now I wonder if Marci's a dyke. Or, a straight girl on a crusade to Save the Gay Boys.

Same as the Women of Serenity Ridge, Marci won't—can't—shut up. "I mean, why should I starve myself? If I'm hungry, I'm gonna eat, right? If you knew me three years ago, you wouldn't even recognize me. In seven months, I went from weighing one fifty-five to two fifteen. One day, I woke up and I was the fattest fucking chick. The *Fattest.*"

I don't believe this story. Marci was always fat. Like the Women of Serenity Ridge, she *imagines* a dramatic weight gain. I yawn, and cover it with a sigh. I smile, nod, "Uh-huh." These girls aren't interested in conversation: They crave undivided (male) attention. Depending on how well the fridge is stocked, this convo could stretch all night. Marci rummages around the sink. Girlzilla knocks over plates and glasses.

"There!"

She holds up a butter knife and wipes it on her shirt. She opens the mayonnaise jar, plunges the blade inside and withdraws it. A testicle-sized ball of glop clings to Excalibur. Expert, she slathers the knife on a slice of white bread.

"One day I woke up, looked in the mirror and saw I had three chins. My body had more rolls than a craps table. I tell you, I was *not* fucking around. The school doctor, he told me to 'drop a few.' He said I was 'at risk.' I mean, come *on.* Who's not 'at risk'? Fuck, *living* is a risk."

She pops multiple Tupperware lids and removes food without looking. I'm amazed. In this dark-as-a-cave kitchen, she *knows* the contents of every container by touch. She could be reading Braille. Or, she works in a deli.

"Voilà!"

A world record, she's made a sandwich in seven seconds. Super-sized, the ingredients threaten to explode: mayonnaise, lettuce, bacon, mystery meat, tomato and pickle slices. But then, she *is* the fattest fucking chick she knows and not about to starve herself. She holds up the fattest fucking sandwich—*ever.*

"Want a bite?"

"Uh, no, thanks."

"*Oh,* don't tell me you're not hungry?" She sounds relieved.

"I'm just . . ." I yawn. I hope she'll get the hint.

She slaps another two slices atop the original two. It's a quadruple decker! I wonder if the fattest fucking sandwich gives tours.

"Are you tired?" she asks.

"Guess so." I shrug my shoulders. I don't say, "Yes." It gives Marci an opportunity to say, "No."

"Sure?"

"I'm sure," I think, "that I'm grossed out. By the sound of dough, whipped eggs, dead animals and wilted vegetables sloshing around in your mouth like a human washing machine."

"Mummmmummm," she mumbles, mouth full. I stand and follow her back into the safe house. The main room's pitch black. I'm confused. Is this a big apartment? Or one room and a kitchen? She swallows, toilet plunger style. "You can sleep up there." She spews sandwich bits all over my arm.

I step forward. My foot steps on something soft.

"*FUCK!*"

"Up *there.*" She takes my hands and places the palms flat on wood slats. Ladder, steps. A bunk bed. I climb up. The word *heights* makes me feel dizzy. But I'm so tired it's all that I can do to lie down and pass out, already asleep.

Chapter 23

" **W**hat's wrong with him?"
Voices. I'm dreaming. Or, people are talking about
me. I might be hallucinating.

My body's twisted, circus contortionist style. My left knee's
pressed against something hard. My eyes flutter, half-open. I see
a wall and, on it, shadows. I'm not ready to meet people.

I sleep. Dream. Automatic writing, imaginary pen to paper.

*I stand outside the seclusion room. I peer through the door-
way looking into the pink cinder block room. A lightbulb burns,
bright and bare, inside its metal cage. I notice there's a heap on
the concrete floor. A pile of trash? Or dirty laundry?*

*The heap moves. I look closer. The form comes into focus:
The heap is not trash but a person. They turn over. A boy. I recognize his face. Me, on the concrete floor near the drainage hole.*

*Vomit covers my Garbage Pail Kids tee shirt. There's a brown
stain on my butt. I've shit my pants. My arms and legs look
funny, too. My head twists to the side. I look like a rag doll
tossed on the ground. Or a corpse.*

*A fire hose gushes water. The stream slams the boy. The me-
boy dissolves into a colorless puddle, dribbles down the drain.*

* * *

Later—hours? minutes? days?—I wake, reach for my note-book and write on the light blue lines.

> in school, one time I remember
> this one guy called san francisco
>
> "planet fag"
>
> i wonder if that's
> what this place will be like
>
> A "Utopia"
>
> like that book we read
> brave new world
>
> all happy and smiley and good—but not
>
> a home room for homos? a world apart?
> or somewhere over the gay rainbow?
>
> A "QUEER-topia"
>
> where we speak our own language
> i mean if there's e-bonicks
>
> we'll speak in queer-bonicks
> secret words nobody else gets
>
> or maybe people speak english
> but then they give you
>
> A Look—zap!—
> queer telepathy
>
> you get what they say means that but
> that is means something else too
>
> maybe everyone will love everyone else
> maybe I've landed on some queer planet

Chapter 24

Something presses against my bladder. Blade? Gun? Nothing so dramatic. I need to pee. I consider my options. I can let go and flood the sheets. But that warmth will turn cold, Snap!

I crack one eye and look around. The safe house is hella small. Last night, it looked vast. Last night, or the night before last night? In daylight, it's a tiny, one-room studio.

A cluster of sleeping forms cover the floor. Good. I won't meet anyone. I roll over, swing my legs off the side and ... Nothing. Air. I'm confused. Then I remember. I'm on a bunk bed. My need to pee trumps my fear of heights. I climb down.

Ground level, I remember Marci said, "The bathroom's by the front door."

A cardboard square with hand-lettering hangs on a string draped over the knob. OCCUPIED. Damn! I gotta pee. I hop, tightening my pee muscle. Ear to door, I hear shower water. Squeak. Off. I knock, and whisper, "Hi?"

The door swings open. White steam rushes out. This happens as if by magic. Coz I don't see anyone. A figure emerges from the steam. A slim Eurasian boy, hair slicked back and towel wrapped around his tiny waist.

"Yes?" His voice is laced with contempt. He *radiates* hostility. Awww, hate at first sight. Whereupon "Ben" meets Mean Asian Gay Boi.

"I need to *go.*"

He steps to the side. A little bit. I try to squeeze by without touching his wet, muscular hatred. I lift the toilet seat and—relief! Firefighter, I aim. Pee gushes out. *Whomp, whomp, whomp!* But the sound's wrong. Instead of hitting water, the pee bangs turds. Eww. Someone forgot to flush. And the water must be warm. It stinks. I reach for the knob.

"*Don't,*" Eurasian boi says. I look back. He's dropped the towel. I can't help but stare. His naked body's off-the-hook *gorgeous.* Water droplets tumble off his dark gold skin, tiny jewels.

I turn back to the john. Look. Someone's stale junk's still in there. Give me a break. I reach—

"No! It's not time."

"Time for what?"

"If we flush too much, we run up the water bill. The landlord will figure out seven people live here."

"Oh."

He steps into a pair of tight briefs, pulling them up, over his lean, muscular legs. The waistband hugs his tiny hips and looks like a cinched ribbon. He looks me in the eye, shoves his hand down the front and arranges his package. His goodies look like a big, balled-up fist. There's not enough steam to hide my embarrassed face.

"Can I take a shower?"

" 'Course."

"Are there any clean towels?"

"Sure." His eyes flicker, down, at the towel on the floor. "You can use mine."

His attitude, voice and girlie gestures remind me of the queeny boys at Serenity Ridge. Their attitude was, "If you don't like it, *fuck you,* I'm a bitchy girl. If you don't like it, hand me that knife. Coz I'm gonna stab yo' face." The counselors left them alone. But whatever. I'm not about to use someone's towel, especially when I see . . . (light brown) scootch marks?

I return to bed, climb back up top. Back to dreamtime. I'm an honorary Aborigine. Creating reality as I walk it. I step into the room. The door muffles sound, seals out light, numbs feeling. Numb. Yes, I feel numb. That's fine. But I can't shake the nervous feeling. The presence of *one* Mean Girl suggests there will be others. I burrow, deep, into sleep. I want to avoid waking. They're waiting. Catfights, claws, cuntiness.

I'm a hot (tense) mess, even in my sleep.

Chapter 25

"**W**ass'up?" and "Muthafucker *don't!*"
I lie there, silently listening to the verbal IMs. The safe house doesn't just smell like junior high school, it sounds like one, too. I bury my head under a pillow. Silence, sleep, whereforartthou? The voices persist.

"You escaped?" A finger jabs my ankle. "Yo! Yo! Yo! I'm Peanuts. And I *know* yous awake."

Peanuts. Aiight. Yous a hims or a hers? A hes or a shes? A s / hims or a s / hes? Yous name doesn't give mes any clue as to whos the hells or whats *yous* is. My head rolls to the side. I crack my right eye. Peanuts. Like the social worker, like Marci, Peanuts arrives armed with questions I don't want to answer. I want shut-eye. I glare, Skippy Peanut Butter, be gone! S / he doesn't budge.

"Yo! Dolls! Yous just escape?"

Yeah, dolls, yous fishing. I'm not biting.

"I had hella lotsa g.f.s. See, I was in this state hospital, right? They put me in there 'cuz I'm butch. Yous know what that is?" Then, Peanuts makes a weird hand signal that's either gang related or ASL. Maybe s / he shouts 'cause s / he's deaf? Peanuts seethes, ghetto as . . . TV. "My homies *so* scared a me."

I knew it. I should have jumped out the van and ran. I could have lived on toilet paper. Stayed in the bus station bathroom stall. Bathed with liquid hand soap. Currently, I've been abducted and am being held by gang of deaf gay bangers.

"Everybody!" Marci says. "This is Ben."

Fuck, I've been called out. Officially. Can't hide, can't sleep. I roll my head and face the room. Sunlight lines jabs the cracks in the tarp-covered windows. The floor is empty, sleeping bags rolled up, mattresses stacked against the wall. I face the firing squad. Six—seven?—faces look up, all at moi. I wave. "Hola, amigos."

Marci stands next to a Tall Black Girl. T.B.G. *almost* looks like that biatchy TV supermodel. T.B.G. wears a Catholic schoolgirl (pleated) miniskirt, knee-high boots and white dress shirt. Shirt open to the belly button, her twenty-six pack abs pop, black against the starched white material. Her long hair, pulled back into a ponytail, is held back by pink, baby girl barrettes. She tilts her head down, blinks and flashes a brilliant movie-star smile. "Hello, I'm Ahh-nee-tah. *Fixx.*"

I'd title her trans-channel-movie-of-the-week special, *High School Honors Student by Day, Castro Street Hooker by Night, I'ma Teenage Trans.*

"We met." Mean Girl-Eurasian boy smirks. "*Kidd.*"

Yeah, Queen, I'll say we "met." And you forgot to flush. Next!

There's a radiant sun beside Kidd's Death Star. Two pink, perfectly shaped lips have been placed, perfect, on the handsome face. Muscles. Blue eyes. <Sigh> Cue cliché, "Love at first sight." Pink lips move, and the man beauty speaks, "Hammer."

Hammer's an All-American Skinhead. Or, the President of the Aryan Youth Nation. His head glows, a spray of gold fuzz. Hammer takes Anita's hooker look a step further: He's shirtless. A thirty-six pack ripples under his tight, smooth skin. All these six packs. Maybe I'll catch one. The way people do the flu.

I stare. Nobody seems to mind. Maybe the safe house is also a nudist colony. Hammer poses, flexing. His melon-sized biceps pop, tiny waist cocks to the side, abs rippling the gold happy trail. My eyeballs are stuck on his tiny blue running shorts. He could be the model on an enormous Times Square billboard. Hammer, oh ye of the spandex boxer briefs, here's my heart. Smash it.

Hammer rolls his head, neck muscles doing the sexy man dance. His mouth falls open and gives me a wide angle view: perfect, straight white teeth and deep throat. Done, he looks at me and . . . winks.

Hidden behind Hammer's stunning stray (straight-gay: no one *that* good-looking could be gay), there's a girl.

"Hi, I'm Alice," she whispers. "I mean, Nadya."

Alice / Nadya has pink hair and creamy white skin. Light catches the Star of David hung on a gold chain. Little Miss Identity Crisis looks like a Popsicle.

"J.D.?" Marci asks. I wonder if J.D. is (a) male (queer, potential boyfriend), (b) female (dyke, B.F.F. material), (c) Trans, or (d) gender indeterminate (Peanuts).

"Hiding under the bottom bunk," Anita says.

"No, smoking," Kidd says.

Marci walks toward me. She holds up a plate. On it, a muffin.

I shake my head. Just the *idea* of food makes me ill. A second girl steps out the kitchen doorway. She could be Alice / Nadya's sister: She's also pale with bleached blond hair. But unlike Alice / Nadya, there's nothing shy about her. She walks to the bunk and holds up a coffee cup. Another temple offering. Am I the fifteenth Dalai Lama?

"I figured you for one cream and no sugar except—that's my name. So I gave you one blue."

Sugar's Riottt Girrlll punk 'do is at odds with her free love, Rasta hippy chick vibe. Large breasts dance, bra-free, under a sheer blouse. Smiling, she looks up at me, expectant. They all do. They expect me to speak.

"Later?"

Peanuts jumps off the ladder and "runs"—two steps—toward a dresser. "I have the bottom drawer 'cuz *I* have the top bunk." Oh, *now* I grasp Peanuts's interest in my sleeping patterns. The sooner I get up, the sooner s / he can reclaim the top bunk.

"The window," Marci says, "displaying" the tarp with arm gliding, baby dyke, game show hostess savoire faire. "There's a fire escape outside—in case you need to leave."

"Run hella *fast*," Peanuts adds, " 'cuz the cops bust in. Wolf! Wolf! With Dawgs! The bitey breed."

"Great," I think. "Or, the Blue-Eyed Bathroom Rapist finds us and picks the lock." I should get up and leave. I hate dogs, especially the bitey breeds. Absentmindedly, my hand drops down and feels the bite marks. OMG, I bet it looks like I'm touching myself. I jerk my hand out.

"The only time I go outside is the roof," Alice / Nadya says, speaking in a barely audible, little girl voice. She steps back, a visible disappearing act.

"That's about half of us." Sugar sips my coffee and makes a face. Eww. Later, I'll tell her: I hate the Blue, too. "The other half stay here until we turn eighteen. Like me."

The group gaze is stuck on moi. I guess they expect me to say something. I should confess: I'm not the Great and Powerful Oz. I can't think much less speak. T.M.I. Cops? Windows? Bitey breeds? Eighteen? Then it occurs to me. If Nadya is an Alice stuck in the alternate universe *anti*-Wonderland, then I'm a friend of Dorothy. Close my eyes, click my heels thrice and say, "I feel kind of dumb asking this but, um, people get to go home? Sometimes? Never?"

"If—*if*—your parents don't have cause or, more typically, the funds for another involuntary committal," Sugar says, eighteen going on forty, the safe house's Mini-Magistrate. "But, yes, definitely, you can go back."

"Or, you've been gone such a long time they forget about you," Kidd says. "But why would you want to?"

"How long is a long time?" I ask. I need a time line. Some idea of how long I should plan to bunk down in da crib with the other crazy kiddies.

"Two years."

"Me, it's been three years, plus change," Sugar says. "I've been underground for four, but three's about how long I've lived in the closet."

"Security!" Peanuts says. "We gotta tell him."

Security—that will have to wait. I turn away, to the wall, and close my eyes. Thorazine, take me away! I drift, back to my favorite destination of choice:

Bliss, Death, Sleep.

Chapter 26

"Ahh!"

The shriek wakes me. My body's tense. Rigid. Cold. Sweat covers my skin. Animal instincts: Trapped and facing a predator, you (a) run or (b) play dead.

Please choose "B" and proceed to survival.

"*Shit!* That hurts like a motherfuck!"

"What about his ID?"

"Ahhhh!!!!!"

"Hold still, or"—a boy scolds—"I'll cut your wrist."

"Ahhh!" Another shriek. "*Heartless* motherfucker!"

"We should skip this and get a dead baby name from City Hall."

"Or, the Internet?" asks a girl.

Who *are* these people? Gay Teen Terrorists?

"I like the DMV," deep-voiced boy says. "Cops look once and it's like, 'Okay, you can go.' "

"Ahhhh!" A third shriek. "This feels like circumcision."

"Like she'd know anything about that!"

"Don't start with that fucking—*AHHHHHHHH!!!!!!*" A yelp. "—'girl' crap."

"Why are you talkin' shit? You got foreskin for *days.*"

They're talking about dick. *Arguing* about it. So long as it's someone else's dick that's being cut, I don't care, roll over and go back to—

Chapter 27

"What?!"
I sit up. My sleeping frenzy ends. Done. Over. Eyes wide awake. I sit. Up.

Run—

I—

"Where am I?"

Am totally freaked out.

"Hello?"

Not at home, that's for sure. Serenity Ridge, bus station, youth shelter. I talk myself down. Look.

Clothes at the end of the bed. Cargo pants, shirt and safari hat. Outfit Number Three, the one I wore in the truck that drove me to the bus station in downtown Vegas and—

Write it down, make notes, map it out. My story. So when I leave, I'll know what I left. Unlike before when I shut my eyes and jumped.

I feel for the blue notebook. I find it where I left it: tucked in the folded-up pants. I didn't take off those pants. Someone else must have. I sniff the pants. They smell fresh. I wonder if they read my journal. I reach under the bed and pull it out. The pen's tucked inside, right where I left it.

I write:

i am cast out
so far a-way
from a home
that is no longer
home but just
a memory

My good mood blooms and wilts in nineteen words. I close 'n clip the pen, shut the notebook and fall back. Dead or asleep, I can't tell the difference. I stare at the ceiling. Listen to the snores. And try not to choke on the nasty-smelling farts. I hate this. It's almost worse than boot camp. At least Serenity Ridge smelled clean.

The ceiling. I stare at it. I try to will my body to fall asleep or die. How can I? Float away without ever having to jump.

Chapter 28

"What!"

There's a hand on my shoulder.

"Don't!"

I sit up, finger in electric socket shocked.

"Here," she says. "Put this on."

She sits on the bunk, next to my shoulder. A nurse, she's here to give me a dose. I'm back in Serenity Ridge. My escape—the whole thing was a hallucination.

Cold sweat (who needs air conditioning when you have fear on tap) panic attack. I remember Marci's words, "Long-term safe house." I want to know, what part of the house is "safe." There's zero privacy, same as Serenity Ridge.

"I—"

She smiles. Yes, I'm dreaming. Nobody looks like this in the hospital. A princess. Or, an angel. I put the pieces together. Face, voice, touch. The girl who brought me the steaming cup of coffee, no cream, one blue is—

"Sugar?"

"Yes," she says. "There's a good-bye barbecue up on the roof."

That smile is definitely *not* an angel. She's *all* fairy. She reminds me of a life-sized Tink. That must mean I'm a Lost Boy. I'll follow her anywhere.

"Put this on," she says, hands me a black hoodie and slides off the bunk. I follow, to the kitchen window. "Sure," I'll say. "Let's hold hands and jump."

"Wait," she says. I stop. She moves the tarp and peeks. She lifts the tarp, steps through the window and waves me out. I hesitate.

"C'mon," she says. "It's safe."

I step toward the window, ready to leave. Then, I look down and see—

The ground. The fire escape's nothing but rusted pipe held together with thin, metal slots and paint. In my imagination, it buckles and falls off the building. My head hits the ground and splits, cantaloupe style.

I freeze.

"*Come on!*" Tink bleats, impatient.

"I—" I withdraw my foot and let the tarp drop. The only way I'm leaving is the way I came in: through the front door.

The tarp moves. Sugar's head pops through the gap.

"Let's *go.*"

"I can't." I'm a total wuss. Tink looks pissed, about to beat me with her wand. I brace myself, ready to duck.

"We had this other kid, Kevin, he had it, too."

"It? What?"

"Vertigo."

"And what happened to Kevin?"

"The last raid, he got caught. He was scared of using the fire escape. You know, '*Ben!*'" she says, in a sarcastic c'mon-I-know-that's-not-really-your-name tone. "This is a safe place."

"But Marci said," I stall. Maybe she'll get discouraged and leave. "Isn't this a closed safe house? Aren't we all supposed to stay inside forever? Or, until we turn eighteen?"

"Tonight's an exception," she says. "Hey, I've got an idea."

She reaches up, pulls off her Cholita kerchief and wraps it around my head. Great. I live with Gay Gang Bangers. I knew it. Upstairs, I'm gonna be jumped in.

"See? What you can't see, you can't be scared of. Look."

I do, it's true. My blindness has a red hue. She takes my hand

and leads me up and out the window. The bandana solves my fear of heights. Problem is, I can't see the ground below. This means I'll need to trust her. I don't. I don't trust anyone. I left my trust behind, bedside, the day I was kidnapped. She knows none of this. She takes my hands and places them down. I feel two, thin metal pipes.

"*Hold and up!*" she barks, an aerobics instructor style. I step up. "Good. *I'm right behind you!*"

Underfoot, the fire escape slants up, same as the bunk bed's ladder. Blind, I climb up-up-up, hoping we're close to the roof. Or, if we fall, heaven. I'm Muslim enough; I still deserve the seven virgins promised to martyrs. (But I'll settle for three if at least one looks like Hammer.)

"Oh!" she freezes. "Stop!"

"What?!?" I almost shit my pants.

"The neighbor's—they—they just got home."

"Yeah, so?"

"So they might *see* us. Don't move. She just set down her groceries. She just set down the bags and . . . Hurry! Up! Quick!"

"How far"—I say, climbing, fast as one can on a rusty fire escape—"is it to the top?"

"Twelve more steps and—" She helps me up the final step. It feels different, flatter than the others. "You good?"

I nod. I lie. Truth is, I feel nauseous. This step feels somehow different because, I realize, it *is* different. I'm on a ladder that goes *straight* up. Vertical. As in, it's bolted, flat, against the side of the building. Worse, the wind. Cold as a wicca's tit, it whips me from all sides. In San Francisco, even the weather's badass. I'm tempted to reach up and rip off the fucking Madonna "Like a Virgin" bandana. I need to look and *confirm* my fears. To see we hang in the air, high above ground. I swallow. What happens if I faint? Will Sugar catch me if I fall?

My tummy growls, hunger trumps fear, and I follow her— Up! Up! Up! I focus on the sound of her combat boots clomp-clomping on metal and rely on my human primate monkey grip to conquer the rungs. One, two, three, I count. Nine to go. "Eleven, twelve."

We reach the top rung. The bandana blindfold slips off my face. It's okay, I tell myself, the last step is the roof and we're done. No. We're not there yet. We have one more path: a catwalk.

I haul myself up, frozen hands guiding me up the narrow path. I fight two battles. Fear and wind. My palms crush old paint. White flakes curl back and reveal metal, pockmarked with rust the color of dried blood.

Up front, Sugar jumps off the catwalk. Air poufs her white ballerina skirt. For a moment, she hangs in the air. She drops out of sight. To death. There's a reason I was born without wings.

"Where are you?"

"Down here."

Jump!

My body won't move.

It knows.

I can't fly.

Chapter 29

I peer over the edge. An abyss. I'm gonna die. My eyes adjust. It's not an abyss, it's the roof. I hope it's the roof. All I see is The Void. The Madonna / Cholita bandana has slipped and covers my mouth, bank heist style.

Then, I notice—The City—sparkly light cast off by bridges and buildings brightens as night consumes twilight.

"Fuck it." I shut my eyes and jump. I drop off the catwalk and land on spongy asphalt. It's still warm, heated by daylight's Indian summer sun.

Chest high, the first roof creates a protective barrier and hides us. Not that it matters. Nobody looks—or cares—about us. We're surrounded by office buildings. I doubt the lawyers and janitors working the swing shift are the least bit interested in our queer crew.

In front of me, there's an enormous, rectangle-shaped pane of glass. It takes up nearly the whole roof. The surface catches fragments of light. I step toward it and glimpse a boy's face in the reflection. His cheeks are hollow. Dark circles are carved under haunted eyes.

Who is he?

"Sorry," I say, and step around him. He copies my movement. Oh, shit, I think, that boy is me. I look like shit. I need a facial.

Sugar looks back. Her ballerina skirt brushes glass, punk rock fairy princess style.

"What're these things? Skylights?"

"Solar panels."

"Yo!" Hammer raises a big blond arm, waving a beer bottle. Forget the hops, I could get shit-faced drunk on his bro'ish gorgeousness. My heart skips a beat. Maybe there *is* hope. Maybe we'll share the bunk and cuddle.

"Careful." Sugar reaches back and guides me toward the group. A homo homing pigeon, I set my sights on Hammer. I bump into something—someone—else.

"Ah!" I squeal, 'fraid, 'fraid, 'fraid. The hospital's turned me into a pins and needles kinda queen. Everything scares and / or startles me. My nose twitches, and smells perfume.

"Haifa?"

A smile materializes in the dark. White teeth. Another monster who wants to gobble me up.

"No, *Anita*," she says, grand. I can't look away from her face. Anita's face is perfect with this beautiful yet tragic movie star quality. I bet people stare at her all the time.

"Wanna toke?" she rasps, smoke caught in her throat. She holds out a tiny cigarette. Small, smokey puffs blast my face. A sweet smell, the weed makes me wonder if the roof's exempt from the zero tolerance rule.

"No, thanks." The hospital drugs blunted enough of my five senses.

"Dork," Kidd mutters.

"Sweetheart," Anita coos. "Please, ignore the hater. All you need to say is, 'Thank you, hater, that just means there's more for you.' "

I sit on the picnic blanket. The wool makes my ass itch. Down here, the city lights cast a *preternatural* glow on the hazy sky. (Preternatural being one of those snooty vocabulary words I love.)

Nearby, Sugar kneels and prods the barbecue. Red-orange embers spark, dancing in the dark before flying up and away like fireflies. Low, old skool reggae music tumbles out a battered boom box. My eyes adjust. There's Peanuts, Kidd, the deep-voiced boy, and two I don't know.

"Here." Sugar hands me a paper plate heaped with food.

Hunger trumps vegan ideals. I haven't eaten in days. I scarf the barbecue meat, beans and asparagus sticks. Food tastes *so* good. So good, in fact, I choke. Nobody notices.

Chapter 30

"When I get out, the first thing I'm gonna do is"—Sugar announces—"go shopping."

"With what?" Peanuts cracks. "You got a secret trust fund?"

"No. I'll get a job."

"*That* is So. Fucked. Up. You turn eighteen," Kidd seethes. Or is it Hammer's? I tell them apart by their heads. Hammer's a blond skinhead to Kidd's tight, terrorist black beanie. "*What* do you have? You've spent the last three years hiding in someone's apartment. You imagine you have some freedom but in *reality*, you have *nothingggggg*. I mean," he says, spitting out his hard, ugly words, "*who* are you kidding? Only difference between fifteen and eighteen is welfare."

His nothing-to-lose words hijack our attention. The good feeling flees. Kidd's hand drops to his crotch and adjusts, moving a large object under the fabric. Kidd's hella sexy, for sure, but he's scary sexy (vs. Hammer's boy-band / soccer-player / Nazi-guard sexy: Hammer excites me *and* makes me want to jump—into his arms).

"Why the *fuck* are we here?!? *Really,* what's this for? So I can grow up and be 'gay'? Gimme some crystal, a *sugar* daddy, and a cell phone. Yeah, I'll set myself up. Pros-ti-tute my young bubble butt. 'Oh, yeah, Papa, it's eight inches, *uncut,* for reals.' Girl, what *else* kind of work you think you're gonna get? 'Sides bein' a ho? Selling your ass. All this safe house does is put time between now and the in-ev-it-able. *Fuck. That.*"

And the party is . . . over.

Hammer drops a big blond arm on Sugar's small shoulder. Brotherly, he leans down and, with his sweet, pink lips, kisses her cheek. "You're gonna do *great.*" He reaches over and catches me up in a hug. "You, too!"

My head spins. OMG, Hammer smells as good as he looks. I don't know if I can handle all this eighteen-and-under (queer) teen sexuality. If Serenity Ridge was about carving out my desire, the safe house is about letting it bloom. Strike "safe" and I've moved into a *hot*house filled with Web pages, cellies, sugar daddies and meth. Fun!

"*Fuck. That,*" Kidd says, and stomps off.

"Yeah, cellies, *sugar* daddies and meth," Sugar says. "That's so me."

"Yeah?" Kidd says, and turns. He walks back and pretends to read her palm. "*Your* future's . . . mmm, let's see. Web sites, lap dances, snorting blow off dirty mirrors and . . ." Sugar tries to take back her hand, but Kidd won't let go. "Headless in a Dumpster!"

Chapter 31

The barbecue light flashes red, yellow and white on Sugar's face. Nothing—and "nothing"—can erase her beauty. I don't know what else she has to offer.

"That was harsh."

"Maybe." She shrugs. "He's right." Her heart-shaped mouth turns up at the corners, a Mona Lisa smile. "I'd go home, but there's not much of a home to go back to. Trailer parks don't count."

"Home's home," I say, and wince. My words sound like a cheap greeting card. She looks away. For a while, we sit like that, quiet and still. The city lights dance in her blue eyes, on skin white as a movie screen.

"How'd you end up here?"

"My dad." She gives me a sidelong glance. "He wanted me straight or dead."

"Hi, sis!"

"Everybody here's got the same fucked-up parents."

"Right. Mine? After my stepmother read my journal, I stopped sleeping cuz I was scared they'd pour gasoline on me and light me on fire."

"Would it bother you," she says, and holds up a cigarette and lighter, "if I smoke? Sorry. Gallows humor. Knowing I'm going to end up headless in a Dumpster does that."

Head bent into cupped hand protecting a small flame, she lights up and takes a long, deep drag.

"They tried killing you, too."

"Yeah, he heard all *I* wanted was to fall in love with a *beautiful* woman. Then . . ." Her lips tighten on the cigarette, cutting the answer short. Eyes closed, head back, her face in profile against the city lights, Sugar's the Unknown Movie Star. She opens her blouse. A scar runs down her neck and dips into her chest. "He did this. That's how . . ."

Another drag. My imagination fills in the rest. White smoke billows and hides her face.

"It's true? About you living in the closet?"

"Uh-huh." She lights a second cigarette off the first one's embers. "Three years. And you know what I figured out?"

"What?"

"Me being sent away didn't have jack shit to do with me being a dyke. It was more *all* about my mom, Samantha, leaving my dad, Barry, for Arnold, a lawyer she met one night at a bar. Arnold helped whip Barry's ass in divorce court. She got everything and married Arnold. Good for her."

"Barry's a clueless pinhead pig."

"*Word.* I mean, he's basically a fucking clown who's never gonna figure out why his life is such a big piece of shit. Is your dad like that?"

"He goes *looking* for shit. Hunter type."

"Ex-paramilitary, right? Anyway, I remember, after Samantha left, Barry started dating. Women—any woman so long as she had tits and a vayjay. We'd go out and he'd get drunk at dinner. One time, when we were in the parking lot waiting for the valet, he grabbed his latest cocktail waitress mistress by the arm and start yelling at me, 'Get in the car, you infant!' "

"Lemme guess. You look exactly like Samantha."

"Smart boy. You look like your mom?"

"I guess. I mean, I don't know. She left when I was two." I don't tell her about the picture I got in the mail. I *do* look like my mom—if that picture is hers.

"I bet you do. You were a daily reminder. He could take out his rage on you. Close his eyes and—"

"Pretend it was her."

"Yeah, I'm pretty sure that's how it works. For *them*."

"Your dad's a cop?"

"Ex. But the psycho never goes away. Anyone who thinks they're good enough to judge and punish people is crazy."

"Uh-huh, the way they think, we're collateral damage." She's making sense. I hope I'm not this wise in three years. "The money? Is that why Peanuts teased you?"

"Like I give a shit what that lil' crackhead wannabe-gangsta ever says." She grinds the ciggie into the black roof.

"What's up with her? Or him? Is s / he schitzo or—"

"Klepto," she says, pauses and lights ciggie numero three. "Who knows? Whatever Peanuts's problems are, they're real and not getting any better living here."

"Everybody else?"

She looks me in the eye. I'm startled by her gaze. I can tell. She's the girl who never looks at people head-on. A long time ago, she learned that looking invited male attention. I guess my look is low risk.

"Don't do what I did. Don't lock yourself in the closet."

"Because?"

Her lips close around the cigarette. She takes a deep drag and looks up, at the sky. Pauses. Speaks. Smoke escapes her mouth, white blasts illustrate each word.

"I'm fine, don't get me wrong. But there're shadows in my life. I see them. And I know I'll never be able to chase them away."

"I don't understand."

She stands. I look up. Against the night sky, this is her face in the mirror. A ghost, a wraith, a shadow. Three years of living in a closet has leeched out more than pigment.

"Now? See?"

Yeah, I nod. I'm terrified. I see, I see my future in *her* face. Haunted. She'll always have that look. An over-my-shoulder expression. There, but not there.

"I don't give advice," she says. Lights dance on her face, moving colors on a white movie screen. "And I don't trust people who do. They're just telling you what *they* would'a done. But I will say this: Don't ever forget *who* you are. Or, *why* you're doing this. Yes, you've escaped. But you've only escaped into your own poverty. Loneliness. And silence."

Sugar kneels and places a hand over my hand. Her fingers are ice cold. I don't feel a pulse. She looks me in the eye. Vision or a nightmare, I want to jump up and run away.

"Just remember one thing."

"What's that?"

"You can always leave."

She takes my hands, helps me stand and guides me toward the sparkly city lights.

"I hope so," I say, even though I don't believe a word. In my head, I hear that old song, "*You can check in but you can never leave . . .*"

All I know is, I've got to get out and escape before I turn into her.

Chapter 32

"Come on."

Going downstairs is ten times more difficult than getting upstairs. Sugar steps off the roof. I don't move. She looks back. I don't move. There's no way.

"It might be kind of hard."

"We'll just take it"—she says, and returns to my side—"one step at a time."

"I don't think I can do it. Is there another way?"

"Other than living up here for three years? No."

Her answer sounds so final.

"Forget it. I'll sleep under the solar panels."

"Hey, before you get into that, would you be open to trying something I did with Kevin?"

"Depends, no, I don't know . . ."

"Here—" she says, and takes my hand. "*Upsadaisy!* Step up, like that. Good."

I stand behind her. My body trembles. If I were an earthquake, I'd be a 10.0. She reaches back, takes my hands and plants them on her waist. "Lace them together."

My grip is weak. I can barely hold on. My body's turned into Jell-O. She looks back.

"You shadow me on this part."

"Then what?"

" 'Then what?' " She mimics me. Irritating but it makes me forget long enough—we're moving forward. Or, down. The moment I realize this, I seize up.

"I don't wanna," I whine.

"Stop," she orders. I do. "Turn around."

"The last time I heard that was in the RTC. The cavity search," I say. She ignores me. I turn around, old man slow.

"Back up. Uh-huh. Good. Step down, right there. Good. I'm right behind you."

I feel her body's warmth and breasts press against my back. I grip the rusty rails. My eyes open. My heart races. Gonna die, gonna die. Bricks. One. Down. Two. Down.

"This is going to take all night."

"Then it takes all night. You're doing great. Close your eyes."

"It's not like Vegas."

"How so."

"I ran up this mountain. I ran through this dude's backyard and he tried shooting me."

I wonder if it's okay to tell her how I escaped. I don't care. Two sentences equal five steps. We're almost there. I look down, just to check and—

The ground looms—

UP!

"Oh! Oh!" I hyperventilate.

One false move and—

Oh, shit! I'll fall to the street, head banging metal and hitting the pavement, my brains exploding like a pumpkin. I feel lightheaded—*I'm passing out.* As in. *Fainting.* And I'm holding on to a ladder that's stuck to the side of a building. *My hands let go.* She must feel it, seeing as how my back's pressed against her heart.

"Babe! Hey! Can you hang on just one sec?"

Hang on? Bitch, I'm so scared, I can't even speak.

"Whoa! Dude! Stop that!"

Dizzy, I'm about to pass out. My body presses against hers. She's strong but not that strong. IDK. Maybe she's been doing push-ups in the closet. Otherwise, I'm taking us both down.

Destination, Death. Her knuckles turn white. Nausea washes over me. *We're going to fall. We're not going to make it.*

"Is that really true?"

"What?"

"About him shooting you?"

"Uh, yeah. Why—" I forget my question. We inch down the ladder. This is never going to end. I'm going to die. Truly. It's not a death wish. More, a death forecast. Unlike Kidd, I just know. I'll die without ever having fallen in love. That should make my father happy.

"Fuck him."

"Who?"

I flush. She caught me, talking out loud. To myself.

"My mom," I joke. "If I die right now, I'll never get to meet her."

"Uh-huh. So, after that guy shot you, then what?"

"I ran down the other side of the mountain."

"This is way shorter. Couple more steps and . . ." She eases me off the ladder. "Yeah, good boy, just like that. Press yourself against my back."

I've turned into a monkey, or a barnacle. Except, instead of a whale's back, I cling to White Goddess Girl.

"Hold on to my shoulders. That's good. You all right?"

"I guess," I stammer. My eyes are shut tight.

"Good, coz we're there. Open your eyes. I do. As promised, there's the kitchen window."

"It's a collective, bitch!" someone shouts.

A fight.

Chapter 33

"And it's your turn to collect the dishes and wash them!" Sugar slips through the window and disappears into the safe house. The curtains part and she reaches out for my hand. I can't move. I'm frozen. Even I wanted to, I couldn't move.

"Yous nuttin' but a fuckin' coconut!" Far away, on another shore, Peanuts sticks out s / his tongue.

"Coconut?" Another boy raises his fist. I don't understand why he's a coconut, except maybe because his neck's a light brown. I hang back, stay on the fire escape, out of harm's way. "And *how* the *fuck* did you come up wit P-E-A-N-U-T-S? That like nuts on the wall? Or nuts on the chest? Creamy, smooth, I'll *suck ya* in a Jiffy? Or, oh! Oh! I know! It's your craigslist ad. *Pee in my face while the cheap trick sucks ya nuts?*"

"Least my beat ain't *mopped,*" Peanuts says. "Dre said it, said it, true that, *way* better, way back, than y'fuckin' Rumpled-up raisin-stilt-skin. Sheiitt. Southern rap rolls over your disko-ko any day."

"Dolly, all that crack you smoked bore some Swiss cheese–sized holes in your lil' nappy-covered head. But Subject A. Have you ever even *had* any nuts? Or, maybe it's like I heard, they cut 'em off. Hah, hah! Whaddaya do when they reach down there? Real fast, you grab their hand? 'No, sir! Not *that!*' "

"Say it, just *fucking say it*, fucking muthafucka!" Peanuts yells. Fury knots up Peanuts' tidy face. The fight shrinks the kitchen. I might as well be looking at it through a spyglass. Or, a keyhole.

"What could I 'fucking' say about you that hasn't already been said? Ten million times before by the hundred million trolls you've sucked off? Or, rolled. The straight dudes who freak out when they figure out what you are and beat you up? Or, that 'sugar daddy' you're always talking about but who nobody's ever met? Yo momma said it best. You ain't nothing but a fucking *wannabe*."

He turns and walks away.

Peanuts launches s / his small body. Hurls s / hiself toward Coconut's back. Quick as a cobra, he whips around and grabs Peanuts's wrists. Twist-turny, Peanuts struggles to escape.

"Hey!" Marci plays referee and separates Godzilla and She-Ra. "Break it up!"

Coconut lets go of Peanuts's wrists and they slither away.

"Fool," Kidd says, looking at me. "Get yourself inside."

I don't move. I can't. Nothing's changed. It's worse.

"I'm fine," I say. I can't believe that being "seen" is really such a big deal since being *heard* isn't.

"No worries, it's ladies boxing," Marci says, motioning me in and off the fire escape. "It's cold."

I can't. My hands and feet have taken root on the rust. She looks over my shoulder at the apartments. There's a worried look on her face.

"*Please.*"

In the window's reflection, I see an apartment light blink on. It casts a dim glow on the brick.

"C'mon," she says, speaking the way one would to a stubborn cat. "I need to close the window. It's cold."

"It's warm," I say, buying time.

"Someone might see—" She sounds tense. In the background, a door slams, the elevator groans. "You."

I don't budge. Even if my life depends on it, I can't move.

Sugar leans out the window and offers her hand. I step back. With fights, somehow, I always end up getting caught in the middle. Not this one.

"Come on."

"Thank you, I'm fine out here."

Frustration flickers across her face. I know, I'm being difficult. They'll probably throw me out for this. Just as well. I don't trust them. Hands reach out. They try to pull me inside.

"*Craaazy!*" Kidd says, leaning over Sugar's shoulder.

Sugar slips out the window and onto the fire escape. One more step, I flip over the bar. I don't care. I'll fall before I let them catch me.

"He's scared. Remember Kevin? He—"

"Vertigo?" Kidd says. He smiles, pleased by my STD. "He can't stay."

"Kidd, there's nowhere else for him to go," Sugar says. "Basement," Kidd says. Fuckhead's got an answer for everything. He looks at me. Basement. Huh. *That's* an idea!

"Try it," Sugar warns, "and I'll lock *you* up down there."

"We'll figure this out later," Marci says. "You need to go to bed. Sugar, come back. Close the window."

Reluctant, she turns and walks away.

"You sure?" she asks.

I nod. Yes. I'm going to stay out here. She slips inside. For some reason, my heart breaks.

"SHUT THE FUCK UP!!!" a neighbor yells.

Startled, I dart, and duck under the window right before it closes.

"Hah!" Kidd cackles. "Can you make it up to bed? Or do you need help?"

I look down. I peed my pants. I'm ashamed. Not for that or anything I've done. More just for being alive. Kidd's words make me feel like I don't have the right.

I scramble up the ladder. His eyes burn my back. I hide, safe in my penthouse. Close to the wall, I close my eyes, asleep.

Chapter 34

Not.

I lie there wide awake. I'm terrified I'm about to get kicked out. Yeah, I know the safe house and kids are both crazy. But it's the only place I feel even a little bit safe. Worse, I'm so tired I can't sleep. I linger in a sleepy netherworld, aware, exhausted yet still awake. I wish I could ask Sugar if this is how it happens: She lay down brown, and woke up white.

I wait for sleep to knock me off the cliff, send my body crashing down, splintering on the rocks. I wait for sleep to come and sweep me away from this anxious and uncertain reality. Sleep might even take pity and ease me off the bed, returning me to raft and river.

My head races. Thoughts. The safe house might just be ultimately boring. Sugar lasted three years in the closet. I doubt I can handle the next three minutes. Forget turning eighteen. I've got, let's see—730 days until I turn sixteen. Only . . . two more years! Then, I'm free. Least, that's what they say. I can't deal with the roof, so I really am hidden. Or, trapped.

It hits me. Yes, I've "escaped," but I don't have a clue what comes next. Seconds, minutes, days. I don't have a plan. I can't leave. I am alone. I might as well be in solitary. I'd put all my energy into leaving. I'm doomed, the prisoner who escaped and then didn't know what. I can't be unique. I bet most people don't think past what happens after they jump the wall.

I run down my options: school (No), home (No), shelter (No). I do the math. My options add up to a grand total of . . . *Zero!* 713 days total (or twenty-three months, thirteen days).

Sleep. Finally, she reaches out and pulls me down. But I'm so awake, I don't rest, and wake more exhausted than before.

I wake minutes? hours? days? later, flushed and hot. My head rolls to the side. Muted voices. Light outlines the closet door.

Outside, in the hallway, human noise: laughter, door slamming, elevator groans. A woman sings, some foreign language. Spanish? Italian? Or Portuguese? Her voice quivers against the backdrop of sweet music, drums and chorus. The song draws to the end. A man speaks over the last bars, his voice close but far.

I'm being watched. A figure comes into focus. At the end of the bed, a panther. Its onyx eyes glitter, emerald green: Kidd. He yanks off the covers.

"Get up."

"Marci?"

"She told me, 'Help Ben with this while I'm out.' "

I don't trust him, but I don't want to disappoint Marci or cause more problems than I already have. Weary, I climb off the bed. Execution style, I follow Kidd down the ladder.

Chapter 35

"Gimme your hand."

Kidd and me are alone in the kitchen. It's dark except for the study light. The black-and-white-striped table are prison colors, perfect since that's exactly how I feel right now with Kidd: jailed.

"What're you doing—telling my fortune?"

He holds an X-Acto knife between his thumb and forefinger like a chopstick. Smart, he doesn't answer, and takes my hand. I don't resist. He slides gauze under my hand and balled-up fist.

"Open your fingers."

I pretend I don't hear him.

"What happened to the mess?" I nod at the clean, empty sink.

Focused, his tongue slides out his mouth and rests on the philtrum, the concave space under his nose. Is he nervous? He holds a sharp object.

"We *got* to do this."

"Said who?"

"Marci said, that's who. Now, undo your fingers."

I loosen my fingers but just a little bit. He leans forward, raising the X-Acto knife. He's going to cut my hand. I tighten my fingers.

"What is this?"

"Really, loosen 'em up or I can't do it."

"Do what?" I tighten my hand. I really don't trust him.

"You wanna stay here, then we've gotta do this, or you can't."

Damn, I must be talking in my sleep. Because he knows all about my fear of being thrown out. I convince myself, "You need to do this." His tongue moves, wets his lips. They keep drying out. He *is* nervous. But about what?

"Listen, *everybody* gets it. The vertigo—" He gives me a look that says the safe house isn't a sure thing. "I won't lie. It hurts for, like, a week, but most people's skin heals fast. They took your fingerprints in the joint?"

I shrug. "Dunno."

"They might have done it and you didn't know. They do stuff. When they put you there, were you sedated?"

"Yeah, pretty much."

"So they took your prints. Prolly swabbed your mouth, too. DNA. Sent the samples to the cops. They've got a record. If you're caught, that's real bad."

"Okay."

"You don't have a choice. If you *don't* do it and you get caught, then, *man* . . . they can trace you like *that*." He snaps his fingers. "And that would put all of *us* in danger. Here, look, see?"

I lean forward. His fingertips are smooth, prints erased. He *was* the one who warned me about flushing the john. Kidd's a dick. But this makes sense. I don't want to, but I lay my hand on the gauze. Up close, his eyes are not green but black. So black, they burn. The table light flickers. His face—those eyes—they're not black but blue, same as the man in the bus station restroom. I recognize the look. I saw it in a counselor's eyes at Serenity Ridge. He's pissed off. Furious I *dared* challenge his authority. Weird. What part of his power trip am I missing? I yank my hand away, hiding it under the table.

"Now, why'd you go and do that?"

"I don't want to do this."

He drops the X-Acto knife on the table, sits back. He cracks his knuckles, palms out. Done, he reaches back, left arm hooked around his neck.

"Know what?" He sneers, giving me a dirty look. "With that attitude, you're not gonna last one week. I've seen *dozens* of people *come*. And *go*. You're just like all them."

Defiant, I hold his gaze. I hope he can't read my face. Really, he might be right, the way Sugar admitted he was about her. I might not "have what it takes."

"C'mon," he presses. "Let's do this. Living here, it's kinda like being an astronaut. Confined space for a long time. You got lucky with the roof. I don't know if Sugar told you, but most people, it's six, nine, sometimes eighteen months before they get to go outside. Some people *never* get to leave. Live here, you gotta *want* it. It's this way: You've moved somewhere else. A foreign country. They're gonna take your prints. Something. It's procedure, right? But I understand how you feel. If you got caught, you'd wanna go back. Or try your luck on the streets."

The streets, he says, pressing a button. My eyes widen, pupils dilated. Damn it, my body always gives me away.

"Yeah," he nods. "Prostitution. Trust, this is painful, but it's not the street, so you won't get the AIDS and die."

I do my magazine trick. Shift my gaze to the side, looking at him but not. I can see a person's essence: friend, foe, vampire, angel, tease, tormentor. Or . . . left hand. The one dangling next to his right ear. His middle finger's cut. Five tiny red ruby droplets ooze out the razor-thin slice.

"I need a Band-Aid."

"For what?"

"Your finger. Do you have the AIDS?"

His left arm flies off his head. I flinch. His hand, it moves slow, even though I know it'll be quick, I shut my eyes. I don't feel his palm—

WHAP!

Slap my face. I'm numb. I see the boy. In the bathroom. The one I couldn't save. His hand reached up. "Help me," he rasped, and—

I expected him to slap my face. His bottom lip pulls back, front teeth digging into the lower lip.

"Your middle finger's cut. I think it's a bad idea for you to do that. You know, cut me. Don't you think?"

"What the FUCK?!? The AIDS?"

What is it about *me* that makes Kidd *so mad?*

"I'm just saying," I say. "I'd feel better if you put something on your bleeding finger before you cut mine. It's not just *you*, it could be *me*."

His face twitches. Guilt? Something. He picks up a Band-Aid, opens it and wraps his finger. Done, he grabs the X-Acto knife.

"Let's get this over with."

A shadow fills the doorway. Kidd freezes.

Chapter 36

"Hi." Alice / Nadya, the quiet girl with pink hair, stands in the doorway. She looks twelve: She wears jammies with a happy Care Bear print. Yawning, she glides past us, opens the fridge door and leans forward, studying the contents with great interest. "Did you see that pie?"

"No," Kidd says. "It's past your bedtime."

"I have the *worst* cramps," she says, her pink head dipping and vanishing into the fridge's bowels. "Where's that pie?" She forages, the open fridge door blocks my view. "There!"

Beep! Beep! Beep! An alarm. Alice / Nadya's hand reaches around the fridge and presses the tiny magnet clock's stop button. She shuts the door and walks to the table. She sits, puts down the pie pan and sets a pill bottle next to it.

"Here," she says, nudging the bottles toward Kidd and forking the pie. "Mmm! What're you guys up to?"

"Nothing," Kidd says, ignoring the bottle.

"You need water?" she asks.

"We—" I say, and look down. The knife and gauze are gone. "He was telling me about that finger thing."

"She ran out of that stuff."

"Stuff?"

"IDs, birth certificates, whatever we're using. Weren't you"—

she hands Kidd the pill bottle—"the last one? To get your fingers done?"

"Uh-huh."

"J.D. You were asleep when we did it."

I want to read the label. Casual, I reach for it. Kidd snatches it. Under the table, he taps out pills and walks to the sink. He fills a glass with tap water.

Alice / Nadya shoots me a confused look. "You're leaving?"

"No."

"Then I'd wait. The acid's better. It doesn't hurt so much or make such a mess. See, look at mine."

She extends her arms, palms upturned and flat on the table. I examine her fingertips. Under the light, they're smooth as glass.

"Why is that?" I ask, looking at Kidd.

"Oh, you know." She picks up a fork, stabs the pie and takes another bite. She glances at Kidd. "You told him the risks? Mother's milk, vaginal fluids, semen. Blood."

Kidd pops a fat, white pill, tilts the glass and drinks. No. He wouldn't. Mix his blood with mine? Infect me? *No.* No one could be *that* evil.

Convenient, I've forgotten Serenity Ridge, my father, Mr. Jones, the nurses, orderlies, and quack doctors. The Blue-Eyed man who cut the boy in the bus station bathroom . . . Every kid who ever teased me. Based on firsthand experience, I *know*— people can be evil. Kidd's just another shape of darkness. And death.

Shocked, I return to bed and lie down. My body's still, but my mind races—I replay the last five minutes. Alice / Nadya walked in and stopped something bad. Kidd views me as an enemy, for reasons I don't know. Given the opportunity, he'll hurt—or kill—me.

"Defiant." That's what they called me in Serenity Ridge. I fought back. I forget that fact. I always think gay equals weak. But it's not true. I've already been through hell. Met and survived demons fiercer than Kidd.

Can't. Make. Me. Sugar was right. The safe house has brought me face-to-face with a demon: Kidd. And I've turned

him away. Thrown water into his fire-breathing mouth. You.
Can't. Make. Me. Unless he tackles me and, even then, I'd
scream so loud the whole building would hear.

I stare at the ceiling, trying to work out all this new information. Is J.D. Kidd's "man"? If so, then I represent some sort of
romantic threat. Which makes absolutely no sense since I
haven't even met J.D.

I hear strange, beautiful music. It dances, curls up and shim-
mies in the air. I wonder, are those songs meant for me? I touch
my chest. I wish I could jump in a bathtub filled with ice. My
heart burns up. What's this feeling? Love? Death? Sex? The three
sit so close together.

Chapter 37

I wake, look right and see a list taped on the wall. "Dos & Don'ts." Safe house rules. Thus far, all these "rules" are meaningless. People leave. People talk loud. People smoke (dope).

What, exactly, am I supposed to do with this paper after I've read it. Eat it? I'm not some '60s radical with a manifesto. Or, a terrorist, waiting to stir in his sleeper cell and bomb whatever.

Still, I know I can't toss the list into the trash. Someone might find it, puzzle it out and notify . . . who? Who exactly is looking for us? I've vanished into the least likely hiding place. If I'm in danger of anything, it's of being forgotten. Fuck it. I stuff the list under the mattress.

Beyond the bunk, Peanuts pads across the main room, opens the closet door and disappears. The inside flashes bright rainbow colors. Even in the daylight, I still haven't figured out if Peanuts is a he or a she.

For a safe house that's "closed," it's empty. Where have all the Waldos gone? Anita Fixx? Gone. Coconut? Gone. Hammer? Gone. Likewise Marci. Sugar's turned eighteen, "aged out."

Right now, it's just me, Alice / Nadya and Kidd. He sits in a corner, body folded over on itself, reading a book and wearing a Princess Leia (doughnut-shaped) headset. His face is set, a Buddha scowl and Ninja warrior. The flat, beautiful mask warns off even *vague* interest.

I reach for the blue notebook, pen and write—

> *we sit at the table*
> *silver X-Acto knife*
>
> *holds steady under the light*
> *waiting to slice when he*
>
> *slips through the window,*
> *silent*
>
> *Mean looking Latino Boy*
> *with his perfekt black spiky hair*
>
> *edges so damn sharp they'll cut ur fingers*
> *if u dared reach out & ran ur hand over it*
>
> *both his ears being pierced with gold earrings*
> *tiny round hoops make him look piratey, dangerous, sexy*
>
> *my eyes cannot resist, i glance*
> *there is something shimmery about him*
>
> *moving even when he's sitting still*
> *i wonder how someone like him lives here, in smallsville*
>
> *first of all he just doesn't seem the type (queer)*
> *he stands in the dark, in a corner faraway from*
>
> *the kitchen & its bright pool of light*
> *& i squint, peering through that curtain of light*
>
> *into the dark & see his eyes*
> *glittering in the dark & they make me catch my breath*
>
> *'cuz he's an animal,*
> *his eyes alive like a foxx's*

(Done.) I've answered a big question. Now comes the small one: What do I do with my day?

Chapter 38

The kitchen window's tarp has been replaced with a white curtain. It's tattooed with lipstick-red cherries. Nature intrudes. Sunlight seeps into the kitchen and breeze squeezes under the cracked window and ruffles frayed fabric.

I lift the lid, scoop gloop oatmeal out the pot and slop it into a bowl. Milk? In the fridge. I tilt the carton and wet the beige paste. Add brown sugar, raisins and nuts, and it'll almost be edible.

WTF!?! Me? No. *My face?* Yes, I'm hallucinating. Oh, shit, *yes*, that's *my face*—on the side of the milk carton. BIG BLACK LETTERS read, MISSING . . . HAVE YOU SEEN THIS CHILD? A milk carton. It's so '90s. Overnight I became an Amber Alert. I didn't know people still cared about missing kids. Or, not enough to publish bad—or Photoshop free—pix. There's a big zit in the middle of my forehead. It renders me ethnic indeterminate. I'm far from it, but I could be a baby Hindu with a bindi.

Recovered from my shock, I study the pic. Even without Photoshop, I look hella sexy. I am jail*bait*. Too bad there're no digits for cute boys to call me direct. Just 1-800-COPS.

"I had one of those." Alice-Nadya-Care-Bear-Jammie-Girl sits on a step stool opposite the fridge. She's been watching me the whole time. I can't decide if it's creepy or a testament to her spy-girl skills.

"You know what that picture means?" Between last night and this morning, she's dropped the "I'm shy" act and speaks in a normal girl's voice.

"No, what. I won the lotto?"

"It means there's bounty hunters out there, looking for *you*. It's kind of like *American Idol*. But with an arrest warrant issued by your parents. There's probably a reward for your capture."

There goes the idea I've been forgotten. She steps off the stool and sits in the chair under Che (Guevara), the '60s, Rolex-watch-wearing revolutionary, Fidel Castro's B.F.F., today known for his face half-hidden under a black beret and silk-screened on tee shirts, postcards and posters. She opens a book and ignores me. She wears old-fashioned, cat-eye frames outlined with glittery rhinestones and pretends to read Machiavelli's *The Prince*.

"Bounty hunters? Did I rob a bank in my sleep or something? Will they take me home?"

"No. Definitely *not* home. Back to where you came from or somewhere—oh!" She jumps up and runs out of the kitchen. The bathroom door's open: She barfs. Pregnant or bulimic?

I stare at the white curtains, morning—or, afternoon?—sun backlit the red dots.

"Back to where you came from, or somewhere . . ."

I sit there, listening to the awful sounds. I'm pretty sure she was about to say, "Worse. Someplace worse. And this time, they'll make sure you don't escape." I shiver. Uh! I need to conquer my fear of heights. There may come a day when I need to leave—

"Quick."

Chapter 39

"Translate *The Diary of Anne Frank?*"

"Correct."

I drop the book. She snatches it.

My head hurts. Alice / Nadya and me sit at the black-and-white-striped table. She stares, her face unreadable. She reminds me of the staff at Serenity Ridge. They'd sit, quiet, waiting until you broke and opened your mouth and tried to fill the silence with words. I broke myself of the impulse. My bad habit's come back. I want to talk. Say anything. Her gaze is unbearable. I don't want to answer; I know I shouldn't but I can't help myself.

"You speak anything else?"

"Farsi."

I laugh. "You're kidding, right?"

"No," she says, serious. "You *are* the Muslim one."

"Culturally, maybe."

"That is so sad."

"Baby"—I shrug—"kittens die all the time. Boo-hoo."

She gives me a look. I guess she likes cats.

"Here's the thing. I've been through this stuff and I need to . . . write it down. The way she did," I say, and take a deep breath. She'll crucify me for saying this. "I need to know my *own* story before I can make room in my head for other people's stories."

"Okay," she says, and I can tell what I've said is anything *but* okay. "Ben. You better get started on your story."

"I dunno, maybe I'm superstitious. But I've been through things—I don't—I can't."

"Sure, whatever," she says, freezing me out.

"Wait—I—the Holocaust. It's—"

"What. What is the Holocaust."

"There aren't any words for it. I mean . . ." I stutter, trying to explain. But she just glares at me. "I've been through."

"Yeah, what *exactly* have you 'been through' that would even come close to *this?*"

"I'm not sure I'd want to."

"Why? You've got something against Jews?"

My head really hurts. I see where this is going. The political-religious tar pits.

"You're"—I laugh, trying to take the edge off—"kidding?"

"No. You're Arab-Muslim?"

"Whatever. Technically. Culturally, I'm American. But I'm—"

"Then why not. Why wouldn't you."

"Translate this?" I hold up the paperback. She nods, super-serious. "Well, this girl got caught and was . . . gassed?"

"Typhus." She tosses another paperback on the table.

"*The Bell Jar?* No, thanks. I've read it."

She removes a third paperback, places it on the table and pushes it forward.

"*Johnny Panic and the Bible of Dreams.* Maybe."

"In Spanish."

"Fluent."

"French."

"You mean," I say, hesitant. "Learn a language from scratch?"

"You need to figure out what you're doing with your time."

I pick up *Johnny Panic* and flip through it, reading but not really reading the blur of words. I stop. Read a random page. "Dream about these long enough and your feet and hands shrivel away when you look at them too closely—"

"Trust me," she says. For a moment, I do. "You need *something* to fill the days."

The white curtains part. One black, scuffed Doc Marten steps inside. I panic—Ben, not Johnny, stands and trips, running to escape, out the front door. They've come to get me. I don't know where I'm going, but I need to get out.

"Hey," he says in a voice so deep, it reaches down, into my ear, and moves through my body. A hand tightens on my arm, and helps me stand. "I'm J.D."

Chapter 40

By daylight, love at first sight looks like "Jay-Dee," a gloriously cocoa-skinned boy who works the Latin Rebel look. Eyebrows plucked to points. Ears hung with tiny, gold pirate hoops. Jet black hair shaved to the skin on the sides, spiked into glass shards on top. Our eyes lock, my brown-yellow with his yellow-greenies. I lose all sense of time, space and identity.

"What's your name?"

It takes me a second.

"Ben!" I hear my voice and cringe. It's a baby chicken cheep. "Are you, uh, by any chance Persian? Or, Armenian?" I wince. I'm *such* a dork! My question's so lame, he could easily snap back with some arch, gaybonic put-down or rap, "Like it *matters* / I'm not FOB / I'm in the here 'n the n-o-w / Face-to-face. *Bee-atch*."

"In fact, I'm—"

Instead, a huge grin splits his face.

Peanuts steps in and snaps, "Wishes!"

"Peanuts," J.D. says, his voice the sound of a switchblade popping. "You better *shut the fuck up*."

Peanuts plucks a spoon out the sink, sashays to the fridge and opens the door.

"*That one* tells everybody he's Persian, but he's real"—s / he grabs a yogurt, opens it and dips the spoon. S / he licks it, giving us a *nastee* Britney / Lindsay / Paris look—"lee, Gua-te-ma-lan."

"And," J.D. seethes, "*s-hit,* Little Miss Gender We Don't Know goes around telling everybody that it's Miss Misunder—"

"Sh-What?!?" Peanuts sputters, spitting yogurt.

"Yeah, *s-hit.* Short for *she-he-it.* All brown an' *nasty,* sumpin' ya can't *wait* to wipe 'n *flush,* like yo's dirty, fuckin' culo!"

I look away. There are knives near Peanuts.

"S-hit sez," J.D. continues, "shit's a Missy-Mis-Understood foster care lesbo love chil' when, *in fact,* s / he's really a cracked-on, ghetto bitch, speed freak 'ho who simply don't got no place else to go."

"*Fuck. You,*" Peanuts says. "Coconut. All *brown* on the outside an' *white* on the inside."

"Split me, snitch witch, only thing's white inside's my milk, sweet 'n tastee," J.D. trills. "What cum outta *you* when you spill? Skanky coochie juice? Ain't the FDA recalled that toxic shit?"

"You remind me," Peanuts says, tiny pink tongue threatening to execute a slow, vicious lick across s / his lips. "When Mexicans first started coming to El-Lay and doing their top buttons up with those weird pants the lil' hats and all the white peoples were like, 'oooooweehhh ke-he'? And then there was like hundreds of them kicking people's asses and ruling shit and they were like, 'OK, OK, OK.' And *now* they're such a part of the landscape that, when you put a quarter in one of those machines at the supermarket, out pops one of those Chicano toys." The spoon slides in-between Peanuts plump lips and s / he swallows. "And that'd be *you,* brutha, just another fuckin' *Toy.*"

Chapter 41

I leave the kitchen and lie down, pillow over my head. The ghetto poetry-insult slam makes my head throb. I roll to the side, head stuck out from beneath the pillow. I fall into another dreamless sleep. No picture, just sound: conga drums, cymbals, flutes, bells and whistles. Or—maybe—I'm not dreaming. Maybe, I hear music. Spanish lyrics. Over them, a deep, male voice rumbles, "And this one goes out to Mirabelle in Potrero Hill."

A shadow falls on the bed.

"Dollie, it's time to *get up*," Anita says, playfully tugging my big toe.

"Time to get up for what?" I mumble, half asleep.

"Time for us to *die*." She puts out a hand. Silly me. I didn't read the memo. I forgot about signing the suicide pact with a crazy trans girl. Her eyes are hella dilated. She's not moving, and I'm in no mood to argue. I crawl off the bunk. Chunky platform heels turned to the side, Anita takes dainty, downward steps. She bunny hops off, and her hootchie mama miniskirt puffs and goes, Oh! I follow her to the bathroom. She flips the sign over (OCCUPIED), closes the door and gestures to the toilet seat. "Sit."

Then, she runs a bath. I don't see us doing any rub-a-dub-

dub. In the small space, I'm able to nail her scents: Chanel No 19, Breath by Smirnoff, 50 Proof.

She turns away from the tub. Busy, she chooses bottles clustered on the plywood slat laid down on the sink.

I study her. High, arched brows give her a wide-eyed, fuck-me-like-I'm-Bambi look. Biology 101, those eyebrows are plucked high for a reason: Wide eyes signal sexual availability. Eyelashes are weighed down by layers of black mascara. The black gunk fools her eyes, and dilates her pupils. She's excited (!) to see you, me and everybody we know.

Anita draws herself up to her full height and cracks her back. Done, she sways on platform heels. She steps back, away from the tub, and trips. I catch her hand.

"Thank you!" she says. "Mama had a nip. Now, put your head *under* there and wet your hair."

"Yeah," I think, "Mama's had more than a cocktail: She's drunk." I lean into the tub. Warm water washes over and soaks my scalp and hair. It takes a minute: I've got super thick (Fuller Brush) hair. I sit up. Anita's gone. I'm dripping wet. There's not a towel in sight and the bathroom door's open. Right then, the front door opens. A figure steps inside. My heartbeat races, zero to two fifty. A bust! They're here! To get me!

Mystery person shuts the door and turns: Kidd. Er, Kidd dressed in some Booty Bandit getup: wool cap pulled down over his forehead, scarf wrapped around his mouth. I'm puzzled; what look is he working: Foiled Fatwa? Or, the Unhappy Terrorist?

Right then, I remember Marci's words, "Nobody leaves the house. Ever." *Yeah, right,* I think. Nobody *stays* in the safe house, except milk carton boy, Alice / Nadya, and Peanuts. Everyone else is M.I.A.

Kidd's just broken a "nonnegotiable" rule. He pauses, and unwraps the scarf. His face is ashen. Or, is it green? He's either sick or scared as shit, maybe both. He drops his bag, locks the door with not just one lock but *all five.* The keyed chain door lock, brass flip lock, slide bolt, door guard and dead bolt. He walks away, bag left on the floor. I'm *so* curious what's inside and am about to run over when he returns and snatches it. Something falls out onto the floor. I'm already up and snatch the paper. It's folded, a paper square. I slide it into my back pocket. Maybe it's the clue I need to figure out what's behind his hate.

Anita steps into the bathroom, towel draped over her left arm, steaming cup of tea in her big she-man right hand. She hands me the towel. "Here."

I take it and drape it around my neck. On her towel-tea expedition, she's pulled her hair back and up into a ponytail. The hootchie mama outfit's gone, replaced with a knee-length apron and white surgical gloves. She looks shorter, too. She picks up a bowl filled with beige-colored pudding, sets it on the bathtub's edge and picks up a small paintbrush.

"Sit," she says, gesturing to the porcelain throne. Anita's not the type I'd argue with. I bet she's packing. She's one . . . *Fierce. Deadly. Tranny.*

Then, I look down and Anita's profile goes South: She wears fluffy bunny-shaped slippers! Behind closed doors, Anita's way more housewife than prison matron.

"You never met anyone like me, huh?"

"Yeah, in the hospital."

"Uh-huh, who?"

"There were kids who couldn't—or wouldn't—play the role of their Natural Born Gender."

"Hah, hah." She smirks, mixing a bowl of beige goop. "I'm gonna mop and modify that. 'Oh, I'm not feeling like my Natural Born Gender today.' "

"Yeah, right? But at Sere—" I catch myself. "The boot camp. There were the tough girls who refused to wear dresses and makeup. Or, the femme boys who wanted to *wear* dresses and makeup. Their dress code boycott was another fake problem. I mean, who cares *what* you wear? But at Ser—the boot camp, it was a big problem. Because it was so in your face. There were always boys who wrapped a towel around their heads after we showered. It drove the staff nuts."

"I bet none came close to Anita Fixx."

I nod. She's got a point. Anita's living as a woman in an underground safe house. Girl. Works. It. Out.

"Most queens, they'll read your outfit. Me? I'm Gen Next. Coming to a salon near you, Anita Fixx, the Psychic Hairstylist."

"In the hospital, I forget. What do they call it?"

"*G.I.D.* Gender Identity Disorder. Some bullshit trip they lay on you if you're a woman, but you were born a man. Of course, the counselor's always got it wrong. There's Joey who wanted to *dress* like a girl, and Josephine who wanted a mastectomy and a penis. Blue jeans, flannel shirt and combat boots being beside the point. Personally, I'm looking forward to getting mine cut off. Sweetheart, did they use that on you? For your diagnosis?"

"I don't know." I feel really dumb. GID sounds way more scientific than, "I like boys." "My parents said it was coz I had a concussion. Said I was, 'Noticeably different.' "

"Different being how you stopped pretending you wasn't staring at boys?"

"Pretty much."

"Darling." She laughs. "Could you scooch ya'self forward? The tinfoil . . ."

Tinfoil makes me think, baked potato with sour cream and chives. Anita's hands get busy all over my head. She picks up the paintbrush, dips it in the beige goop and glops it over my scalp.

"What's that color?"

"Black. Gonna make you darker than shoe leather." She steps back and studies the back of my head. "Serious. You got any preferences? Besides the obvious?"

"Blond. A really *good* blond."

"Like Hammer? If he let his stubble grow out? Then you can cam ho' and sell it, two fer one. Don't lie! Mama got your number."

I doubt it since I don't even have a cellie but whatev. More silent paintbrush / gloop activity follows. Even if she gets the sex change, what will she ever do about those hands? They're huge.

Breasts, makeup, long hair and hormones will fool a dude (at night), but there's nothing she can do about those hands. Then again, maybe she'll meet a dude who doesn't care. Or, she's a pre-op *lesbian* trans girl. She's gentle. Maybe, with a gift like hers, nobody will notice.

Meanwhile, I fantasize about how I'll look: blond, angel-fairy-boy.

"Strawberry blond is not just a color," she says, folding tin-foil and bobby pinning them onto my head. I worry she's building a satellite dish.

"It's not?"

"No. Strawberry's a street ho who'll do it for a hit of crack."

Anita brushes on more beige glop and folds more aluminum foil triangles. The bathroom functions much like a regular beauty salon. Spurts of conversation. Silence. Physical transformation in-between the two. I wonder, is "the unexamined life" just another version of "ignorance is bliss" but without the blond hair color?

"I must say, you don't really look like the type." She steps back and examines her work.

"Type of what?"

She fusses with the tinfoil. "That hurt?"

"Stings. My scalp."

"Good. Means the glop's doing its thing."

"I better not end up looking like my stepmother."

"No, Cinderella, your black Arab coif's gonna look Uni-porny."

" 'Cause my stepmother's never fooled anyone. She thinks gypsy bitch orange is blond. You should hear her friends' 'com-pliments.' 'Oh, Haifa! Your hair looks really, so, different!' "

"If someone named Anita Fixx don't know the secrets of beauty, then who the fuck does?"

"True." I nod. "What type am I?"

"Well . . ." She washes out the paintbrush in the sink and glances at me over her shoulder. "You look like the type with a hard-on for Hammer who will break J.D.'s heart."

I thought my face was unreadable. A mask. Anita saw right through me. Same as I noticed her boozy breath. Habits or glances, we all give ourselves away.

"*Knew*. It." She slips a plastic cap over my head and sets an egg timer. She removes the plastic gloves. *Snap!* "Now we wait for the miracle of color to do its magic."

In the world of hair color, I guess miracles and magic are like tricks are for kids. She pulls out a pack of cigarettes and lights up.

"How's it we're all drug free but everyone here smokes? Last time I checked, nicotine's a habit."

"Yes, it is," she exhales, smoke drifting out her nostrils. "Smoking's a way to pass the time. Sad cliché, but you'll learn, it's true. In here, minutes can turn into days."

"Are you drunk?"

Without a word, she leans over, her right leg reaches out and a big fluffy toe shuts the door. *Click*. Oops. My bad. Edit. My *real* bad. If the safe house is anything like Serenity Ridge, there are The Rules. And then there are The *Unspoken* Rules.

"Yes, I've had a nip, or two," she says, cool as a serial killer femme fetale. "Which is *my* business."

"Yes, it is." She's been nothing but nice, and I act like a dickhead. A judgmental one. Kidd and me share a character defect. My head fries—in total silence. I count the minutes ticking off the timer. Nineteen and a half minutes. I must sound like a snotty little bitch.

Blond? I can just hear Anita say. No, Ben, I see you closer to your ethnic *roots*. How about gypsy bitch *orange?*

"My parents are obsessed with grain content."

"Here." She offers me the sports "water" bottle.

"No, thanks," I say, and shake my head. Tinfoil rustles.

"You don't drink?" She poses her question in a neutral, shrink voice. The neutral voice is supposed to make troubled teens spill the beans. I learned quick to say as little as possible. They wrote everything down and used it all against me.

"I'm still trying to flush all that junk they slammed in me."

"I thought it was coz you're Muslim."

"No," I say, feeling my face flush. My honorary bin Ladenness is that obvious? "More O.J.'s distant relation."

"Huh." Her fingertips test my hair. She's too much of a pro to fuck up my color. People would see my gypsy bitch orange hair and blame *her*. "Would that be like Liz Taylor playing Cleopatra? Or that blond baby Jesus? The originals, you know they were *all* black."

Anita parks the cigarette between her lips, leans forward and carefully lifts my cafeteria lady cap. Her big hands touch my head. I jump-flinch. Maybe her trans'ness makes me feel more uncomfortable than I care to admit. No matter, the tub water's running. She must have sensed my discomfort (or seen it: How could she have missed it? I almost jumped off the toilet). She puts her fingers under the flow, testing the temperature. She yanks off the plastic cap and steps aside. "Rinse. Keep your eyes shut tight."

I lean forward, head under the faucet. *Whoosh!* I love the feeling of the warm water flooding my head with Anita's big fingers giving me a scalp massage.

"K, upsie!" She tilts me up, towel dries my head. She finishes me off, styling my new 'do with a blow dryer and shiny goop scooped out a metal tin. The attention makes me feel like the Prince of the Safe House.

"There," she says, giving me one last dab. She steps back, admiring her work. "Take a look."

I turn and face the mirror. See. Me. And . . .

"Well?"

"I . . . love him!"

"Beautiful," she says, and slips out. "I'll let you two get to know one another."

Makeover madness! I don't recognize my reflection. I'm so beautiful I'm . . . *someone else*. For sure, I'm *not* the snot-nosed seventh grader whose picture is plastered on a milk carton. I lean toward "him." I'm the boy who I've always wanted to kiss. Too bad the closest I'll ever get to him is my reflection in a dirty bathroom mirror. Anita has a point. I *am* good enough to sell.

A second face emerges in the dirty mirror. I know that face, but I can't recall from where.

I rub my eyes. I open them. The other face is gone. Good thing, too, since seeing other people's faces in the mirror—when you're supposed to see your own—means you're crazy, for reals.

I touch my head. I've seen this color before. But on another boy's head. His eyes look back at me in the mirror. Face in the brushed, silver metal door—

It opens—

He—

Opens his mouth—

Creak—

He's here—

Opens more—

And—

Screams—

I feel faint—

Open my eyes—

Same as—

The Dead Boy in the Bus Station Bathroom.

Chapter 42

"Hey, hey—"
I lie on the cold tile floor. I either was in a fight (and lost) or fainted. Left hand to tub, I push and try to stand.

"Here," he says, grabs my hand and pulls me up.

"Embarrassing." I laugh weakly and sit on the toilet seat.

"I walk in. You were up. And then, you weren't."

Instant replay. I was so caught up with admiring my trés sexy reflection in the mirror I don't hear footsteps on the tile floor.

" 'Scuse me, I need to use the john." I stand and walk toward the door. "Hey, I'm not kicking you out."

He sits on the tank, reaches back and opens the tiny window.

"You gonna rinse off?" His voice sounds like bubble gum. Or that old, famous actor. What's his name? Brando?

"Rinse?"

"Hands." I look at my hands. "Unless you're ready for surgery?"

"Yeah," I say, desperate to avoid his gaze. He leans toward the open window. Thumb to match, he pops a flame, holds up the ciggie and inhales. The ciggie's tip sizzles, red. I stare, mesmerized by how he works the cancer stick.

I give him a *subtle* boutique once-over. He's got The Look: black skull cap (overlapping, white letters, "N—Y" on the front), oversized white tee and baggy jeans cinched tight on a wasp waist. Hot, J.D.'s a Real Live Gay Gang Banger.

"Wass'up?" he says, reaches down and, looking me in the eye, adjusts his package. Yeah, Holmes, I know, your cajones are *That Big*. "You strictly dickly?"

"Am I what?"

"Do. You. Suck. Cock? Or swing both ways? I'd ask, are you trans, but you're not giving that."

Giving? Trans? IDK, I flash my Ferrari, a closed-mouthed smile. In my head, I summon a fashion police lineup. J.D., Kidd and Hammer. They're *all* sexy but hella different. I rate them, one, two, three. Fire, Ice, Airhead.

He picks the paper (the one that fell out Kidd's backpack) and holds it up.

"Thanks," I say, and reach to take it. "Marci's Rules."

He rolls his eyes and holds on to the paper. "Yeah, her 'rules,' " he says, leans back and takes a drag. "That's her trying to be 'straight edge.' She 'claims' she's all stepping it."

"Stepping?" I use the neutral shrink voice. J.D. holds the paper. How do I get it back? "Like stairs?"

"Sober," he says. "No drugs or Anita's Jesus juice."

"Like Evergreen." He shoots me the WTF look. "You *know—Twelve Steps to Overcoming Homosexuality*."

"Oh, yeah." He bluffs. I don't care. I vibe him: "Give me the list . . . Give me the list . . . Give me the list . . ."

"They never tried that shit on you?"

He leans back and rests his skull on the ledge. A thin stream of white smoke escapes his lips. It curls up and out the tiny window. If a stranger sees the smoke, will they think, S.O.S.?

"For reals." He nods. I don't believe him. "Last time we got raided—"

"*Raided?* Like, Raid, a roach bomb or—"

"No, raided cops and dogs. But cops and roaches, hah hah, there's not much difference. This one kid, Kevin, he was so stoopid from smoking a blunt, he ran out the *front* door."

"*Damn.*" I whistle. I act like I'm caught up. In his story and faux—F-A-K-E—ghetto speak, that's straight outta Compton. No, wait, MTV! Well, we do live in a roach-infested walk-up. Some would count that as "ghetto."

His hand—the one holding the cigarette—hangs out the window, in the air shaft. He takes a drag. His Adam's apple bobs. Maybe I can distract him. Lick his neck and steal the paper. His head snaps up. Our eyes meet. Somewhere, in the electrified air between us, if I'm feeling this, then he must be, too?

"*Damn* ain't the half of it. Last I heard, Kevin got sent down to solitary. I heard he's all droolin' 'n shit from the 'tropes 'n the EST. So. You *do not* want to get your ass caught. Not now. Cuz, they'd feel *obliged* to *learn* you, like some ax murderer. Or pedophile."

Arms overhead, he stretches. The deep yoga breath forces the nicotine in real deep. His body's limber, like taffy. Or, a cat's. He folds himself over, head on knees, arms alongside his legs. Show off.

I turn to the mirror and stare at my new look. I don't care if he sees.

"Why didn't you use the fire escape?"

"Occupado and, besides, it's hella cold out there."

He offers the pack.

"No." I shake my head. "But that just means there's more for you!"

"You and Anita been hanging out."

"She says that to everyone."

"Basically but—" He takes another deep yoga drag. "That'll change."

"I made up my own No Smoking policy."

He hops off the toilet, stands behind me and rests his head on my shoulder.

"Why does that color look *so* lame on me and *so* damn good on you?"

Flattered, I admire my reflection. No shame!

"There should be laws against people like me looking this young and this cute. It's sick, though, huh."

"What?"

"What what?"

"Sick?" He lifts the toilet seat. "You need to?"

"No, fool." I laugh. "*Kewl.* You been in here that long?"

"Guess." He tilts his head and shrugs, Don't Know / Don't Care. "I've lived here almost eight months."

He reaches out and runs his hand through my new hair. Spine chills. He may not know today's teen lingo, but he's got the touch.

"Feels like mink," he says, steps back, sits on the tank and takes a drag. Slow and sexy. He gives me a *look*, fucking me with his eyes. His head drops back, Marie Antoinette style. Say the window drops, there goes his neck, chop!, guillotine style.

"You from here?" His voice ricochets in the air shaft. I want to jump up and follow the sound up, to the sky.

"Mmm?"

"You're from here?"

"No, I'm—"

"Don't tell me. They catch us, we can't tell them what we don't know."

"Right." I nod. I don't know what the hell he's talking about.

"Fool, what *school?*"

"Oh, like, where'd I escape from?"

"Yeah."

"Aren't we supposed to keep it a secret?"

"I promise not to tell."

"Serenity Ridge."

"No way! Me too!"

We look into one another's eyes. Deep. You'd think we'd fallen in love on the spot. That spot being a skanky bathroom in a ghetto safe house. But J.D.'s *way* too cool to simply give himself over to the moment. Not that it matters. I don't like him. I like Hammer. Right?

"Dude," I say, and point at his hand. Ash trembles, about to break and fall off the cigarette. "Time to put that out of its misery."

"You remember that girl?" J.D. takes one last toke and drops the ciggie in the toilet water. I look away. I don't want to think about the ciggie's filter tip, glazed with his saliva, soaking in the yellow piss water. He shuts the lid. "I forget her name."

"Little Miss Permission Slip."

"Uh-huh."

"That girl, whatshername, always running around, saying, 'You are *so* gross and *so* vulgar and you are so going to *pay*,' " I say, mimicking Shelly, the girl who was famous at Serenity Ridge for sucking up off the male staff's members.

"Damn, you do her good."

"Hah, hah, hah." We laugh. I'm amazed I can laugh about *anything* associated with Serenity Ridge.

"I could never figure out. Why was she there for so long?"

"Oh, you never heard?" He takes a quick drag and flicks the cigarette out the window. "She was fucking that orderly. I forget his name. But did you know? That fucker tried doing me!"

My body seizes up. I hope he doesn't notice. I wonder if there are muscle relaxants in that medicine cabinet. The way he says it makes me think he can tell. See it on me. There's *no way* anyone can know. "That orderly" didn't just *try*, he *did*. All the time. I force the memory, down, out, away. Forget, forget, forget.

"What's wrong?" he asks, peering at me.

"Nothing."

I look away and study the tub. The green paint on the bottom peels. I want to plug the drain, turn on the faucet, get in and slit my wrists. ("Time to die!" cries the voices in my head.) I won't answer his question. I'll make something up. I will not tell him the truth. I'll tell him what I think he wants to hear. Better, I'll tell him what I'm feeling. Problem is, I've forgotten how to speak. I've lost my voice. He gives me this funny look. The "Hey, are you retarded? Say something" look.

"No, it's just that place. Talking about it. I was trying not to think about it, that's all. Brings back, you know, stuff."

"Yeah." He nods. "More kids she ratted on, more points she got. I bet she wanted to be on staff."

I'm not buying it. J.D. hasn't told me anything he couldn't have heard, guessed, or made up. There were several Shellys at Serenity Ridge. She was a type.

I study his face. I don't remember seeing him at Serenity Ridge. If he's lived *here* for eight months, we would have met. Or, we might have just missed one another. He could have been on another unit—there were five. Or, was I so doped up, we *did* meet and I forgot.

"What?"

I open my mouth, about to ask, "Wasn't Shelly there about eighteen months?" But I don't ask. I keep my mouth shut. I'm so confused. I was never good at math. Still, I have this nagging feeling. He's lying. Who'd lie about being in Serenity Ridge? He touches my arm. I jerk. An electric shock. *He never said her name.*

"You're thinking."

"Nothing." I lie. Is it still a lie if you just can't explain the thoughts you have or second thoughts about sharing? I test him. "Did Valerie really leave in a body bag? Dead? Like everybody said?"

"Geez." He shakes his head, "acting" like he's "remembering." Or, trying to. Now it's so obvious he's lying. There was no Valerie, and if he'd been there, he'd know. "Valerie, Valerie, Valerie. Dunno. Musta been after my time."

A knock on the door. Startled, I jump. J.D. slides the window shut, hops off the tank and turns on the faucet. He splashes water on his face. Head up, he reaches for a toothbrush, wets it and swipes away the cigarette breath. Done, he moves the mirror. The reflection catches our faces in the chipped silver surface.

J.D.'s rests his head on my shoulder, face next to mine in the reflection. He gives me a small smile, like he can't be bothered to make the effort and part his lips. He's not being friendly in a friend way. He's being friendly in another way. I don't get it. His arms tighten around my body. I like the feeling. And his look, whatever it is, makes me feel . . . nervous? And excited. He turns away from the mirror and faces me. I'm in his arms. I don't like this feeling. I want to leave. He blocks my exit.

I look away, then back. His face says everything and nothing. I get it. He's got game. J.D. thinks he's some junior high school Casanova. I need to leave, now, or I'll start laughing.

"Excuse me." He moves, just enough for me to squeeze by. The closeness wavers between hostility and intimacy. He breathes on me. My skin tingles. I'm sure he sees the goose bumps. I look away, avoid his gaze. Something might happen, and I'm not ready for it. I've almost slipped away. He catches my arm and spins me around. Guess he *is* ready. He leans toward me, eyes closed, lips ready to kiss.

"You want to."

I slip away, step forward and reach for the door. I open it and step out.

"Sorry, but I don't. Smoke makes me sick. For reals."

wishful thinking

on the love or lust front
nothing's developed

yet

as for me
I am still love free

more of my virginity returns
everyday

J.D.
Hammer
sky brightening

reminds me of
that singer's
hard voice

aching with desire,

"hopeful embraces
& wishful thinking"

Chapter 43

Twilight slips to night. I sit on the floor. The radiator kicks in. Steam oozes out the grill. The sound breaks the early evening quiet. The closet door squeaks, opens. My heart still skips every time a door opens. I live prepared to run and dive out the kitchen window.

A figure steps out. Hammer. Naked from the waist up. I stare at his perfect abs. His face and torso are sweaty. He opens his mouth and sinks his perfect white teeth into a Pink Lady apple.

"If you want," he says, juice dribbling down his square chin, "jump on it." For a second, I imagine his offer's to jump on his jock. He looks at my puzzled face and grins. "*Internet.*"

Inside the closet, a lavender scent hangs in the air. Sex? I can't see Hammer and Peanuts getting it on. Small, the closet has walls painted a pale purple color. Usually, I hate purple. I don't mind this shade—it's more eggplant purple (vs. tacky, Teletubbies purple). Oversized pillows, covered with sparkly Indian fabric, are piled up on the corner bed. It's Harem decor, Ali Baba, baby, all the way. Something glittery catches my eye. I push apart the clothes hanging off a wood rod. Gianormous, sparkly letters—SUGAR!—are painted on the wall with a flourish, Vegas style.

"There." Peanuts motions me over. A sleek PC sits atop the

desk. A Webcam's perched on its razor-thin monitor. The browser's open to craigslist.

"See, that's how we found you," Peanuts says. "Right under their fucking noses."

The picture on-screen is what gets my attention: a boy's naked, muscular upper torso. Peanuts clicks the mouse and shuts the window. I don't understand the craigslist / sex ad / bus station connection.

"Wanna surf it?"

"Hell, yeah!" I sit on the stool and face the monitor.

"Don't move it—it's Wi-Fi. Signal's iffy."

I move the mouse. Of course, the first thing I do is open bookmarks and history. Click. The window opens.

san francisco craigslist > men seeking men > Hot
Str8 College Cock on Cam!
last modified: Sat, 21 Oct 23 PST

please flag with care:
(miscategorized)
(prohibited)
(spam)
(discussion)
(best of)
email this posting to a friend
Hot Str8 High School Jock Cock on Cam!—15

Reply to: pers-111111111@craigslist.org

Ive been having some financial problems
lately and so I decided to start charging for
webcam shows to help me pay some of my
bills. I am a str8 high school kid but I do things
such as jerk off, play with my ass and even
suck my own cock. These shows are through
either yahoo or msn messengers and range
anywhere from 30-100 depending on the

show. I am good looking and in shape and
have never had a complaint for my shows, if
you feel like helping out a cool high skool kid
for a little online excitement, get in touch with
me at sucking_self on yahoo or hotmail
message services.

I study the torso. It's Hammer. Weird. I've never seen Hammer write or read. No matter. I clear the search history and wipe
evidence of my snooping.

The closet door opens. J.D. slips inside.

"Hey."

"My time's up?"

"No, but would you mind, can I jump on?"

"Sure." His arms reach around my body.

"Peanuts is a real hard-ass about scheduling." His fingers
dance on the keyboard, quick, rat-a-tat-tat taps. He stands, feet
and elbows wide, and blocks me in. "Wait, do you mind—"

I look at the screen, read: "*No screen name available. Your
mail has been returned as a mailer daemon: undeliverable.*"

"What do I do if I want to find someone and their screen
name's been deleted?" He's so close his lips brush my ear. I
shiver. "Cold?"

I nod. In reality, my groin tingles. I'm excited. Closer, J.D.'s
chest presses, flat against my back. He tightens his arms. I'm
supposed to feel warm; I feel trapped.

"What service are you looking on? Yahoo, Gmail, My-
Space—"

"Facebook."

"Try name search."

J.D. types. Done, he drums his fingers on the desk. The re-
sults pop up.

"There!" He clicks the mouse, talking as he types. "*Oskar.
Where. The fuck are you?*"

Bling!

"*ey wh u?*"

"It's him!" J.D. type / talks. "*You still got the Ghia?*"

I can't move. Unless I shut my eyes and, even then, he reads as he types. I'm eavesdropping. "Maybe I should—"

"No," he says, "please, don't. Peanuts."

Bling! Oskar's responds, "*2tlly . . . im wait ing 4U :) gots to run . . . xoxox*"

I stay, but look away. J.D.'s excited, type-talking, "*no knot yet. . . . ! PLS!!!! i need 2 talk 2 U!!!*"

Bling!

"*kant besos ciao*"

"*wait! wait! one sec, bro!*" J.D. types, frantically pressing "SEND." *Bling!* "SIGNED OFF" pops up.

Oskar's gone.

I follow and go back to bed.

Chapter 44

"*Noooooo!!!!!*"
Screams. The sound wakes me. I sit up, drenched in sweat, tangled up in sheets. My body flashes *hot, cold, hot.*

His hand reaches out the dream, punches through reality and grabs me by the throat. The hand tightens. I can't breathe. Him, I know it's him. The feeling's real as my father grabbing my arm back in the desert. The moment he reached out and maneuvered me into the bathroom.

"Baby, hey . . ." he says, stroking my back. "It's okay. You're safe. Up for a smoke?"

I open my eyes. I am awake. Not awake-in-a-dream-awake, but awake in life. Eyes, hazel and beautiful, look into mine. J.D.'s. Liquid, those dark orbs are pools. I want to jump in, swim to the bottom.

"Sure." I'm still not up to speed with "Yes," stuck in the non-committal "Sure" mode.

"Here." He hands me a jacket, skull cap and gloves.

"What about these?" I finger the flimsy pajama bottoms.

"Take 'em off," he says, and leers at me.

I move back. I was wrong about him. He's no different from the rest. He'll have his way and I've got no say.

"Psyche!" He laughs and tosses me jeans. I pull them up, over the jammies. He stares. I knew it: He wants to see me naked.

Take advantage. They all do. My guard is up. I slide under the covers, shuck the jammies and pull on the jeans.

"Ready?"

He takes my hand and guides me off the bunk and through the main room. Ever since I ran, people have been taking my hand. They lead me here, there and everywhere. Day or night, everybody treats me like I'm blind.

He opens the kitchen window, parts the curtains and motions, "Go! Go!"

I step up to the window, look out the fire escape and freeze. "We're not supposed to go out there," I say, hiding my fear of heights. He doesn't need to know about that.

I step back. I can't do it. I won't.

Chapter 45

"Fuck that. You're with *me*. Safe, y'know?"

"Sorry," I say, and back away. "I can't."

"Can't-can't? Or won't-can't?"

"Can't-can't."

"Here." He turns and offers his back. "Climb on."

"You're strong enough to carry me?"

"Man, you weigh like, what, eight-eighty pounds soaked? Get on."

I don't want to—and have every reason to refuse—but that's how we climb up. I hang on his back, baby monkey clinging to its daddy. Or, mama. Some bigger, stronger relative. The cold night air helps. Numb, I'm less afraid of what I can't feel. I realize I could have just as easily ended up dead in an alley, or sleeping in one. I force my eyes to look up. Overhead, the full moon. It's an enormous, blood-orange orb.

Up, up, up. His legs devour the fire escape. He's a machine. Under his baggy, El Vato Cholo ropas, J.D's all fine and young and lean, pure muscle. His back flares out, two solid wings, neck taut as steel. Then there's his booty. My crotch sits on the ledge that juts out between his back and legs. Those, in turn, are powered by a V-8 engine.

We reach the roof. Graceful, J.D. lifts me up and sets me

down on the roof. He hops over the ledge and lands, quiet as a cat, beside me.

"Here's good," he says. Immune to full moons and heights, he wastes no time, pulls out cigarettes and lighter.

Click-click, a tiny flame pops up.

Chin down, his hand cups the orange flicker and lights up. Puff puff, white ciggie smoke swirls up and away. He's focused on smoking. He busts one out and lights up another. I've gone from riding a race car to sitting next to its exhaust pipe.

"What's J.D. short for?"

"James Dean."

Lips clamped down on cigarette, he takes a drag, eyes studying the solar panel. The moon's blood-orange light hits the mirror surface, giving our faces a sunset glow. My teeth chatter.

"Cold?" He reaches around my body and pulls me close. I want to resist, but he feels warm. Good and familiar.

"But serious," he says, sucking on the tail pipe. He looks like a Latino James Dean. He's a Stone Cold Fox. Already, I feel like I'm cheating on my One True Love, Hammer. "When you woke me up—"

"I'm sorry."

"I heard you screaming, and you reminded me. When I first got here. I had nightmares, too."

"But serious—" He takes another drag, true to his matinee idol namesake.

"About what?"

A thin line of smoke oozes out his full lips, white devoured by black. The scent lingers. Strange, I hate the smell, but I like how he smokes. Sexy, low-key, matter-of-fact. Just like James Dean, J.D. smokes without a smile or sell.

"Dunno." He shrugs. "I forgot. I just stopped having them."

"How long did that take."

"Months—three? Then, I dreamed . . . what'd I dream?" He looks away. His eyes search the night. I imagine, he's looking for those dreams. He takes a drag. The ciggie's tip sizzles. Ash splits, falls off the tip and drifts down, gone in the black. "So, what's haunting you?"

"Not what, who," I lie without hesitation. "Dave and Seth."

"What'd they do to you."

"In real life, or in my dream?"

"Either."

"Broke down my door with an ax," I lie, again. Really, it was the cops, and I never knew their names. I don't question why I rewrite my story as I tell it. The first sign of trust is telling the truth. Instinct guides me. I don't trust J.D. I don't trust anyone. Plus, unlike Serenity Ridge, I can say anything, and no one can interrogate me, check my story or punish me.

"Dang, bro'," he says, and stubs out the cigarette. The gesture's trés straight, *so* dude. "That's some harsh shit. An *ax?*"

"Yeah." I nod. "How'd they find out about you?"

"They?" He sounds surprised by the question. Impossible. I doubt there's any exception to Marci's "taped and transcribed" interrogations. They're the price of admission.

"Your parents?"

"Oh, *riiiggghttt.* Moms found me in my bedroom having sex with another boy."

"Boy boy boyfriend or hookup?"

"He was fourteen."

"In your *house?!?*"

"Sure," he says, resting his head on my shoulder. Heavy lids with long, dreamy lashes are half-closed on beautiful eyes. Close-up, he's too pretty to pass for straight. His head moves, lips ready to kiss.

"Sorry," I say, pulling away. "I can't. I have a boyfriend."

"What!?" He laughs, "searching" the roof. " 'less he's hiding up here, what's the problem?"

"Problem is," I lie, on a roll, # 4 or 5, I've lost count. "I'm faithful. Coz I *love* him. Even if he's not here."

"Oh," he says, firing up another ciggie. He lights up. Inhale. Spew. Eww. Compared to J.D., Sugar's habit was amateur hour. "What's so special about this person that you won't mess around with me?"

"Geez!" I grab the ciggie. "Gimme a drag."

"Oh! Oh! I love it, Mister Nicotine Anonymous knows the smokers' lingo."

He hands it over. I take a drag. I cough. Instant nausea.

He pats my back. "You okay?"

"No, I'm gonna—"

Chapter 46

"Y-y-yeah," I chatter. I shiver. Barfing felt good. I hope it purged more toxins. I want to ask, "Was it cold the night you got caught?" and "Who the hell is Oskar?" I want to know, but I can't bring myself to ask. Not direct. My Arab side retreats.

J.D.'s slung his arm over my shoulder. He pulls me close, but this time, the gesture's totally bro'. He wants me to know, this gesture's "nothing special."

"Man, that night? Yeah, now that you ask, it was freezing. I was s'pposed to meet my boy at the club. The same night, his parents kicked him out. Which was fine coz we planned to run away."

"Who were you in this little homo-romo? Romeo or Julieto?"

"You *didn't*," he says, mock-surprised. "Oskar, *he* asked me the same thing. So t'was kinda, you know, 'déjà vu!'"

"So who were you: Romeo or Julieto?"

"Duh, what do you think? *Romeo.*" He looks at me head-on. "And *you?*"

"Me?" I look up and "study" the sky, thinking about that phrase, "People only know what you tell them." The only "fact" is, I can be whoever I want to be with J.D. I'm a blank slate.

"Yeah, *you.*" He's mopped my strategy—hiding behind questions, asking questions being the best defense against answering them. That's my strategy. If I gather enough stories, maybe I can make sense of my own. He presses, "What about you? How'd they find out?"

"Teacher called my parents, ratted me out. 'I am concerned about your son.' Blah blah blah."

He nods, "Uh-huh," eating up every word. This lie doesn't feel as good as I'd imagined. I toss out a half truth. See how it feels. To reveal myself.

"Teacher read my journal. I wrote some poems, and she figured it out. The way they are, they assume, if you're not running around shouting, 'I'm gay! I'm gay!' or, talking about it twenty-four seven you're 'at risk.'"

"Yup, yup. When really, it's your parents who are the risk." I relax—a little. He gets it. "You still do that?"

"What?"

"Write love poems."

"No," I say. I never said they were love poems. Silent, I recite the one I wrote about him, yesterday. White puffs escape his lips. What's it about those lips? Plump, they look ripe as summer fruit. I struggle, trying to resist the temptation to lean over and kiss them. I slide my hands under my legs, pressing down hard on my hamstrings. I need to keep myself away from him, on *this* side of the roof.

"What went wrong?"

"When?"

"That night. It was cold, you and Oskar . . ."

"Yeah, yeah," he says, "so I go home to get clothes. My boy had the car keys. He was waiting outside my house in the car. I had told him, 'Kick it if I'm not back in five minutes.' But I didn't really think anything would happen. I mean, we had wheels. Dude, we'd *MapQuested* our route. My bags was *packed*. But then we got caught. His parents called mine. Dad was not having me even *thinking* about leaving. Two days later, my ass was triple packed with Thorazine and my dick was getting those electric zip-zap shocks." He stops, pauses and takes a drag. I feel him wait for my reaction. When I don't give it, he asks, "So. Whattaya think about my escape plan?"

I want to know what happened in the *first* story (him getting caught hooking up with a fourteen-year-old).

"You thought you could run away?"

"Sure, why not? He had a driver's license. Me, I had learner's permit but, you know, still. We even had enough money to get somewhere."

He takes a drag. I think, "You've gone over this story, relived your foiled escape a thousand times. Or, you're like me, lying, making it up as you go?" Fuck it, I decide I don't care. I'm talking to a *real, live boy.* You can't fake that. Reality check, I don't have a boyfriend. I'll practice on him. I scooch closer.

"You two were in love."

"Yeah. But then—" He looks at me with those beautiful eyes. "I saw you."

Yeah, those beautiful eyes are wide and open, filled with . . . bullshit. I cough. I hope the sound hides my laughter. He bats his eyelashes and says, all innocent, "What?"

Just for a second, I take him seriously. "No," I tell myself. "This is just another pose, fake as his dead Movie Star smoker's cool."

"You're *such* a Latin lover." I giggle. "A *real* Casanova."

"And your heart," he says, laying his palm on my chest, "is racing. Anyway, Casanova was French, not Mexican. Don't take this the wrong way, but you're kind of uptight. There's nothing's wrong with a lil' romo. Straight or gay, young love makes the world go 'round."

"Love"—I roll my eyes—"is not a roof top booty call."

"Don't *lie*," he says, giving me a look that suggests he knows everything I've said has been a lie. "You're lonely in that top bunk. All by your lonesome?"

"No," I lie, again, effortlessly. Any trust I might have offered, evaporates. Sure, he's "romantic." In a Reality TV, I'm-full-of-shit, here's-your-plastic-roses-choose-me sort of way. Sad but true, I am lonely, so lonely I ache. Every night, I sleep curled up with my pillow. I hold it, pretending it's the love of my life. But J.D. will never know that. I can front with the best of them.

"I'm too young to be lonely." I yawn, looking over my shoulder at nothing. I stand. "Listen, I need to sleep."

Without a word, we walk down the narrow steps to the fire escape. I try not to think, it's ninety degrees *down*. I swallow the fear, bile in my throat. I mount his back.

"Hold on tight," he says, like I'd do anything else. Say, *wave* to people? Eyes shut, I let him carry me down the building's ladder. The moment a "shade" drops over my inner eye, I know we're halfway there. We've dropped below the city lights. I peek. Yes, we're on the dark side of the building. He moves down the fire escape, fast as an extreme athlete—or, someone escaping a fire.

"It's like you and Kidd," I say. "I mean, once you find someone, you don't want to fuck it up, right?"

"There is no 'me and Kidd,' " he says. I feel his body stiffen. "That boy will *always* want more than I can give him."

"Then—"

"Shhh! People are sleeping!"

"That sounds all mature, but what does it mean?" I release his body from my death grip. I'm ready to end this nighttime game and step through the window. The curtains move, whiffing in the breeze.

"No," he says, and grabs my wrist. "Don't go. *Wait*."

He turns me around and pulls me close. Close enough to kiss and close enough to smell his breath. It reeks of cigarettes. Tragic much, the combination of elephant breath and bad dialogue must be what soap opera actors deal with on a daily basis.

"Will you sleep with me?" he whines.

Instinct, now *my* body stiffens. I might like J.D. (a lot) but I'm not ready to give him that.

"Just cuddling," he presses.

I look down, shake my head, afraid to say, "No."

"But you would with Hammer. I see how you look at *him*."

"Yeah, well, Hammer, he's *hot*," I admit. He can't argue that point. Hammer *is* hot. J.D.'s arms drop. I'm radioactive.

"Hot," he scowls, "if you're into *white* boys."

"Hotter," I hiss, ducking away from him, through the window and into the kitchen, "than people with boyfriends who don't tell them they need breath mints."

Chapter 47

Night. The room is bright. My pants are down. "Bend over," Nurse commands. I lean forward. The steel table is cold under my stomach. I feel a finger. It slides inside.

"Ah!"

"Now," Nurse says. "Cough."

I do. I'm done. I reach down, pull up my pants. A hand stops me.

"You think I'm hiding a roach up my butt?"

"Orderly," Nurse says.

I look over my shoulder. A gap tooth grin and meat hook hand. It holds a syringe with a big needle.

I back away, into the corner. To them, I am not human. I'm an animal. They know I'll do anything to avoid the needle. And that knowledge gives them pleasure: their noses twitch, excited by the smell of my fear.

Nurse leaves the room and shuts the door.

Sharp, it punctures my skin. Mute, I struggle, fight, try to get away. The orderlies pin me down. The needle pricks—it's a needle?—slides into my ass. Then, each one takes a turn.

"Wait," I wail, "what'd I do?"

Chapter 48

"What did they do to you? In there?"

Alice / Nadya's looking at me, tapping a pen between her front teeth. They're perfect, straight and white. Braces 'n bleaching. Rich girl.

"Do what to me where?" Maybe she'll get the hint. I'm not eager to talk about what happened at Serenity Ridge with her or anyone.

"Your treatment plan," she says, rephrasing the question, the way an attorney cross-examines a witness. "What was it?"

I ignore the question and doodle. A flower.

"I'm only asking because your nightmares wake up everyone in the middle of the night."

"I don't have nightmares."

"What do you call screaming and crying?"

Her words sting. I feel hot tears spring up and blur my eyes. I know exactly what she's talking about.

"I wouldn't know where to start."

She says nothing—of course—and stares. I feel rude. I need to say *something*.

"I—" I start, then stop. I can't tell her. Not her, not this girl. She "knows" something about me. But instead of saying it, she wants me to. I can't lie to her. She'll see right through me. I press hard, dig my fingernails into my wrist, and I force my hand down. I really want to slap her smug face.

I'm onto her game, and I hate her for playing it. In Serenity Ridge, I learned silence is a weapon. And I have more practice staying silent than she has with questions. Another part of me aches to speak and tell someone the painful, unvarnished truth (or, like the song goes, *"will set you free."* Yeah, right . . . just look at what happened to me because I wrote the truth in my journal). Problem is, I don't know where to start. *Nightmares?* I know. And, yet, I don't want to know.

"You realize what it was about."

"No, I don't realize. Tell me, what was it about?"

"I think you know."

"No," I say, resisting every question. "I don't."

"Really? You don't?" I shake my head. I refuse to help satisfy her curiosity. She sighs. *"Power."*

"Power?" I say, neutral. Inside, I flinch. I know exactly what it's "about." And I hate myself for not saying it. They did it to me *there*, and she's trying to do it to me *here*. I close up. I don't trust her. She's another Kidd. A bully with attitude in one hand, and a self-help book in the other.

"What was his name?"

I shake my head, refuse to fill in the silence.

"He had a name."

"No," I say, my voice small, "I—"

Even if I wanted to, I can't say it. She sees me, my pain, whatever. Why does she need to hear it? What he did to me. I haven't thought about him since I left Serenity Ridge. I refuse to give him free rent in my head. He's as good as dead.

She's worse, in some ways. Maybe because some part of her knows. As in, *really* knows. I sense that. She wants me to feel the same way as her—Obsessed, Vigilant—and I don't want to. Let her play with someone else's feelings. I've had enough humiliation at fifteen to last a lifetime. Unlike them, with her, I can refuse. Say, "No." Or, *"You can't make me."*

"Well?" she says, impatience underscores her voice. Like she's ready to stand up and leave. She has "somewhere" (nowhere, really) to go. I resist, I don't speak. I look at her. Silent. Meanwhile, the voice in my head screams, "It's none of your fucking business!"

"You know, *Ben,*" she says, giving me that stare-glare, "you're going to keep having nightmares until you talk about it."

"Oh, like talking about anything ever did anyone any good. Talking doesn't make it go away. That's a lie. I—"

I can't bear to say what comes after the "I." I refocus my attention on a paper clip. I unbend one end and twirl the metal twig between index finger and thumb.

Twirl—

Twirl—

Twirl—

I cast my spell,

Choke—

Choke—

Choke on your silence, you nosy girl with a hard face and cruel voice. Beat it, bitch 'cause I can twirl way longer than you'll ever be able to hold your stare-glare.

But no matter how hard I vibe her, I still feel her eyes. I feel her dismay. She studies me, the way you would a butterfly pinned to cork. I hate this. My whole life, a "topic," me, stripped of privacy.

I might as well be back in the hospital. I dare myself, "Look up." But I can't. I keep my eyes down and focus on the whirly-twirly paper clip. I roll the tiny metal tube between my fingertips and make it go, go, go. Sunlight glints on the silver, and hits her eye *Pow! Pow! Pow!*

"Stop that."

"Stop what?" In Serenity Ridge, they'd call my answer "defiant." Or, "oppositional." But here, I know I can use this tone with her because there's nothing she can do. Solitary? Puleeze. Meds? Sold out! *Time* out? Clock out.

"Mean girl," I think, staring at the paper clip, pleased to have annoyed her. "Take your nosy questions and *Fuck Off.*"

"*Please*, I—" She stops, gives up midsentence. I guess she realizes that she's lost. I can tell. It's her voice. The way the "I" got caught on her throat. I respect surrender. I stop. That's the moment I realize, This is not a game. She's serious. She sounds like a bitch, but some part of her's really trying to help.

I look up. I'm not prepared for what I see. She's not a shrink. She's a young girl who wears a funny face. A face twisted up and filled with Pain.

Chapter 49

Knock, knock. My heart jumps. Someone's at the front door. *Creak.* The door opens. I press my body against the wall. A shadow moves inside. The door shuts, locks, *click.*

"Hey, Ham," Marci says. I exhale. It's not a Bounty Hunter. "Where's Ben?"

" 'sleep."

"You awake?" she asks, tugging my big toe.

"Nap."

"Takes time for all the drugs to come out."

"But," I think, "that's *so* not the problem." The grocery bags crinkle. She picks them up and leaves the room. The closet door shuts. I reach under the mattress, grab my journal and write. I don't feel it. I shut the notebook, careful to place it under my feet, away from my head. I like knowing my dreams unravel far away from the daytime events. The ones I drain out my head and spill onto the paper. I feel free to lapse into a sleeping frenzy. Lonely has its pluses—I dream without guilt. Dreams keep me off the street.

The elevator groans. I wake, exhausted yet alert. The sound means someone's in the building. "They" could easily be headed to the safe house. Armed with, well, whatever. Me and Everyone, we're sitting (or, sleeping) ducks. Just "waiting . . ." Capture, imprisonment, torture. Coz that's the American way. We lock up anyone who's different, poor, or young.

Game on, I lie there, obsessing, plotting, planning. My escape. I imagine complex scenarios. Where I'll go, what I'll do. Freedom doesn't figure into this—I live in low-grade panic. The feeling chews through my peace of mind, till there's nothing left.

Chapter 50

"**H**uh! Huh! Huh!"
Grunts wake me.

Hammer's kicks are propped on the window ledge, palms flat on the floor. He busts out push-ups, a shirtless, blond skinhead. Sweat coats his golden skin with a delicious gaze. Loose, b-ball shorts drape over his rock-hard ass. Arms pumping, pistonlike, he moves, efficient as a stopwatch.

Up, down. Up, down. Up, down.

Heaven! He ignores me (on purpose), or, he wants me to stare. I imagine myself under his perfect body. He pulsates, pink lips come close to mine and . . . kiss. They part, he returns. Repeat. Over and over.

Looking at Hammer is too much. I feel overwhelmed by desire, what I want and cannot have. I look away. I close my eyes and touch my mouth—I'm not drooling, my tongue doesn't hang out. I press my hands against my body. Otherwise, I'd be tempted to jam them into my pants and jerk off.

Chapter 51

A bear-sized hand rests on my shoulder. I lie still and play dead. I worry it's the wolf (or, in my version, the Blue-eyed Bob). Maybe I've been mistaken for Goldilocks? I *am* blond and there *is* porridge in the kitchen.

"You type?"

I open my eyes. Hammer's face is close, so close we could kiss.

"Do I what?" I heard him, but I didn't. Maybe I heard something else. Do I type? What is my blood type? Or, *who* is my type?

"Do. You. Type," he says, slowly, like he's speaking to a child. "I need help."

He needs a typist. Eager to please, I launch myself up, off the bunk, and follow him to the closet. Inside, he shuts the door and gestures to the laptop.

"People write stuff and you read it to me and I *tell* you *what* to say." He looks at me, flashing beautiful, blue eyes under hooded lids. The extreme color and shape makes him look alien.

I'm confused. "Tell them how?"

"*Type*," he says, impatient. He believes typists should keep numbskull questions to themselves. He stands in front of the laptop, faces me, and turns the Webcam around. I still don't grasp the camera–typing connection. There's something Home

Shopping Network about the setup. "We're going live in thirty seconds."

"Aren't we—"

"*Live*," he says, an Aryan Youth look with a cold voice. "On the *net*."

"Why?"

"I'm doing a show."

Ten, nine, eight, seven, six, five, four, three, two, one . . . zero . . .

The screen morphs and comes to life. On it, a digital Hammer unbuttons the flannel shirt, ready to peel it off. Something about this makes me sick. I want to leave. I don't want to see this. Or, the show.

His hands and hips move. There's a delay between what's in front of me and what's on-screen. The picture's herky jerky versus the "live," fluid, flesh-and-blood Hammer.

He tosses the shirt. Stops. Stands still. His torso bulges under the tight, white ribbed, cotton wifebeater. The push-ups have pumped his chest and arms. He reaches up, yanks down the baseball cap, and hides his face.

In seconds, he's gone from real, live sexy to fake and robo-pornish. His hips move, slowly gyrating. Live! Naked (not yet)! Boy! I stare, mesmerized by his moves.

Bling! Bling! Bling!

I ignore the sound. It's probably Oskar, trying to reach J.D.

"Dude!" Hammer grunts.

"What?"

"*Read*."

I look down. Crazy. IMs pop up all over the screen, an epidemic of electronic weeds.

"What're they saying?" he asks, head down, mouth semihidden. Well, hidden unless you're me, sitting in the room, and see him speak.

Scanning, I reading the IMs out loud, " 'Welcum back,' 'Missed YOU!!!!!' 'where u been?' 'don go way' "

He lowers his head and shoots me—or, really, I realize, the Webcam—a seductive look. Muscles bulging, face semihidden,

Hammer's all the hot bro' types I've ever seen riding a bike, walking down the street or shooting hoops. He's the gorgeous guy you want to talk to but can't. The boys whose beauty invites you to look but never, *ever*, touch. Your mind's eye sees him, burned with an image of beauty and youth you'll never be able to erase.

"How's that?"

"How's what?" I'm so lost in the pleasure of looking at him, I forget I can, in fact, talk to him and he'll answer.

"How's that *look?*" he says. He pouts and adjusts his pose.

"Great, but don't you want me to type? Your answers? Or is that—"

"No, not right away. I always make 'em wait. Then, they'll *beg* for it. How do I look?"

I compare Hammer's image with Hammer, the person.

He's handed me a tire pump. And with it, I'm in charge of filling him up with compliments. If I don't, we run the risk he'll deflate and then—IDK. I don't understand the importance of this cyberstrip. But it's important to Hammer, and I'm along for the ride down 'Ho Road.

"Perfect," I say.

"I'm not moving too fast?"

In person, Hammer barely moves. On-screen, the itty-bitty movements look just right.

"Excellent. What is this, anyway?"

"Cam whoring," he says, matter-of-fact. Nauseous, I swallow hard, forcing the vomit to stay down.

"Cam *whoring?* Is that, like, um, prostitution?"

"No," he says, swiveling, sensually turning his body sideways. "That's when you meet them in person."

I shouldn't ask, because I don't want to know. But I need to know if my blond angel's tarnished. It's the whole serpent / Apple tree-Adam-Eve thing. Weird, too, since I don't even believe in the Bible.

"Have you ever done that?"

Hammer raises his arms. Back muscles flare. He moves his shoulders, one up, one down. His ass moves, too, separate from his shoulders, this way and that. Slowly, he turn-turn-turns around until he faces front. Focused, Hammer's very coordinated.

"What are they saying?"

I look at the screen. A dozen more IMs have sprung up. I scan the clusters. They all say pretty much the same thing. I wonder if I'm here to "type" or as a buffer between Hammer and the sexually charged words.

"You want them one by one, all together or—"

"Together." He rocks his hips side-to-side, hooking his thumbs into his jeans' belt loops. "How's that?"

"More," I say, summing up the theme of the mushrooming IMs. I get the feeling that, if they could, these cyberpervs would reach out, break the monitor and rip him to pieces. It's the Devour Hammer Hour. I shiver. "They keep saying they want more."

"What else?"

"You want me to type that?"

"No, what else are *they saying?*"

"More but—Wait, I—it looks like, every time you move or stand different, they say they want more of that."

"Right. Good," he says, pleased. It dawns on me, Hammer knows exactly what he's doing. He stokes the fire with reason and purpose. Gross. I wanted him for myself. But, turns out, he's already spoken for—by hundreds, if not the world. This is a horrible feeling. I've been betrayed before I ever got a chance to fall in love.

"And the hat. They want you to take off the hat."

His thumbs remain in place, hips pulsing. His fingers move, creep down and cup his crotch. I ignore the IMs. I can't believe I'm seeing Hammer do *this*, in person.

Hammer *really* knows how to work it. It's a good thing that I sit. My dick is hard. This voyeurism is prolly going to scar me for life, another bad habit I'll have to overcome. Sexually charged images being this year's theme. If I wasn't in this closet—and had a credit card—I'd pay to watch Hammer do his thing (and hate myself for it!). Once—if, ever—I find a real therapist, I'll cloth, feed and put her / his children through private school and college.

Bling!bling!bling!bling!bling!bling!bling!bling!bling!

The IMs go crazy. I space out.

"*Hey!*" Hammer barks. "I'm counting on you!"

I refocus. The screen's solid with IMs. "Hammer, Cam Whore for President." He could win. I mean, he's *that* popular.

"Who are these people?"

"Dads, regular people, pervs."

"It's always like this."

Silent, he shoots off a series of slinky-sexy moves. If he's annoyed by my ADD lapse, he doesn't show it. He's focused on his performance.

"Yeah," he says, his answer, like his on-screen image, a couple beats late. "It's always like this. What else?"

I read the screen, "They want to know—"

"Don't tell me that," he says, "I know they're asking questions. Read them. Type my answer and press Reply."

"That'll take forever. There's—"

"Everyone gets the same answer. I'm the Go-Go God."

"What's in the hour?"

" 'I do *everything* . . . if you know what I mean.' Put those dot, dot, dots in there. Between 'everything' and 'if.' "

I'm impressed. Hammer wouldn't know an ellipse from an eclipse, but he knows which one works in cyberspace.

"They all want to know, how much—"

"Three hundred," he says. "Three. *Hundred*. Donation. Put that in caps. Three. Zero. Zero. Spell it out."

"I can't use numbers?"

"No, spell it out. Then put in those dots."

"Ellipses," I say. Somehow, I need to let him know, I'm more than a typist.

"Yeah, then write, 'To *start*.' Make sure you slant, you know, the word—start."

Italicize, I think, but keep my mouth shut. One grammar lesson a day.

"When?"

"Tonight. Put those dots. Then, 'When my bro goes to sleep.' "

"Your brother?" I type, hit Reply and look up from the keyboard. "But you live *here.*"

"Dude." Again, he could be talking to a retard or a child. "They don't know that. This is them. Looking at me. I can say, like, whatever, and they'll believe me."

I'm starting to appreciate Hammer's natural grasp of cyberspace.

Bling! Bling! Bling! Bling! Bling! Bling! Bling! Bling!

" 'Take off your belt.' And 'Why are you not typing?' "

"Tell 'em, 'I got one of those voice machines. Speak 'n spell,' " Hammer says, and I fall back in love, a little. Who knew. Hammer's a triple threat: beauty, brains, and brawn. Done talking, he fires off a series of sullen looks. Stop. Stand. Pose.

I love looking at him (standing in front of me) and comparing him to his time-delayed image of him (on-screen). I can't decide which Hammer I like better.

I study his moves. Jiggle. Move. Slide. Turn. Gyrate. Hammer's mastered the art of making it seem like he *might* do something. Suggestive. Seductive. But then he pulls everything back, pauses and—leaves you hanging. Somehow, in the gap between doing and doing nothing, he makes you *think,* "Okay, *now* he'll do it." ("It" being whatever you imagine.)

"Have you done this before?" I ask. "That's me asking."

"Back home. I had all these girls looking at me. My dad found out."

"Your *dad* knew about this?"

"*Dude,*" he says, using word that lets him speak without communicating (or, my "Sure"). His fingers creep down and play with the belt buckle. The blings jump from active to insane.

"That sure got 'em excited," he says, and lets his hand drop.

"Wait, who are you talking to?"

"*Duh,*" he says, "my homie." He looks me in the eye. I'm meant to know, I guess, *I'm* his homo homie. Insta-blush. Far as I know, only straight dudes use the word *homie.* Maybe I've misread him. He's just a really chill straight guy. I feel like a total dork.

"What're they saying?"

"What's your name?"

"Make something up. Or don't." I don't. He glances at my motionless hands and smiles. "*Now* you're getting the idea."

"What idea?"

"It's better when—" He slides the belt out a little bit and looks down, pink tongue to lip. He better stop that or his typist's going to whip it out and bust a nut. "Make 'em wait."

"Your dad found out."

"Yeah, o of 'em, a trick—you know what that—" I shake my head. "A trick, can be your hookup. Or your sugar daddy. So this one is my sugar daddy. He rents an apartment near my house. Sweet. Every time I wanna pull a show, I tell my mom, 'I'm visiting my friend down the street.' What now?"

"Huh?"

"What do they want to know."

"Oh, right." I read, " 'Show us your feet . . .' and '. . . wanna see you in boxers' and 'when are you gonna stroke it?' and 'touch your nips.' Nips?"

"Nipples! '*No* special requests.' "

Bling! Bling! Bling!

"Please Please Please."

"Takers, users, time wasters, this boy needs some give."

Bling! Bling! Bling!

" 'Check your wish list.' "

"Yeah, today's wish list is hella different."

I type exactly what he says. I feel weird having a convo when I don't have a clue what it's about. If this is all about "give 'n take," what am I getting for my voluntary carpal tunnel? A front-row seat. Kind of like an "All you can eat" buffet.

Bling! Bling! Bling!

"They want to know, 'Enough for today?' "

"We get to that when . . ." His voice trails off as he unbuckles the belt. "We get to that—"

I start to understand why Hammer and Peanuts spend so much time in here with the door shut. There are shows to perform, clothes to remove, and wish lists to fill—"fans" to satisfy.

I feel sick to my stomach. Hammer—*My* Fantasy Boy—has morphed into Hammer, My Worse Nightmare. I hate this. I feel trapped. Same as Serenity Ridge? But a boy stripping in cyberspace is nothing like Serenity Ridge.

"You okay?"

I want to leave.

"Yeah," I say, lying. I hope he can't tell. "Your mom . . . she followed you?"

Chapter 52

"This guy made a reel—clips of my shows. He threatened me. He said, 'I'll send it to your mom if you don't get with me.' I told that bitch, 'No *fucking* way are *you* blackmailing *me*.'"

"And he sent it?"

"Yup."

"That's when your dad found out and got mad?"

"Hell, no! Dad wanted in. Fuckin' deadbeat. Dude *loves* trannies. Anita's his idea of Miss America. He didn't give a shit about what I was doing. It was about the Benjamins. He's the one who busted me and set me up to do more shows. We made *bank*. I was *way* fucked up on drugs. He started pimpin' me out for reals."

"Pimp *you?* Like, sell you for sex?"

"Girls, boys, their dads, grannies. For Sale. Stamped it on my body."

Hammer's so matter-of-fact about incest and his Pimp Daddy. My father, Moustapha, is a monster, but I doubt pimping me out ever crossed his mind.

"Wait, so you're bi, or—?"

"I'm whatev. Hole's a hole. But then—" Hammer's attention shifts back to his performance.

"Can I guess?"

"Go for it."

"He wanted in on the action?"

"*Dude!* How'd you know? I split. Back to mom's house and that's when—" He punctuates his thought with a move. "I got sent down, dude, *down.*"

Compared to Hammer's story, mine feels lame. Maybe it wasn't so bad? Reality check: closet, cam whore. For a moment, I consider. Stand. Walk out. Call home.

He stares at me, unbuckles the belt. He's got this weird half smile on his face. I can't read his expression. Blank. Cam whore? Or, serial killer? He's here, but not. I know that face. If not the same face, then the feeling underneath. Dead. I bet he learned it from being with his dad. Or, it settled over his face, like a scarf. *Working* for his dad. Doing. The way I—

"No!" I shout out and cut off the thought. Hammer's so far gone, he doesn't notice. Then, I remember: He's looking at the Webcam over my forehead. Duh. "Blank" is his show face. But there's nagging questions. What came first: the blank face? Or, the cam show?

"Peanuts types for you?" I ask. I want to grasp the "how" and "why" of this cam whore show.

He slides the belt out, slow as a rattlesnake on the creep. Done, he dangles it off his index finger.

"I had the number one ranking on this portal. This other kid knocked me down. Peanuts sends him an e-mail and says—hey, can you move the camera so it's on my hands?" I play with the toggle and move the camera eye down, to his hands. I like being in control. Deciding what the "audience" sees. "The next day, that kid's site was gone. *Gone.* After that, me and Peanuts, we *tight.*"

"You're not worried about your dad finding you?"

"Whatta you mean?"

I twitch. My mind's eye flashes on Blue-Eyed Bob's face.

"Track you down."

"Naw." He knocks back the baseball cap. Chin up, he reveals his face. He curls his upper lip. Snarls. Now, he looks more perfect than perfect. Part man, part boy and all sex. "I know he's seen me. *For sure.* One time, he tried getting me back, but he knows—*knows*—if he says one word. *One* word. The End. Told him, 'I go to the cops and you, Daddy, will go to the joint. Some gang banger's meat puppet *biatch.*' Ain't heard from him since. Now, Mom, she—"

"She never knew. But if she found out, she'd send me back."

"Where?"

"Juvey. RTC. Foster case. Those are all the same fuckin' place. Just a different sign outside." He turns. "Can you bend down and move over that way?"

I look over my shoulder. My face looks back at me in a mirror's reflection. All this time, I thought he was a natural. Really, Hammer's been working his moves in the mirror over my shoulder.

"How's the pervs."

I scan the IMs piled up, one atop another. "Lots of, 'We *love* you.' "

"Love?" He snorts. "What they *love* is lookin' at what they can't have."

"You want me to write that?"

"Go for it."

I type.

Bling! Bling! Bling!

"They *love* it. Lots of exclamation marks and hearts."

He sticks his left thumb under his waistband, raises his right hand, and gives the camera the finger. He runs through a new series of hot, sexy poses. He has an unlimited supply.

"You want to say something?" I ask. He ignores my question and continues working his poses. I sit, mute, hands on thighs and watch him. IMs go unanswered. He tilts his head, rests his chin on his shoulder, looks to the side. "Some dork found my pictures and passed them around school."

"Copies."

"Yeah, so I tell my mom I'm gonna home school myself. When the school calls, I was flunking out everything but football and shop."

"Your mom let you drop out, no questions asked?"

"My dad and me split. What now?"

I decide to digest this information later. I scan hundreds of messages, looking for an average, skipping the weirdo requests: bathroom business, clean up my mess, and doggy style. "Basically, they all wanna know when your shirt comes off."

"Tell 'em I need three grand in *two minutes* or I step off. No, no! Wait! Don't write that. If there's—how many peeps I got watching me?"

"About five hundred."

"What's that into three thousand?"

"Into? You mean divided?"

"Yeah."

"About six."

"So write, 'Torso Special. Fourteen fifty. *No face.*' "

"No face?"

"Say, 'Three minutes, or I step off.' You time it."

I post the torso special and note the time. Hammer's eyes are closed. He moves, slowly, in a trance. On-screen, he looks like he's dancing. But in the safe house closet, he's somewhere else. Not here. Present but not accounted for. I'm not sure I buy that life-after-death crap. But if he has a soul, his is gone. Hammer's a meat puppet. Invisible strings make him dance.

I know the feeling. I felt that way during "treatment" (electric shocks to my dick every time I got hard looking at the nekkid pix). Leaving your body's all you can do when your body's trapped.

Meanwhile, the money counter ticks. Up, up, up. Fourteen fifty plus fourteen fifty plus fourteen fifty. It'll hit three grand in two minutes.

Moving, always moving, Hammer's hypnotic, hypnotized and hypnotizing. His left hand drops to the shirt's bottom edge. He lifts the frayed fabric, flashing his perfect stomach. He lets it drop. Moving, moving, always moving. He lifts the shirt, flashes some ab and drops it. Moving, moving, always moving. He lifts the tank and flashes the skin under the boxer's waistband.

"You know what that"—fingertip to tongue, he wets the tip and draws it along the ridge that runs deep between outer blond pubes and abs—"is?"

"No, what?"

"It's called," he says, tracing the ridge, "a cum gully."

Stops, pauses.

"How much now?"

"Seventeen thirty-five, fifty." I can't keep up coz it's going so fast. There's a cotton triangle in a dark blue frame. The numbers climb faster than I can count.

"How much time's left?"

"Nineteen seconds."

" 'Not fast enough,' tell 'em that." His eyes crack, opening slightly, but not all the way. He might be waking up. On-screen, his eyes look sleepy-sexy. Or, like he's having sex with his reflection. His right hand slowly climbs up, over his chest. Massaging his pecs, he plays with the silver nipple ring.

"Say, 'Hit it peeps or we go dark.' "

I type the warning.

Bling! Bling! Bling!

The money line shoots up and crests over the two—three— four thousand mark.

"We hit it?"

"Yeah. Now they say they want to see it." I smirk. "It" means one thing to me and Hammer's hundreds of fans.

"Tell 'em, I said, '*Five Minutes*.' Put that in big letters. Tell 'em, 'But.' Then do that dot, dot, dot thing. 'Behave yourselves. Or I might change my mind.' "

His left hand drops, hung over the white triangle. His big fingers graze the cotton. They creep over, left, to his thigh. His hand moves up and down. Even though he's fully dressed, Hammer's hot and makes bank.

I glance at the monitor, back to him, "live." He looks sexier on-screen. I look in his eyes. Present? Absent? I can't tell. Absent might work better. People want what they can't have. Hammer couldn't give present even if he wanted.

"How'd you get so good at this?"

"Practice." His hands hold down the sides of his shirt. He pulls one side up a little and one side down a little, stretching the fabric, gyrating his hips. Thumbs hitched to underwear, he slides the fabric down. His Hammerhood presses, hard, against the shirt.

Creak—

Sound—

I turn, look—

See—

The front door open.

Great, we're gonna get caught. One of us, literally, with his pants down.

Chapter 53

My hands can't move.
"What's wrong?"

I open my mouth. But I can't speak. I turn my head, look. The door clicks, shut. Hammer nods, index fingers to lips, a silent "Shhh."

He steps away from the cam and peeks through the closet door.

"Marci. Music? The box is in back'a you."

I reach back, press Play and music—tribal, house back beats—pours out the speakers. I feel light-headed, filled with helium. I'm about to float off, too.

"Who you got the hots for?" I type his question. "No, I'm asking *you*."

His shirt plays hide-and-seek, flashing gold skin, muscles and sex. He plants his feet and takes a wide stance, moving his hips side-to-side. Hammer's a human sextronome.

I can't look, I look away. The way he's moving—two feet away from me!—makes me excited. Dot, dot, dot: *again*. I reach under the desk and adjust myself.

Bling! Bling! Bling! Bling! Bling! Bling!

The computer goes ape-shit crazy. The activity saves me from answering and extreme embarrassment.

"They're say—"

"No talk," he says, hollow voiced, head elsewhere. "I'm *all* action."

"You want me to type that?"

"Yeah."

I do.

"You didn't answer my question," he says, breaking his vow of silence. I forget: I feel like his audience but, really, I'm his *typist*. I guess a little chitchat with me is our give 'n take. I know—it's not real, and kind of grosses me out—but his attention feels good.

"Question?"

"Who do *you* have the hots for?"

"Where, here, or . . . ?"

"*Here*."

Quick, he reaches back and pulls the shirt's fabric in-between his legs. He tugs the fabric, and it rips, splitting down the opening, up, and middle, creating another V.

Oh, oh . . . I gasp. The show feels dark, exciting, confusing. Gold. Bare. Skin.

The white shirt jumps. His abs dance. Golden hairs dusted over smooth, tight skin. The fleece doesn't show on-screen. I pinch my arm. This is real. I'm really *here*. Something switches. What seemed sleazy becomes fun.

"You."

My answer pops out, against my will, itself on a three-second time delay. I want to reach out, grab it, take it back.

He smiles, huge, hips quickening. Now, *he's* the excited one. Abrupt, his movement grinds to a slow, hard side-to-side slide. I want to believe, this is for me. But my smarter self knows better. This is just a show. Only a test. If he can work me—audience of one—then he knows he's doing his job.

"*Me?*" He smiles, pleased. "You got the hots for *me?*"

"No, I meant—" I stammer, more confused. Hammer's my *fantasy* boy. He's not supposed to brush reality. Yet, it sounds like he agrees with me. Thinks I'm a hottie. Or, he's just leading me on? Or—the scariest—he offers to make my fantasy a reality.

My head's about to explode.

"What if I told you—" His tongue pops out his mouth and runs over his lips, covering the plump, pink flesh with a wet gloss. "I want to kiss you?"

"I—" I'm ready to. Then, I notice he stares at his reflection. Oh. No. I might have mistook his convo with Narcissus, the God of Love Thyself, for one between him and me. Embarrassed, much . . .

"You could, you know. Fact, I'd like that," he says, looking at me—and the mirror—while moving the white shirt up—down—OFF!—over his torso. Hammer, heading to naked . . .

Knock! Knock!

Hammer stops, his body freezes.

Knock Knock.

"Hello?"

A woman. Marci's already inside.

Chapter 54

"Hello?" Hammer pulls up his jeans, cracks the closet door and looks out.

"Hey, *you*," he says. His face relaxes and he smiles. "I'm doing a show."

He steps out the door, careful to close it. I press my ear against the door.

"Oh! I'm sorry," a girl says. "The door was open."

"Later."

Click. The front door shuts. Closure does nothing to slow my heart's fast rat-a-tat-tat.

The closet door opens, Hammer steps inside and looks at me.

"You okay?"

I nod, freaked out. My face feels like it seized up.

"Shelia's cool. She lives upstairs. One time her client—"

"Is the camera off?"

"Oh, shit!" He grabs the Webcam and turns it away from the room.

"Your commercial break."

"Yeah, so one time her client comes to our door. 'Shelia!' he says. 'It's me!' We tell him, 'There's no one here by the name Shelia.' He keeps knocking. Real loud, he says, 'Shelia! I know you're in there!' I opened the door and told him, 'Bro, there's no

Shelia here.' He stuck his foot inside. I can't shut it. I know his type. He'll push to get inside. Needs to see for himself. Right then, Shelia shows up. That's how we became friends."

"You do shows with her?"

"Hell, no! She's got fake tits. 'Sides, she only does *private* shows. You know . . ." he says. "You're really cute."

He steps forward. His voice, his body, his smell—he radiates sex. And pleasure. When I watched him doing push-ups, this is what I imagined. We wouldn't talk. Our kiss would just . . . happen. I close my eyes. I'm ready.

His big left hand touches my forehead, fingertips trace my face, temples to cheekbone and jaw, lips. Kinda rough, he thumbs my lips. My body shudders. My head feels light. He sticks his right hand in my hair and roughly pushes it back. The blond color's fake. Who cares. I don't. Hammer *wants* me.

"Yeah?" he says, his voice low, sexy and dirty. He steps close. Heat peels off his body. I reach out and hold my left hand over his chest. Hot, he burns. "You like that?"

"I do but . . ." Yeah, dude, BUT WHAT? That's not what I'm supposed to say—not to a sixteen-year-old hottie who's perfect. And wants *me*.

"But what?" A confused look crosses his face. Hammer's *never* dealt with romantic doubt or sexual hesitation. Hammer knows he's hot and has known this since kindgergarten. Girls chased him around the playground. Boys wanted to be him. He knows that everyone who sees him wants to fuck him. Like, me. I want him *so* bad. But I pull back. I want to turn and run.

He's not put off. I hope he's not the type who believes "No" means "Yes." His hand pushes through my hair. Meat-hook-sized fingers move down and grab my neck. He pulls me forward. He even smells good. Lemony fresh with a hint of violet.

"Foxy boi," he says, voice sexy and dirty. His lips graze my ear. I can't resist: I want him. I reach up, caressing his hair. Oh. My. God. Blond, buzzed and *thick*.

"I don't know—"

"Shhh." He places an index finger over my lips. He pushes my lips apart and forces me to suck his thumb. His other hand travels down my neck and over my back, to my butt. His big hand cups it. Instinct, I arch. I guess this makes me a bottom. His touch feels so good. He's gentle, so different from—

Stop. Everything stops. My body seizes up. I freeze. I want to shout, "Stop!" but the word's stuck in my throat. I pull away. He won't let go. He holds me tight. I choke. I want to throw up. "Let me go!" Where'd my voice go? He pulls me closer. Peach fuzz brushes my skin. I don't want to kiss him or his pink lips, just—

Chapter 55

"What?"

He steps back. That's it. Now I've done it. Really fucked up. Hammer Fail. I'm such a fool. He never really liked me. He's just good at *this*. Fake desire? Velveeta? I feel so stupid. He's a tease. That's his *job*. Worse, I *watched* him. Give a glimpse. Pull back. Stir up desire. I feel so stupid. I've been played. Used. *Again.*

"I—" I duck down and slip out of his arms. I don't care about his soft touch or heat. I feel trapped. I want to run away. I panic. I feel disoriented. Where am I? How'd I end up here? Again.

"What's wrong?"

I want to tell him everything. Explain. But every time I open my mouth, the words won't come. I can't even *look* at him. I look down. I'm ashamed. Tears sting my eyes. I'm gonna cry. This is *not* how I pictured us hooking up. Me crying, him puzzled.

"Forget it," I mumble, turn and reach for the door.

"Hey," he says, and grabs my arm. "Don't you like me?"

I hear uncertainty in his voice and my heart melts. Headline, *Seventeen* magazine, "Boys Have Feelings."

"Well, there was . . ." I'm frustrated. I can't find the words I need. They're buried, leaves tossed in a heap. I thought, if I left those words alone, those feelings will decay, fade away. But then, something curious and surprising happens.

Hammer doesn't move. He says nothing. He just is. He's given me a space. It's bigger than the distance between the desk and the door.

"Was what?" he says. Two words, kind of amazing. This has nothing to do with sexy, turning me on, or taking advantage. No, he's handing me an opportunity to speak. If I want, I can seize this moment, take a risk and be *heard*.

I shake my head. No way can I *tell*. Even Hammer the Mahn Whore would hear my story and think I'm filthy. Disgusting. That's what *he* always said. And it must have been true, too. Because if it wasn't true, then the people in charge at Serenity Ridge wouldn't have let it happen. To me. The way it did. Over and over. Everyone knew what he was doing to me, yet they did nothing to stop it. Therefore, I must be a worthless piece of shit.

"I knew I was gonna run," I say. "The day I got there, I was already planning my escape."

"Uh-huh." He shrugs. I can tell it's not that he doesn't care. He's interested. He's just not staring me down. Or, taking notes. And that makes it okay for me to tell. Easy. Not about *him*. No way. I'm not ready for that. But the other stuff.

Chapter 56

"I—" I don't know where to start. Deep breath. Hammer doesn't move. He listens. "I-I knew. I *knew* I was gonna run. The day I got there, I started planning my escape."

Colors and sound blur. Now, *thinking* about the hospital makes my head light. Like it might spin off.

"Like my mom. She split. I knew, I had to leave. As in, Did. Not. Have. A. Choice. I didn't. R—that guy, he sealed it. First time he held me down, middle of the night and did that . . . stuff. I knew, knew I'd do *anything* to get out. Away."

"You tricked 'em."

"Yeah, with my tooth. I faked how much it hurt. No, did I? I forget. But I knew I could use the tooth excuse. It was a good one. They didn't have dentists. My mom taught me it's about the when. My dad didn't know it, but he told me how she did it. Said, 'The bitch *waited.*'"

"The day they came to pick me up and drove me away, it was like a movie. Speeded up. At first, I didn't have a plan. Not really. Just that I had to wait. Let them drive me away. Jump out and run. The day before, this kid told me, 'Look for this one sign.' I had help. People picked me up. Rescued me.

"Growing up, I always wondered how did *she* do it? 'The bitch waited.' But *how.* I never knew. Did she look at a clock and call a cab? What?

"I found out. You just know. There's that moment. The door, it opens. Some people stand there and look. My first step, I *knew*. Ohhhhh, this is how she did it."

"Did what?"

"Left. If someone looks away, even for a second, you can run. Like my mom. I woke up one day and . . . she was gone. Haifa Number One took her place. My father never explained. There was no reason *why*. I don't think he knew. There was no, 'Your mother left because . . .' Just, 'The bitch waited.'

"Right away, I knew she was gone. The screams stopped. She was done. With lying to everyone about the black eyes and bruises. We lived in a ranch house. She was always, 'falling down the front steps.' Always 'hitting her head' on the car door. Nobody believed her—turned out, we shared that, too. I wish she took me, you know, with her. Once *I* left, I knew why she didn't."

"Why didn't she?" Hammer asks. I don't need to ask *why* he asks. He asks because someone in *his* life left. Same as me, he wants to know why they didn't take him. 'Why'd they leave me? *Here*? Alone with these horrible people?'

"I knew," I say, "because the second *I* left, I learned. You travel faster if you travel alone."

"Right," he says, nodding his head.

"But even though she couldn't take me, just by leaving, she'd carved out this path. For me. Made a way for me. May I—?"

Hammer steps aside. I need to leave. I'm not trapped. But I don't move. I can't. I'm stuck. I look down, focusing my gaze on his big toe. Blond hair sprouts on the knuckle. He's got hella ugly feet.

"Stuff. Night. He. I—"

My words get mixed up. The words are slimed with silence and shame. "The truth will set you free," I tell myself. I don't believe it. Another cliché, my reality being far removed from gospel choirs, church and the Bible.

The monster springs up, out that dark place, a grinning ghoul jack-in-the-box. Mocking me.

"Motherfucker!" I shout.

Hammer backs off.

"Not you. *Him*. He—"

"That guy?"

"Yeah."

"Tell me?"

I shake my head. I can't.

"Look at me?" His big paw reaches out and touches my chin. I flinch. Shut my eyes. Tight. I know what comes next. "Gentle," they're always, GENTLE. His fingers tilts my head. I force my eyes to look up, meet his. Our eyes meet and, without one word, I know that he *knows* what I'm trying to say.

"Same thing," he says, "happened to me. Happens to a lot of us. Some people . . . a room's filled with kids. They look out and they see *you*. They chose you coz they *know*. They can take advantage."

He knows.

My head and heart split in two. Battles—"Shut up!" "Speak!" "Quiet!" "Talk!" I try silencing the voices. I crack. Hot tears bubble up, spill out my eyes. My soul shudders; a silent sob rakes my body.

"Can I give you a hug?"

I nod. He takes me in his arms. He holds me, just holds me, with such a simple, pure love, I feel like my entire being might dissolve. I don't know if I can bear such pure love. I know, I don't deserve it.

Hammer's put away his warm, sexy self. The *real* him holds me, like that, for how long? I don't know. I decide, I'll let him. Just a bit. I'll trust him. I'll *allow* him to. I don't cry. I don't dare cry. I keep the tears bottled up inside, pushed down, sealed in. Takes all my power. Violent, I force those feelings down, to stay *down*. Because I know—if I start crying, I can't stop.

He pats my back. That feels nice. But all this—effort to keep it cool, and *maintain*—leaves me feeling . . . tired. So, so tired. I might ask him to lift me up, carry me back to bed. He lets me go, reaches for the Webcam, and turns its eye upside down. He presses a button on the computer. "The show" goes dark.

"Tell me."

Nothing. We just stand there. Like that. Silent. I know I can:

tell him my story. Or, kiss and touch him. I can do whatever I want. He'll let me. He's invited me in. The door's shut. Nobody can see or hear us. It's not complex, or "hard." The way they predicted in Serenity Ridge. This isn't a sign of "resistance." It's me, being me. In the presence of another human being. Who loves me, in some way I've never imagined possible.

There's nothing wrong with me. I'm not clogged up. They've taught me to doubt myself. To watch. I hesitate. Speaking my "truth," I know, will not set me free, like instant coffee. Or, Jell-O. The past is the past is the past, and nothing I do or say will change it except I'm not sure I should say. It might sound corny. I smile, sphinx with a secret.

He senses something—in me. Maybe that's the reason I don't ask, Why? Yes, I don't *need* to *tell* my story, the one that's all bottled up, to something—someone—other than my journal. The park, that was the "record." From this moment forward, Ahmed will describe—or, not—his life to who *he* chooses. Who *I* choose.

I don't. Don't tell Hammer. Don't volunteer my story. The hospital, Ralph, running—nothing "tumbles" out, there's no revelation. I don't know long it takes. Five minutes? Or, five hours? Who knows but when I'm done, I feel like I've dropped dozens of heavy bags.

"Better?"

I nod. Touch my face. It's wet. I wipe away the tears. I reach for him. I trust Hammer. He takes me in his arms. *So* uncool, but I need a hug.

"Hey!" Peanuts stands outside the closet. Hammer drops his arms.

Peanuts looks hella *confused*. I know that look. *Oh, now I get it:* Peanuts and Hammer are a couple. I wonder if Hammer knows.

I step forward, to walk out. Peanuts grabs my arm.

"Hey! Where you think—" I wriggle away. Behind me, the door closes. "Don't! It's . . ."

Their voices rise, but I don't care. I feel light, clear. For the first time in months, a long time, I feel my age.

Young.

Chapter 57

I step out the closet. Alice / Nadya stands beside the front door. She pulls a black chador on over her head.

"Since when did you become the undercover Muslim? Or are you planning on bombing Fisherman's Wharf?"

"I'm one hundred percent Jew," she says, draping the veil and hiding her face. "So it's the *perfect* disguise. They're not looking for a Yid in a chador."

"It's Shabbos—should you really go out?" I don't want her to leave. I have a bad feeling. Maybe it's the milk carton thing we have in common.

"Back before sunset."

" 'k, I gotta go," Marci says, closes the cell phone and pushes off the sofa. "Ready?"

"Yes."

"Wait!" I scramble up the ladder. I hand her my lucky orange tennies. "They got me here. I want you to wear them. Let them bring you back."

She lifts the chador's black-skirted bottom and holds the kick's rubber sole to the Docs. "Perfect."

"We'll be late," Marci says.

For what, I want to ask, but it's none'ya (my) business. If I can have secrets, so can everyone else.

"One sec." Alice / Nadya removes her heavy clunkers, slips on my magic kicks and drops the chador.

"They're"—she kisses my cheek—"*brilliant*. I left something for you on the kitchen table."

Then, they're gone. I feel anxious. Ill. I worry, anxious I won't see them again.

In the kitchen, my journal sits on the table. Someone's moved it. I didn't leave it out. There's a bump in the middle—something's stuck inside. I open it and find a slim device. Alice / Nadya must have put it there.

I peel off the yellow Post-It stuck to the silver case. "TRACK TWO. LISTEN UPSTAIRS." A wool sweater's draped over the chair. She's thought of everything. I pull it on, tuck the iPod in my front pocket and part the curtains. I'm reach for the window, ready to lift it.

"UPSTAIRS"

I'll never make it up the fire escape.

"UPSTAIRS."

Coz really, there's no difference between listening to this at the kitchen table and listening to it on the roof. Unless . . . this is a test?

Allah, I pray, how do I find my way up there? By touch, he instructs, *feel* your way. Okay, so I don't believe in Allah (or, any other invisible father beings) and I'm probably just psyching myself up. Still . . . eyes shut tight, I feel the windowsill's wood frame. Right away, I cheat. I crack my eyes and peek. I need to make sure that when my feet step out, they land on something solid. Like, metal. I'm not stepping out, eyes closed, only to drop, coconut to pavement. Hit, crack, split, splat. Brains everywhere, food for stray cats and dogs.

Step. One. Outside. Hands on metal rails. I. Step. Up. Two. Okay. Step. Up. Three. Repeat. I know it's only twelve steps to the roof.

"You," my inner Allah coaches, "you're closer than when you left."

Bang! Ouch. My head's hit . . . the next landing. Great, I'm almost there. I open my eyes. Doing so forces me to surrender the illusion I'm anywhere but hanging off a building. Gulp. *Seven flights up*.

"You are," my inner Allah observes, "that much closer to heaven and seven virgins." I'm not so sure. I'm pretty sure the virgins are reserved for martyrs. Suicide bomber types. I don't have a blow-it-sky-high bone in my body. The only person I'm capable of terrorizing is myself.

"Inner Allah," I ask, "I need to speak with you about customizing my virgins. The way people do birthday or wedding cakes. Can you make them all look like Hammer?" Allah chuckles, "Ahmed, heaven's filled with *virgins*, not ho's." Interesting. My Allah's gay friendly and has a sense of humor. "Yes, my child," he says, "you *are* crazy."

"LISTEN UPSTAIRS"

Fuck her. No. Fuck *me*. Why am I obeying instructions written on a bloody piece of paper? Not even paper—a *Post-It*. Allah coaches, "Ahmed, it's only one more flight. You *can* make it."

Or, I can't. I step back, into the kitchen and walk to the front door. I open the front door. I'll never make it up the fire escape.

The forbidden stairs.

I don't have much time. If I want to get back, undetected. Eleven—or twelve but who's counting?—steps and I scale up the stairs like Arnold friggin' Spider-Man. I pretend I made it to the top. I'm on the slanted path! Killing it! I hop down and—

There. I land on—

The door swings open—

I've made it! I'm here! Victory!

I hold up my arms, Rocky Balboa style. I hope people in the office buildings see me, think, "That kid's out of our reach."

I look up, half expecting to see Saint Peter hovering overhead, clipboard propped against his waist, pink feather pen in one hand, low tar cigarette in the other.

I walk the roof, passing the solar panels. At one end, I dare myself, "Dude *look*." I do. Wow. The street's *way* the fuck down there. I'm so far up the traffic—cars, buses, trolleys—look like toys.

There's a corner next to the little elevator engine "house." It's hidden from sight and offers shelter.

Overhead, clouds gather, darkening the sky. I'm no wiser about the afterlife, but I'm pretty certain it's gonna rain. I don't have much time. If there's a storm, I can't use the fire escape.

I sit, plug in the headphones and listen.

Track Two:

Chapter 58

"When I got here, the whole city was out. Gay Pride. Who knew, not me. Even if I had, I wouldn't have cared. Me? Gay? I'm not gay. I was still rolling on the whole 'I'm bi' thing.

"All day, I was the wandering Jew Girl. Totally lost. My family had come here for vacation. We drove to tourists spots, looked and left. We stayed in the car, doors locked. My parents were terrified we'd catch something. Like gay was a cold and you could catch it.

"I remembered looking out the window and seeing tons of gay people. From inside the car, 'they' looked so strange, I might have been watching a TV show about this alien species, 'The Gays.'

"The day I ran away, I landed on this Queer Planet without a survival kit. I snuck into a bar and was thrown out. Then, Pride was over, people were leaving and it started raining.

"I didn't know where I was. I kept walking. Wandering. I ended up on Polk Street. I didn't know Polk Street was Ground Zero for the city's punks and runaways and addicts. The teen boi hookers ignored me. Except one, who hissed, '*Fish!*' The punks scared me: They looked hungry, like they'd eat anything. I stayed away from the trannies. They looked like crazy girls with bad makeup.

"One car drove by *so* slow. A station wagon. My family's car. Stupid, but I thought that meant something good or 'safe.' Weird, too, since I was running away from my family.

"I looked down. My eyes met the driver's. At first, I thought he was my dad! He'd found me! Before I could run, the passenger window rolls down, he leans over and smiles. 'Hey, can I ask you something?'

"I think, 'He needs help.' I was a Girl Scout. I walked over to the car. He looks friendly. I have nothing to worry about. I step forward. Close up, I realize, 'His smile isn't friendly. He's a weirdo.' I look down. His pants were open and he was jerking off. 'Ten bucks, bitch, suck this.'

"OhmiG-d I was *so* grossed out! I ran up the street and hid in a doorway. It was pouring rain. The wind was blowing—hurricane style. The rain wouldn't have been so bad, but it was freezing. My clothes got soaked. I knew I had to get inside. A red light.

" '*There*,' I thought. 'You'll be safe there.' I ran across the street. By this point, I'd seen enough sex shops, I knew that it wasn't a synagogue or church. I thought, 'Maybe it's a shelter.' Closer, the neon letters came into focus. 'Ming's.'

"I stood on the sidewalk outside big, wall-sized windows. I screwed up the courage I needed to open the door and walk inside. I didn't know it, but my life was about to change.

"Forever."

Chapter 59

"The smell. I'll never forget the smell of those greasy hamburgers and fries. My stomach did backflips. Cold *and* hungry. I realized, I hadn't eaten for two days.

"A Chinese guy stood behind the counter. I thought, 'He must be Ming.' I smiled; he scowled. Five minutes inside Ming's would be a lot. Just my standing there cost.

"I pretended I was thinking about what I was going to order. Really, there was nothing on the menu I'd eat at home. But then, I wasn't at home.

" 'Hey!' Ming yells. 'What you order!' I assumed he yelled so I could hear him over the disco music. The song was—get this—'I Will Survive.'

" 'You no order,' he barks. '*Go!*' I turned to leave when I remembered the vouchers the shelter lady gave to me.

"Oh, I left out that part. Before I ended up on the street, I went to this shelter. They told me I could sleep there, but after seventy-two hours, they had to call my parents. There was no way I was tipping *them* off. I knew bounty hunters were looking to capture me, and claim the reward. Twenty-five or fifty thousand dollars. For my 'safe' return. I'd vowed, 'I'll never go back.'

"I had a way to pay. Now, I took my time. I *studied* the

menu. I knew Ming wouldn't say anything. My suburban girl attitude worked. I knew how to act like a paying customer.

"*Grrrrrr*. My stomach growled—loud. Ming must have heard it. He said, 'What's that?' His pen hovered over the green-and-white order pad. Ming was patient. He'd wait. All he cared about was money. And it didn't matter if the cash was crumpled up ones, five hundred pennies or vouchers.

" 'Double cheeseburger with fries, hold the onions. Chocolate milkshake. Small.' If he didn't want the vouchers, I bet he wouldn't toss the food. I bet he'd soften up and give it to me.

"Ming gave me a number. Seventy-two. I don't know why. I was the only one in there. I took it and sat down on a plastic orange swivel chair. There was nothing relaxing about Ming's. The air conditioner was turned on full blast. Icicles grew on my clothes and hair.

" 'Seventy-two!' Ming yells. The vouchers were still in my jeans. I walked to the counter, pulled them out and reached for the white bag. Food! Just in time, too. I was about to faint from hunger.

"Ming snatched the white bag. 'Cash!' he shouted. 'Five dolla fitty-two!'

" 'I'm sorry,' I said. 'But that's all I have.'

" 'You no pay, you go!' he shouted. His hands made shoo-fly-shooh movements. There was no let's-talk-about-it. I looked up and recognized a Christian calendar. It was tacked to the wall over the grill. This month was covered with grease.

"I turned out my pockets. Showed him, 'Empty? See?' I hoped he'd take pity on me. He shook his head. No. Fucking. Way. He said, 'Out.' I would have grabbed the bag and ran, but Ming had stowed it under the counter.

"I turned and walked to the door. The phone rang. Ming yelled, 'Hey, you!' I looked back. Maybe the call's for me. He pulled out the white bag and set it on a red tray. I walked back to the counter. I planned to take it and leave. The front door swung open. A smiley dad type walked in. He grabbed the white bag. 'Hey,' I go. 'That's mine!' He said, 'C'mon.'

"Ming was quiet. He wouldn't look at me *or* the smiley dad guy. Clue Number One. But I was so hungry, I ignored it.

" *'Like a lamb lost in the woods'*—the song playing on the radio—I followed smiley dad guy and sat down. He pushed the white tray across the orange tabletop. 'Eat.' I didn't eat the burger and fries fast, I inhaled it. It'd take a stomach pump to get it back.

"I wasn't really listening, but he was talking. Real casual. He *knew* how to talk to a kid without it seeming weird. Even though he was doing all the talking, I felt like we were having this normal conversation. Somehow, he made me forget he was a smiley dad type. Yeah, nothing strange about a thirteen-year-old girl sitting with a chatty middle-aged man on a rainy night. Clue Number Two. Coulda, woulda, I shoulda known. He was good at this because he had practiced.

"Plus, I forgot or ignored that he'd didn't just stumble in off the street. He'd *called*. But who thinks like that? When you're starving and wet.

" 'Hi, I'm Bob,' he said. He asked me all these questions. 'You just get into town?' and 'Are you a runaway?' Fuckhead would *not shut up*. But he'd bought my burger, so I felt like I owed him something. Attention. I felt sorry for him. A guy his age, so lonely he buys thirteen-year-old girls burgers. 'Are you gay?'

"I almost choked. 'Well, *are* you?' I said, 'Bi.' Bob got this real 'concerned' look on his face. A real social worker, that Bob. Or a priest. Someone who wanted to save me. Missionary Man. G-D on his side. He shook his head and said, 'Geez, you kids got it hard.'

"The way he said it—OMG, I was such a sucker—I stopped. This was when I believed cops were public servants, not Nazis. 'Bob,' I said, 'are you a cop?'

" 'Cops,' he says, 'don't go buy burgers and milkshakes for kids.'

"Don't take sugar—candy or *milkshakes*—from strangers. I had left my common sense outside. Clue Number Three. I ig-

nored how he *studied* me. All I did, get this, was lean forward
and suck on the straw. I ignored the bad feelings. I thought, 'No
way, this can't make someone excited.' I didn't care. Milkshake
tasted *good*. Slid down perfect, too. Landed, plop, right on top
of the burger and fries.

"His questions made *me* wonder, 'Is Bob gay?' One of those
Good Gay Samaritans who drives around in the pouring rain on
the lookout for gay runaways?

"He looked so much like someone's dad. A *real* dad. I didn't
think to ask, 'Why is Bob *alone*? Where's his family?' Oh, yeah,
maybe they're buried in the basement.

"I must have fallen into a hamburger, fries and milkshake
coma. 'Cause here *I* was, talking to strangers, the *big thing* they
warn you about in Girl Scouts. Did I remember? No, I was worried about dying from trans fat.

" 'Saw you standing there,' he goes. 'And it just about broke
my heart.' His voice cracked. He sounded so sad, so . . . sincere.
I swear, I thought he would break down and bawl. Little Miss
Skeptical didn't stop to question why he was driving around
Polk Street, at night, right after Gay fucking Pride.

" 'Try living my life,' I said, all *tough* and streetwise. I was
about to learn I was anything *but* tough. 'That's the heart-
break.'

"He looked at me. His face was wrinkled with 'concern.'
Looking back, Bob the Big Bad Wolf was a *real* actor. He'd stud-
ied Hallmark movies in his spare time. Coz, he had the whole
'Kiss Daddy Good Night' act down. Voice, face, touch. He says,
'What are you running away from, little girl?'

" 'Dunno,' I said. I hadn't totally lost my Jewish mind. There
was *no way* I was telling him—or anyone—my real story.

" 'Everybody's running away from something,' he said. It felt
like he *cared*.

" 'You wouldn't believe me if I told you.'

" 'Are you sure?' he said. 'Try me.'

" '*Try me*.' I felt like I was the guest star on some reality TV
show about runaway teens. And, 'Don't be sure'? He made me
doubt *myself*.

"It's amazing I lived to tell. Bob wanted something from me. It wasn't a secret. He laid it out. It was so planned. Down to the food. If I hadn't ordered the burger, fries and milkshake, he would have. He *knew* the food would send me into a carb coma. I wouldn't be capable of logical thought. I felt lucky he didn't grab my hand and put it on Bob's Hot Dog. Or jerk off under the table. I felt bad for him. Bob was so pathetic. This big, creepy dad type with sad, blue eyes. I'd totally fallen for his puppy-dog-in-the-window act. But he confused me. With all this stiff formal stuff. He put out his hand, like we were meeting for a business appointment. 'Hello, my name is Bob. Or Dad. All the kids on Polk Street call me Dad.'

" 'Lorraine,' I said. Lie number whatever spilled out my mouth. Effortless. I acted so tough. I knew I'd survive on the street *just fine*, thank you very much. 'Yeah, Bob, but one father was more than enough.'

"His eyes. I couldn't get over them. They were hypnotic. *So* blue. A *good* blue, too. Like blue eyes 'meant' something. I ordered myself, 'Forget the eyes and sweet talk.'

"First, he hadn't laid a finger on me. He'd been honest. There wasn't much to lie about. His name? Being worried about runaways? The food he bought, now that was something real and good. He'd *fed* me. That counted for something. And there was just *something* about him. I trusted Bob. I wanted to trust him. Probably, I *needed* to trust him.

"I thought, 'Maybe Bob's my . . . guardian angel.' I'm Jewish. We invented angels. Or Bob's a *Prince!* So what if he was old enough to be the prince's grandfather? I'd watched *The Little Mermaid* and *Sleeping Beauty* so many times, I was a walking Disney casualty. My head was filled with rescue fantasies and unicorns.

" 'If you want,' he said, 'we could just drive around till you dry out.' No pressure, very casual. He gave me a choice: *that* got my attention. I studied him. I knew I could see what was wrong with him or bad, if I only looked hard enough. Problem was, I had nothing to compare him to. Except, maybe, pervs on the Internet.

"So I said, 'Sure,' and he said, 'My car's parked by the curb.' How convenient, right? Now, looking back on it, he wasn't taking any chances.

"He opened the door. I got in and sat in the passenger's seat. Bob drove a new Range Rover. Big. Warm. *Hella* warmer than Ming's. I leaned toward the heater and tried to soak up the warmth and dry out. It felt so good in Bob's car. I relaxed. I let down my guard.

"I felt better now that there was a car window between me and the street. The car pulled away. The speakers surrounded me, wrapped me in classical music. Bach. I didn't like it, but it was stuff my parents would listen to. It felt familiar. 'Lorraine, if you need a place to crash, I have an extra room.'

"His offer was so . . . generous. I relaxed. Now I knew I'd made a good choice. Only a *good* person would be willing to take in someone like me. Yeah, I felt a little pathetic. A little girl lost in the woods. Red Riding Hood stood outside, on the curb, jumping, trying to get my attention. Warn me about the Big, Bad Wolf. Stupidly, I ignored her. . . .

"My head rolled to the side. Gave Bob another look. Bob wore a blue Windbreaker. Khaki pants with a crease down the middle. His deep voice, gosh, he sounded just so *sincere*. And he was the only person in a city filled with queers celebrating Gay Pride who'd bothered to look at me or even say, 'Hi.' I'd walked around the city and the whole day, I felt totally invisible. Looking at him, I thought, 'Really, Bob could be *anyone's* dad.'

"Bob turned the wheel. The car pulled into a dead-end alley. 'Are you really one of those artist types who's just fronting with that suburban dad outfit? Pretending you're a cop?' He'd smiled. 'Yeah.' I knew it! I'd worked it all out, his story. Based on nothing more than the fact that he'd parked his car in an alleyway. I told him, 'I bet you've got some hella cool loft.' He smiled. I said, 'I knew it!'

"He put one hand behind my head and the other on my left knee. I was ready for him to lean over and give me a kiss on the cheek. 'I'll let him,' I thought. 'Princesses are good, sweet and kind. They're gracious. Even to old princes who should know better.' He turned to me and said, 'One question.'

" 'Yeah?' I said. Secretly, I was worried he'd fallen in love with me. He was a prince, but there was no getting around the thirty-year age difference. I didn't want to break his heart.

" 'Who's your daddy?'

"I ignored the question. Asked, 'Aren't you taking me upstairs to your loft? I'm really tired. I need to sleep.'

"He smiled. The little voice said, 'Get. Out.' I reached for the door handle and pulled. It was locked.

"I knew. He dropped the dad act. Revealed his creepiness. 'You suck cock.' Not, 'Do you suck cock?' But '*You. Suck. Cock.*'

" 'Bob!' I said. I was shocked. But my heart sank. I hoped he was kidding.

" 'You said you're bi,' Bob said. His hand stroked my leg. 'Bob, stop that!' He ignored me. He leaned over, pulled my face to his hands and mashed his mouth against mine. I tried to scream, but his mouth was eating mine. Bob might have *looked* old, but he was strong. Bob pinned me down. . . . I tried to, but I couldn't get away. Believe me, I *tried*. I kicked my feet and clawed his face. I bit him—he socked my jaw. I heard it crack. My clothes, Oh My G-D, he ripped them off! I gave up. I did.

"I hit him with my fists, but I knew. I wasn't getting out of that car until he did it to me. Held me down. Pushed my legs apart. Climbed on top. Stuck it in. I'd never done it before. I was a virgin. Down there, felt like someone was stabbing me with a dry knife. Felt like it was *never* going to end.

"When it did, end—when he finished and the electric locks clicked, he said, 'Get out, *whore*.' He pushed me *so hard* I fell out and landed facedown on the asphalt.

"The ground was wet. Puddles. My panties and jeans were down around my knees. I tried to pull them up.

" 'Don't move,' he said. I looked up, into his eyes. Scary, Coz they'd gone from blue to red. 'I'm *going to kill you*,' he said. It went, 'Click.' A switchblade. He leaned over the seat and out the car and grabbed my hair and pulled me back and tried to cut my throat! I felt the metal blade on my skin. I closed my eyes. 'Just get it over with, cut—'

Chapter 60

I press Pause. My arm's wet. I look up. It's sprinkling. The gray skies gone black. Rain's on the way.

Crack!

Lightning. The sky blinks. The man's face flashes on the clouds.

Crack! Lightning. The switchblade catches the light.

Crack! Lightning. Quick, Bob slices the boy's throat.

"No!" I shut my eyes, shake my head. Maybe that will erase the image from my mind's eye. I wonder. Are Bathroom Bob and Burger Bob the same Bob?

I press Play.

Chapter 61

"—**M**y throat. It happened so fast, I don't know. He'd got stuck in the seatbelt. Or his arms weren't long enough to hold on. Whatever, I sensed an opening. A moment. It meant I had to move.

"I jerked my head, and kicked. The knife dropped. I fell back. Tumbled out the car. Landed back on the ground.

"I reached down, touched myself and felt something warm. I held up my hand.

"Thunder, lightning, flash. Mother's strobe light, the world went white. On the Blood. Red. Liquid. *Click,* off, back to black. I hoped the rain would wash it away. Bob's car was gone. I sat, bare ass on the ground. I sat next to a Dumpster.

"I didn't bother to pull up my jeans. I crawled to the Dumpster and scootched underneath. I ignored the maggots and the smell. I knew it would be dry there.

"Hours—or days—later, I woke up. Anita had found me. She brought me back."

Chapter 62

I remove the earbuds. Alice / Nadya's story? I get the point. The "lesson." *Me* listening to *her* story. It's meant to help me reflect on my own. Substitute therapy. And that's all fine but . . . whatever.

I try to stand. Wobble. While I was listening and reflecting on our pain, my left leg fell asleep.

A door slams.

Click.

Click.

Smoke. The smell poisons the air.

Click, click, click.

Whoever's down there is walking around the roof. I'm being stalked. Like Ripley in that movie, *Alien*. The monster *knows* I'm here but isn't 100 percent certain where. Except their victim's close.

I'm trapped. Or, maybe not. The fire escape's nearby. I could make a break for it and scramble down.

I stand. My legs go bezerk. Cosmic pinpricks. I can't walk without making shuffling sounds.

Frantic, I search for a new hiding place. My only way *out* is *up*. I wiggle out my hiding place and climb up, onto the elevator roof. I lie on the tiny pitched roof, frozen with fear. I stare at the black sky. Drizzle flutters down like dark feathers.

Click, click, click.

Alien is on the move. But I can't see him. I roll over. Gravel tumbles off and goes *Ping!* I might as well be banging giant Chinese gongs, those pebbles sound *that* loud. Fuck! I'm a goner, for sure.

"Caw! Caw! Caw!"

Overhead, a flock of crows flies by. Wicked Witches, they circle the roof, beady, black eyes peering down at me.

"Caw! Caw! Caw!"

The dive down. Near my body. They plan to eat me. I probably look like a dead cat.

"Caw! Caw! Caw!"

I unfold my body. Stretch. Open my mouth, stick out my tongue and make scary faces. Maybe that will stop them from swooping down and pecking me to death.

"Caw! Caw! Caw!"

The gargoyle faces work. The beasts back off. If only the *Alien* was so easily shooed away. I've lost track of his whereabouts.

Voices—

They come close—

Shadows on the solar panel—

Somebody's pissed.

Chapter 63

"*Stop* that!"

I look over the edge. Marci jabs her index finger at Anita's chest. "There's *other people!*"

Then . . . crickets.

Blue-Eyed Bob either slit their throat(s) or Anita's lost her voice.

I peer over the roof. There! There he is! The rapist! The killer! He stands in the shadows! Bizarre, we're both eavesdroppers. He steps back. I strain to see him without being seen. He pulls out a cigarette pack. He toys with the lid. His bald head moves. He glances up. Oh, shit! He's seen me! No, he didn't. Because he doesn't jump up and grab me. I do, however, see his eyes. Blue. Blue-Eyed Bob.

I'm tempted to warn them. But if I do, he might get me, too.

"This afternoon—" Marci's voice, broken up by the loud street traffic. "I follow—" . . . "—to a bar!" and "saw . . . I took you in for *that?*" she says, fully audible. "So you could turn *tricks?*"

I remember Hammer's two categories of tricks: hookups and sugar daddies.

"I didn't do that!" Anita squeals. She's a bad liar, and I can't even see her face.

"*Really?* So those men *don't* pay? I mean, *come on.* I know *all about* that place."

"You know *what* about that place?!? Don't tell me *you* tricked it—there. All you said when I moved in was, *no drugs.* It's my life. You're always saying that. Now you *spy* on me?"

"No, I'm not 'spying' on you," Marci says. "Nadya and me were coming back from her clinic—"

"What's wrong with her?"

"You found her in the alley, *bleeding*, hiding under a Dumpster, figure it out."

"Oh, girlie girl got the AIDS?"

"Abortion. *She* saw you and—"

"*Nadya's* the damn spy?"

"She was *excited* to see you. She wanted to say, 'Hi.' I asked her to wait. *I* followed you. She didn't have a clue where you were going so don't get defen—"

"*Defensive? Bitch!* You saw *shit!* All I did was—" *Click, click.* Anita's Bic. Ciggie smoke drifts up. "*All* I did was go in that bar, sit down and let some guy buy me a drink."

"Fine, it's your life. But if you get picked up for, oh, *whatever*, you're on your own."

Too bad I'm not down there, on the roof. "Watch out!" I'd warn them. "His name's Bob. He's five feet away from you and listening to your argument while cleaning his fingernails with a switchblade."

"Living here means coming home after school. *Straight* home."

"*When* am I s'posed to get my fun on?" Anita whines. "Sounds like some damn shelter. Or house arrest."

" 'Nita, in case you didn't notice, living here's *not* about getting your fun on. You *know* what happens to those other kids?"

"What happens is," I think, "Blue-Eyed Bob follows you downstairs, steals a wig and goes Lizzie Borden on your asses."

"If *they* get caught because *you* had to 'get your fun on'?"

"Tell me, girl, what is this 'about'?"

"Please don't blow smoke in my face. It's about *you* getting *your* cosmetology license and getting a job. Then *you* can sup-

port yourself and get *all* the fun on *you* want. Party twenty-four
seven."

"I get it."

"No," Marci says, "since you remember our first conversation, then you also remember what I said about using in the safe
house. Obviously, you didn't bring any booze *into* the house
but, c'mon, Anita. Some of those kids. Ben? They're nowhere
near as, uh—"

"Lil' Benny's bought his hooker training wheels."

My back stiffens. Excuse me? *Hooker? Training* wheels? Forget Blue-Eyed Bob, I'm gon' *cut* Lil' Miss Two-Faced Tranny Biatch!

"—acting all innocent! L. O. L. Tricks are for kids!"

"Ben and Nadya *study* all day. They—"

"Sit, take up the kitchen table like they own it."

" 'Nita, you can be such a bitch."

"Don't get me started! You missed the night little Mr. Prep
School fucked J.D. right here, baby, up on the roof—"

"*What?*"

What is right.

"That's right. One night, I *saw* them stand on the escape, kiss
and crawl back inside. Kiss the way people do after they been.
Fuck. Ing."

"For some reason," Marci says. "I doubt that."

"What *else* would they be doing on the roof?"

"Talking?"

"Oh, there's a lot you miss."

"Please, tell me, what else has Ben been up to?"

My question exactly! What *else* have I been up to?

"*Well!*" Anita says, huffing and puffing, ready to blow that
ciggie down. "He *followed* Hammer into the closet, and those
two pulled a show! Peanuts told me. Kidd and Peanuts heard
everything. Finally, Peanuts couldn't take it no more, got up and
caught them! Peanuts told me, they looked *guilty* as hell."

"Hammer's doing shows again?" Marci sighs.

"Didn't hear it from me."

"Ben's not the type."

"Honey," Anita says, "they *never* do. Those types are the ones who *always* the type. You didn't know me then. *I* started out that way. Hammer's a whore to the core. Got some fresh meat. I bet he made *bank*."

None of this is true, but still I feel ill. I lie there, plotting revenge.

"Don't look down on Hammer. He's the reason we'll have heat this month. Promise you'll come straight home after school?"

"*Nevah* straight, Gaily Forward, girl, I'm rhythm in motion."

"The other reason you really need to stay away from those fern bars."

"Really, what reason?"

"'Cause, *girl,* you sound like an old queen."

"*Fine,*" Anita says, a pout in her voice. The conversation moves away.

Bob steps away from the elevator house and a corner. A door creaks, opens, groans and shuts. *Click.*

I crawl to the other side and peek over the edge. Blue-Eyed Bob's gone. A cigarette's been left on a dry spot. Red embers consume the white paper.

Plop.

Water hits my arm.

Rain. I look over the elevator roof. They walk around the solar panel. If they look up, they'll see me. But they don't. I guess they're not curious about the rain.

"Gross, everybody smokes up here." I see Marci kneel and daintily pick up Bob's cigarette. She flicks it away, onto the roof.

The door squeaks, opens and slams. They're gone. I start to follow and stop. I don't want to run into Blue-Eyed Bob. He's the type who hides in stairwell shadows.

My right leg's fallen asleep. Crazy, pinprick sensations shoot down my legs. I forget about being scared. I won't need to psyche myself on the fire escape—I'll be lucky if my legs work.

One step at a time, I obsess on Blue-Eyed Bob turning up on the roof. I debate whether or not to warn Marci. If I do, I rat myself out. I bet Bob does all his dirty deeds in public. That's probably part of the thrill for him. Besides, twenty-five locks keep us safe. Right? I convince myself, Yes, we're safe, and step into the kitchen. The front door opens. Marci follows Anita— *she* sees me and flashes a big, fake smile.

"Oh, you're wet, baby," she coos. "Hiding out on the escape? Come in and take that off. Don't want you sick."

She doesn't ask why my jacket's wet. And I don't tell her how close she stood to death.

I decide to keep my mouth shut about what I saw on the roof. Because, really, what can Marci do about Mr. Switchblade, Blue-Eyed Bob. Call the cops?

Chapter 64

Dawn. The kitchen curtains are suddenly sheer. I peer over the bed. Below, Kidd and J.D. sleep. At night, they curl up together, two spoons. By morning, they sleep apart, separated by a wall built from sheet and pillows, "... *like brothers on a hotel bed.*"

I reach under the futon, fingers feeling for the hard rectangle shape. The journal's blue lines are in the faint morning light, nearly invisible. Doesn't matter. I put pen tip to white paper and let the black ink spill.

white ankle, black plastic

next stop is—
blank, a pastry face with black handlebar mustache

his job's "security"
tho i have yet to meet anyone who feels safer
he pulls me out, into the empty hallway & a small cell
i keep my mouth shut, i know better than ask, why me

see all my experiences at Serenity Ridge
were baffling or violent or both

"up" he says pointing to my right pant leg
no reason why never is

he fascinates us—we think he's a tard
who talks r-e-a-l sloooooo 'cuz hes so fuckin stoooopid

makes u want to yank down on his black 'stache
yeah we all know 2 that hes a pedophile

that dont make him gay
just another perv like all the rest

he kneels & hikes up my cuffed jeans
baring my bare ankle his crusty hands reach stroking

the white in-between
orange kick & deep blue denim

his hands are busy doing his creepy perv thing on me
& i look down eyes shocked to see the white skin strip

'cuz last year when they brought me here my ankle was
a golden tan brown licked only by the sun

Ralph stops with his desperate sad touching strokes
wraps a band on my ankle & snaps it shut

rolling the hard blue denim down over the white skin
& black plastic

"*case u try leavin' *" *he says standing excited hard*
prick pokes out his pants 'we know where to find ya'

great
I got my own LoJac

he swipes the white card key with a black magick stripe
stroking my back my skin crawls walking out the cell

In back i hear the door shut & click
alone

i realize i have just been left alone for the first time
since i got here

i sit on a lemon sofa & touch a green plant feeling
the leaf a dead plastic frond thick with gray ghost dust

i lean forward reach down & touch
the black plastic thing on my white ankle

i look up a mirrored insect eye's stuck between ceiling
& wall like an alien probe

They watch.

I slide move my hand up down pretending
to scratch my calf

i do this b.c I know the gesture
will trick them

till im gone ill be
scrutinized searching for any sign of rebellion

Chapter 65

"Hey," I ask. "What about my tooth?"

Marci ignores my question.

"Gas and electric?"

"Twenty-two forty-one," Kidd says.

Alice / Nadya notes the amount on scrap paper. Marci counts out the bills, hands them to Kidd who slides the money into an envelope and hands it off to Alice / Nadya who affixes a stamp. We live off the grid, but we pay bills like everyone else.

Eleven letter-sized envelopes are lined up on the kitchen table. I stare at them. I don't care about the heat. Lately, my tooth aches. The wisdom tooth that got me *out* of Serenity Ridge *now* gives me constant pain. I floss, and brush, but the pain's only gotten worse.

"Phone?"

"Fifty-six thirty-three," Kidd says. Count, money, envelope, stamp.

"What does that leave us?" Marci asks.

"After rent? We've got . . ." Alice / Nadya taps the amount in a calculator. "Two hundred and one dollars and seventy cents."

"Let's see," Marci says, motioning me over. I open my mouth. She peers inside. "I'm sorry. We don't have money for a dentist."

"What am I supposed to do?"

"Tie a string around the tooth, hook it over the knob and slam the door. Wait," Marci says, stacking the completed envelopes. "I'm forgetting something. We still need to spend two hundred on Pony's bus ticket."

"Fuck him." Peanuts scowls. Pony's moving in. I forgot. I already hate him. I *live* here. Two hundred would pay to fix my tooth. Pony, *he* gets a bus ticket; I get more Tylenol.

"Huh," Peanuts says. "I thought we was full up."

"We're saving lives." Marci shrugs. "Desperate time, desperate measures."

"Who's leaving?" I ask. Maybe it's one in, one out.

"Nobody," she says, sliding the envelopes into the backpack and walking to the front door.

"Where's this one gonna sleep?" Hammer asks, looking at Peanuts. "Coz there's no room in the closet."

"We'll figure it out," Marci says. The door shuts. She's gone. With my dental two hundred.

"Hey, you forgot . . . !"

Marci left an envelope on the kitchen table. It's addressed to "Karen Smith." The postmarked's Nashville, TENN. I open the envelope and slip the letter out. Before I read it, I pause. I'm the same as Haifa snooping in my journal. The print is blocky, childlike. I read.

> Dear Karen,
>   Just got your letter today! I was so glad to hear from you! Karen, I need help and I need it fast. I'm still in the Central County's Youth Center. No one in my family wants me until I get "cured." Please, can you do anything? Oh, and are you allowed to tell me your last name?
>
> Love and thanks,
> PONY

A memo (typed) is paper-clipped to the first envelope.

Please destroy this memo after reading it. PL will
be driven down and arrive in the early evening of
October 25. He'll be at your place for
approximately one month, and then another safe
house in the area for another undetermined length of
time directly after he stays with you. You asked
about food. He can't stand (and refuses to eat):
mayo, yogurt, milk, tuna, bananas, apples, cottage
cheese and sandwiches.

I guess Pony plans to live on Ming's burgers, fries, chocolate
milkshakes and oatmeal.

Chapter 66

Mouth. Ache. I've had it. The throbbing tooth must go. I sit on the edge of the tub and massage my gums with ice cubes and oral anesthetic. I poke the soft tissue. Numb. Nothing. I feel—

Quick, before the numbness goes away, I wrap floss around the tooth, hook the end around the knob and kick the door. I hear something rip and scream—

"AAAHHHHH!"

The pain's incredible. Blood, *real* blood, pours out my mouth and runs down my shirt. I should ask Hammer to set up the camera. Surely, someone would pay to see, "The Boy with the Bloody Mouth."

The rotten tooth hangs off the floss. It dangles from the knob, horror movie style. A dark, red droplet hangs and shudders, one last sigh, and drops. Lands on the white tile and explodes and I—

I wake up. I'm in bed. Someone tucked me in. It's night.

I remember—I passed out.

I grab the plastic bottle, take a swig and taste. Cold, bubbly liquid. Good.

The mind-numbing pain's gone. The 7UP feels good in my mouth. I feel woozy. I bet someone gave me a pill. That's why I can't remember my dreams.

I collapse, back, and pass out. I need to dream a dream, or two.

Chapter 67

"**P**eople!" Marci shouts.

I sit up and look around, ostrich style. Fist to eyes, I rub and try to get the sleep out. My mouth's packed with stuffing. I reach in and pull at it. The giant tampon's soaked with blood.

"Girrrl." Kidd cackles. "You a woman. *Don't flush it!*"

"Fabric!" Marci dumps a pile of bright scraps on the floor. Everyone swarms. Arts & Crafts Day must be big in the safe house. "And *this* is Pony."

I'm the only one who looks. A scrawny kid stands behind Marci.

"Hi," I say. He ignores me. I climb down and hover, watching the fabric feeding frenzy. "What's that about?"

"Halloween costumes," Marci says. "Our High Holy Holiday."

"Holy? Hardly." Alice / Nadya rolls her eyes, holding a piece of blue chiffon up to her face, Mata Hari style. "All we do is go out and walk around."

"Hey," I say to Pony. Maybe he didn't hear me. Close up, Pony's beautiful. I guess anyone named Pony would be pretty. His little body is perfectly shaped. His face is cut like a statue's. Pony's a white marble angel covered in black soot. A hard journey's etched on his sweet face and aqua eyes.

I lean into his left ear and whisper, "Isn't Halloween for little girls in princess outfits?"

He ignores me. Traumatized, I guess. He reminds me of me. But I'm pretty sure I've lost that glazed-eyed, freaked-out look. His nervous energy shows me how much anxiety I've shed.

"Do you feel like taking a shower?" Marci asks.

"Hell, yeah." Pony's voice is deep, with a twang. He looks like an angel, but he sounds like a pit bull. He feels my stare. "What the *fuck* you lookin' at?"

I shrug; he grunts and follows Marci to the bathroom. I want to pull her aside and warn her, "He's a mistake. Send him away. This won't work out. He's crazy. All he wants is attention. And he doesn't sound gay."

In Serenity Ridge, I met lots of Ponys. Their eyes burned bright furnace bright. The Pony type has just-don't-know-what-to-do-with energy. Between the Halloween fabric crisis and Pony's arrival, I feel ignored. I slip out the front door and run upstairs, to the roof.

I walk toward the solar panels. The panels' catch light—from the street, cone-shaped aircraft red warning lights perched atop of skyscrapers and a moon the color of tea-stained teeth.

I stand on the roof's edge and stare. The city. I want to see— *really* see—what lays beyond the safe house. Far away (or nearby, I can't tell), there's an odd-shaped building covered with a blue-green glass skin. The shape and cartoon colors make me think of a stranded whale. Or, a dyslexic's idea of the Great Pyramids. On the green side, colored lights travel up a column, morphing red to purple to green to blue.

"C'est romantique, c'est magnifique," a deep voice says. The song kicks in, "*This is what it sounds like when doves cry.*" The D.J.'s hidden but close. Over my shoulder? Or, in my head? Maybe this is my "he-crazy" moment, the first sign being, hearing '80s music 24 / 7.

The elevator motor groans. I peer through a small window covered with metal mesh. Inside, it's dark except for one reading light hung over turntables. The D.J. sits in the shadows on a milk crate. Hunched over the gear, he wears a thick parka, hoodie and wool cap. I can't see his face. He leans forward. Light catches his eyes, nose, mouth.

I step back. Of course. All those nights I lay in bed and listened to the deep, marble voice and house music, J.D. was the D.J., podcasting to the world, the galaxy, the universe and beyond.

The song crests. I turn and face the city. The column's lights fade to black. The sequence ends and starts over, colors brightening and fading. Add music. Mix. Drink Hypnotic.

Time to go.

I slip inside. The "safe" house is scandalously easy to enter. So easy, in fact, I wouldn't be surprised to find Blue-Eyed Bob in the closet getting a lap dance from Hammer. I lock up and climb up the ladder, eager to rest.

Pony's in my spot, curled up, dead, or asleep. Drool dribbles out his pink, bow-tie-shaped mouth. A tin sits next to his head. I pick it up, unscrew the top and sniff. Tobacco. Gross. That explains the dribbling drool. I climb off the bed. Tonight, I'll sleep on the floor.

İNVİSİBLE

Chapter 68

Halloween.

Sixty minutes to freedom. Everyone runs around the safe house, laughing and screaming. We spent the day getting dressed. A few hours ago, we started putting on makeup.

J.D.'s costume is simple: sky blue midi (tiny tee cut off right below his breastbone), plastic vampire fangs and white face. His lips are dark red with temple-to-temple black slashes across his face. His mohawk's dyed magenta. Spiked, his 'do looks like an underworld security fence tipped with purple razor blades. A cross between Dracula and Futuristic *The Last of the Mohicans*. I'm running a Best Costume Contest in my head: J.D. wins First Place.

The closet door opens. Hammer steps out. Boberella bends over and zips up knee-high boots. Hammer's costume isn't much more than a tiny, rhinestone-covered thong and iridescent paint smeared over his body-by-Michelangelo.

The closet door's open. I peek through the crack. Peanuts. Topless, she turns and sees me. *Whomp!* The door slams shut.

Hammer slips a CD into the old boom box, jacks the volume on a generic house track ("Alice / Nadya / Sell me . . .") and dances, turning the safe house into a strip club. I'd guess he's going as a go-go boy (or, working as one?). He grabs a sparkly cowboy hat and white gloves lined with fringe, Madonna (circa, a while ago). Moving, grooving, his body shimmers and shines, a human rainbow. The glam body makeup catching the light.

I wear tight pants, identical to J.D.'s, except mine are white. Anita wanted me to go shirtless but (a) I've got a dork chest, and (b) I get cold easily. Anita made a sheer (see-through) shirt thing. It's not really warm, modest (or, my style), but it's better than naked.

Earlier, she nudged my shoulder and motioned to the bathroom. "Time to dye." She calls my new hair color "dead movie star blond." My hair was barely dry when she switched on the clippers and buzzed my scalp. Chop-chop, five minutes later, I was mohawked.

"What the hell are you?" Kidd cracked.

"Angel-A," I said. "My costume's more of a look."

"Yeah, if you're in seventh grade and that's your idea of sexy."

"If you're gonna mop my look," J.D. said. "You need product." He whipped out a giant tub of green gel and styled my 'do into a proper homo'hawk.

"Close your eyes," he said, setting it all in place with a rainfall of toxic hairspray. "Look at us, bro'. We're ebony and ivory."

"Or, alterniverse twins," I said, referring to the Xena Warrior Princess Twins, Crazy Sandy and Elena, those crazy-beautiful dykes who rescued me.

"Done?"

"Almost. Makeup." Careful, he drew lines across my face.

"Accessories." Alice / Nadya drapes a fake pearl necklace around my head, a minicrown. Marci slips wings over my shoulders. Kidd tried to wear the wings, but they didn't fit. Watching him struggle to pull them on over his broad shoulders, I think, "Evil Stepsister."

When everyone's done tarting me up, I look in the mirror. I'm more like Angel-A than Punk Rock Jailbait.

Done and dressed, I sit back and watch. Alice / Nadya works on her costume: layers of blue, chiffon material, matching veil and crown. She sticks twelve candles in the crown. Using Anita's fish bowl makeup mirrors, Alice / Nadya fills in her pursed lips with bright red lipstick.

"What's that thing on your head?"

"A minora."

"A wha'nora?"

"You'll see," she says, tracing her lids with kohl and blue eye-liner.

"What are *you?*" Kidd jokes. "The angel with a birth defect?"

"Remember Joey?" Alice / Nadya says, daintily adding three tiny lines just outside her left lid. Marilyn Monroe did that, too.

"I do," J.D. says. He sits, perched on the kitchen's windowsill, smoking a joint. He's getting high. Preparing to take flight. He holds out the roach. I shake my head.

"Hell, ya, gimme some'a that," Pony says, and takes the Mary J. He's a cross-dressed Daisy Mae: blue-and-white ging-ham print dress, ruffled cocktail waitress top and wig—blond pigtails. Anita painted red circles on his cheeks and dotted his face with mascara. It looks like he has really bad combination skin: blackheads and chicken pox. His fire engine red lips shine, hard and beautiful, dipped in shellac.

"Was Joey the crazy guy who let you spit in his mouth at par-ties?" J.D. exhales. I don't partake, but I like the scent: incense with an edge.

"Joey's the one who let you spit in his mouth?"

"Help." Peanuts steps out the closet, pointing to s / his head. "They won't stay on."

"He's the one," Alice / Nadya says, mid-eyelid, reaching over and adjusting Peanuts's headpiece, a dozen green, rubber snakes. "You could put anything in his mouth."

Peanuts nods. The snakes shimmy. "The boy who swallowed the spider the size of a cellie?"

"Yeah," Alice / Nadya says, returning to lining her eyes. Cos-tume plus makeup, I'm guessing Scheherazade. Or, Liz Taylor's Cleopatra (the real Egyptian monarchess being many, many shades darker than these two). "And remember how he had that extra nipple?"

"—*really* good at crank phone calls."

"—triple back flips."

"And could suck his own cock."

"Ready?" J.D. says, stands and looks at me.

"Boys," Marci says. "We're not ready."

J.D. grabs my hand and walks us to the front door.

"Hey! Guys!" Marci calls out. "I told you, *wait up!*"

"Shouldn't we—"

"Hell, no," J.D. says, opens the front door and steps out. I follow. He pauses and lights a cigarette. "We 'wait' for them, we'll be there all night."

I don't tell him, but I'm a little worried about going outside-outside. Everybody's nervous. We were ready to leave hours ago. He propels down stairs, taking two, three, four steps at a time.

"Dude, you ever seen Marci wait for us to *eat?*"

Chapter 69

We step down off the stairs into the lobby. I look at the floor-to-ceiling mirror. It takes me a second before I realize the two boys in the reflection are . . . us. The two cutest bois in *all* of San Francisco. We're destined to get more looks than Louisiana food stamps.

"Fuck prom," I say, parting the front door's dirty lace curtains and peering out at the street. It's packed. (Surfing the Web, I read Burning Man started here, at Land's End.) People shout, laugh, dance. Bare flesh flashes under barely there costumes. I reach for the doorknob. I want to dive into this beautiful, moving tide of humanity.

"Hey," J.D. says. "Let's wait a few."

It's been a while. Anxious, I look at the stairs.

"Does everyone think Halloween lasts three nights?"

"People!" Marci marches downstairs. The kids follow. She installs herself, guard style, at the front door. "We leave the building in pairs, one pair every five minutes." We surge toward the front door. Marci blocks it. "Wait! Where's Anita?"

"Fuck that," Peanuts grumbles. "We're not livin' on *drag* time!"

But s / he doesn't move, and I know why. We want to see Anita's getup. Sewing it was a top secret project, the Area 51 of Halloween costume manufacture.

Kidd glares at me. No mystery why *he's* mad: His costume's lame, a brown papoose (really, a stuffed backpack), corn husks and feathers sticking up, out his head. He's shirtless—and hot (yawn, Hammer's way hotter)—and wears moccasins with his loincloth. He's a post-op, she-to-he Pocahontas.

A stethoscope's draped over Marci's Doctor Marvelous white overcoat. A tiny digital camera hangs on the cord. She holds it up. "Before you leave, disclose your psychosis."

"Punk Rock Jailbait," I say. A flash pops and bathes me in white light. I feel famous for a second.

"Next."

"Dwaculaaaaa!" J.D. hisses, bares his fangs, lifts his arms and turns his black cape into giant wings.

"Pocahantas!" Kidd steps out, twirls, left hand in the air, right foot out, bouncing down into a lap dancer squat.

"Or," I think, "the Skanky Squaw."

"Squirtle," Peanuts says. "The stuff *dreams* are made of!"

"Or nightmares?" Kidd says. "Anyway, who gives a fuck about Squirtle? Star-Belly Sneetches'd be all over him, beating—"

"Girrrlll!" Marci says, staring at the stairs. I look at J.D. and mouth, "Let's go?" He doesn't see me. He and everyone else are transfixed.

A shadow darkens the wall. A foot wrapped in a green high heel steps down.

Pauses.

"Work it, girl!" Hammer shouts. "*Woooorrrrkkk!*"

Anita's legs are fantastic, all long and showgirlie, wrapped in shiny nylons. She draws it out, revealing her showgirl self *very slowly*.

Peanuts was right about drag time. We'll be leaving five hours from now. On full display, Anita stops. Dramatic. The top of the stairs being the pinnacle, forcing us all to lift our eyes. Arms up, left foot turned out, knee cocked, it's the Tah-dah! moment. The Showgirl slowly moves, turning like she stands on an invisible, rotating pedestal.

We hoot and holla, make catcalls and whistle. Anita merely

nods, a queen barely aware of her subjects. She doesn't smile. Glamour is grim.

"Aiiigggt, fa-fa-fa-furrrrrrsssssttttt!" Kidd barks.

I go, "Huh?"

J.D. leans over. "Famous fierce." Word.

Anita moves among us costumed mortals. Her outfit dazzles: headdress, mini-microbikini, heels, and freaky fluorescent colored tribal makeup.

"You are?"

"Dahhhhling . . ." she says, drawing out suspense over her true-secret self. "I am The Interplanetary Brazilian Samba Zone Goddess."

"Rules. One, back by dawn. Two, stick together. Three—"

Chapter 70

We burst out the Cretan. The sidewalk's crowded. I stop, breathless, a combination of brain-body freeze and shock.

Freedom. I forgot. Half-alive, tiptoeing to and fro from bunk bed and bathroom and back has changed me. Half-naked in the Tenderloin, I feel *free*, really and *truly* free. Giddy, glorious, gay and glamourous, costumes don't matter, it's the intention.

I dismiss all thoughts of bounty hunters. Let them lurk on side streets. Me and J.D., we're going to go get lost. Blend into city streets overflowing with partiers, revelers, dreamers, mystics, witches, warlocks and fairies. J.D. takes my hand and pulls me into the throng of magick, mischief and mirth makers.

"No—" I say, and hold back. "Wait."

I want to absorb the energy given off by these creatures. I shut my eyes, take a breath and say, "My people." I open my eyes, a smile on my face. My gaze is immediately drawn to a cluster of faeires. Our wings light up, and twinkle. They suck drinks through straws, spitting mischievous fountains at passersby.

"Look," J.D. says. Alice / Nadya and Anita sweep by, larger than life. Anita reigns, the Queen of the Night. "Check it out. Alice / Nadya's on fire."

The crown's candles are lit, flames dancing in the breeze.

"Yo, Golda Meir!" I call out.

"Hah hah!" She laughs, stops and strikes a pose, arms thrown up into the air. The gesture splits the blue chiffon fabric down the middle. "I'm the Flaming Menorah!"

"Wow." J.D.'s eyes widen. "What a rack."

Under the blue chiffon, Alice / Nadya's *buck nekkid* (except for a floss-sized G-string). Two Playboy centerfold–sized breasts sit high atop her body, bare except for gold Star of David pasties glued to her nipples.

"C'mon!" J.D. says, tugs my hand and pulls me away. "Time to move. We'll see them later."

"But—" I look back. Alice / Nadya's gone except for the trail of Hebrew camp songs she leaves in her wake.

"Wait. I want to look."

I feel like I'm missing out on seeing thousands of other in-sanely cool costumes and creatures.

Maybe people see us and, right before we vanish, say, "Those beautiful boys." Tonight, we're blurs, captured in stolen pic-tures and flashes, memory.

"We've got a date."

"With who."

"It's a surprise."

I don't like the sounds of this. It maybe Halloween, but I'm not into three-ways.

Chapter 71

"That's it," J.D. says, excited.

"McDonald's?"

"Yes!" he says, rushing toward the puny, yellow (not golden) arches.

"Ronald. McDonald. That's your date?" I say, careful to make it his, not mine. "I think I wait this one out."

Nearby, there's the Civic Center. I'll go explore the wide open space and fountain.

"Wish me luck," J.D. says. I watch him walk away. My heart sinks. I *know* the reason why he's walking into Mickey D's: Oskar, the supposed love of his life.

Until he leaves the fast-food fluorescent cube, I'll wait. I remind myself, for what? The tenth? Hundredth? Thousandth? time—J.D. and I, we're *not* in love.

Fuck that.

Denial fail.

I push open the glass door. I'm the lost Charlie's Angel. I want to see the competition.

Inside, I search for J.D. His magenta mohawk and black cape move through the crowd.

Two guys follow him. They look like pedophiles from that show, *To Catch a Predator*. The types who agree to meet a 13 y.o. for a burger and side order of diddle. (And when they're caught say, "I just came here for something to eat!")

I've seen them before, but I don't remember where from. Are they wearing costumes? Or, are their oversized parka jackets and combat boots real work clothes? Viewed from the rear, the duo could be the same Rent-A-Escort-A-holes who nabbed me from my bedroom, shoved me into a backseat and drove me to Serenity Ridge.

They stop, pause and look back. I see their faces: Dave and Seth, a.k.a., the Pigfuckers!

Maybe it's detoxing off the tranks or being away from Sadaam "Dad" Hussein, but my intuition's come back. Something bad's about to go down. The little voice in my head chimes, "And you'd better do something about it!"

Outside, Hammer poses. He's a Market Street sidewalk show stopper.

"Help!" I grab Hammer's left, cantaloupe-sized bicep. "J.D.'s in trouble—"

Hammer turns and walks toward the Mickey D's.

"Find a pay phone, call 911 and make a bomb threat. *Now!*"

Chapter 72

X-nay on the pay phone. Where's AT&T when you need to make a bomb threat? I run back inside. The Pigfuckers' big asses spill over soda-pop-sized seats. Their feet jiggle, nervous as girls on first dates.

J.D. sits with a woman. If Oskar was the bait, Mom is the hook, Pigfuckers are the fishermen and J.D.'s the prize.

Mamacita. Let's just say, if Dracula's nephew had gone in drag, he would look something like this woman's daughter. The Addamses' family reunion.

"*Mijo.*" Her voice oozes insincerity, "This new place will *help* you."

"I'm fine! *You*—you and *your* fucked-up ideas. *That's* what needs a cure!"

Hammer walks to the table between the Addams Family and bounty hunters, plops his butt-naked ass down, go-go boots dangling off the side. I wonder if the boots are steel tipped. I'd *love* to see him break some Pigfucker face.

His legs wide, Hammer's big basket spills out onto the table. He plants his palms on the surface and pushes his chest out, pure, 100%, All-American Boi Beefcake. He moans, drops his head and gyrates his ass.

To keep J.D. in their crosshairs, the Pigfuckers are forced to look at Hammer's exaggerated cam whore / stripper moves.

"Oh, baby—" Hammer groans, bouncing his body and rapping out a Lil' Ru ditty, *"I love the way she freak with no panties on. . . ."*

Pigfuckers shake their heads, grossed out by Hammer's homo-porno-rap. Pigfucker #1—Dave? Seth?—hollers, *"Shut up!"*

"Acting?" An alarmed voice refocuses my attention. She's been nominated for her leading role as Most Dreadful Mamacita. Her startled face suggests she thinks she's on TV. "Acting like *what?*"

"Acting all 'innocent,' " J.D. says, sharp. "Don't play games with me. I know why you sent me there. Why can't you just be honest about that?"

"I don't know what you're talking about!"

"Oh, *come on!*" J.D. says, shoulders rolled forward. I feel bad for him. He wants to fight but, facing her, he's deflated. He sits back in his chair, arms crossed. "Yes! You do!"

I'm tempted to jump up on the orange table and join Hammer on his makeshift go-box. Dirty dancing, I can make J.D. jealous *and* detonate the Pigfuckers' heads.

A little voice cautions me, tells me to hang back. These bounty hunters might be out to score an RTC runaway Twofer. After all, I *was* featured on the side of a milk carton.

"Mami, how would *you* like it if someone put their hand up your ass? You know, they did that to me in there."

We're surrounded by dozens of Adams and Steves who probably think we're dumb twinks, forget about our civil rights. Fuck gay marriage. We need help. *Now.*

"Where did you go?"

"Work," J.D. says. "But Mami, that was two—"

"They said you left early."

"—years ago. What about—"

"Night after night," she says, tone-deaf to J.D.'s words. Their conversation sounds like one between me and my parents. Everybody's talking, nobody's listening.

I move around the column to a spot where I can see "Mami's" face. She's a Latina version of Haifa, my stepmother. For an older lady, she's hot. Tonight, she's dressed to the nines:

red suit, gold hoop earrings and big hair. She's either going to a fund-raiser or dressed as Nancy Reagan.

"*Lies!*" she wails, black eyes narrowed to slits, the j'accuse! look borrowed from a telenovela. *Muy* dramatica. Just like my stepmother, she wants to act out bad soap opera dialogue. Logic, reason and facts are for suckers. These women "win" through emotional display.

"Mi'jo," she says, insect-sized, false eyelashes fluttering. Flirtatious, she places a gnarled hand over his. The diamond ring catches the hard light. I shudder, creeped out. She's worse than the Pigfuckers. J.D. can't see it, but he must sense it. His hand jerks back. This telenovela's episode is "Bed-time for Oedipus at Mickey D's—Hello, Jocasta!" "I'm your ma—"

"Not anymore!"

"I *knew*"—she hisses, enraged by his "rejection"—"where you were going!"

"What? That stupid club?"

"Mi'jo!" she says, sweetly, switching personalities the same way *The Exorcist* girl's head spun 360 degrees.

"It's not *just* a club," she says. I get the feeling they've had this conversation before. I'm watching a revival of a long-running show, and they're reciting lines off scarred hearts.

"Mami, I like to party! I—"

"They *told* me—"

"Yeah? What'd they *tell* you? Who is they, anyway?"

"—was a *lion's den* of—" She waves her diamond hand toward the street. "*Homosexuality*. Look at them! What do you—"

"People, Mami, I see—"

"No, Mi'jo, you *don't* know—" She pauses, pre–bomb dropping moment. "They just want to *use* you and throw you away after they give you AIDS!"

"Clubs can't give you that."

"This about what I *believe*," she says, bejeweled hand waving away his words. "And until you're eighteen, you'll live by *my* rules."

"Mami, I haven't lived with you for almost *two* years. I

barely—" he says, and I mouth the words, lyrics to a song I know by heart. "Know you."

Mamacita looks away. The window's reflection captures an expression that's a mix of disgust, self-righteousness and sadness. Disgust at her monstrous desire. Self-righteousness over something she can't understand. And sadness over the painful truth of what she's lost.

"You'll never be happy in that 'lifestyle.'"

"Jota. Maricon. Vestida. Taco. Burrito—"

"Such words!" she cries. "Where did you learn them?"

"Luis!" His voice cracks, he shakes his head and looks away. The light catches tears in his brown eyes. "*My* faggot son. Sometimes, I think you sent me away just so the neighbors wouldn't know. How'd you explain? Tell them I died? How will you explain my return? The Immaculate Resurrection?"

"Return? You're—" She catches herself, doesn't say, "not coming back," cautious about alerting J.D. to the Pigfuckers.

"Ai, Mami—"

"Stop calling me that!"

"Okay, how's *Puta*. Dressed like some cheap street hooker's idea of 'classy.'"

"*Cayate*—"

"Mami, since we're spreading our legs so the truth can spill out, answer me this. Who's my father? The real one. Not one of my 'uncles.' Do you even know?"

"This is *why!*" she cries. "You lie. You lie."

"I watched you pick them up. Married—"

"*Nev*—"

"*Yes*. One time in a Denny's, I saw you uncross your legs, flash him and stand, knowing—*knowing*—that he'd follow—"

Jeweled hands fly to her ears, eyes shut and lips press together, watertight. He reaches across the table, pries her hands off her ears, pinning her wrists to the table.

"Every time you say—you *claim*—you know 'what' I am, I feel like you're talking about an alien species. Lady, I know exactly what *you* are. A telephone number palmed off. Twenty minutes later, on your cell. An hour later, three hundred dollars to 'see' the bedroom."

"I want my boy back," she rasps.

"Who's my father?"

She shakes her head. Black, mascara-stained tears run down her face.

"*Why*, Mami, if you can't be honest about that, why'd you do that to me? Did you know what they'd do? Am I—really even—your son? I mean," he pleads. "Do you even know who he is?"

"Because . . ." She struggles to speak having tossed the bad-faggot-you'll-just-get-AIDS-and-die script. She reaches out. He pulls back. "I wanted you to go to the seminary! Become a priest! Our hope! Yes, *our* hope. There's time. You can save *us!* You can save *yourself!* You—"

Cue, Pigfuckers.

Chapter 73

The men push back their parkas. They're both armed—handcuffs, interrogation hoods and syringes—ready to end the Addamses' family reunion.

Hammer jumps up and busts a series of high-speed, go-go boy moves. He's the whirling dervish of male strippers, a combination of the Tasmanian Devil and Fabio. Mamacita stares, horrified and aroused. The crowd moves toward the "show," a clusterfuck that slows the Pigfuckers. Jackets back, they're ready to go: plastic handcuffs, mace and hood. I guess people are so jaded by American Torture, nobody blinks. Rendition? Black Ops? Who cares.

"*See* what I mean?" She points to Hammer.

J.D. turns and glances at Hammer. Calm, he turns back.

"Right," J.D. says. "Coz this is church."

"Excuse me?" She looks at him, startled to see and hear him speak. In her world, Hammer's behavior is a conversation stopper. In our world, it's, "*Heeeeyyyyyy! Let's get this party started!*"

"When I called mi abuela," J.D. says.

"Don't call me that. I'm your madre."

"Madre, smadre," J.D. taunts. "Elena—"

"Is *not!*" she spits, hatred cracks her face.

Elena. I've heard the name before. Then, I remember. Elena

was the Latina half of the superdyke duo who rescued me back in the desert.

"This was Luis's," she said, handing me the brass buckle. I just assumed she meant her brother—not her son. Impossible. I couldn't have met J.D.'s mother in the desert, a lipstick lesbian with a crazy stripper girlfriend. But then, I never thought I'd live "underground" like a runaway slave.

"What did you tell her? Did you tell her they shocked my penis? Showed me pornographic pictures?"

The Pigfuckers have pushed through the crowd. I wait for Mamacita to end the scene. It's their cue to yank J.D. off the stage. OH. NO. I realize, I'm the deluded one. I've been watching J.D. with his mother like they were a show. She had me sitting on the edge of my seat. The drama, the heat, the . . . reality. J.D.'s about to get caught.

"You can make this easy—" Pigfuckers grab J.D., pinning his arms back and pulling on the hood. They drag him toward the door. "Or you can make this hard."

J.D.'s kicking and screaming, but he's no match for Pigfuckers taller—fatter—asses.

I grab the tiny hammer, break the glass next to the EMERGENCY door. I pull the handle down. The alarm rings, *WUNH! WUNH! WUNH!*

"*GET YOUR FUCKING HANDS OFF ME!!!*" J.D. screams, his voice louder than the blaring alarm and Halloween Happy Meals loop.

Thirteen whipples turn to look. Mamacita's eyes widen. She sees bearded men with clown white faces, glitter lipstick, gaudy Lacroix crosses—all dressed as nuns.

While the—mostly gay—crowd stands and passively watches J.D.'s abduction, the whippled ladies are lawbreakers and shit-kickers who *act*. As in action. Forget waiting for answers to your prayers, the sisters provide immediate assistance. The orange tabletop eating area becomes a blur of black robes, fishnets and flashing dicks.

Hammer leaps and lands *Thunk!* in a crouched position atop J.D.'s table. He grabs his package and sticks out his tongue, serpent style. Mamacita tries to disguise her hot and botheredness with "horror." I'm sure, if this goes on long enough, she'll pop her handbag and tip him a buck—or, slip him her number. Hammer hops off the table, stands behind Pigfuckers and reaches around their pinheads.

SSSSSSSSSHHHHHHHH

Pepper spray. "Hot sauce with Pigfucker Eye." Ming's Special, next week.

"Ahhhh!" Pigfuckers scream, hands to faces, fingers clawing eyes. J.D. wriggles his arms away from Pigfucker #1 and escapes. Pigfucker #2, eyes squeezed shut, holds on to J.D. Blind, he's determined to leave with his package. Pigfucker must have a drug habit or owe back taxes. Pepper spray *hurts.*

"Let go!" the chorus of man-nuns trill. A man-frocked mass—church, flash mob style—they block the exit and peel the Pigfuckers off J.D.

Pigfucker #1 looks at me with swollen, red eyes.

"Ahmed!" he shouts.

Ahmed? Who's that? I don't know any Ahmeds. Does he mean, Ah-men? Or, Ah-choo? I'm Ben. Then I realize. Pigfucker's seen *me!* Called me by my real name and—

He grabs me.

Oh. So this *is* a twofer. That *was* the plan. Ahmed & J.D. Easy, breezy and Pigfuckers are 100K richer. I'm happy for Pigfuckers. They're entrepreneurs. They *deserve* the J.D. & Ahmed jackpot. I bet the combined revenues from our capture will buy them three years in Thailand with enough money to molest dozens of twelve-year-olds virgins.

My family's in on this. I bet Haifa's worked some insurance scam: recapture or refund. I'm flattered she's bet on me.

Tiny problem.

I don't care.

I'm sick of "the struggle."

Besides, I kind of deserve this. I was dumb enough to walk into their trap (and, worse, stayed when I could have left).

I feel helpless. My determination to move Pigfucker #1 and 2 off J.D. doesn't translate to me. I give up. Numb is a hugely underrated state of being. I *know* I'll never manage to worm my wrist away from this guy's grip. He'd break it before he lets go. I'm money in the bank. There's nothing I can do.

Except—

Open my mouth, tilt forward and sink my teeth into Pigfucker #1's wrist. I bite . . . *hard*. I draw blood.

"Arrrgggghhhh!" I snarl, a real live Wild Thing. *"Arrrgg hhh!"*

Pigfucker screams. I think, we should forget this abduction stuff and form a band. Primal Scream, the sequel. He holds me tight. He lifts me up and carries me to the door, The Child Bride. I look back. My eyes meet J.D.'s.

Crack!

A switchblade pops.

"Over here!" J.D. shouts.

Pigfucker turns and slams my body sideways against the door frame. I grab the door—leverage, anything to escape. My will to survive has come back. Pigfucker's left hand dropped and clutches his butt—J.D.'s stabbed his fat ass.

Logically, this would be my chance to escape. No, Pigfucker's right arm holds me tight, carrying me off like some ogre waltzing away with the princess.

Hammer drops to the ground and slips, unseen, in-between Pigfucker's legs. Pigfucker walks into Hammer's flat hands. Contact. Pigfucker sways, a human Leaning Tower of Pisa, and crashes back. I go with, and his head hits the floor, *thump*.

I squirm, try to get free, but Pigfucker's grip is absolute.

"Faggot!" he rages. Oh. He's mad about being humiliated by a bunch of men dressed like nuns and a teenage go-go boy. Metal grazes my left wrist. Pigfucker struggles to shut the handcuffs.

Fuck it. Forget it. I give up. I'm not going anywhere. If he wants me this bad, I'll let him.

"LET HIM GO!" J.D. jumps on Pigfucker. He growls, werewolf style, and straddles Pigfucker's thighs. He raises the switchblade, holding it to Pigfucker's crotch.

"No, please," Pigfucker begs, terrified.

J.D. unzips Pigfucker's pants. His hand dips inside and pulls out the saddest, droopiest-looking pair of balls. *"Cajones!"* J.D. laughs, cackling. "Eh, vato, don't *ever* touch another kid. Cuz *next* time, I'll cut off your pinga."

Zip! Another horror movie scream, Pigfucker drops me, his face squeezed tight. He grabs his balls. Blood spurts. Well, it *is* Halloween.

I take J.D.'s hand. Now we can go splash like water nymphs in the fountains outside the library.

"AHMED!"

Oh, Allah. Now what.

Hands grab my shoulders. Pigfucker #2's grabbed me and J.D.

I panic. I leave. I run. Spring out the door. I don't care. I don't look back. I've learned *that* lesson. I've remade my DNA. Escape is in my blood.

Blind, I run. I push my way through the crowds until there's real distance. *Space* between me and the Pigfuckers, loca Mamacita, the male nuns and J.D. I decide far is far enough when the smell of weed and carne asada carts overpowers McDonald's beef tallow fries. Only then do I look back for J.D. Did he make it out? Is he following me?

I don't see him, only loca Mamacita, her ravaged face and confused eyes. My backward glance doesn't turn her into a pillar of salt.

My body moves forward, toward an invisible horizon.

I run. I need to run. I need to run until I'm safe.

And then, before I know it, everything's gone, the crowds have thinned and I wander the streets, alone.

Chapter 74

I get my wish. Now I'm free to stare, look at anyone for as long as I want. Everyone's a target. I spring my inner voyeur. I look and look and look until my eyes are exhausted.

I realize I hate being alone. Worse, I feel like everyone looks at me. I probably look like what I am. A runaway.

I turn, try to find my way to the McDonald's. It's gone. I'm lost. I'd go back to the safe house, but I don't know where it is.

I look for signposts and landmarks: Hammer's tall, shimmery form or J.D.'s black cape. Count Dracula's spawned hundreds of doppelgängers. I tap a few dozen capes.

"J.D.? J.D.? J.D.?"

They turn and I face . . . J.D.'s cousin / brother / uncle.

Cold, I press my forearms together, hold them up to my heart and try to warm my body. I spy a spot between two cars. I sit. It's warm here. I sit above a steam vent.

Chapter 75

Saddam and I sat in the car, inching toward the TO GO window. Forty-five minutes ago, we'd arrived in a "new" city. Except, nothing is new. It's the same strip mall, chains and fast-food joints.

That year, I was thirteen. American Bedouin, we'd moved every other month for years. Cleveland, Fort Lauderdale, Silicon Valley. My father was a computer engineer, proudly selling his skills to the highest bidder. "Our" life was a series of tract houses, ex-wives, and hotel rooms. One day, I realize, moving isn't about money but memory. Sadaam's attempt to erase the past, more specifically, my mother.

That day, I was exhausted. We'd driven all night. The hotel room wasn't ready. We were "killing time." Our turn, the car rolled up to the window. Saddam thrust a furry forearm out the window. Sausage fingers exchanged $7.99 for two XXL milkshakes, fries, and double cheese with everything whatever dead horse / cat / dog byproduct hamburger.

I sat in the backseat. From there, I saw his eyes flicker down and left, about to eye fuck the girl's tits. But then he saw something else, a name tag. "Mary." He never knew where she'd turn up. That moment, it was the girl in the white uniform with the red cone hat and pretty smile.

"Cunt," he raged, gunned the car and drove straight to the

freeway. He drove, demanding she come back, suck his cock, be his whore. She never did. Didn't call or write. Wherever she'd gone, she stayed there. She sat in the shadows and drove him completely insane.

He'd tossed the food over the seat. He forgot I was there. The milkshake exploded on my lap, the burgers split and fries scattered like matchsticks. *Click.* I was locked inside. He hadn't forgotten me. He held on to me. Bait. So long as I'm nearby, he might lure her back and destroy her. The way he wasn't able to the first time.

Up until now—or, thirteen months ago—I was a stand-in. A prop. For his rage. Rage over the one fact he cannot change. She left. She left him. He never says it. My presence causes him pain. I'm a visible, constant reminder—of the day she stood at the front door, turned the handle and walked out. She chose. Most of all, he hates her choice. And still, there was nothing he could do. No way to stop her from turning him into a raving beast.

Until, quiet as she'd vanished, she used the mail to sneak back into my life. I opened the envelope. Three items fell out. Photo, envelope, money. Mona Lisa's daughter taught me: Survival sits square on silence that's hard and smooth as black marble. Don't give in. Keep quiet. There are no guarantees, Ahmed, but if you listen, read between the lines of invisible ink, you have a chance. You might live.

Hand to neck, I open the locket and remove the photo. I stare at the image. Tonight, if I saw her, would I recognize her? Walking by, is she that woman? Or, that one?

Saddam left the job. He never bothered to call. He said, "I never quit because I never started." That's when I knew. He was *spooked.* My mother was everywhere. She haunted him and drove him crazy with her spectral presence because *there was nothing he could do.*

Chapter 76

"Get up," my inner voice says. "Time to go."
I stand, careful to avoid the bumper, and walk. I don't
have a clue where to. Cold and alone, I recall my theory of soci-
ological physics. Tonight's been an excellent illustration of the
theory. It goes: "for every wonderful social encounter, there's an
equal and horrible opposite."

I believe humanity's plastered onto a cosmic Rubik's Cube.
We don't know it, but everyone's all stuck on one of nine
squares. Each of us hopes some "invisible" force (The One who
turns the cube) will match up our other squares and create a
solid color panel. (Or, Nirvana.)

"Ahmed?"

Who dares to call me by my name?

"Ben!"

I don't think.

I run.

"Wait!" cries the voice—not the one in my head—and I slow.
"It's me!"

"Me" grabs my hand, spins me around and gives me a sweet
kiss. I'm confused, but I don't resist.

"J.D.?"

He pulls my hand.

"C'mon, we're late!"

In seconds, we rejoin the crowd and merge into the flow.

"*What*," I demand, "the *eff* were you thinking? Back there? With the scary Latina Lady in Red?"

"Scary, that's funny." He doesn't laugh. "Forget it."

Up ahead, Hammer waits on a corner, sole propped against an octagon-shaped YIELD sign. He sees us, and pushes off. J.D. and I follow his enormous muscle ass. I keep my eyes fixed on the white G-string dividing his Clydesdale buttocks and tiny waist.

Hammer's Ass serves as our personal lighthouse. So long as I can see it, I know we're heading somewhere. A destination.

The Gay Moses, Hammer, parts the crowd. People stop and stare at his scandalous getup and flawless body. Flashbulbs pop, people whistle. They ignore us. We're the entourage for The Halloween Prom King.

I tap into my fortune teller genes (crystal ball, Ali Bababulous, lacquered lids, my inner *I Dream of Jeannie*) and predict: "In twenty years, people will look at these Halloween pictures. They'll add a digital fade feature or 3-D'ize it and, for the first time, notice the boys walking behind the Go-Go God—and say, Look at those beautiful boys."

"What?" J.D. says. Even if he heard my prediction, I doubt he'd understand it. I've cast us in the past while living in the present. Sentimental memories aren't in J.D.'s wheelhouse.

Another corner. We turn and walk down a narrow side street. We join the pilgrimage of beautiful freaks. A Kofi roll on a Nefertiti-shaped head; glossy boy lips slide off a mouth like rainbow-colored push-up Popsicles.

"Where are we going?" I ask. "Or is that another surprise?"

"Center of the Universe," he says, ignoring my dig.

I hear the club before I see it. Loud bass rumbles underfoot. Closer, blue lights twinkle, scattered like fairy dust on the dull gray pavement. We stand outside a three-story brick building.

"That's it. You dance?"

"Sure," I lie. Really, for me, dancing's a big, Huh? I'll fake it. Belly dance my way down the dance floor.

At the door, Hammer turns and waves. We walk to the front of the line. Security give us the nod, and we step inside.

"I love it."

"Yeah, the music's totally on," J.D. says, pulling my hand. If I live in a past that hasn't yet happened, he's somewhere else, too. Here.

I smile, don't bother to explain I love our Lolito and the Bandit act. It trumps the law, age of consent, everything be damned.

Chapter 77

We walk down a slanted ramp into white fog. Churning colored lights turn the white to blue and pink and yellow. Giant fans suck up the fog, creating a rainbow-colored tornado.

"Dude, we're not in Kansas no more!" J.D. shouts over the loud music. I doubt L. Frank Baum knew Oz would become the philosophical foundation and color swatch for a rainbow nation.

Next stop, the igloo room, a frosty pass-through with walls made of blue glass bricks and metallic icicles hanging from the ceiling.

The music stops.

"But I don't hear no music!" a boy whines over the PA. "Ohhhh, that's better! Turn it up! I'm waiting for the music and then I can feel it."

The music kicks in.

Over it, the voice loops, "*Work me, work me, work me—*"

We must be closer to the dance floor: instinct, J.D. moves. His limbs and torso catch the beat.

"Here." J.D. puts out his right hand. Two tiny, white pills sit in his palm. "Want?"

I shake my head.

"Trust," he says, "you'll love it."

"Thanks, but I don't want to trip tonight."

"Whatever." He shrugs.

Truth is, even if it's J.D., I'm tired of people giving me pills and making me feel the way *they* want me to feel.

We turn another corner to face a vast grotto. The dance floor's huge, three football fields. And packed. Rave on, children!

Overhead, a galaxy of blinking lights dance and pulsate. Music comes at us from every direction. Now I know how captive dolphins feel. My ears quiver.

"See?!" J.D. says, his voice swallowed up by the artificial cosmos. "The center of the universe!"

"Typical Western decadence," Moustapha would sneer.

"The Milky Way!" I mouth. Even though, in space, nobody can hear you scream. Or, talk.

Boom! Boom! Boom!

The music's simple, a four-four beat headache. I might need to reconsider the white pill. It could help me get through the night.

Hammer appears and hands us bottled waters.

"Laters!" he shouts, spinning off, a Sun God ISO satellites and stardust.

Again, J.D. holds out an open palm with pills. Tempting.

I shake my head and mouth, "No, thank you."

"It's a party! Let's party!"

He might be right. I calculate the odds. The club's big. But so's the world, and it hasn't exactly been "safe." If I take the pill and lose my mind, the club's an enclosed space. I can't wander off or get lost.

I take it. Looking in one another's eyes, we pop the pills, tilt the bottles and swallow. And . . . I feel nothing. I knew it. Aspirin. The water bottle triggers a memory of being—

Whoosh! My heart opens up. Springtime in my chest. Ten million flowers blossom. All my pain and hopelessness and fear drops away and I'm left with one feeling—

Love

I look at J.D. and send him my love. I project my love up, to the lights. I hope they'll catch my love and spread it around this beautiful universe. The lights do what I wish and spread my love, Magick Milky Way butter slid over layers of everything— J.D., the guy next to me, Hammer dancing on a box and all souls gathered here in the dark.

Dancing's easy. My body moves, effortless. J.D. and me inch closer to the true center of this miniature universe. My feet feel light. I look down: We hover, a few feet above the floor. No magic carpet, just the ride. J.D. steps forward, his smile forming the words:

I've watched your face for a long time

On the first—

love

He spins away—

love

I'm excited. I want to tell him I *feel* it.

love

And on

—us

The song brings him back. Hand out, finger-shaped molecules touch my shoulder, caress my chest, travel down to my hip. He teases me, seduces me. I move to him, ready to surrender.

He steps away, his body plucking petals from the flower of my heart. "He loves me? He loves me not?" He spins me around and 'round in his arms. Maybe it's the pill, maybe it's him. He's gone, I'm back inside the song and J.D.'s a satellite, spun far, far away from my orbit. His cosmic coming and going has wound me up.

I wonder. "Romance?" Is it something like teetering over a spiked iron fence post? Or, crossing a rotten drawbridge over a moat stocked with hungry alligators? Am I ready to leap? Or, am I in free fall—

love

into J.D.'s arms? Will he be there to catch me? If I should fall? Or, am I about to land in ravenous, razor-sharp jaws. End up chewed to bits, swallowed and spit out.

The music quickens. J.D.'s back. I know this even though my eyes are shut. Because I feel him, his warmth. His red heart light burns bright in his chest. His brown skin slides over me. He leans toward me, lips brushing my left ear, and whispers, "Mi'jo, like this."

Hands on my waist, he moves my hips. I belong to him.

"Move, yeah, like that, good."

Joined at the hips, we move as one with the song.

I know, this whole thing's a joke. I expect him to leave with a laugh.

But this time, he doesn't leave. He stays. He stops. I stop. We stop. We stand still. Our bodies vibrate, still moving to the music. He takes my head in his hands and leans toward me. Eyes closed, lips pursed, ready to kiss.

"He loves me . . . he loves me not."

And why not? All I have to lose is my heart.

I part my lips. His tongue jumps inside. I feel a warm, flickering flame. It lights the tiny cave. His eyelashes flutter, and butterflies land on my cheeks.

My hand drops and lands on his back. My fingertips trace the muscles, following the path down, into his ass crack. Our lips part, I close my eyes and rest my body against his.

"Abre los ojos."

Chapter 78

Iopen my eyes
And see

Giant mirror balls spinning, throwing off light. Rainbow-colored explosions. I peer into infinity. Gaze into forever.

We stand at the center of the universe. Eye witness to everything. Birth. Death. Creation. Destruction.

Blackout

Silence

The crowd takes a breath, thousands of souls pulling in prana, life.

Time stops

Limbo, we hang between a vast nothing and mysterious something

Time stops

Beauty Horror Love Death Hope Fear

Eternity reveals

Everything and its opposite.

I look back, into the past. Forward, into the future. I lift my arms, and reach. I stand on the midline. A current—time—runs through my body.

Everything and Its Opposite.

I am

Pop!

White

Flash!

A line shoots across the top of the room. A white horizon equal to the Universe. The white turns into greenpurpleorangeredyellow and fades to Sunset. Night. Dawn. Oranges, yellows, pinks.

J.D. and I hold one another. We sway. We're not alone. Other hidden ones join us. Tonight, we walk among faeries, angels, demons and ghosts. Creatures, many inhuman.

I could dance for hours. I'll never tire. The pill amplifies the feeling. Ecstasy. Spills over the edge. The moment of. Consciousness.

Reality steps up, cuts in.

"Hey," I say. "I need to pee."

J.D.'s mouth moves. Huh? I shrug, I'm deaf. He points, Up, UP. Someone's stolen the sound. What was speeded up has slowed down and become silent. Is this. Mental telepathy. Astral projection. The fifth dimension.

"I need to . . ." I want to say, but the words fall away.

"I know!" J.D. yells. "I'm taking you there!"

He tugs my hand, leads me off the dance floor. Away from the cosmic center. Buddha's belly button. Bathroom, I don't see the point. I resist. I don't want to go. I want to stay. Get lost in the music. Dance, forever and ever and ever. I wonder if the club's open until then.

Chapter 79

Dimly lit, the bathroom's vast, a rectangle bookended by red walls lined with mirrors and black floors. Stalls with silver metal doors opposite a long row of silver sinks.

We step into the hall of mirrors. Five hundred thousand faces. Our reflections, faces brushed with sweat, glassy eyed from gazing into infinity.

A gentleman, J.D. opens a stall, ushers me inside.

"I'll wait for you."

I'm filled with bliss and gratitude. The stall is *incredible*. Music filters into the space. I close my eyes. Swaying. Still moving. Happy.

My bladder threatens to burst. It knocks me out my trance-dancey-ectasy-haze. I'm gonna pee my pants if I don't take care of business. In the cosmic scheme of things, I could wet my pants and it wouldn't matter. However, I don't want to smell like piss.

Unzip, *UNZIP!* The space station's about to explode. I need to eject. Frantic, I search for the zipper. Anita must have put one in. I search my crotch, hips and—there it is—on the ass. I squat-hover. The pill didn't take away my bacterial phobia.

Done, I stand and reach for the door. Before I step out, I pause and look through the crack. Habit? Maybe. The last time I was in a bathroom stall, I saw—oh, never mind.

J.D.'s head. No biggie except—he's kissing—a girl? *Feeling her up*. The girl's head tilts, back, turns to the side. I see her face: Pony.

I close my eyes. No. This can't be. Another murder. Only this time, the knife's been stuck in my heart.

Fumbling, I open the door. My emotions have switched. Adrenaline surge. I'm ready to run. Or, fight. Yeah, I'll confront Pony. Thrown down. Fuck. Him. Up.

I open the door. The love is gone.

"Hey!"

J.D. turns, looks.

"Hi." He smiles. He's alone. My blood runs hot. I look for Pony. I'm ready to fight. Or, fuck. Something. My body's all messed up.

He reaches out, fingertips tracing my face. "What's wrong?"

"I—" I can't say what's wrong. I'm embarrassed. "Nothing. Let's go back."

He takes my hand. His natural warmth melts my hard heart. I never knew: Anger's not hot, but cold.

Am I so high that maybe—*maybe*—I *imagined* I saw the kiss? Or, did I just see what I *wanted* to see?

Chapter 80

We climb a narrow flight of stairs, following a trail of sweat. At the top, we step out a tiny door and onto a rooftop. It's overrun with plants, flowers, ferns. I should feel safe in this garden of earthly delights. But my vertigo swells. I swallow to push down the barf.

J.D. leads, and I follow him to the edge. A matchbook-sized ledge separates us from the city. Slip and there's nothing to grab. Vast, the city's a tidal wave of twinkling lights.

I turn away and back, toward Eden. Miniature orange trees are wrapped in snowflake lights. Buddha fountains gurgle. Loungey chill music tumbles out hidden speakers. Nearby, the blue-green pyramid and its rising columns of colored lights.

"You like?" J.D. stands behind me and wraps his arms around my waist.

So many mixed feelings. I can't answer. He is with *me*, not Kidd or Pony. "Remember," I tell myself, "back in the McDonald's he *did* cut off Pigfucker's balls and risk his life to save you."

"Yeah," I say. His head rests on my shoulder, the same way it did in the bathroom, after Anita dyed my hair. I smile. It feels fake but looks real enough to hide my distrust. "I like it a lot."

He lets me go and walks to the edge of the roof. His legs dangle over the dead drop. I join him, and sit, a few feet away, back against a concrete square. The bass vibrates under my palms.

"Look"—I say, running my fingers over a web of tiny cracks—"at what the music's done."

J.D. leans away from the edge and kisses my neck. "How d'you feel?"

"Great." I smile, this time for real. The night's too short to hold a grudge. 'Sides, I can't remember what it is I'm holding on to. I let it go. A kiss. That's no crime. Besides, we're out of our minds. High on the Love Drug. "*Amazing.*"

"I knew you'd love it."

I lean toward him, take his hand and pull him to me. I don't want to leave. I refuse to sit on the edge. He comes to me. I could lie here, like this, his body against mine. We don't need the fake universe. We have the real one overhead.

"Look, all those stars."

"Inside?" he says, and jumps up, antsy. "One more spin on the dance floor!"

I crack up. My laughter infects him. We collapse on one another, overcome with the giggles. But under my happy exterior, I've cooled. I watch. I know I can say anything and he'll do or say what I want. It's so obvious, he wants to please me. He wants something, and there's not a long list of things I have to offer.

He kissed another boy behind my back—*and thought I wouldn't see.* Even so, I want to join my good, pure part with his good, pure part. I see them. They're a perfect fit.

I remove my cool gaze, step forward and join him. Bound to end? Maybe. I might be settling for something less than love. I'm aware, our dreams are drug induced. I haven't felt this good in months, for over a year. It's been so long. I didn't notice, but one day I forgot how to feel good. Tomorrow, true, I might wake up hung over or brokenhearted. Right now, I crave happiness. Yes. I decide. It's worth it. I'll pay the price.

Chapter 81

"One more, baby," J.D. raps under his breath, anxious to leave and return to the dance floor. His thumbs press my lower back, palms over my butt, fingers fanned over my waist. Behind me, he guides us back to the dance floor. Overhead, the lights shift, ceiling filled with upside down synchronized swimmers.

Here, it's ground zero of the *queer* universe. We're surrounded by bouncing boys with glistening bare chests. Ethereal hippy chick girls and dark-eyed gypsies. Swirling, they churn the air, skirts blown out, gold jewelry lighting up the air, fingers throwing thunderbolts.

Our universe is filled with happiness and laughter. Mouths part, teeth flash, wet dreads flay. Feathers flutter, slick bodies glitter with gold dust.

"*We are family*," blares on the speakers. The crowd sings along, raising their arms and a mass of handheld lighters, flames flickering in dark. The song makes me eyeball the club. My temporary family is present and accounted for. Abduction free. Over there, Kidd and Hammer share a go-go box, get down and make out. Maybe Kidd's moved on. Maybe I'll be able to stop worrying about watching my back. Anita—she's on a box, absolute center of the dance floor. She shares the square with The Flaming Minora. Their lips are locked in a passionate kiss. All that's left is ménage à trois: Peanuts, Marci and Pony. Three sistas, just like the song.

I lean toward J.D. "What's that song?"

"Disco classic." J.D. gestures at the crowd. "For a queer monster mash-up. Gotta love a room filled with circuit queens, skin heads and diesel dykes and femme bots. Forget Gay Pride, Halloween's the shit!"

BAM!

Lights out—

Pitch black—

Overhead, another flash of white light, bright as an atom bomb and—

"Noel!" an announcer's voice booms.

Spotlight blinks, ON, and hits a towering black woman. Anita's Auntie? She walk / floats across the stage. White fabric's draped over her gleaming, mahogany skin. Her Macy's Day Parade–sized afro's back lit, a follicular rainbow.

Wind-blown, the material flutters, Noel opens her mouth and she sings. A forest filled with morning bird song. A snap, crackle, pop. Beauty, funk, harmony, edge. Noel's voice takes me there.

Mesmerized, J.D. stares at her like he's seen the second coming of the first Madonna. Overhead, giant TVs come to life. Our faces—mine and J.D.'s—appear. On-screen, every single image is . . . *us*. We're larger than life. Eros and Apollo.

The screen blinks, wipes us away. Blue eyes blink. I know those eyes. I scan the crowd. There. Him. Pony. He stands on a balcony and points to the crowd. Beside him, the man's gaze searches for us. Our eyes lock. My blood runs cold. I'm suddenly sober. It's him. Blue-Eyed Bob.

"C'mon!" I say, pulling on J.D.'s hand.

He ignores me. Oblivious, eyes shut, he dances, lost in the music.

"We need to leave!" I plead. Blissed out, he smiles, ignores my warning. Think. What are the words that will make him leave with me.

"Pigfuckers—"

He dances, stuck in a trance. I grab his shoulders and shake him, hard.

"The bounty hunters, they're *here*."

"What?"

"The bounty hunters, the Pigfuckers, they're here, coming to get us."

"Where."

"Up—up there!" I shout, and point to the balcony. J.D. looks with interest equal to a groggy freshman on spring break.

Pony and Blue-Eyed Bob are gone.

Chapter 82

"Where is everybody?"

Frantic, J.D. looks for our crew.

"They—" I say.

Blue-Eyed Bob's on the dance floor and headed straight toward us.

"Fuck them!" J.D. pulls out his switchblade. It pops open. He's looking for the Pigfuckers. I try to grab it. He turns on me. "What the fuck?"

"Put it away. Security sees you with that, they'll kick us out *and* call the cops."

I move him off the dance floor toward the igloo. He staggers and weaves, mumbling, "Don't wanna, don't wanna leave."

"Hey, mister, me neither." He stops. I pull. He won't budge. "Listen, there's always next year."

"You love me?" He looks at me with big, puppy dog brown eyes.

" 'Course I do." I say anything to rescue him, even if it means lying. (Or, telling the truth earlier than I planned.)

"You do?" he slurs, waving the switchblade. "Do you?"

"Sure, I—"

"*Sure?* What the fuck is *sure?!?*" he cries. "*Do you love me?!*"

"Yes," I say, quiet, backing away, forcing him to step forward. "Love."

He takes the bait and follows. I'm a bullfighter with red cape, I rattle off silly stuff. Nonsense, it's mumblecore manipulation.

"What about you?"

We near the exit. I look back. A shadow darkens the igloo wall. Blue-Eyed Bob is close, a homing pigeon, knife in its beak.

"Yeah," J.D. says. Shy, he looks down.

"Let's go outside." We can do the homo-romo later. I take his arm, trying to coax him forward. "Come on."

"No!"

"But, baby, if we—"

"What, leave Paradise? Go back to that *shithole*. I don't wanna—"

"Mi'jo!" I pretend I'm talking to a child. Or, a crazy person. "We need to get home before dawn."

"Says who." He pouts.

"Say you!" This is what it must feel like for a straight guy. The logistics of getting laid, and leaving.

"And leave *this?*" He tries pulling me back to the dance floor. Two steps forward, one step back, we're dancing the Tango da Morte. "It's incredible!"

Blue-Eyed Bob's closing in, just around the corner. I smell him. Cigarettes breath and booze. His knife tip pokes down and out his left sleeve.

"Over here." I move us into a corner. J.D. falls onto me, cape draped over us. We're perfectly hidden.

"Mmm," he purrs. Two hands have become twenty, and they run over my body. Sex, yes—

Click

Blue-Eyed Bob's shoes tap on the floor. He stands three feet away from us. J.D. places his palm on my chest.

"Your heart's racing."

"Yes."

"It's like you're so scared, you think you're gonna die."

"It does. I feel like that a lot."

"*Everything*," J.D. slurs, "looks different in the light. When the X wears off, you'll crash. You think you're dead."

"That's what happens?" I say, bland.

"Yeah." He leans toward me. His tongue darts out and licks my neck. My back arches. My foot slides. It kicks something. I'm scared to look. The something might be Blue-Eyed Bob's foot. I force myself, look down and see a mask. I scoop it up and press the white plastic mold to my face.

"It's cold in here," I say, faking a shiver. I look over J.D.'s shoulder. Blue-Eyed Bob's two feet away. "Can I wear your cape?"

He drapes it over my shoulders.

"Where are you taking me," I say. He's in charge. "I wanna go."

J.D. grabs my hand.

"How did I look?"

I pull back and look into J.D.'s eyes, saucer-sized pupils. He smiles, wobbly, and I can tell that he doesn't care. "Your pupils are—"

"*HUUUUGGGGGEEEE!!!*"

"Okay," I tell myself, "he's making a scene. Maybe Blue-Eyed Bob won't notice. Halloween is a scene. Deep breath. Chance it. We need to leave our hiding place if we're going to escape." Blue-Eyed Bob looks at me. I almost faint. Then, I remember, I'm wearing a mask. He can't see my face. I give him a once-over. He came as himself: businessman slash serial kiddie killer.

I clutch J.D.'s hand.

"Let's jet."

Somehow, we make it up the ramp and out the entrance. The crowds spill off the sidewalk onto the street. I want to look back, but I don't dare. I'm afraid I might conjure him up.

"You know the way back?" Mindful, I substitute "home" with "back." I don't want to trigger J.D.'s stubborn side.

"Yeah. It's the special route."

"Okay," I say, docile. Inside, I'm wound up, tight as a spring-loaded bear trap. He takes my hand and squeezes it. I like the feeling. When he held my hand, before, he felt like a tour guide. Sometime during the night, I got made. We're together. An item. I have a boyfriend.

That was easy.

Next comes the hard part.

Keeping him.

Chapter 83

It's the Magic Hour. The air's washed with blue. I look around. I want a pic—

The Pigfuckers stand at the club's entrance, arguing with the bouncers. Badges are flashes, voices are raised. The bouncers don't budge. We're not out of the danger zone. Not yet, far from it. Still, I feel calm. I don't mention the Pigfuckers. Instead of running, I decide we'll play it cool and walk away. By the time they get inside, the party will be over and we'll be long gone.

The morning air's damp and sweet. Our breath makes fog. Another reminder that this moment and every one that follows slips away.

"What?" J.D.'s "I'm high" voice reminds me why drugs are illegal: They deny what the working (money, money, money) world wants you to buy—that life is nothing but sacrifice and working-till-you-drop. Wandering the streets at dawn is for wastrels and losers and runaways.

"Yeah." J.D. smiles. "Easy breezy."

Okay, either I'm hearing things or he can read my mind. Either / or, something's shifted. I feel great, but I worry I've given in to everything I hate and reject. I've got to speak, break the silence in my head.

"Maybe it's not the pill. Maybe we feel good coz we gave ourselves permission?"

"Hell, yeah," J.D. says. "The pill pulls out the mood. But you make the music and love."

"I—" The mask garbles my words. I pull it off and set it down, on the curb. "Will you make me a promise?"

"Sure." He's on autopilot, with me but not. I don't care. What I want to say needs to be said.

"Later. Remind me. Everything's going to be okay. I want to take that feeling into our regular life."

"Aiiight."

He takes me in his arms, spinning me around. He pins me against a wall. The brick cuts my skin. It hurts. The feeling is intense. I love it.

"In the club, I felt everything and its opposite. I mean, if we don't believe in fear, then it doesn't exist? Right? Only love does because—"

He leans forward, quieting me with a kiss.

Chapter 84

The morning air spooks my torso. I shiver. Holding hands, we walk, our path zigzagging through empty city streets. The asphalt's littered with confetti, beer bottles, silk blossom petals and little net wings. An orphaned cigarette sits, perched on a curb. The tips embers wheeze. A swirl of smoke drifts up and away. An engine backfires. Top down, the old Cadillac's packed with screaming queens.

"Hey!" the boys holla. "Need a ride?"

Then, they're gone, a flash of baby blue, pink and silver tail fins. I'm learning what it is to be a couple. We hold hands, but we're alone with our thoughts.

Grrrr, a gear shift grinds. Another car. I turn, look. I'm paranoid: I need to make sure it's a car, not a Halloween creature, lost and stumbling around in the blue light. Until dawn, demons and undead still roam free.

"Pigfuckers on the right. Yellow Hummer."

J.D. looks. The tank car barrels toward us.

"If they can't catch us, will they just run us over?"

"I bet we're worth the same—"

"Dead or alive."

The Hummer closes in, a giant metal bee, Pigfuckers visible through the windshield.

"Should we run?"

"Did they see us?"

The car drives by, a slow blur. Yellow body with black tires, roof and bumper. A bus pulls up. It groans, belches a cloud of black exhaust and stops. The doors swing open.

"Who'd you boys piss off?" the driver asks. "C'mon."

Dazed, we board, and take opposite seats. We sit, staring out the big picture windows. The yellow Hummer bee makes a U-turn, rolls over a concrete roundabout, crushing a stop sign. Last time they came to get me, they drove a Pontiac. I lean back, resigned. I know they'll get us, eventually.

The bus turns left, onto a one-way street. Narrow, it's lined with parked cars. The Hummer can't cut in front. The bus slowly climbs the hill. Fog, white and thick as glue, erases the outside world. The bus pulls up to a curb. The back doors open.

"Go on now, run into the park! I'll wait a few."

"Thanks!"

We jump off the bus.

"Run!"

I'm terrified of getting caught.

I look back.

Lazy, the Pigfuckers stay in the Hummer, laying on the horn. It's all good.

Chapter 85

The park's path takes us deeper into the dense fog. It's perfect cover. J.D. sticks out his tongue.

"What does it taste like?"

"Weird. Try it."

I stick out my tongue. The fog tastes like . . . nothing. Light explodes in front of us. Closer, the source comes into focus. Fireflies. They must be cold, too, because they lead us out of the fog. We pass through the white veil, back to Earth, and down another path. Here, the trees are washed with light, a brighter periwinkle blue. J.D. walks fast. I struggle to keep up. He grabs my hand and pulls me along. We leave the park and walk down another empty street. The city feels like a stage set.

"You know where we're at?"

"Uh-huh."

I don't buy it. He doesn't know anything. Unless he memorized a map before we left the safe house or has a photographic memory, I suspect we're lost. And I worry we're not heading somewhere, just wandering everywhere. Worse, Blue-Eyed Bob lurks around every corner, bush and car.

Blind or stupid, I trust J.D. to find our way back. My thoughts drift back to the bathroom stall and seeing the kiss. Do I forgive J.D. or put him on probation?

We reach an intersection, a fork in the road. J.D. looks both ways. "Huh."

The pill's worn off. I know this because my body's weary. More than fatigue, I feel like I'm on the verge of collapse. My heart, limbs—everything feels woozy. I could lie down, right here, and sleep on the sidewalk. Or, die.

Worse than exhaustion, there's the sunlight. My pupils slam shut. I know, I never got around to asking J.D. what was in those little white pills or how much they cost. But I'm learning there's a price to pay for intergalactic euphoria, music and romance. He warned me. Fool, I should have stuck to "Just Say No."

"Better to have lost and loved," I say.

"What?" J.D. gives me a look.

I was unaware I spoke out. Maybe I am—still—a little bit high. I notice J.D.'s brown skin is pulled back tight on his face.

"Nothing," I say. Mouth shut, finishing the stanza—"Than to have never loved at all"—in my head. It feels heavy as a diving bell, lizard brained. My eyes drill the street, counting steps. We turn, walking down an alley. I expect Blue-Eyed Bob to jump out of the shadows. Abrupt, J.D. turns and shoves me against the wall. I guess this is his "passionate"—date rape—gesture. Take me! I want to tell him, knee cocked and ready to slam his crotch.

"Is that your big move?"

"What?"

"Backing me—" I don't finish. His face comes close to mine, hands all over my body, the scent of his sweet breath—

Chapter 86

Our music video moment. J.D.'s hands cup my face. Around us, the world swirls. His red lips touch mine. Wet, they taste like raspberry and—

He lets me go. The klieg lights and crew scatter.

"What?"

"Not here." He wipes his mouth. I worry, am I the one with bad breath? "Inside."

J.D. jumps, his fingers catch the ladder's bottom rung. He pulls, holding it down with his body weight.

"What? Am I sup—"

"GET ON!" he shouts, face red, veins popping out his forearms.

I jump, and land on the ladder. I just do it. I don't know how, but I do. Last night, I dropped the sum of my fears. We step off and the ladder pops up, guillotine style.

I look at him. He nods, Up. My stomach lurches. I want to barf. Nope. I didn't drop all my fears.

"You can do it, mi'jo, I got your back."

"I can't," I say, unable to move. Paranoia and fear poison whatever's left of my euphoria. I would jump and end it all, but we're not high enough. I'd just break my legs. "No, there's *no* way."

He peers through a glass door. I look over his shoulder. A hallway. He turns the knob. Locked.

"Give me the cape." I do and he takes it, wrapping the material around his fist. He punches the glass. "Fuck!"

"Let me try." I wrap the cape around my ankle, lift my leg and slam my foot. The glass shatters. But I lose my balance and fall forward, into the jagged edges.

"Hey! Careful!" He pulls me back. "Don't cut yourself."

He reaches through the gap, lifts the latch and opens the door.

"After you," he says, ushering me into the hall.

I shake the cape over the street. Glass shards rain onto the ground. The sun turns the pieces into fistfuls of yellow diamonds.

I step forward. J.D. grabs my arm and holds me back. His index finger traces my cheek. Morning light crawls over the fire escape. He pushes me back, against the brick and leans forward, eyes shut, ready to kiss.

I turn away.

"What?" He takes my face, forcing me to look. His eyes are filled with love, lust and betrayal.

All our feelings lurk, just below the surface.

My heart, my skin, my whole being feels raw. And nervous. I want to run away. Sugar couldn't leave. Me, I can't bear to stay. This might be how the safe house leaves its mark: me, forever in flight.

"What?" he says, fingertips under my chin, tilting up my face. He doesn't have a clue, not a single G-D damn clue what I feel.

"I—" I start. But I don't know where, exactly, *to* start. Feelings and thoughts, they're all jumbled up inside. "Let's go."

I look down, avoid his gaze, and push past him. I can't help it. I need to punish him for kissing Pony. Love begets tough because love kills. He needs to learn he can't kiss whoever he wants. But I won't tell him that. He'll have to figure it out.

He leans back against the metal railing. One push. That's all it would take to him flip over and onto the street. I look away. The thought makes me nervous. I scare myself.

" 'k," he says, and sighs. "If you say so."

He squints, looking at me with snake eyes. He smokes. He takes his time; he's got all the time in the world. He places his bet. Ben won't wait. Ben won't go back to the safe house alone.

"I'll meet you up there," I say, calling his bluff. He kills the ciggie, pushes his body off the rail and steps past me. Just like that, he thinks he's put me in my place. I follow him into the hallway. We walk up. Two, three, four flights.

Halloween ends with me, in a zombie state, barely able to keep my eyes open, the walking dead. I try the safe house's door. Locked. I collapse against the wall.

"How do we get inside?"

Sly, J.D. smiles, left hand to ear and earring. He unscrews the ankh. Something drops out. He holds it up: a key. I'd say, Congratulations, but I can't speak. He unlocks the door, picks me up and tosses me over his shoulder. I don't mind. Otherwise, I would have crawled.

He stops, one foot inside, and slides me down, till my feet touch the ground and my body's pressed up, against the door frame. He tries to kiss me. No. I turn away. He needs to learn.

"Oh," I say. Vagueness, I'm aware, drives him nuts. "I'm not sure."

"About *what?*"

"Everything."

"*Everything?* In the club, you said, 'Oh, yeah, baby, I looooovvvvee you.' "

"Dunno." I shrug. I don't have the energy to explain how it's Blue-Eyed Bob, Pony's kiss, the drugs. "The music, the—the, you know, *everything.*"

"The moment."

"Yeah, I guess."

"You guess."

"Me. You. I don't know. I don't know if you really like *me.*" I look him in the eye. "Maybe you just want me for sex."

"Hey," he says, holding my gaze. There's my answer. He does like me. It's no act. I knew it. No wonder I'm so nervous. "What are *you* afraid of?"

"You."

"Afraid of me? Why?"

"I don't know . . . who's the boy, who's the girl?"

"Oh!" J.D. says, with a huge smile. "I can tell you *that*."

"But that's not the *only* thing I'm afraid of."

"Halloween's over," he says and leans forward, Casanova with plastic fangs. "What else scares you?"

We stand, face-to-face, chest-to-chest, crotch-to-crotch. His body pulses, far from being one of the living dead, he's warm, oozing sex and life. Tempting. Young, lean and fine, J.D. flicks a switch, turns on my desire. Still, *I need to know*.

"You being poz."

J.D.'s body goes cold. The smile fades. His eyes shift. He bites his lower lip.

"It's true?"

"No."

"So you're not poz?"

"No."

"If you can't tell me the truth, I don't care if you're the best kisser in the world."

"What do you want to know?"

"Are you HIV-positive? Or aren't you?"

"Let's go inside."

"Sure," I say. I'm casual. But now, nothing is casual.

Chapter 87

J.D. stands outside the kitchen window, leaning against the fire escape. I sit at the table. We're separated by five feet, but it might as well be five million. That's how far apart far apart feels. He lights a cigarette.

"Fear and ignorance." He exhales. "*You* probably think you could get it from kissing me. Or cuddling."

"You can't blame me. Who'd have sex—sex without condoms—knowing it was a death sentence?"

He looks at me and takes in my words. Or, I imagine he does. Maybe I'm more interesting to look at than the wall.

"Everybody acts like they're so cool about it. But they're not. When my other grandma died, my mom freaked out. And *she* was the one who was still alive."

"Didn't you just yell at your mother for telling your grandmother?"

"Yeah, but that was a couple years ago," he says. I almost believe him. "Anyway, *that's* why I don't accept labels or categories. I need to show people that it's *not* a death sentence."

"It's a virus. You either have it or you don't."

"We all have it."

"You *are* positive?"

"Nope."

"You would have sex with me without a condom?"

"Nope." He twists his head, cracks his neck and smokes.

"You know . . ."

"No," he says. He glares at me. "I *don't* know. Tell me."

"Everything and its opposite," I say.

"What?" He looks at me through narrowed eyes.

"Well—" I start, then stop. "I didn't want to say it, because then I'd be calling you a liar." He opens his mouth. I put up a hand. "It's my turn. Half of what you say sounds like a lie. And the other half sounds true. So I'm standing here, looking at these two piles. One pile, lies. One pile, truth. So I made a third pile."

"What's in that?"

"The I-don't-believe-*anything* pile. And—" I can't say it. My pride won't let me. Plus, I'm terrified if I do say it, I'll feel vulnerable to him in a way I can't ever take back. So I muzzle the words. "It doesn't matter, I *still* want you."

J.D. flicks the ciggie, and it flies out, into space. He doesn't give it a glance. I watch it fall. He ducks under the window, into the kitchen. Inside, his left leg swings over the chair. He stands, crotch level with my chest. He looks down, mouth turned up at the sides. I gaze up into his eyes. Morning light hits the yellow flecks. Gold in green pools. I fall under his spell. Thing is, I *know* I'm falling. Hypnotist or magician, J.D. doesn't need words to get what he wants. He smiles, sexy and seductive, "You wanna."

"*Sleep*," I groan. "All I want is sleep."

"Go," he says, swinging his leg over and off the chair. He walks away. I miss you. "Don't flatter yourself," his body language says, "I don't want you anyway."

I know—*know*—he's manipulating me, but I still want him. My body—it must be chemical. I've lost control. My legs—not me—stand and follow. I catch his arm.

"Really? You know you don't want to."

"You don't know what I want," he says, and pulls away. Like that, we've switched roles. Now he's the one who plays hard to get.

"I don't know what you want, because you won't tell me the truth," I say, and let him go.

"Really." He walks to the bathroom and turns over the sign. OCCUPIED. I wait. He leans back, beckoning me with a look.

I step into the dark. He lights candles and runs the water, scattering powder for a bubble bath. Steam rises off the water and fills the cold room.

"Well?"

I nod.

He shuts the door.

Chapter 88

I look in the mirror, check my hair. When I turn back, J.D.'s naked. He puts out a hand and pulls me close. I don't resist. He reaches around my body and unzips. I let him peel off the skin-tight pants. I stand there, naked. But I feel more than nude.

His left toe dips in the tub. I mirror his movement, and dip my right toe. Mute, our bodies mime one another. Tell one another what the other wants. Till we stand, water knee high, in the tub. We kneel, submerging ourselves, sinking down until we've disappeared under the bubbles.

I lean back. He holds up a sea sponge.

"Close your eyes."

He squeezes. Warmth floods my face, neck and shoulders. It dissolves the layers of night. Washes away makeup, sweat and smoke. My weariness slides off. I reawaken. He reaches out, over the tub.

Click

A horn, mournful and low, fills the room. It swirls, a dancing genie freed from her bottle. Drums join the horn. Chills run down my spine, legs, out my feet. A woman's voice, low and mournful, comes forth and sings.

Take this kiss upon the brow
And, in parting from you now,

Thus much let me avow—
You are not wrong, who deem
That my days have been a dream;
Yet if hope has flown away
In a night, or in a day,
In a vision, or in none,
Is it therefore the less gone?
All that we see or seem
Is but a dream within a dream.

Her voice fades, the horn goes crazy and J.D.'s body moves up, his tongue running over my skin. Song matches music, and pleasure with sensation. *Held*, now I understand. J.D.'s hands are strong, gentle, knowing. His touch lacks fear—of my body or desire. Everything is possible. He's bold. I can follow him into the dark, and know I'm safe. J.D.'s arm holds me, his embrace ties me to this moment and each one that follows.

"Am I dreaming?"

"Yes," he whispers. "We dream together."

I get lost in him. The feeling of water and warmth. Reality and imagination blur. He slides under me. His hands—big, square, certain—hold my hips. His lips brush my ear.

"I'm real," he says, pressing himself, rock hard, against my ass. He pushes. Inside. He wants to enter me.

"You got a condom?"

He reaches over the edge of the tub and rolls himself over, his body on top of mine.

"Here," he says, and hands me the rubber.

My teeth tear the wrapper, I slide it out and roll it on. He leans forward and pushes back. I enter him. It happens without effort. Our bodies are a perfect fit. I know what to do. How much and how fast.

"Ah!" he cries, hands gripping the tub. Ass arched, his body pushes back, demanding, "Take me."

"You feel so good," I rasp. My voice catches. I shut my eyes. I want to feel. He gives himself to me. Completely. He tightens his body. I caress him. I want to know him, every inch of him.

His smooth skin. His body is the new world. A landscape to explore. He catches my hands and holds them over his heart. We inhale, reciting the prayer said between lovers.

Our arms and legs are wrapped in and around one another. I've lost track. I don't know what's "J.D." and what's "me."

Our pulse, our blood, our bodies, we become one. I thrust, deep into his body—and his into mine. I lose myself. I don't know where—or who—I am. I'm lost in the *us*. Pleasure builds. I feel it. Rising from my source. I cry, "Ahhhhhh!!!"

We shake, violent and shoot—me into him, him into the air. Pleasure pours out our bodies. Pleasure radiates through our body. Pleasure is possibility. Possibility is pleasure.

We hover. There. In. Between. Held aloft by the water.

I lean forward, over his shoulder. He turns his head. Our lips touch. We kiss. Hungry, our mouths close the circle. Energy flows through our bodies. We. He. I. Vibrate. Cells light up. We are a bright beautiful being. Love here, love there, love everywhere.

I eat from the tree of knowledge. Pleasure. Sin? The apple nourishes. Sustains me. Gives me pleasure and life. The snake eats its tail. The circle is complete. Heart racing, my palm hovers over his chest. His heart races. He slides his body over me, a magical sea creature. His movements slosh foamy water over the edge of the tub.

I've never felt this close to another person. Maybe when I was born. We breathe. Our breath is one. And as our pleasure ebbs, our bodies relax and float, dropping down, into dark, watery depths. Our hulls settle, and rest on the ocean floor.

We stay there till the water chills. J.D. pulls the plug. The water drains. We stand.

"Wait," he says. He returns with fresh towels. "Arms up."

Obedient, I stand there, naked as a child after a bath.

Satisfied as an adult after a hard, tender fuck.

Chapter 89

We sneak back, into the safe house. A digital clock glows, red numbers marking the hours since we left.

We climb up, into our bed. Gravity and exhaustion pull me down to the sheets.

My heart. My head. My body. My soul. I vibrate. I feel connected to everything, and everyone.

"Listen." J.D. puts headphones over my ears. Music. A singer's voice echoes, seeps into my head:

... with stars of brightest gold ...

Daylight seeps through the window coverings, stains the dark safe house. I close my eyes. I breathe, deep, into my core. For the first time in my life, I feel safe, and I fall asleep in his arms.

i listen to them fight
i did not know he'd

be so angry
about second place

i want to stand up
& take kidd in my arms

if it were up to me
i'd give him the gold medal

"here" i'd say
"take him"

but i am not
in charge of his heart

so it's not mine nor
can I give it away.

GONE

Chapter 90

"I wanted to know," I say, unsure how to ask.

Marci and I stand at the sink. She slops the soapy sponge on the dirty plates; I rinse and dry.

"About what?" She hands me a plate.

J.D. sits on the window ledge, strumming a guitar. After Halloween, he went acoustic.

Click click click.

Dead bolts tumble. The front door opens.

"About sex. Are there any rules about, um, you know, people hooking up?"

Kidd steps into the kitchen, peels off a ski cap and drops his backpack.

"How'd it go?" Marci asks.

He doesn't answer, lost in a bad mood. He drops to the floor, legs spread. He reaches down, fondles his crotch and looks at me with an evil grin. "We can do what we want with our bodies."

"Cuz there's always condoms lying around!" Peanuts shouts from the main room.

"But it can get complicated *if*," Kidd says. His eyes make me wonder if he's been hanging out with Blue-Eyed Bob, taking serial killer lessons. "There's a friendship between two people and one of them starts having a relationship with somebody else."

He twists his body, speaking to me but looking at J.D.

"People call each other on their shit. So," he says, turns and glares at me, "if somebody's having sex coz they're *lonely* or *bored*, that's *definitely* gonna be out in the open."

"Yeah," Peanuts says, walking into the kitchen. "People *talk* about it."

"Like, for example, Coco—" Kidd says, eyes fixed on J.D. "Nut."

"Hey," Marci warns.

"*Ben*," he says. "I'm speaking to *you*. Or you gonna act like you don't hear me?"

"I hear you," I say, and look him in the eye, running a carving knife under the hot water. I hold it up and dry the blade. "Everyone does."

"Just like everybody knows you're *fucking* him because you're bored shitless and you don't know what else to do. Right?"

The question / accusation was one of Moustapha's favorite tactics. I ignore him. This makes him furious. Were we alone, Kidd would grab my head and drown me in the soapy water. Peanuts cracks up, doubled over with laughter.

"I don't necessarily think that's a bad thing," Marci says. "I mean, if everybody knows what's going on, it's all out in the open. Nobody gets hurt."

"Ben, you prolly know about the buddy sleepover," Kidd says, ready to rant. He loves nothing more than the sound of his voice. He loves it the way other people worship their dicks. He stands, walks to the fridge and opens it. "It's harder for us to pull them off since we're 'Co-Ed,' but not impossible. What does he tell you? When he crawls up the ladder and slips into your bed? '*Dude*, I'm wasted. I'm so drunk! I'm so fucking horny! My dick is *so* hard!' "

He leans forward, foraging in the fridge. I visualize him falling inside and the door slamming shut. We try to open it, but it's stuck. He suffocates. End of Kidd.

" 'Ahh! Hey! Wha' . . . Oh! Oh! Oh! Papacito, *that* feels good, yeah, mi'jo, fuck I'm *so* damn wasted. Whoa! I'm *so* wasted. I'm. Ah, ah, ah . . . AAAA!!! Dude, what just happened? My ass burns. I gotta crash!' "

I summon my mental powers. *Push*. A charity truck picks up the fridge. They can't get it open, either. Another truck drives it to a landfill and dumps the fridge. Years later, Kidd escapes. Serial killings ensue. When he's caught, the headlines read, "I Was a Teenage Mummy."

"If that's what it sounds like having sex with you," I say, hand tightening on the knife. "No wonder he left."

Kidd holds the O.J. carton to his lips and drinks. His throat bobs. I hate the sound—the glub-glub-glub. Done, he burps, the way people harsh a fart. I hand a clean glass to Marci, who passes it to him. He looks at the glass. Will he smash it? Or use it? He pours O.J., drinking glub-glub-glub. Done, he burps.

"*Then*, you wake up the next morning and the one playing the man sits up and goes, 'Fuck! Dude, I don't remember *anything*. Last night? I was *so* out of it, bro'.' "

"I don't think sex with more than one partner is necessarily bad," Marci says. "I mean if—"

"You don't know *shit*," Kidd explodes, drops the carton on the sink, slamming the fridge door. "You fat, nosy bitch, he's *mine!*"

"—if *everybody* knows what's going on," she finishes.

"*I do* know what's going on," Kidd says. "I'm not making up this shit. They keep me awake at night with their stupid, fucking frat boy nonsense. That *is* a problem."

"Yo, Kidd? I don't belong to *nobody*," J.D. says. Calm, he props the guitar against the wall. "Not you. Not him. Nobody. I belong to *me*."

Kidd steps forward. J.D. mirrors him.

"Time out," Marci says, stepping in-between them. They *could* move around Marci, but her body barricade gives them an excuse to stay apart. "J.D., go to the roof. Kidd, wait there."

Still, I expect a fight. At the last second, either one could snap and throw down. J.D. parts the curtains and opens the window. A gust of cold air blasts the kitchen. He pauses.

"I need my jacket."

"I'll get it," Peanuts says, jumps up and runs out.

"I want to say one thing," J.D. says. "Why do you 'suddenly' have a problem with *me* having sex? It's not any different than before except—"

Peanuts returns with a puffy, Frosty-the-Snowman jacket. J.D. pulls it on and ducks out the window.

"Your cig's in the pocket."

"—that it's not with you."

"J.D." Marci sighs. "He won't say it, but he does."

We all know what "it" means. Love. I sneak a look at Kidd's face. He's angry and scared. He turns away.

"When he was fucking Jeremy," J.D. says, speaking to us but mostly to Kidd. "*Everyone* knew. I never said a word. Fucking in the closet, 'accidentally' leaving the door open. You never, *never* heard *me* complain."

"J.D., you're not going to like hearing this," Marci says. "But sometimes you play with people's—"

"I never played with nobody or their heart."

"I didn't say that."

"But you were going to, weren't you?" J.D. pats the pockets, feeling for lighter and ciggies. "I tell people exactly—*exactly*—what they can expect. *Always*. But some people, *some people* hear what *they* want. And there's nothing I can do about that."

Cold wind ruffles the curtains. J.D.'s gone. I start to follow. "No," Marci says, grabbing my arm. I pull away, but there's no point. The window slams and shuts me out. "Bed."

Chapter 91

"Get up." Kidd tugs on my tee shirt. "We're going down." I sit up.

"For what?"

"New stove."

"Going down?" Another game. Hide-'n-seek. I'm tired of playing. Maybe Kidd's trying to trick me. I look over the bed's edge. During my nap, seven lives were erased. The safe house is empty.

"Wait up." I climb down, nervous about being left out (or, left alone). The front door's open. Everyone waits in the hallway. I hesitate. I don't see Marci. "Where are we going again?"

"Basement."

"I thought we were supposed to stay inside."

"Inside the *building*," Peanuts says.

I pull on my orange kicks. By daylight, the corridor looks the same as it did the night I arrived. Only now, I can see the filthy carpet, scuffed walls and burned-out fluorescent lights. It's a bad horror movie. I walk out. Behind me, the door clicks, shuts. We're locked out. Single file, we follow Kidd. His legs take the steps two, three, even four at a time.

"Wait."

The line stops. I bump into Peanuts. Kidd creeps down to the first floor and looks both ways. He motions, waving us down.

"C'mon, move, move it!" One at a time, people turn a corner and disappear. It's a *The Sound of Music* moment (at the end, when the kids walk offstage just before the Nazis catch them).

My turn. I step down. Light flashes on the lobby walls. Beyond the glass door and metal gate, I see the Real World. "You can always leave," Sugar said. I remember her words.

"Hey!" Peanuts shouts, pulling me back. "Come on!"

S / he stands in the doorway, between light and dark. I'm tempted to turn and walk away. "Leave," Sugar said. "You can always leave." Peanuts holds the basement door open. I look at the street. It's bright, filled with life. I look back, at Peanuts, standing at the entrance of the underworld. Stay? Or go? No, I realize the question is not here or there. It's whether I'll ever stop running. And find home.

"*Come on!*"

S / he must have read my mind. "I don't want to leave the light. I want to leave this place. I want to go home." I feel squeezed between my desire for safety and for freedom. Better to live my life with mistakes than live someone else's life perfectly.

"*Hurry up!*"

I turn and walk away. As I step down, and leave the daylight to enter the gloom, I'm aware, painfully so, I've made a choice.

Chapter 92

The basement door slowly closes and . . . shuts. *Click.*

Peanuts is gone. I'm alone. I inhale stale air. If it's not exactly death, then it's something close to. Cold and alone, it's awful here. My instinct tells me to turn and run.

"No!" Peanuts hisses. "*This* way!"

S / he stands there, invisible in the dark. S / he grabs my hand and pulls me down. Truly, s / he believes this is being "helpful."

"Wait," I say, trying to buy time. "Let my eyes adjust."

Cautious, I put out my foot and I step down. Wood creaks. I take another. And another and another and soon I'm at the bottom, swallowed up by the dark. *Halloween II,* I'm Persephone headed off to greet her guy, Hades, and hang out for the winter.

I try to remember something from one of my stepmother's self-help books. Haifa bought them by the carload. I "walk into my fear." Two steps, my body stops. This is a test, I tell myself. Or, to use one of my father's favorite expressions, "What doesn't kill you makes you stronger." I often thought about that in the days leading up to my abduction. It's only true if—and it's a *Big If*—"it" *doesn't* kill you. I step off the flat wood. My foot touches concrete. I'm blind. I reach out. My hand touches stone. It's cold. At least the Crypt is air-conditioned.

Squeak! Squeak!

I want to think otherwise, but I know the squeaks are not a dog's toy. I shudder. Squeaks mean *rats*.

"No, go away!" I shout. I'll scare them. Of course, this is when I would remember the animal trainer on a talk show who said, "Rats are the most difficult animals to train because they're most like humans."

I squeeze the thin metal tube. I forgot—I have a flashlight. I press the button. A tiny beam lights my way. I move it over rough concrete walls and bare floors. Rusty pipes and cobwebs crisscross the ceiling.

Sound bounce off walls; they're faraway and close. The human noise pulls me toward a doorway. Laughter and voices. I'm surrounded by thousands of ghosts.

I step forward. A voice takes shape. Kidd.

"Why can't you just love me?" he asks.

I stop.

"You keep backing me into a corner," J.D. says.

"Where am *I* supposed to go? Listening to you two?"

"So wear earplugs," J.D. says. "I don't remember asking you to sneak around, eavesdropping and shit."

"You don't even know," Kidd pleads, "how hard it is."

"Yeah, I *know*." J.D.'s voice is laced with boredom, the filing your fingernails, rolling your eyes and letting out an exaggerated sigh sort. "I *know*. You feel bad. You told me and I keep telling—"

"You make it sound so easy," Kidd whines. "*I* can't escape. I'm stuck. Listening to you two—"

I can't get over Kidd's sad, little girl voice. It sounds like him. But not.

"You knew what you were getting yourself into," J.D. says, hard and cold. I take note. Several weeks ago, they were a couple.

"Sure, 'No strings attached,' " Kidd says, bitter and bitchy.

"Have you *told* him?"

"The way he looks at you makes me sick. And you—*you*—playa, toggling his feelings like a video game."

Click.

Silver glints, flint strikes a hammer, a lighter's flame bursts. The ciggie's lit, a red blot on the black backdrop. They're close. Five feet? Or, two? I might be Bat Boy, but I can still hear.

"Did you tell him?"

"Whatever, it's none of his business," J.D. says. Again, that voice. Flat and hard. "And I don't plan to."

They walk away, and J.D.'s last words sound less like an answer than a threat: "And you better not either, or I'll fuck you up."

Footsteps.

I'm not alone.

Chapter 93

"I think the question is . . ."

I shrink back. You'd think there would be a lot of places to hide in the dark. But, no. His voice is *right here*. My heart quickens. Kidd scares me. And excites me. I look for J.D.'s cigarette. The red is gone. We're alone. He steps forward. Oh, shit.

"Would you still *fuck*—"

I step back, using my hand to guide me around a corner. Escape. Maybe I can duck down, slip away from his grasp, run.

"*Someone*—"

Streetlight, a bitter yellow, pours through an overhead sewer grill and cuts through the dark.

"If you *knew*—"

The figure steps out. I bite my lip, muffling my cry.

"They were going to—"

Now, Kidd's voice is low, husky.

"—*die?*"

A flashlight pops on. He holds the bright beam under his chin, throwing ghoulish shadows up over his face. Kidd's gone native. He belongs down here. My body seizes up. Shivering body. Chattering teeth. Dry throat. "He knows, he *knows*," I think. "Now he's going to punish me. Rape me. Kill me. Leave my dead body. He could. No one will look down here. I'm neither present nor accounted for. The milk carton said, MISSING CHILD. Kidd's not just strong, he's smart. He could pull it off."

"Ben?" he'd say, casual as a hello. "Don't know. Must have got lost. Or left. Yeah, he was the type. Always had his eye on the door, ready to leave."

"Hold your ground," I tell myself. "He'll use any sign of weakness against you. He's a bully."

But I can't help it. I inch back. Now I get it. When my stepmother(s) fled—and they all did, eventually—in the middle of the night, they took everything *except* the self-help books' advice. That, they left behind, untouched, because *they didn't work*.

"This is part of the game."

"Yeah." He points the beam in my eyes. I close my eyes, imagining I'm a Saint. The flashlight clicks off. I open my eyes. Blind.

"You know . . ." He strokes my head. I shudder, creeped out. "That blond looks like *shit*. Fake. But then, I guess that means it's *perfect* for you."

He turns and walks away. I realize, I'm lost. I run after him.

"Are we—you—meeting up with the others?" Now, my voice betrays me. *I'm* the one who sounds like a scared little girl.

"Bitch, step off. Find your own way."

"Please?" I beg. Humiliating. I'm more scared of being alone in the dark than being alone in the dark with Kidd. He doesn't answer. I don't care. I follow him. I count the steps. One. Two. Three. Four Five Ten. Then . . . Voices. The others! We're close. I'll ditch Kidd and run to J.D. Kidd turns another corner. I don't follow.

"Hey! Hey! Her—" I shout. "Over—"

A hand covers my mouth and muffles my voice. I fight. I struggle to escape. But Kidd's stronger and bigger. He lifts me up, carrying me away from the voices.

"I heard this story once," he says. Hot, stale breath blasts my ear. "About this guy on a hospital unit. All he heard was the fan. Spinning, spinning, spinning. Drove him crazy. Pretty soon, he thinks this fan's talking to him. And this fan, you know what it tells him? What he should do?"

I shake my head, No. He holds me up, arm stuck in-between my legs.

"You like that, huh?"

I love it. Or, my body does. Without asking permission, my body's excited. My pelvis rolls over his hard, muscular forearm. Fear? Sex? Pleasure? Pain? Emotional overlap. I'm confused. Is he going to kill me? Or, fuck me? Logically, I know Kidd's a horrible, evil person. But he's sexy, too, and my body can't resist. In the quiet, I hear my heartbeat. It's loud, fast as hummingbird wings.

"Kill, the voice told him," he says. "*Kill* that kid. There's another one with him in that room." His lips tickle my ear. "You know what happens to you? Down here? If you got lost?"

He sets me down, removing his hand from my mouth.

"S-s-s-ome—someone—would find me."

"Oh, you think."

"Yeah. Or the rats will eat me."

"Hee-hee." He points the flashlight beam in my eyes.

"Hey!" I hold up my hand and block the light. "Knock it off!"

He switches off the beam, drops me and walks away. Fast. I scramble to stand and run to catch up. My foot catches. I stumble. "Turn around, fool, run back." I have no idea why, but I run, desperate to catch up with Kidd.

I'm slow. He's gone. I'm lost, truly, with no way out. I wait. I know he'll come back.

"Please, come back," I whimper. "Please."

Chapter 94

"I know the rest of that story!"

My voice echoes in the tunnel, "*I know, I know, I know . . .*"

"You do."

He steps out the shadows. He was there all along. He walks. I run to catch up.

"Yeah?"

"After the guard does the midnight check, the kid took a soda can. Aluminum one. He bent it over and over until it broke. Sharp, like—"

He grabs my wrist. Metal's drawn along the skin. He's going to cut me, bleed me, kill me.

"Hey!" I try to yank away. "Don't cut me!"

I stick my finger in my mouth. I expect to taste blood. The skin is dented. He pressed the metal hard—but not hard enough to cut.

"Fan, fan's still talking to him. Telling him, 'Cut that guy. His finger.' "

"He'll die," I say. "The other guy wakes up. And believes the fan's talking to him. He goes ape shit, cuts the other guy open and pulls out his heart?"

"There's the other part. He pulls out the other guy's eyes 'cause he thinks they're grapes?"

"No," I lie. I've heard the whole story. Several versions circulated around Serenity Ridge. In one, the do-it-yourself heart transplant is followed by eye surgery ("The eyes! The eyes!").

"Don't take this the wrong way, but I have to ask. He's a legend. Are you—"

"*Yesssssss!*" He lets rip a ghoulish laugh. Maybe, now that he's "scared" me, he'll take me back. The others are gone. He walks away. Fast. I jog to keep up.

"Wait," I say. "Are we walking *away* from the first room?"

"Ahahahahahahahaha." Another voice cackles. I grab his shirt.

"Don't. Clutch."

"Who was that?"

"Fuck if I know."

We turn the corner. A fire lights up a dark nook. A figure's hunched over the flames. Kidd ignores it and keeps walking.

"Who was that?"

"Mole people."

"Mole people?" I ask. "Like genetic mutants?"

"Naw, just people with nowhere to go. They live down here. It's safe."

I need to keep the conversation going. Engage Kidd. I know my survival depends on it.

"I guess J.D. told you that we found Oskar?"

"You did," he says, trying to act blasé-blasah.

"Yeah," I say, hoping to bait him. "On the Internet. But wasn't Oskar J.D.'s boyfriend, you know, back home?"

"Never heard of him. 'Sides, why would you care?"

"Coz, um . . ."

"I know you were back there, lurking, all stalkerish an'—"

"*Why* you hate me?"

"Because," he says, turns and jabs a finger against my chest. "*You* don't give a shit 'bout nobody but *you*."

"Like you're any different."

"What's *that* s'pposed to mean?"

"It means—never mind. Who cares." I wish I had the courage to walk away and find my own way back. I have a flashlight. We pass under another sewer grill. This is my chance to escape. I look: ladder? I'm so desperate, I would crawl up and climb out a pothole in rush-hour traffic. Cars could smash my head, pumpkin style. But there's no ladder or, if there is, I don't see it. There's no chance to take. I stick with—or, am stuck with—Plan "A," Kidd.

"You know the way back, right?"

"Yeah," he says. "You wanna get back to fuck J.D.?"

The tunnel splits. Kidd stops, looks left. Then right. He's deciding. Or, acting like it. He torments me, making me wait.

Keep up the dialogue, I tell myself. Maintain the connection.

"You never told me."

"Told you what?" He holds up the flashlight, moving it left, then right. "This way? Or that?"

I know it. There's no way out. We're lost.

"How you got here."

Abruptly, he walks away. I don't move. I cast my bait. "You couldn't handle it if I told you."

Chapter 95

"Wrong. Fact, I'll do you one better. I'll *tell* it."

"What?"

"Your story. And if I get it right, will you show me the way out?"

"Uh-huh."

"You probably started out in a hospital. You've been hospitalized on and off since you were five. Or six? At least, up until you escaped?"

"Eight. I was eight when they sent me away."

"Twelve or thirteen, you were depressed. The meds stopping working. They gave you electroshock. 'Hey, kid.' That's what they'd say. Coz you couldn't remember your name and it stuck."

He's silent. I was right.

"There," he says. The flat voice makes me nervous. Either I'm wound him up or we're about to bond.

"You got older. You couldn't remember your family's face. When you dreamed, you dreamed about escaping the social workers and foster homes. You were sick of being a case number. Tired of moving from one place to the next. You thought about—"

I pause. "What doesn't kill you . . ." True, I think, but sometimes there *are* warning signs. And it *does* kill you.

"Keep going," he says.

"But escape scared you. They'd brainwashed you, told you couldn't even think about—"

"What. Think about—"

"Escape." I pause, make him want it. "Because you were doped up on one thing or another. They'd drop random questions. You worried you might slip. 'Cause it was hard to think fast enough to lie."

I know Kidd's story, but telling it's exhausting. There's so many Kidds, all with the same story. The walking wounded. Trapped, 'cause they'll never understand. I'm no different. I've just fooled myself into thinking I know more because I write it down. Or, stripped of specifics, our stories are all the same. We're all throwaways, locked out, lost. Doomed to wandering without knowing what really happened because knowing would destroy us.

"Don't be an idiot," I think. "Save the world another time. He's your ticket, he knows the way back. *Say anything*." There isn't a "way back." Marci calls it "long term," but the safe house is temporary. A band-aid and—

"You were dreaming about—"

"Running," he says. "Dreamed about running down the streets. Of the town. The last one. Away from those foster parents. I lost count. There'd been so many. I was running away from them, all of them. I dreamed—in my dream, I felt my sneakers hit the pavement. Cold air on my face. Night. Street lamps. Month, month and a half after I started having these dreams, I sat in another social worker's office. I don't know why it was that day, but it was and I decided. I'm gonna change all this. I had enough."

Overhead, sunlight hits his head and turns his hair a deep, indigo blue. He walks fast. He could be running in the dream of the night. I run to catch up. The sunlight hits my blond hair. Nobody sees it, but I'm still embarrassed. He's right. It's not beautiful. It's fake.

"What made you think you could change everything?"

"I remember . . ." He slows down. Not much, but enough for me to catch up. "I looked up and saw the clock. The social worker left. Walked away. Just left me sitting there. Alone. You know how they do. She'd left the door open."

"Yeah," I say. "Like she was inviting you to leave."

"Uh-huh." He nods. "There was no one to stop me. Never was. Nobody ever cared if I stayed or if I left. I heard this voice in my head. You know what it said?"

"No."

"Said, 'Kidd, you think it'll never end. Really, you're just getting used to it. Forget *them*. Now it's *you* who don't care.' But some part of me still *did* care. I stood up and ran. I ran down the stairs, out the side door and I kept running. I never looked back."

I shouldn't, but I do. I relax. If Kidd feels comfortable enough telling me something this personal, then he doesn't hate. I exhale, relieved. This is our "bonding" moment. We're going to walk out and up, into the light.

"Then you walked in—" He turns on me and swings the flashlight to smash my head. "You *fucked it up*."

My stomach drops. I duck down. He smiles. The happy face turns him into a killer. I stumble, trip and fall back. I land on my ass.

He jumps, sits on my chest, knees pressing my arms to the ground. He's gonna kill me, I know he is.

Chapter 96

"Me?" I don't fool him. But I give it a shot. Maybe I can buy time. Wiggle away. "Fucked up what?"

"You don't even give him the time of day and he's all over you!"

He waves the flashlight, a miniature light saber. My hands fly up. I try to block the beam. Too late. My pupils close, tight as a virgin boy's butthole.

"That's not true, I—" The flashlight gave me a headache. Fuck it. If it's the "truth" he wants, I'll give it to him. Go ahead, kill me. You'll be sorry. I'm giving you something to think about for the rest of your life. "You're right. The second we laid eyes on one another, we knew."

"Knew what?" His voice shrinks, suddenly small and scared. I stand.

"I wanted *him* and he wanted *me*."

I laugh. I make myself. It sounds false and brittle, but I want to hurt him. I back away.

"*Fucking liar!*"

"Yeah," I say, lowering my voice. I know how to drive him insane. Unleash jealousy, the green-eyed monster, to attack him. Bite him. Infect him. "We *smelled* it. I knew I was gonna fuck him the second I saw him."

There. I've said it. But once I've said it, I regret it. The words don't make me feel better. Or like I've won. No, I stand in a mold-infested basement, playing a supporting role in some dumb homo-romo triangle. I'll pay for my cruelty—pay for it with my life. Well, I think, maybe in the next life, I'll be a nicer person. Live longer.

Kidd rushes toward me. But instead of running away, I reach out and grab him. Hold him in my arms. Hug him.

"Fuck! Get off!"

He tries to shake me. I hold on tight. Strange as it sounds, I draw my strength from our shared love: J.D.

"*Bitch!* You *heard* me! What'd I say *first* time I sent you to hell?"

"What?"

"He's pos-i-tive," Kidd says, sounding out the word. Hooked on phonics, this is how we say, H-I-V.

"Positive?" I play dumb. Even though I knew. J.D. told me, but—

"*Positive.* He's positively positive. Fun, huh?"

"You're a really sad dude." My heart sinks. He laughs. The sound's outside my head. His words echo, "You couldn't handle it if I told you."

True, I *know* the virus has no morals. But the truth is *the truth*. Facts are facts. I'm negative; J.D.'s positive. Never shall the two meet. But wait. J.D. and me did—we had sex. As of last night, we are (okay, were) still having sex. I've been infected and I'm positive and I don't know it? That's not possible. We used condoms. Well, *most* of the time. My head spirals.

Meanwhile, J.D. is elsewhere, off-stage from our homo-romo triangle. A chasm's opened up, and it's bigger than the one between me and my parents. Kidd did me one better and saw something in *me*—that my sense of survival trumps everything, even love. He knew. Knew that I'd give up, turn and go back. I could choose to refuse to "believe" Kidd. I could act like I don't understand what he's said. I might feel like shit, but he was right. I give up.

"He's positive about *what?*"

"He's got the bug, baby, do I need to spell it out? The pre-AIDS, the H.I.V.," he says, rhyming "HIV" with "give."

"The *what?*" I ask, playing dumb coz I'm in denial.

"Stick around. Loverboy's gonna get *real* sick. That map you stole?"

"What map?"

"The one that fell out of my bag. I leave the house for doctors' appointments. He won't do it. He thinks he's special. Immune. He thinks he'll never get sick. Me? I plan to live. So it's pills and checkups and medicine for the rest of my life. *All* courtesy of loverboy."

He points the flashlight at a pool of water. The beam hits the surface. The tunnel lights up, wavy shadows dancing on the ceiling and walls.

"It makes sense for *us*. My advice? *Give him up*. Trust, you can't handle it. You're not immune. You're not special. You'll die if you catch it."

Finished, Kidd studies my face, checking to see. "Did I make my point?" And, "Will he walk away?"

"What you're saying is—" I've got cotton mouth. "J.D. infected you?"

"One night, he fucked me, didn't use a rubber, and this would be—" The flashlight clicks off. Darkness falls over us like a shroud. "The end of your ride."

"Ride? What ride?" I ask, even though I get it. I've got to keep him here. I can't be alone. The mole people, the rats—I won't survive. I need him to show me the way back. My "ride" was an emotional roller coaster. Next stop, hell!

"Part of the game," he says and, just like that, he's gone.

"You don't scare me!" I yell. My voice bounces off walls, echoing, endlessly. You. Don't. Scare. Me. There's fear in every word.

"I was a nice person before I met him!" he shouts, words ping-ponging *ding! ding! ding!* and lighting up the inside of my head.

Then, nothing. Reality check. Kidd's gone.

"Ah—" A tiny sob threatens to slip out. I press my hand against my mouth and muffle the sound and stand there, left not just alone but terrified.

Chapter 97

I stay like that for a long time. Alone, in the dark. I don't know what else to do or where to go. I wait for someone to turn up and "save me." I could try to retrace our path. Or, I could just start walking. Five steps later and I turn a corner. There's a shape in front of me. Giant rat? Mole person? I reach out. My hand brushes wool. A coat.

"RUN!!!" my brain screams. "RUN!!!"

My legs are weak with fear, but they obey. Or, try to. Running, I feel like that Greek character. Lot. A Lot. As in, A Lot to Lose. Lot escaped hell. But right before Lot left, he was told, "Don't look back. If you do, your wife turns into a pillar of salt." Of course, Lot did look back and saw his wife morph into salt. Forget the wife, I know Lot's story. It's human nature dressed up as myth.

So, I turn and look back. Eyes glow. Lot's wife? No, these eyes are blue. Blue-Eyed Bob.

I turn, run and bump into—

"Ah!!!"

I recognize the shriek.

"Anita?"

"Girl!"

Laughing, we fall into one another's arms. I know she's a lying bitch (who goes around telling people, "Ben's a dirty ho."). That's ancient history. We join hands. We're going to find our way out. I have faith. Anita knows.

We're about to turn the corner and—I can't help myself—I look back.

Bob's blue eyes are gone.

Chapter 98

"I'ma Gla-*More* Girl." Anita giggles. "Capital *G-I-R-L*."
Despite being several feet taller than me, she hangs off my
arm. We've become BFFs who could be heading home after a
late night out (party, club, party, club).

"I am *not* taking those stairs." We take the elevator. On the
fifth floor, I knock on the safe house door. No one answers.

"Honey," Anita says, placing a big hand on my tiny shoulder.
"It's locked."

We cross the roof and climb down the fire escape. Last step,
we stand outside the kitchen window.

"I mean," she says, unspooling a nonstop monologue stud-
ded with lines stolen from last month's *Vogue*, "I would sell
anything for a new haircut, ya know?"

"In here!" Marci shouts, motioning us inside. It's a wake.
Everyone wears the same bored, miserable face.

"Girl." Anita's curled up, laughing. "Who died?"

Chapter 99

Peanuts and I kick it on the sofa. We're in the middle of our daily dose of afternoon reality TV and talk shows. After noon, I abandon the *Johnny Panic* translation. I need something else to relieve my boredom. Nothing's better than listening to someone else's problems.

"Gimme!" Pony lunges for the remote. "I wanna watch cartoons."

" 'sides Pony," Peanuts says, holding the remote up, beyond Pony's reach. "Who votes cartoons? 'cept the seven-year-olds. *Shiiiittttttt.*"

We crack up, falling onto one another. It feels good to laugh.

"Aw." Pony makes a try for the remote. "They relax me."

"Hey, Pony, knock it off," I say, "We got a date with Oprah."

"Yeah, yeah, yeah. We're gon' watch my girl," Peanuts says.

Cue, theme song. We shift our gaze to the show's spectacular sci-fi graphics opening. Oprah steps out, curls bouncing and working her razzle-dazzle smile.

"*Heyyyyy!*" we chant, and wave. Oprah waves back. "Love you!"

Pony stands and walks to the kitchen, kicking our ankles.

"Hey, Bigfoot!" I shout. "*Watch out!*"

"I am *so* fuckin' sicka your shit, Pony," Peanuts says. "You go 'round all bumping into people, demanding they be *nice*."

"Yeah, bro'," Kidd says. "What the fuck's your problem?"

"*You* try hidin' under a buncha trash in the back of a pickup all the way from Texas!" Pony screams. He stands in the kitchen doorway and waves his arms.

"You were in the hospital like, *what?* Two weeks? That's *nothing*," Kidd says. Lately, he's been an equal opportunity asshole.

Thump! Thump! A neighbor pounds on a wall. "Keep it down!"

"Do they think we're having a party?" I ask.

"You know what?" Pony looks around, crazy-eyed, "searching" for something. His sanity? Good luck with that. You'll never find it. Pony runs across the floor, scrambles up the ladder and leans over. I know what he's planning. I panic. But before I can stop him, he's pulled out my blue notebook. Crazicle's psychic. He reads:

> i love the way J.D.'s hair
> feels in my fingers.
>
> it is black & thick.
> silky smooth but so tough.
> there is more hair on his head
> than there is grass on most lawns.
>
> or wheat on fields.
> his head is just covered in hair.
> then, i realize that it is black. no color.
>
> i ask him, 'why is ur hair still black?'
> he looks up at me with those brown eyes & smiles.
> ''cuz Anita said it'd just turn out orange.'

I jump off the sofa and run to the bunk. A hand grabs my ankle. I trip and fall.

"Oh, no, *honeeeeee!*" Kidd banshee screeches. "This too damn *good!*"

Click, click, click. The dead bolts turn, front door opens. Anita walks into the safe house. She shuts the door.

"*Let him go.*" Her voice is stone-cold sober. She's home early. This is another Anita. She's drunk. Pony and Kidd stupidly stands in her crosshairs.

"Or what?" Kidd says.

"Or—" Anita slides a switchblade out her purse. "I cut your face, you dumb fucking wannabe militant."

Kidd open his mouth—

Click!

The switchblade pops, shiny, silver and sharp.

"Case you don't notice," Anita says, "I'm *not* fucking around with the likes of you."

Note to self, re: safe house rules. Switchblades?

"And *you*, retard, up there, hiding." Anita waves the switchblade. Sunlight glints on the blade. "Give the man back his journal."

Pony leans over the bunk. Polite, he hands me the journal.

"Get off that bunk," she orders. "That was *Ben's* bed before you got here."

I love Anita. She'd make a fantastic bank robber.

"*Motherfucker!*" Pony screams, back to white trash psycho. He leaps off the bunk, *George of the Jungle* style. He slips past Anita and stands in the hallway. "I fuckin' *hate* livin' here! I *hate* all these stupid rules! I *hate*—"

"Then maybe, homeboy—" Anita says, steps forward, switchblade up, near his face. Pony stares at the tip. He's got one foot out the door. "You *should* leave. Like, right now."

"You're all a bunch of losers with AIDS!" he shouts, and bolts. "*Fuckin' Commies!*"

Anita calmly folds the switchblade, walks to the door and closes it. Casual, she flips the dead bolts, and locks up. Done, she turns to us and gives us a tired smile.

"I'm always so glad when the trash takes itself out."

Chapter 100

"Anita?"

I knock on the bathroom door. Behind me, the closet door opens. Hammer sticks his head out.

"Dude, you gotta check this out."

He wears a cam whore outfit: tank top and loose shorts.

"Is this one of your Webcam things?"

"No." He motion me inside. Peanuts sits in front of the laptop. On-screen, a reporter, microphone in hand.

"The shooting occurred outside the Polk Street restaurant. Witnesses said the argument was over 'Who's prettier?' "

Cut to, a grainy surveillance image.

"Isn't that—?"

"Yeah!" Hammer says. "And look! She's got a gun!"

"The suspect is a black, teenage female. The gunshot was not fatal."

The "suspect" wears oversized sunglasses, a silk wrap dress. She holds a black clutch and a small gun.

"Wow," I say. "She even managed to work a look."

"Which one?" Hammer asks.

"High-fashion model slash Black Panther circa nineteen seventy-five."

"Can you *believe* this shit?" Peanuts says, clicking the mouse, channel surfing. The shooting is headline news. "Over who's prettier!"

The bathroom door opens. We all turn and look. Anita emerges out of a cloud of white smoke. At first, I almost don't recognize her. Her long hair's gone, shorn to the skull. Without makeup, she looks like a boy.

"Hey, 'Nita." Peanuts laughs. "What'd you do with the piece?"

Anita may look like a boy, but she still acts like a queen. She ignores Peanuts, opens the front door and leaves. She left her purse on the bathroom floor.

"I hope the cops don't come to get her," Hammer says.

"Depends on how good a shot she was," Peanuts says. "She killed somebody, probably. Assault, naw. There's so much shit that goes down on Polk. Nothing ever happens."

I grab Anita's purse, about to follow her out.

"Hey," Peanuts shouts. "Where you going?"

For some reason, I turn and look for J.D. He's gone. Maybe he's smoking or on the fire escape. I walk to the kitchen, part the curtains and look—it's empty. Voices. I look up: Kidd and J.D. are together, one flight up. They kiss.

J.D. looks down.

"Mi'jo!"

I hear him, but I've already turned and run back. I want to open the front door and run even farther, but right now, I don't know where to go.

Chapter 101

J.D. crawls up the ladder and onto the bed. I'm turned away and face the wall. I know it's him because I know his weight, how his body feels on the bed. He raises his hand, a shadow on the wall, about to rest it on my shoulder.

"Mi'jo, please!" he pleads. "Can we talk?"

I don't move. Even though I want to turn over and ask. Why. I stare at the wall, listening to him breathe. I wonder how long he'll wait. Five? Eighteen? Thirty days?

"Can I at least explain?"

I roll over. I don't look him in the eye. I look to the side, at everything but: chin, ear, temple. I want to kiss him. But now his lips seem used. Dirty.

"Explain what?" I say. "I *saw*. What else is there to say?"

"No. You. Just. Saw. Can we talk about this?"

"I'm here. Talk."

"In the closet?" I wipe the tears off my face. "Okay."

Hammer and Peanuts leave the closet, silent. The door shuts.

"We're alone,"

I tell myself. "We could work this out." I shake my head. "No, he lied." My body says, "I don't care."

J.D. steps forward. I step back. I don't want him to touch me. I back into a corner. He comes close. I put out a hand. Stop. I know that if he touches me, I won't be able to resist—his touch, his lips, his kiss.

"Are you listening?" I nod. "Then what'd I just say?"

"Dunno."

He reaches out and squares my shoulders, turning my body toward his. "What do you want?"

"You," he says.

"Fine. I'll leave my body. You can have it. But you can't have me."

I wish he'd leave. I want to lie down and go to sleep.

"Look at me." I do, but my gaze drifts to the side. He takes my chin, forcing me to meet his gaze. "You don't get it. Kidd? He's like living with a stalker."

I watch him struggle and try to explain. I want to hear him, but my heart is deaf. I feel betrayed to the core by the one person I chose to trust. "Compassion," I tell myself. "Forgiveness." I look at him. I can't help it. My heart is cold.

"Why do you talk that way?"

"I knew it." He drops his hands. "You'd never understand."

"Understand what? You're a liar? A poseur? That you're full of shit?"

"What's that s'pposed to mean?"

"What that means is you can just stop with the rap flavaed whatevah." Now I glare at him, head-on. My fake blond hair stands on end. I'm ready to fight. "I *know* the truth. You're about as get-tow as me. And I'm about as ghetto as Mickey fucking D's."

"I grew up *poor*," he says, defensive. "You don't even fucking *know*."

I pause. Take a breath. "Maybe you should stop," the little voice in my head says. "Maybe you've said enough." But I can't.

"I *know* your stepfather got caught diddling your—"

Crack!

He slaps my face. It stings. So much for being "right." Next time, I'll use a smug, nonverbal look. I step toward the door. He blocks me.

"Let me out."

"Who told you that?"

I thought that throwing the truth in his face would feel good. I just feel like shit.

"I'm sorry. Forget it—us. Let me go."

"How," he asks, refusing to move, "did you know?"

"Sugar's journal. Am I right?"

He steps aside. I got my answer. I'm free to go.

"She don't know the half of it."

"The other half? That true?"

"Pretty much," he says, looking down and away.

"The story you told me—about getting caught having sex with the fourteen-year-old. Or, the one about you and 'Oskar' planning to escape—"

"I knew someone," he says. "Maybe, it wasn't *exactly* like that. But, mostly, it was."

"Exaggerated, or lied? What about you and Kidd: true or false?"

"You have to, like, *trust* me. Okay? There's a lot of other stuff you don't know."

"Start with one fact."

"Okay."

I look him in the eye. Now, he's the one who won't return my gaze.

"Tell me, who are you. For real?"

He looks up and takes a deep breath.

Chapter 102

"I can't tell you my bio. None of us can. Not even you. And I wouldn't ask. It's more important to you because you're closer to the truth because . . . you still remember. Me? My family? My 'real' life? That's what I remember least. You live here long enough, you'll see. It'll happen to you. You move things around in your head. Or you forget. Otherwise, you can't get up in the morning. There's life—what you remember—and life that you live. You can only live one if you forget the other. What happened with us . . . I *never* meant to hurt you. That's the truth. The first time we talked on the roof, I wanted to be with you. And now, every night, I sleep with you and hold you in my arms . . . there's truth in *that*. I know it. You know it."

Done, he looks at me. His face is flushed. I see the effort it took for him to tell this "truth." My head's jumbled with thoughts. Sleeping together. Holding one another in our arms. He's right, it's true. There's no denying. He sleeps with me every night, all night.

"Those kids?" he says, gesturing toward the safe house. "They *act* like they're all ghetto, but they're from the suburbs. Like us. But look around. We're not in the suburbs. It *is* the ghetto. And the longer you live in it, the more it becomes you and your reality. Your reality stops being what you remember.

Or where you came from. It's where you are *now*. So, you tell me: What's the truth? What's a lie?"

"I dunno," I say. I'm confused. Some of what he says, it makes sense. The rest gives me a headache. "You tell me."

"I like you," he says. "I really, *really* like you. That's the truth. That's for real."

I believe him. But I can't help it. My heart breaks a little. There's a gap between "like" and "love." He looks at me. Black eyelashes blink. One. Two. Three. The last time, his eyes stay shut, lashes resting on his cheeks. He leans forward, lips ready to kiss. I let him. We part. Our lips tremble with hope and fear and excitement.

"So?"

The moment of truth. I look him in the eye.

"You don't love me."

I walk to the door. My hand reaches for the knob. He doesn't try to stop me. I can leave. The little voice in my head says, "You're making a mistake." I ignore the voice and step out the closet. I know I've been cruel and . . . foolish?

I'm dazed. At first, I don't hear the fist pounding on the front door. Or, the voices.

"Let me in! Let me in!"

Chapter 103

Peanuts peers through the keyhole. Nobody moves. It's happening. A raid.

J.D. grabs my arm and pushes me toward the kitchen.

"Run!"

Blur, movement, bodies rush out the room like water sucked down a drain.

The front door shakes. Someone kicks—

Whomp! Whomp! Whomp!

"Run!" J.D. screams.

I can't run. But I can hide, I think, leaving my body and—

Watching—

The door crack—

Split—

My bedroom door. It's all happening again. They're here. To take me away. Lock. Me. Up.

My vision fades. I'm blacking out.

"Run!" J.D. yells. His voice is far away.

I step into the closet. I dive down. I burrow, hiding under a pile of dirty clothes.

"Ben!" J.D. cries, *"Ahmed!!!"*

He calls me by my name.

"Ben! Ahmed!"

J.D. keeps calling me by my name. Both of them. He's broken a rule. There are no rules. This safe house is closed.

"*Ben! Ahmed!*"

He wants me to follow. I would, but I can't. I'm hidden.

"*Ben!!!*"

J.D.'s voice sounds so sad. Faraway. I peer out, my nose in-between a jockstrap and jeans. A blade splits the door.

"*Ben? Ben! BEN?!?*"

J.D.'s voice is close. He came back. The door cracks.

Whack—

Light hits the blade.

A man steps inside. He wears a helmet, uniform and boots. He holds a gun. Wow. A Real Live Cop.

"*Freeze!*"

"*BEEEEENNNNN!!!*"

I cover my ears.

Cops pour into the safe house.

Click-click. Handcuffs. I know that sound. They lead him out, wrists cuffed behind his back.

Passing the closet, J.D. turns his head and looks down, at my hiding place. Our eyes meet. His mouth forms the words—

"I love—"

And, then, he's gone.

Chapter 104

My nose is stuck inside the jockstrap's plastic cup. It smells. Oh la la. Hammer's sexy self. I gag on the odor. It's revolting. A nasty combination of dried cum and skank. Why didn't Hammer take it? Isn't his sperm-stained jockstrap worth hundreds—or thousands—of dollars on eBay?

It's noisy outside. I peek through the tee shirts, running shorts and socks. The pile smells so bad, I might vomit. There's a price Hammer pays to look like a muscle god: His clothes smell like a garbage dump.

My left hand's cramped. I flex, feel a telephone cord.

Creak.

The sound stops me. I look up. A figure stands in the doorway. A gun's barrel nudges the door. It swings open. A head look inside. Blue-Eyed Bob steps into the closet. He's huge. Monster sized. He grabs the telephone cord and yanks. The cord snaps, and it hits my face. It hurts, but I don't move. I don't breathe. I don't make a sound. He scans the closet. His eyes land on the dirty clothes. He smiles. He bends forward. His fingers plunge into the pile. He's going to rip off my face.

I shut my eyes.

Chapter 105

"Ohhhhh!" he moans, orgasmic.

I look through the hole left by the jockstrap. Blue-Eyed Bob could see me—if he looked. But his face is buried in the jockstrap, his mind in an imaginary locker room, hand rubbing his crotch.

I move and a pair of shit-stained briefs fall, draped over my face.

Blue-Eyed Bob turns and leaves with the jockstrap.

I stand. Dirty clothes fall off my body. I plug the cord into the jack. I hope the phone works. It vibrates. I flip the lid. It's an old walkie-talkie model. The Star Trek communicator model.

"Hello?" I whisper.

"Where are you?" Marci's voice.

"Closet."

"Cops."

"Yeah."

"Who'd they get?"

"J.D."

"Shit! He's gonna get deported."

"Deported?"

"That's it?"

"They axed the door and tore the place apart and, and—" I

feel horrible. I start crying. My last words to J.D. were, "You don't love me."

"They're gone?"

"Yeah."

"We're downstairs. Leave the closet and run down the hallway. When you get to the fire escape on the first floor, jump."

"Unit four fifty-six, status check, Market Street raid?"

"Over, 806 in progress."

"Pigs," Marci says. "They're outside. They have dogs. You have two minutes before they come back. They're looking for drugs."

Drugs? What about the kiddie porn? If they examine Hammer's computer and find his pictures, I'll get the blame! I imagine life imprisonment without parole. Men with bad breath, rough hands and smelly crotches. I'd rather die. All this had to happen just when I was starting to like sex.

"Still there?"

"Yeah."

"They entered the building. Get out."

Ten minus ninety, ten minus eighty, ten minus—and I know this—I mean, I *really* know this, but I can't move. I'm stuck. My body won't stand. My feet refuse to budge.

"I can't."

"If you don't, the dogs will smell you, you'll be caught and sent back."

"*Clear!*"

The cops march down the hallway. Holsters bounce, guns slam, walkie-talkies squawk.

"This is your moment," I tell myself. "*GO!*"

Now or never.

What'll it be?

Chapter 106

The safe house is silent. I drop the cell. All I need to do is . . . Move. *Fast.* Well, probably not even fast. Cops are always late to bank robberies. They'll probably be late with—

Woof! Woof! Woof!

I look back: German shepherds strain at their leashes, fangs bared and barking. They smell me. See me. And foam at the mouth.

"*Hey, you!*" shouts Piggie Number Whatever. "*Stop!*"

I ignore him and run. I jump out the window and land on the fire escape. I climb up, faster than Spider-Man on crack. On the roof, I look over the edge. Cop cars outside the building. A dirty Impala's parked at the end of the street. This isn't the fire escape or the second floor. I can't jump. Well, I could, but seven flights up, I wouldn't live. I'm trapped.

I need to go back, down the fire escape. I start to and then I see the Storm Troopers and the dogs. They're trying to climb up the fire escape, but they're slowed down by batons, gun holsters, walkie-talkies. The dogs' feet slip on the metal stairs.

One flight down, I see an open window.

The cops look up, see me.

"*Halt!*"

I ignore the order, scramble down the metal steps and slip through the window. The apartment is empty. I slam the window shut, lock the latch and walk away. I hear them pounding on the window, "*Open this window!*" I give them the finger and run out the front door.

The moment I step into the hallway, two coppers walk up the left stairwell. I turn right. Spider-Boy's wrist unspools web. In free fall, I drop down five flights.

Ground floor. I stand outside the emergency exit. I realize I hold something in my hand: Anita's purse. She needs it. I need to warn her. I owe her that.

I open the basement door. It shuts. I walk into the dark.

Chapter 107

The door shuts. I'm back. The place I said I'd never return: the basement. I step down. The wood creaks. I hope Anita's down here. I step off the wood. My bare feet touch cold concrete.

Click. Click. Click.

Rats? Lighter? I pray it's Anita.

Click.

My hair stands on end. I pretend I'm Hansel looking for Gretel. I pretend the *click-click*'s the sound of crumbs landing on concrete.

Click.

I focus, trying to source the sound. It could be coming from here. Or, over *there*.

Click. Click. Click.

The sound's a pack of rats, nails skittering on concrete. In seconds, they'll swarm over my body, thousands of fangs digging into my flesh.

Click.

"Who, who's there?"

Click. Click.

No answer.

Click click click.

"Hello? Hello? *HELLO!?!*"

No answer. I know I'm going to die here, in this awful basement. I escaped from Serenity Ridge, survived assault, *and* my parents. For what? Flesh-eating rats and Death. Something furry brushes over my foot.

"Ahhh!"

Click click click.

I put out my hand. My palm touches a . . . wall?

I use the flat, rough surface to guide myself toward the sound.

"Motherfuckin' lighter!"

I exhale. I'm safe. Well, for the moment. Rats don't bitch about lighters.

Chapter 108

"They gone?"

"Yeah."

Ahead, light. I creep forward, look around the corner. The lighter sparks, and I see her. She sits on the floor holding a glass pipe. Her lips are wrapped around its end. She suck-suck-sucks *hard*. Her cheeks collapse, craters. She looks ancient. She holds her breath. The pipe slips out her lips and she looks up, seeing me but not.

Silent, she waves me closer.

Click click.

The flame pops, flickers, trembles and sputters. Dark, Death, it's all the same. I'm trapped in the black. I can't get out.

"What the fuck brought you down here, child?"

Anita, the animated Buddha. She exhales. Thick white smoke pours out her head. It swirls, circling her head like dragon's breath. Or, fog. The air reeks. I stick out my tongue, curious to taste. Tacky-heavy on my tongue, it tastes like lead. I feel lightheaded.

"What are you smoking?"

"Between you and me?"

"I don't see anyone else here."

"See, don't see that, is—" The light blue flame dips, gone. "Shit!"

"I brought your purse."

"Oh, baby, thank you! Gimme that, would you," she says. Dead lead smoke blasts my face. I cough. "Sorry, baby."

"Here." I hand her the purse. She opens it. *Zip*. Plastic compacts clink against metal lipsticks.

"There!"

A blue flame explodes against the black, a mini–blow torch. It speaks, too. *Sssssshhhhhhh*.

" 'Nita, what're you doing with a blow torch two inches from your face?"

"Sweetheart," she says, using her G-L-A-M-O-U-R-O-U-S voice. "What does it *look* like?"

"Um." She sticks the glass pipe between her lips. "Smoking crack?"

She sucks, inhaling, filling her lungs with more dead lead. She holds it in. Exhales, tilts her head up and aims her mouth. The white blast drifts up, toward the ceiling.

"Oh, baby boy," she says, and shakes her head, No-No-No. "Crack's *so* eighties. Girl, I wouldn't even know where to get that shit. *Lies*. 'Course I would. This here's—" She hacks, spewing out smokey leftovers. "Tina."

"Whatever, Anita Tina Fixx, it smells awful."

"Speed, crank, meth, tweak—all the same."

"Crack and speed are the same?"

"Here," she says, offering the pipe. "Why don'tcha take a hit. Decide for yourself."

"Thank you, but no," I say. "There's more for you."

"Riiight?" She smiles. She holds the blue flame under the pipe, warming the glass. "You remembered."

Her brow furrows and she sucks, hard, like she's trying to pull the last drops of a chocolate milkshake up, off the glass bottom. I want to look away, but I can't. It's so dangerous. And exciting. And a little bit depressing. No. A *lot* depressing.

"You swear," I say. "Your face looks like Buddha when you do that."

"I'm guessing, but Buddha prolly didn't smoke Tina. Ganja, maybe. Or heroin."

" 'Nita, why do you smoke that stuff?"

"At this point, it's—" She moves the torch's blue flame away from the pipe and exhales. "So I can act normal."

I stare. At her. The pipe. And I totally get it. They feed off one other. PipeAnitaPipeAnita.

"Bring it on," she says. "Here's your big opportunity."

"Oh, no, thank you but—"

"Got it. More for me. I see you have *quesssstions*. Might as well, you know, *ask*. You sit with a real live drug ad-dick!"

"Questions? Like what?"

"Somethin' real Oprah. 'So *tell* me, Ah-nee-tah, *why* are *you* smo-king speed?' "

"Oprahtobehonestwithyou," she says, back to herself, taking a quick hit, "an' allIcandoisbehonest'cuzyouOprahIswearcan youhandme some tissues?' And then, you know, I'd stop, slow it down, you know, like how they do."

"She doesn't have issue shows anymore," I say. "We were just watching her and—"

"Okay, so Old Skool Oprah. Early Oprah. *Rerun* Oprah. Greatest Hits of Oprah! Crack pipe in one hand, microphone in the other Oprah. 'Yo! Oprah! Lady! It be *true!* I am the world's *original* Crack Baby. I'm whatchacall Crack Baby Numbah One.' Yo, Ben, yo mama smoke crack?"

"My mama'd get upset it didn't smell like French perfume," I laugh, imagining Haifa with a crack pipe. "Is that you asking? Or Oprah?"

"You talking to me? Or Oprah?"

"You! Ben! You! D'Oprah in d'crack house!"

"*My* stepmother's hair would melt."

"First time I smoked, oh, *honey*, it was *on*. I found *it*. The answer. Whatever wasn't there before, suddenly it was! How you do, Miss Tina. See you brought your BFF, too, Miss Addicktion. Yes, Ben, I was hooked. Love. I did it once and, baby, I *never* looked back!"

"That's what Kidd said," I say, absentminded. "About running. Never looking back."

"Honey, that's what we all say. You too, you—"

She turns her attention back to the pipe. Blue flame, torch to end. She suck-inhales like a baby on a mama's breast. Her physical need is intense. Desperate. No shame. I don't look away. I want to see what she's doing. I mean, *really* see it. I want to see what it is so I'll never need to look at it again.

"Why do *you* like drugs? Why *don't* you?" She waves the blue flame. I step back. The flame looks like it could melt skin. Anita's so caught up she doesn't notice.

"I still don't get it. Why you do that when you've got so much going for you?"

"Can you sit there," she says, "and honestly tell me *you* love yourself?"

"Well—"

"Sweetheart, it's either a Yes or a No," she says, leveling those dead-crazy-alive eyes at me. "You don't know, do you?"

"Know what?"

"If *you* love you. Forget"—her hand flies up, waving away invisible insects—"*him*. Do *you? Love* you?"

I don't. I don't know if I do.

"Sometimes I don't 'cause . . ." Maybe Kidd was right about me. That I hide behind questions. "Sometimes—sometimes, I wish. No, more like . . . I keep wondering what would my life be like if I was straight. Nobody would have noticed me. I'd have started dating girls. Everyone, they would have *encouraged* me. But 'cause I'm different, I'm forced to live through *this?*"

"Girl." She puts down the pipe and drops the attitude. "Now, before we say good-bye, it's time for us to get real."

Chapter 109

"One day I remember," Anita says. The G-L-A-M-O-U-R-O-U-S voice is gone. "I came home from the waffle shop. Someone seen me, you know, *dressed*. They told my grandparents. Who sat me down and said, 'Chil', long as you live *here,* you will *dress* like a boy.' And I told 'em, 'I just spent the last five months learning how to act like a girl!' "

"That's how they found out?"

Maybe her story holds a clue. Maybe I'll learn that I'm not really as alone—or, damned to shame and loneliness—as I feel.

"Chil', they didn't find out *once!*" she says. "No, more like they *kept* finding out. Till they couldn't pretend no more."

She lights up, sucks, smokes. I'm mesmerized by her ritual. How she holds the blue flame to the end of the pipe. How she sucks it. How she holds it in, how she exhales. How her mood tick-tocks with each puff.

I'm tempted. I'll try it! Take the edge off. Nothing wrong with that, right?

The blue flame lights up Anita's face. She sweats and her hands shake. N.P. (Not Pretty.) No, thank *you*, there's more for you. And, oh, yeah, 'Nita, don't meth rhyme with death?

"I was little. Five? My dad walked into my parents' bedroom," she says. "Dancing! And, girl, I was *all* dressed up. In my mom's clothes. I even had on one of her wigs. He scared me.

I saw him and jumped under the covers. Like I could hide from him. He stood over the bed and said, 'What's that you have on?' I said, 'Nothing!' Then, you know what he does?"

"No, what?"

"He drags me off the bed, marches me out the house and drives me to school."

"*Damn!* That's hard."

"I loved it. I thought, 'Now all the people can see how pretty I look!' " The blue flame cuts out. She puts down the torch. We sit in the dark. She rummages around in her purse and pulls out lipstick. "So, sweetheart, what's your story? I know you're dying to tell it."

"I don't have one. I'm the victim of extraordinary circumstances."

"I know *exactly* how you feel. Fact, I feel you so deep, I thought you might like—"

Crack-pop, the blue flame comes back to life, illuminating our cave. Ladylike, she holds up a homemade cigarette. She lights its white tip on the blue flame.

"What's that?"

"Somebody didn't graduate D.A.R.E."

"Yeah, I did. You're holding a gateway drug."

"Maybe?" She takes quick, short puffs on the joint. "Don't believe everything the government sells. One puff and—boom!—you're an addict. You're not like me."

"What makes you so sure?"

"You didn't grab this out of my hands, for one. You didn't open my purse, for two. You didn't open my purse and *run off* with my purse to some alley and get high by yourself." She exhales, a fine line of sweet-smelling smoke. "Remember the first time we dyed your hair? I asked you if you wanted a nip, you said, 'No.' You didn't think about it. No, 'Hey, 'Nita, gimme a toke.' It'd have been like, 'Yeah, gimme the bottle. And what *else* you got?' "

"Okay, I see."

She offers me the joint.

"Listen, your head's not gonna explode if you take one toke."

Cautious, I take the joint. I pinch it in-between my thumb and index finger. I don't know what the hell she's talking about, but I don't want to sound like a total dweeb.

"Speed? I mean, if you want to stay *up*, why would you smoke *this*? Doesn't it make you sleepy?"

I raise the joint, take a little puff and hand it back.

She shakes her head. "No, no, sweetheart, take a *toke*. Suck in real deep, hold it long as you can and let it go."

I follow her instructions. Inhale. Hold. Cough on the funny bunny smoke.

"Good." She laughs. "Coughing'll get it down there real good."

Unlike the ecstasy, I feel the pot right away. But it's a different feeling from the pill. Pleasant, but not euphoric. More foresty than exploding heart chakras and galaxies. Calm. A spacey feeling settles in. Like I'm sitting on the moon and my ass is about to slide off the surface. I stare at the red tip, mesmerized.

"Wow, check it out."

"Huh."

"How the embers chew up the tobacco and white paper."

Anita polishes off the joint. Turns out, she was "sharing," but only out of politeness. More for her . . .

"You think it's a gateway drug?"

"One time? No. Here," she says, puts out a hand. I help her stand. Her palm is rough with big fingers and long, curved nails. My hand disappears in hers.

"What're we doing?"

"You're leaving."

Chapter 110

Blind, without light or lighter, Anita leads me out the basement labyrinth.

" 'Nita, are you part bat?"

"Shhh," she whispers, and pulls me close. "Be *real* quiet!" She inches us forward. Stops.

Click. Click.

Dress shoes on concrete. I know that sound. Twenty? Thirty? Steps. We stand at the bottom of the stairs. The dress shoes halt. I look up. A sliver of light's forced its way through the basement door's crack. I stop and pull her to me.

"He's here!"

"Been there the whole time. He followed you."

My mouth flies open. I'm about to scream. Her hand clamps down and covers my mouth.

"They're waiting for you upstairs by the side of the building," she says, voice urgent and low. "And this is what you're gonna do. Walk up those stairs, walk past the pigs and walk out the side door marked EXIT."

"But—"

"Sweetheart, if you act like it's the most normal thing in the world, they won't even see you."

"What about you? Won't he—"

"Go on, I'll take care of myself."

I step up. I look back. There's just enough light to see her hand reach and dip into the purse.

Click.

The gun.

I scramble up the steps, escape the basement for the final time. At the top of the stairs, I reach for the doorknob. I turn, and look down.

Anita looks up, her beautiful face framed by the dim light.

"Santa Anita," I whisper, giving her a small wave and choking on my tears.

"Not everybody has the same key!" she shouts, loud enough for Blue-Eyed Bob to hear. "Cuz they don't have the same lock. My motto's always been—"

I hesitate, reluctant to turn the doorknob and step out, into the hallway. I may be the last person who sees Anita before the Angel of Death comes to take her away.

I turn the knob.

"Honey, I always said, if you can't find the key, *bust down the fucking door!*"

She steps back into the dark and her fate as I step out into the light and mine.

Chapter 111

The basement door closes. No click. Right in front of me, the exit.

Noise. Cops or immigration officers, it doesn't matter, they smell blood. Their voices filter down from upstairs. Maybe the side door's a magic portal. I sure as hell don't remember seeing that green, glowing EXIT sign.

I push the bar, open the door and peek outside. Two cops sit in a patrol car. I can't tell if they're chatting, jerking off or looking at Internet porn. Down the alley, the Impala's trunk. It's parked on Market Street. The back door's open. I run down the street.

"Get in!" Marci grabs my arm and pulls me inside. The door slams. The car peels around the corner.

"They almost got you." The driver's the same boy who drove the VW beater van. He holds up headphones. "The audience *is* listening."

We're moving. I look out the window, at the city. Day for night. I see everything I missed the first night, and on Halloween.

I consider his words. Fact is, I almost *let* myself get caught. I almost gave in to my fear. I turn forward. I won't look back.

Chapter 112

The new safe house is temporary. Kidd calls it "a *fucking flophouse!*" He's right. I'd describe it as a roach-infested nightmare. The walls are peeling, the carpet's tattered with torn-up bald patches and the front door hangs off the frame. It makes the old safe house look like a five-star hotel.

Everyone—except J.D. and Anita (and Pony, but he doesn't count; he left on his own)—escaped.

I'm overwhelmed with guilt. I don't dare tell anyone or write it down. J.D. saved me.

He really loved me . . . and I doubted him.

Chapter 113

Night.

Marci and I lie on a bare mattress. The fabric's shiny from overuse. The surface feels exhausted from fucking and sleeping. She offers a cigarette. I wave it off.

"Why'd you come back for me?"

"I didn't realize," she says, taking a drag, "I had a choice."

"Weren't you afraid of being caught?"

"If I get caught and put in jail," she says, blasting white puffs, "I can use the phone to call someone and post bail. But if *you* get caught, they'd send you back. No phone, no bail."

"What about J.D.?"

She looks away. I don't ask why. Not that it matters. I don't have a rescue plan.

I close my eyes and "sleep." I can't really call it sleep. Every morning, I'm the first one up. I live in a panicked state. I'm a roiling cauldron of feelings. Nervousness, excitement, dread. My heart races. Even though the room is freezing, I'm always hot. My body burns.

The next morning, I sit on the window ledge, peering out the filthy pane. After months of hiding, I thought I'd be curious about the world. But I can't see anything through the glass. The grime is too thick. I'm not even hungry, and it's been ages since I ate. A shape appears in glass.

"J.D.?"

"No," Marci says. She sits on the mattress and lights a cigarette.

I turn back. Fist to glass, I wipe away the grime and look through the spot. There's a girl down on the street. She's young, maybe fourteen, and stands on the curb.

"You miss him?"

"Hell, yeah."

A station wagon pulls up. The door swings open. The girl slips in and the car pulls away. My body shudders. Is the driver Blue-Eyed Bob? Or, some other creep? What will happen to her? I'll never know. She's gone.

"I found a new place. I'm going back to the old one and pick up some stuff. What's the *one* thing you want?"

"My journal. I left it under the futon. It's blue."

She drops the cigarette, grinds it under her heel and leaves. I fall back on the mattress and look up, at the ceiling. It's endured thousands of eyes: awake, shut, surrendered.

Mine grow heavy and I slip into a deep, dreamless sleep.

Chapter 114

"Get up!"

A hand shakes my shoulder.

"What?" I sit up. Outside, it's dark and so cold my teeth chatter. I look around. The room's empty. The door's open.

"Where is everybody?"

"Hurry up!" Marci tosses me a jacket. "We're leaving. Here, put this on." She hands me a red wig and green fabric.

"A dress?"

"Your picture's all over the news. You're an Amber Alert."

"No way."

"Way. Put it on."

"You're kidding."

"It's your disguise."

I claw at my clothes. I know all about disguises. I'm a quick-change artist.

"No, pull it on *over* what're wearing. Girls do that now. Wear dresses over jeans. And don't forget the wig."

I follow her out, looking less like a girl than a nutty boy who didn't know the difference between a skirt and pants. We run down a dimly lit hallway, passing a series of open doorways. People fucking or shooting up. Angry people. Crazy, high, dead people. The air reeks—rotten food, vomit, speed.

We're halfway down a narrow flight of stairs.

"Wait by the door," Marci says. "I need to get the car."

"Alone?" I shake my head and look up. Her eyes follow. A figure stands at the top of the stairs. His pants are crumpled at his knees. His hand moves, jerking off.

"C'mon, girls, cum up here an' suck Daddy's cock—"

Marci grabs my arm, pulls me out the door and onto the street. She threads her arm through mine. "Look down and pretend we're girlfriends."

"Hey! Hey! Bitchs I's talkin' to you!"

A hand clamps down on my shoulder. I turn, look. It's E-Gore, the masturbating ogre from the top of the stairs. Marci spins around, holds up a canister and shoots pepper spray in his face.

"Get the fuck off us!"

"You fucking bitches! I'll fuckin' kill you!"

We run. A siren wails.

"Stop!" A cop's voice.

Marci ignores the command. We dash down the street. I look to the left and see—No! Yes! Blue-Eyed Bob? Am I imagining things? Magical thinking. If I look to the right, he'll disappear. I see the Impala. It's parked by the curb.

"Wait!"

"No, we can't!"

We run past it and down a stairwell.

"Run!"

I lose the wig and rip off the dress. We run down steps.

"JUMP!"

We hop a turnstile and tumble down more steps. The train waits, parked at the platform. She pulls me inside, the doors close and the car lurches. We're moving forward.

" 'Scuse, 'scuse us." Marci pulls me through the crowded car to another exit. The car gathers speed. "Hang on!"

Bam! She slams her fist against the emergency button.

Shreeaaaaakkkkkk

The trolley's wheel screech and stops. The lights cut out. Marci forces the door. It opens. She leaps into the dark.

"Jump!"

I leap, landing on the platform connecting the cars. The tunnel air's stale. Below, I see a blur. Ground, track.

"Get off! *Down! Down!*"

I jump off the platform, shoes crunching on gravel. We run down a tunnel. Toward flashing lights and through echoes. Train wheels squeal, screech and groan. Headlights, bright and white, barrel toward us. I knew it. We're going to die, crushed between metal wheels and railroad tracks.

"*UP! UP! CLIMB UP!*"

I climb up a ladder and crawl onto the floor. My face meets a million questioning eyes. I look back. Marci struggles to pull herself up, onto the platform. I put out a hand.

"Hey—"

WHOOSH

"Marci?"

She's gone.

I stagger away from the scene. Dazed, I trudge up the stairs, elbowing my way through the crush of bodies moving, gushing, down like a river.

I reach the street. Think back. The violent screech. The loud thunk. The flash of arms. Body snatched. And the screams. The screams are nothing like a horror movie.

My knees weaken.

"Hey!"

I look over. My gaze keeps me upright. The Impala, its open door. The boy. He motions. "Get in! *C'mon!*"

"But—"

He reaches across the seat and hauls me inside. The door slams shut, the car speeds away, my head hits the seat and—

I don't want to see. I need to. I crawl up, turn, look back.

Lights flash. Ambulance sirens wail. I did, I did see it. The accident. The men in white carrying a gurney, head downstairs to—

"She's dead," I say. "Dead."

I don't think he understands what I'm saying.

Am I saying it?

"Dead." But he doesn't stop the car. He keeps driving. He glances at me. His hands tighten on the wheel. He looks away. He doesn't stop the car.

I turn back, face forward and remind myself.

Don't look back.

Chapter 115

I look up. Alice / Nadya. She strokes my head. It rests against her tummy. I feel a kick. She's pregnant?

"It's Thanks-*fucking*-giving and all I want to do is . . ."

"Get high?"

Wait, I *know* that voice. Where am I? I try to lift my head, but I'm too weak.

"Is that her?"

"Who?"

"Sugar. What's she doing here?"

I close my eyes. I must be waking from a long sleep. Or, I'm in another dream. A bad one. Yes, I dreamed what I saw. Marci, hit by the subway car, ground up under—

"No!"

I jerk my head and move my eyes away from the horrible image.

blood ragged flesh death death death

Magical thinking: If I can't see it, it doesn't exist.

"What?"

I look over. I *know* him. But I don't know his name or how we met. Then I remember. He drove the VW beater van. And the Impala.

"Anita's back for a tryptophan fix?" Marci's dead, Anita's gone and he's joking.

"All—" I struggle to speak. My mouth is dry. Alice / Nadya gives me a sip of water. "I want to go home."

"I keep remembering the year before I was locked up," Kidd says. *His* voice, I know, it's impossible to forget. Why didn't he get caught in the raid?

"You thought, 'Maybe if I went home,' " another voice says. "It would all be better."

"But you forget all the times it was bad. Okay, bedtime!" *That* voice belongs, unmistakably, to Marci.

I cry. I *am* dreaming. None of this is real. It can't be. I'll wake on a filthy mattress in an empty room. Alone.

"I know, honey, but—"

I force my body to sit up.

"Marci?!" I reach out and touch her arm. She *feels* alive. I scootch over so I'm close to her face. I hold my hand out under her nose. "You're *alive!?*"

"What!" She laughs. "Why wouldn't I be?"

"Are you a dream? Or are you alive-*alive?!*"

"Living and breathing."

"Then what was that?" My voice rises. "Back in the train station?"

"Hey there," she says. Alice / Nadya eases me down. "Take it easy."

"But I *saw* you—"

"I crawled up onto the platform. The person you saw—hit, by the train—that was one of the mole people."

"But what about the ambulance? I saw them going downstairs to get you."

"For him, honey," she says, patting my back, comforting me. "For him."

Chapter 116

New bed, new room. I look under the curtains. Night. I let it drop and check the clock. 3 a.m. Halloween's a memory. We're traveling through the lost, lonely days that fall between Thanksgiving leading to Christmas. I grab my journal, flip it open and scribble,

> The darkness is more final in the winter months. It's
> as if a velvet curtain is drawn across the sky. I think
> this activates our primitive brains. We seek the
> warmth of a safe place.

I swing my legs over the bed. My feet touch wood. I walk down the long hallway to the kitchen. Marci sits at the table. It's covered with masses of wrapping paper, ribbons, tape and presents.

"Hi. What're you doing?"

She holds a felt-tip pen. She writes on tags and ties each one onto a stocking.

"Is there milk?"

"Yeah, I just bought some."

I stand and touch her shoulder. I need to make sure she's here. I pick up a stocking.

"Nancy?"

"Stockings have people's real names written on them."

"I thought our identities are secret."

"They are, but it's a holiday thing. There's something about writing your real name. I mean, if you think about it, your name separates you from everyone else. It's part of what makes you unique. So, one day out of the year, we use our real names."

My eyes are drawn to a small, neatly wrapped present. *Ahmed* is written in Arabic on a tiny envelope. I slide the card out. It's a reproduction of a famous painting. I turn it over. "Frida Kahlo, Self-Portrait with Thorn Necklace and Hummingbird." I open the card and read.

Dear Ben,

 The Hummingbird is used here as a "love"
amulet because this bird is considered to have
special powers to attract matters of the heart.

 At least that's what I read somewhere. In fact,
some Mexicans will wear amulets of hummingbird
dust as a love potion . . . or so my sources say!

 Where I'm living now, I have a hummingbird
feeder hanging from a hook outside the kitchen
window.

 There are three customers.

 Lolita, my cat, "bird" watches them like she's
hypnotized. She makes weird noises and whisker
twitches as the hummingbirds pass by for a drink.

 I hope you have a Merry Christmas! When I saw
this card, I couldn't think of a better one.

 Love—

"*Luis?*" I look up. "J.D. is back?"

"Thank God," Marci says, "I thought I'd lost it. Go ahead. Open it."

I unwrap the gift. Inside, there's a silver-framed picture of J.D. Er, "James Dean" (or, "Luis"). I stare at the photo. His face sits in the palm of my hand. All that's missing is . . . him.

Stunned, I slump back. Memories flood my brain. Kissing

those lips, seeing his warm, bright smile and resting my cheek on his shoulder. All of it so, so long ago. I stare at the picture. J.D.'s face. My life turned into a dream. A dream that evaporates with time, itself an illusion. He's here, he's not. Halloween night. We step onto the dance floor . . . led out of a foggy forest by fluttering fireflies . . . and slide down, into warm water.

The images pass in front of my mind's eye. Like film run too many times through a projector, the images are scratched and faded.

"Is he okay?"

"What did the card say?"

"He's good."

"Tomorrow, meet me up on the roof."

I nod. I stand. The frame weighs heavy in my hand. I stagger back to bed. I decide I'll leave the bed empty until J.D. returns. I lie on the floor. My cheek rests against the silver frame, the hummingbird card pressed to my heart.

Chapter 117

I wait until everyone's asleep. Then, I slip out of the bedroom, pull on a coat and walk down the hallway. The new safe house is the second floor sandwiched between three railroad flats. I step out the kitchen's back door and walk up the stairs. Marci waits on the roof. She stands next to a hibachi barbecue. A full moon rises on the horizon.

"Here." She hands me a fistful of name tags. "Burn these."

I feed the tiny slips of paper into the hibachi. The paper lands on the coals, curls and catches fire. Ahmed, Nancy, Edward, and Kai. Our real identities burn out, ash swept away by the breeze.

I hold up the silver-framed picture of J.D.

"Did he give this to you?"

She parks the cigarette between her lips and warms her hands over the hibachi's heat.

"Why do you ask?"

" 'Cause that note," I say. "It's your handwriting."

She takes a drag, pauses, exhales.

"You *know* where he is?" I press.

"Sort of."

"Where?"

"You can't help him."

"I can't fucking believe you! You know where and you—"

"Serenity Ridge."

"Come again?"

"Serenity Ridge. Ben, there's nothing you can do—"

"My name's not Ben!" I scream, loud enough to wake the city. "It's Ahmed! *Ahmed!*"

"He *let* them catch him so *you* could escape. You need to . . ."

She talks, but I don't hear. Her voice is an echo. I stand, run across the roof and down the stairs. I don't care who hears. They *betrayed* me. They took him away. The only boy I loved. I *ever* loved.

"*Remember.*" Sugar's voice guides me to the front door and down the steps. "*You can leave anytime.*"

I stand on the sidewalk. I face the street, away from the safe house. I've left. I'm outside. I look back. Marci's shadow hovers in the window.

My eyes move up. Beyond her. Beyond the safe house. Beyond the roof to the sky.

A star streak across sky.

I close my eyes—

Make my wish—

Find J.D.—

Find my mom—

Live.

Please turn the page for a
very special Q&A with
Tomas Mournian.

Q: Is there any new information in *hidden* that's never been disclosed or that very few people know about?

A: Underground railroads. When I was researching "Hiding Out," a non-fiction piece about safe houses, I came to see that an underground railroad is a vital American tradition: for slaves before Emancipation, of course, but also for women escaping domestic violence, and for draft dodgers, as well as for others. I would say *hidden* tells the story of a little known yet latest version of this underground railroad.

Q: How does *hidden* (the novel) relate to the article "Hiding Out"?

A: "Hiding Out" was a news article I wrote for the *San Francisco Bay Guardian*. The piece served as the origin for *hidden*. I dropped a lot of the informational graphs that were in the article. For both the article and the novel, I took certain elements from different safe houses and combined them into one: the San Francisco setting from one; the one-room safe house from another; and the fire escape to the roof from a third. However, the fire escape in the novel is actually taken from my building. When Ahmed stands on the roof and looks at San Francisco, the view he sees is really . . . L.A.!

Q: Are the characters in *hidden* based on real people?

A: The characters in *hidden* are inspired by real people, but they're not exact portraits. Over the years I've heard hundreds of stories of young people—gay, straight. When I wrote *hidden,* I drew upon their stories for inspiration. I was careful to shed the particulars and express the underlying struggle.

Q: What elements of the article "Hiding Out" did you choose to keep in the novel *hidden*?

A: "Hiding Out" told the story of one safe house but drew upon a larger pool of people. *hidden* is my imaginative reinvention of those people and places. I'm always curious to see how patterns emerge among people who have split off from mainstream culture. I fully expect accusations of "You based that character on me / my friend!"

Q: Would you describe *hidden* as a gay or queer novel?

A: I was intent on making sure *hidden* could be read by the queer reader, but by any other reader, too. There were language choices I made that open up the narrative to everyone.

Q: Readers tend to identify the main character with the author. Are you Ahmed?

A: There's a big part of me in Ahmed. Like him, I spent years running away, and hiding. My experience was a central reason why I needed to write *hidden*. I hope young people who need to read *hidden* will take what's useful and make good decisions.

Q: The romantic element of *hidden* was a very minor part of the original news article "Hiding Out." Why did you chose to enlarge the love story between Ahmed and J.D.?

A: I made the choice to tell a love story because Ahmed needed to fulfill the reason *why* he'd gone to such lengths to escape and hide. Ahmed's struggle came at a price but also a payoff. Compared to ten, five years ago, mostly because of the AIDS epidemic, there are so many more gay / queer people on television and in movies. I feel like it's time authors tell gay or queer stories that are read equal to other stories.

Q: Why does Anita Fixx, a trans person, play such a central role in *hidden*?

A: Trans people, Anita Fixx in particular, are important to *hidden* because I believe trans people are equal in life and are becoming ever more visible. Anita reflects the emergence of people's desire to determine their gender. What I think trans'-

ness really points to is (a) how arbitrary or fluid gender is, and (b) that it's a social construct. Like race, gender serves power. Trans people, by virtue of their choice(s), confuse this modern attempt to classify everyone. Trans'ness is a definitive statement and an exercise of several rights guaranteed by the Constitution: the right to happiness, the right to self-definition, the notion of reinvention, and sovereignty over one's body.

Q: Are you trans?

A: No.

Q: Then how did you write about trans'ness?

A: *Orlando,* by Virginia Woolf, asks the same question. In essence, how does one write about what one *doesn't* know? I came of age around trans people. I've known people who've transitioned. I've seen their struggles as difficult and equal yet different from my own.

Q: Yes, but where did the idea for Anita Fixx come from? Or, to you?

A: Anita Fixx came in a brief, thirty-second moment, when I held hands with a black trans woman. It was quite amazing. I don't know if it was a spiritual experience or a matter of instant perception, but I felt her story in that moment, and she expressed herself through me.

Q: Anita reminds me of an Almodóvar character.

A: Exactly! I love Pedro Almodóvar's films. I grew up watching Almodóvar's movies, and they're filled with trans people who always play a central role in the narrative. And though they're fabulous, Almodóvar's trans people are exceptionally human: generous, lovers, and tragic figures. Yet their stories are equal to those of the other characters.

Q: What about Hammer?

A: (Laughs) Right? Because I'm not tall, blond, or anything like that. But a friend of mine, David, who I knew when he was a teenager, looks like Hammer. David's a huge fan of Grace Jones, and before everyone else was mopping her, he was clued in to her singularity of appearance, her embrace of the extreme. In David, I saw a young person struggling with being this sort of queer ideal. And it's been interesting to see him grow up and play with that stereotype, to fuck with it, as it were.

Q: Are you still in touch with teenagers from "Hiding Out"?

A: No.

Q: Talk about the process of being contacted and hired by George Michael to make a short film based on "Hiding Out."

A: Two years after "Hiding Out" was published, the piece had been syndicated (reprinted) in several magazines, one being the UK-based *Attitude*. One morning, my phone rang and a British voice on the other end said, "Hello, this is George Michael." I laughed and said, "Yeah, right," and hung up. My best friend, Andrew, lives in London, and I thought he was playing a prank. Later that day, I got a message from Andy Stevens, George Michael's manager, explaining that the call was, in fact, real—and that George was performing a four-song set at Equality Rocks . . . two weeks from the date. He wanted to produce and show a video during his set and would I put them in touch with people so they could produce it? That was impossible, but I offered to produce the video myself, contacted John Keitel, an L.A. filmmaker, drove to San Francisco and, over four days, taped interviews with kids from that safe house. We returned to L.A. and edited the material in five days. The morning of the concert, John flew to D.C. and delivered the tape.

Q: What happened to the *Hiding Out* documentary after that?

A: The documentary *Hiding Out* was subsequently shown at film festivals, and MTV contacted us about making a reality TV show based on the safe houses. But that proved impractical and didn't happen.

Q: What made you decide to adapt a news story about underground safe houses to writing a novel about the same topic?

A: Certainly the documentary was a central motivation: I saw, in a larger way, how the story of kids escaping from these boot camps and living underground resonated with people. It was eerie seeing an audience watch the documentary at film festivals. I was surprised by the emotions it brought up for the audience. The MTV thing happened and then it didn't. For a while, John and I planned to make a film about the safe house; I wrote and rewrote dozens of screenplays, each one further from the original intent.

Q: Why did you choose to include sex work (prostitution) in *hidden*?

A: That's a reality that a lot of teens—gay or straight—who run away experience. Cam whoring, for example (which the character Hammer does in the safe house's closet), is real, but it's not widely known about. Or, it hasn't been written about in any way other than the most sensational way. People don't generally know this, but the word *gay* comes from the demimond of courtesans in nineteenth-century Paris. So, there's an epistemological relationship between gay and sex work. It's literally written into the culture. I consciously included sex work in *hidden* because it's dismaying to see how far right the LGBTQ community is trending. Toward this sort of conservative modality. And I see that tightening up as diminishing one vibrant element of the community, forcing it underground and flattening the culture at large. I wanted to show what I knew and have seen and know continues to exist.

Q: Likewise, why is *hidden* filled with drugs and drinking?

A: Where I live, in Los Angeles, or have traveled and lived (San Francisco, New York City, London), drugs have always been present. And most people, I think, in the gay community partake, to whatever extent. Again, back to history, drugs have not always been about addiction—and death. In the sixties, LSD was a central part of the human potential movement. Prior to the eighties and Reagan's "War on Drugs," "Just Say No," and extremely punitive sentencing laws, drugs were seen as gateways to other states of consciousness. Certainly I was conscious of presenting both sides: the addictive side of drug use and the liberating, wonderful side.

Q: Is there a "dirty"—i.e., sexy—part of the book that people should look for?

A: Yes!

Q: Why did you choose to show teenage boys in romantic relationships that also feature sex?

A: I don't know about you, but in my life and in novels as some expression of life, sex and love are the pulse. Sex is a central way people connect.

Q: But why sex and romance between teenagers?

A: Most people—straight people—don't tend to think about this, but most gay/queer teens don't have the same opportunity to date. So until they've graduated from high school, queer people tend to start dating five or six years later than their counterparts. As a gay teen, I was in that boat and, as a gay adult, I wanted to write a story for gay teens that was both romantic and sexual.

Q: A role model?

A: No, I'm not a sociologist or a policy maker. And I don't buy into that whole idea—"gay writers save lives." If anything "saves" a life, it's a person knowing oneself. All humans are hardwired for stories, but without those stories to inspire, teens—especially gay teens—are forced to forever reinvent their stories. I hope *hidden* can become a story or template that all teens, gay or straight, can take from.

Q: It's difficult to imagine a suburban teen relating to *hidden*'s cloistered environment.

A: *hidden*'s closed, safe-house setting removes the teen from the typical high school setting. Popular culture is filled with examples of teens in teen-only spaces. *hidden* reinvents everything from *Clueless* to *Degrassi* to *The Breakfast Club*, all peer-centric universes.

Q: How do you imagine a gay / queer teen will benefit from reading *hidden*?

A: I think the question is, what pleasure will any reader take from reading *hidden*?

Q: Do you plan to write a sequel to *hidden*?

A: *hidden* is published as a stand-alone book. That said, if the book's a success and people want to follow Ahmed's story, I have thought about what might happen to him.

Q: Why did you chose to write what is, essentially, a "dystopia"?

A: Recent LGBTQ literature has been so universally utopian. I decided to write *hidden* because I saw an opportunity to write something more urban and dark.

Q: Yes, *hidden* isn't set in the suburbs. Why is that?

A: For the dystopic element of *hidden* to work, I knew I needed to set the narrative in "the city." As a place, the city occupies a large place in the queer imagination. The city's a destination that holds the promise of freedom and self-expression.

Q: Right. You put together a teenager running away from home and the city.

A: Exactly, but *hidden* isn't indulging the characters' general dissatisfaction with life. They all have real and urgent reasons to run away. They all need a place to hide . . . and what better place than the city, a place where one can get lost. So, "the city" was a logical place for Ahmed to go. But this city isn't perfect. It's also rife with danger, even death.

Q: What was the idea behind separating the book into four sections?

A: I decided to divide *hidden* into four sections to create a sense of time passing. Until the last rewrite, I struggled with how to tell a story that covers a period of time that's both active and static. And I happened to read an interview with an actor (Robert Downey, Jr., in *Rolling Stone*) who referred to four words—escape, hidden, invisible, and gone—that worked perfectly to divide the sections.

hidden

Tomas Mournian

About This Guide

The suggested questions are included to enhance
your group's reading of Tomas Mournian's *hidden*.

Discussion Questions

1. How does the safe house in *hidden* become a character? Describe how the author uses a place as part of the story.

2. Time both accelerates and stops within *hidden*—fast in the opening sequence (Run), and slow in the second sequence (Hidden). How does the writer indicate the passage of time in the second sequence?

3. The period of time covered is never explicitly stated, yet there are clues to its passage. What span of time does *hidden* cover?

4. Suspense underscores *hidden*'s narrative. What storytelling techniques does the author use to create a sense of suspense? How does that suspense express the consequences of the characters' choices?

5. Many characters in *hidden* use fictional names. What are those names? How do those names serve a practical function? Symbolically, what do those names express about the characters?

6. When Ahmed first sees the other kids in *hidden*, he makes immediate judgments. How true / false do those assumptions prove? Have you ever seen something and made an assumption that's proven less than accurate?

7. Food serves different purposes in *hidden*. For example, both Ahmed and Alice / Nadya describe chocolate milkshakes, but to different effect. What is the difference? What are other examples of food's importance in *hidden*? What roles does food play in your life?

8. The author makes a specific language choice to show the romance between Ahmed and J.D. What is it? How does it allow any reader—i.e., female, male, gay, straight, etc.—to imagine one's self in the story?

9. Ahmed's mother is a powerful—yet unseen—character in *hidden*. What purpose does her absence / presence play in the narrative?

10. When Ahmed first sees Hammer, it's love at first sight. But this changes. What happens to shift Ahmed's interest? What is the role of desire in *hidden*?

11. During the Hidden sequence, Ahmed continues his journey, but it's confined to one space, a contrast with the physicality of the novel's opening sequence (Run). Discuss how Ahmed's journey shifts from external to internal. Also, how does Ahmed change during this period of time?

12. Ahmed's story is central to *hidden*. However, his story exists in relation to other character's stories. By character, describe these other stories. Discuss how Ahmed's own story is changed by hearing these stories.

13. Alice / Nadya's story shifts between present and past tense. Discuss why the author may have chosen to tell her story this way. Also, does the use of past / present tense add or detract from the style of the story and character? Why is / isn't it confusing?

14. How did the story impact you on a personal level? Which character did you most relate to? Explain.

15. "You can always leave," Sugar advises Ahmed. The phrase reappears several times throughout *hidden*. How is the advice both physical and spiritual? How does

Ahmed use the phrase to frame his final, crucial decision? Have you ever heard a piece of advice that you've taken to heart and acted upon? Why / why not?

16. In *hidden*'s opening section, Run, Ahmed looks out the van window and sees a boy his age. The boy climbs into a car to commit prostitution. At that moment, Ahmed makes a promise to himself that he won't make the same choice. By the end of *hidden* Ahmed's attitude toward sex workers has shifted. What happens?

17. Have you ever considered running away? Why? Could you make the same sacrifices of lifestyle described in *hidden*?

18. Ahmed makes the same choice at the beginning and end of *hidden*. What is that choice? How are the choices the same / different? At different points in your life, have you ever made a same but different choice? Discuss.

19. What was the ultimate life lesson Ahmed learned in his journey? If you feel there's more than one lesson, what is it? Did you relate to these life lessons?

20. The ending of *hidden* and Ahmed's story is open-ended. What do you imagine happens to Ahmed?